The TROUBLE WITH RAMONA AND BEEZUS

Beverly Cleary

OXFORD

OXFORD
UNIVERSITY PRESS

Great Clarendon Street, Oxford OX2 6DP
Oxford University Press is a department of the University of Oxford.
It furthers the University's objective of excellence in research, scholarship,
and education by publishing worldwide in

Oxford   New York

Auckland   Cape Town   Dar es Salaam   Hong Kong   Karachi
Kuala Lumpur   Madrid   Melbourne   Mexico City   Nairobi
New Delhi   Shanghai   Taipei   Toronto

With offices in

Argentina   Austria   Brazil   Chile   Czech Republic   France   Greece
Guatemala   Hungary   Italy   Japan   Poland   Portugal   Singapore
South Korea   Switzerland   Thailand   Turkey   Ukraine   Vietnam

Oxford is a registered trade mark of Oxford University Press
in the UK and in certain other countries

Beezus and Ramona first published 1955
Ramona the Pest first published 1968
Ramona the Brave first published 1975
Ramona and Her Father first published 1975

First published in this edition 2010 by arrangement with
HarperCollins Publishers Inc., New York, USA

British Library Cataloguing in Publication Data

Data available

ISBN: 978-0-19-275521-6

Printed in Great Britain

Paper used in the production of this book is a natural,
recyclable product made from wood grown in sustainable forests.
The manufacturing process conforms to the environmental
regulations of the country of origin

CONTENTS

BeeZuS aND RaMoNa

CONTENTS

1

Beezus and Her Little Sister

Beatrice Quimby's biggest problem was her little sister Ramona. Beatrice, or Beezus (as everyone called her, because that was what Ramona had called her when she first learned to talk), knew other nine-year-old girls who had little sisters who went to nursery school, but she did not know anyone with a little sister like Ramona.

Beezus felt that the biggest trouble with four-year-old Ramona was that she was just plain exasperating. If Ramona drank lemonade through a straw, she blew into the straw as hard as she could to see what would happen. If she played with her finger paints in the front yard, she wiped her hands on the neighbours' cat. That was the exasperating sort of thing Ramona did. And then there was the way she behaved about her favourite book.

It all began one afternoon after school when Beezus was sitting in her father's big chair embroidering a laughing teakettle on a pot holder for one of her aunts for Christmas. She was trying to embroider this one neatly, because she planned to give it to Aunt Beatrice, who was mother's younger sister and Beezus's most special aunt.

With grey thread Beezus carefully outlined the steam coming from the teakettle's spout and thought about her pretty young aunt, who was always so gay and so understanding. No wonder she was mother's favourite sister. Beezus hoped to be exactly like Aunt Beatrice when she grew up. She wanted to be a fourth-grade teacher and drive a yellow convertible and live in an apartment house with an elevator and a buzzer that opened the front door. Because she was named after Aunt Beatrice, Beezus felt she might be like her in other ways, too.

While Beezus was sewing, Ramona, holding a mouth organ in her teeth, was riding around the living room on her tricycle. Since she needed both hands to steer the tricycle, she could blow in and out on only one note. This made the harmonica sound as if it were groaning *oh dear, oh dear* over and over again.

Beezus tried to pay no attention. She tied a small knot in the end of a piece of red thread to embroider the teakettle's laughing mouth. 'Conceal a knot as you would a secret,' grandmother always said.

Inhaling and exhaling into her mouth organ, Ramona closed her eyes and tried to pedal around the coffee table without looking.

'Ramona!' cried Beezus. 'Watch where you're going!'

When Ramona crashed into the coffee table, she opened her eyes again. *Oh dear, oh dear*, moaned the harmonica. Around and around pedalled Ramona, inhaling and exhaling.

Beezus looked up from her pot holder. 'Ramona, why don't you play with Bendix for a while?' Bendix was Ramona's favourite doll. Ramona thought Bendix was the most beautiful name in the world.

Ramona took the harmonica out of her mouth. 'No,' she said. 'Read my Scoopy book to me.'

'Oh, Ramona, not Scoopy,' protested Beezus. 'We've read Scoopy so many times.'

Instead of answering, Ramona put her harmonica between her teeth again and pedalled around the room, inhaling and exhaling. Beezus had to lift up her feet every time Ramona rode by.

The knot in Beezus's thread pulled through the material of her pot holder, and she gave up trying to conceal it as she would a secret and tied a bigger knot. Finally, tired of trying to keep her feet out of Ramona's way, she put down her embroidery. 'All right, Ramona,' she said. 'If I read about Scoopy, will you stop riding your tricycle around the living room and making so much noise?'

'Yes,' said Ramona, and climbed off her tricycle.

She ran into the bedroom she shared with Beezus and returned with a battered, dog-eared, sticky book, which she handed to Beezus. Then she climbed into the big chair beside Beezus and waited expectantly.

Reflecting that Ramona always managed to get her own way, Beezus gingerly took the book and looked at it with a feeling of great dislike. It was called *The Littlest Steam Shovel*. On the cover was a picture of a steam shovel with big tears coming out of its eyes. How could a steam shovel have eyes, Beezus thought and, scarcely looking at the words, began for what seemed like the hundredth or maybe the thousandth time. 'Once there was a little steam shovel named Scoopy. One day Scoopy said, "I do not want to be a steam shovel. I want to be a bulldozer."'

'You skipped,' interrupted Ramona.

'No, I didn't,' said Beezus.

'Yes, you did,' insisted Ramona. 'You're supposed to say, "I want to be a *big* bulldozer."'

'Oh, all right,' said Beezus crossly. '"I want to be a big bulldozer."'

Ramona smiled contentedly and Beezus continued reading. '"G-r-r-r," said Scoopy, doing his best to sound like a bulldozer.'

Beezus read on through Scoopy's failure to be a bulldozer. She read about Scoopy's wanting to

8

be a trolley bus ('Beep-beep,' honked Ramona), a locomotive ('A-hooey, a-hooey,' wailed Ramona), and a pile driver ('Clunk! Clunk!' shouted Ramona). Beezus was glad when she finally reached the end of the story and Scoopy learned it was best for little steam shovels to be steam shovels. 'There!' she said with relief, and closed the book. She always felt foolish trying to make noises like machinery.

'Clunk! Clunk!' yelled Ramona, jumping down from the chair. She pulled her harmonica out of the pocket of her overalls and climbed on her tricycle. *Oh dear, oh dear,* she inhaled and exhaled.

'Ramona!' cried Beezus. 'You promised you'd stop if I read Scoopy to you.'

'I did stop,' said Ramona, when she had taken the harmonica out of her mouth. 'Now read it again.'

'Ramona Geraldine Quimby!' Beezus began, and stopped. It was useless to argue with Ramona. She wouldn't pay any attention. 'Why do you like that story anyway?' Beezus asked. 'Steam shovels can't talk, and I feel silly trying to make all those noises.'

'*I* don't,' said Ramona, and wailed, 'A-hooey, a-hooey,' with great feeling before she put her harmonica back in her mouth.

Beezus watched her little sister pedal furiously around the living room, inhaling and exhaling.

Why did she have to like a book about a steam shovel anyway? Girls weren't supposed to like machinery. Why couldn't she like something quiet, like *Peter Rabbit*?

Mother, who had bought *The Littlest Steam Shovel* at the supermarket to keep Ramona quiet while she shopped one afternoon, was so tired of Scoopy that she always managed to be too busy to read to Ramona. Father came right out and said he was fed up with frustrated steam shovels and he would not read that book to Ramona and, furthermore, no one else was to read it to her while he was in the house. And that was that.

So only Beezus was left to read Scoopy to Ramona. Plainly something had to be done and it was up to Beezus to do it. But what? Arguing with Ramona was a waste of time. So was appealing to her better nature. The best thing to do with Ramona, Beezus had learned, was to think up something to take the place of whatever her mind was fixed upon. And what could take the place of *The Littlest Steam Shovel*? Another book, of course, a better book, and the place to find it was certainly the library.

'Ramona, how would you like me to take you to the library to find a different book?' Beezus asked. She really enjoyed taking Ramona places, which, of course, was quite different from wanting to go someplace herself and having Ramona insist on tagging along.

For a moment Ramona was undecided. Plainly she was torn between wanting *The Littlest Steam Shovel* read aloud again and the pleasure of going out with Beezus. 'OK,' she agreed at last.

'Get your sweater while I tell mother,' said Beezus.

'Clunk! Clunk!' shouted Ramona happily.

When Ramona appeared with her sweater, Beezus stared at her in dismay. Oh, no, she thought. She can't wear those to the library.

On her head Ramona wore a circle of cardboard with two long paper ears attached. The insides of the ears were coloured with pink crayon, Ramona's work at nursery school. 'I'm the Easter bunny,' announced Ramona.

'Mother,' wailed Beezus. 'You aren't going to let her wear those awful ears to the library!'

'Why, I don't see why not.' Mother sounded surprised that Beezus should object to Ramona's ears.

'They look so silly. Whoever heard of an Easter bunny in September?' Beezus complained, as Ramona hopped up and down to make her ears flop. I just hope we don't meet anybody we know, Beezus thought, as they started out of the front door.

But the girls had no sooner left the house when they saw Mrs Wisser, a lady who lived in the next block, coming towards them with a friend. It was too late to turn back. Mrs Wisser had seen them and was waving.

'Why, hello there, Beatrice,' Mrs Wisser said, when they met. 'I see you have a dear little bunny with you today.'

'Uh . . . yes.' Beezus didn't know what else to say.

Ramona obligingly hopped up and down to make her ears flop.

Mrs Wisser said to her friend, as if Beezus and Ramona couldn't hear, 'Isn't she adorable?'

Both children knew whom Mrs Wisser was talking about. If she had been talking about Beezus, she would have said something quite different. Such a nice girl, probably. A sweet child, perhaps. Adorable, never.

'Just look at those eyes,' said Mrs Wisser.

Ramona beamed. She knew whose eyes they were talking about. Beezus knew too, but she didn't care. Mother said blue eyes were just as pretty as brown.

Mrs Wisser leaned over to Ramona. 'What colour are your eyes, sweetheart?' she asked.

'Brown and white,' said Ramona promptly.

'Brown and white eyes!' exclaimed the friend. 'Isn't that cunning?'

Beezus had thought it was cunning the first time she heard Ramona say it, about a year ago. Since then she had given up trying to explain to Ramona that she wasn't supposed to say she had brown and white eyes, because Ramona always answered, 'My eyes *are* brown and white,' and Beezus had to admit that, in a way, they were.

'And what is the little bunny's name?' asked Mrs Wisser's friend.

'My name is Ramona Geraldine Quimby,' answered Ramona, and then added generously, 'My sister's name is Beezus.'

'Beezus!' exclaimed the lady. 'What an odd name. Is it French?'

'Oh, no,' said Beezus. Wishing, as she so often did, that she had a more common nickname, like Betty or Patsy, she explained as quickly as she could how she happened to be called Beezus.

Ramona did not like to lose the attention of her audience. She hitched up the leg of her overalls and raised her knee. 'See my scab?' she said proudly. 'I fell down and hurt my knee and it bled and bled.'

'Ramona!' Beezus was horrified. 'You aren't supposed to show people your scabs.'

'Why?' asked Ramona. That was one of the most exasperating things about Ramona. She never seemed to understand what she was not supposed to do.

'It's a very nice scab,' said Mrs Wisser's friend, but she did not look as if she really thought it was nice.

'Well, we must be going,' said Mrs Wisser.

'Goodbye, Mrs Wisser,' said Beezus politely, and hoped that if they met anyone else they knew she could somehow manage to hide Ramona behind a bush.

'Bye-bye, Ramona,' said Mrs Wisser.

'Goodbye,' said Ramona, and Beezus knew that she felt that a girl who was four years old was too grown-up to say bye-bye.

Except for holding Ramona's hand crossing streets, Beezus lingered behind her the rest of the way to the library. She hoped that all the people who stopped and smiled at Ramona would not think they were together. When they reached the Glenwood Branch Library, she said, 'Ramona, wouldn't you like me to carry your ears for you now?'

'No,' said Ramona flatly.

Inside the library, Beezus hurried Ramona into the boys and girls' section and seated her on a little chair in front of the picture books. 'See, Ramona,' she whispered, 'here's a book about a duck. Wouldn't you like that?'

'No,' said Ramona in a loud voice.

Beezus's face turned red with embarrassment when

everyone in the library looked at Ramona's ears and smiled. 'Sh-h,' she whispered, as Miss Greever, the grown-ups' librarian, frowned in their direction. 'You're supposed to speak quietly in the library.'

Beezus selected another book. 'Look, Ramona. Here's a funny story about a kitten that falls into the goldfish bowl. Wouldn't you like that?'

'No,' said Ramona in a loud whisper. 'I want to find my own book.'

If only Miss Evans, the children's librarian, were there! She would know how to select a book for Ramona. Beezus noticed Miss Greever glance disapprovingly in their direction while the other grown-ups watched Ramona and smiled. 'All right, you can look,' Beezus agreed, to keep Ramona quiet. 'I'll go find a book for myself.'

When Beezus had selected her book, she returned to the picture-book section, where she found Ramona sitting on the bench with both arms clasped around a big flat book. 'I found my book,' she said, and held it up for Beezus to see. On the cover was a picture of a steam shovel with its jaws full of rocks. The title was *Big Steve the Steam Shovel*.

'Oh, Ramona,' whispered Beezus in dismay. 'You don't want that book.'

'I do, too,' insisted Ramona, forgetting to whisper. 'You told me I could pick out my own book.'

Under the disapproving stare of Miss Greever, Beezus gave up. Ramona was right. Beezus looked with distaste at the big orange-coloured book in its stout library binding. At least it would be due in two weeks, but Beezus did not feel very happy at the thought of two more weeks of steam shovels. And it just went to show how Ramona always got her own way.

Beezus took her book and Ramona's to Miss Greever's desk.

'Is this where you pay for the books?' asked Ramona.

'We don't have to pay for the books,' said Beezus.

'Are you going to charge them?' Ramona asked.

Beezus pulled her library card out of her sweater pocket. 'I show this card to the lady and she lets us keep the books for two weeks. A library isn't like a store, where you buy things.'

Ramona looked as if she did not understand. 'I want a card,' she said.

'You have to be able to write your own name before you can have a library card,' Beezus explained.

'I can write my name,' said Ramona.

'Oh, Ramona,' said Beezus, 'you can't, either.'

'Perhaps she really does know how to write her name,' said Miss Greever, as she took a card out of her desk. Beezus watched doubtfully while Miss Greever asked Ramona her name and age. Then the librarian asked Ramona what her father's occupation was. When Ramona didn't understand, she asked, 'What kind of work does your father do?'

'He mows the lawn,' said Ramona promptly.

The librarian laughed. 'I mean, how does he earn his living?'

Somehow Beezus did not like to have Miss Greever laugh at her little sister. After all, how could Ramona be expected to know what father did? 'He works for the Pacific Gas and Electric Company,' Beezus told the librarian.

Miss Greever wrote this down on the card and shoved it across the desk to Ramona. 'Write your name on this line,' she directed.

Nothing daunted, Ramona grasped the pencil in her fist and began to write. She bore down so hard that the tip snapped off the lead, but she wrote on. When she laid down the pencil, Beezus picked up the card to see what she had written. The line on the card was filled with

'That's my name,' said Ramona proudly.

'That's just scribbling,' Beezus told her.

'It is too my name,' insisted Ramona, while Miss Greever quietly dropped the card into the waste-basket. 'I've watched you write and I know how.'

'Here, Ramona, you can hold my card.' Beezus tried to be comforting. 'You can pretend it's yours.'

Ramona brightened at this, and Miss Greever checked out the books on Beezus's card. As soon as they got home, Ramona demanded, 'Read my new book to me.'

And so Beezus began. 'Big Steve was a steam shovel. He was the biggest steam shovel in the whole city . . . ' When she finished the book she had to admit she liked Big Steve better than Scoopy. His only sound effects were tooting and growling. He tooted and growled in big letters on every page. Big Steve did not shed tears or want to be a pile driver. He worked hard at being a steam shovel, and by the end of the book Beezus had learned a lot about steam shovels. Unfortunately, she did not want to learn about steam shovels. Oh, well, she guessed she could stand two weeks of Big Steve.

'Read it again,' said Ramona enthusiastically. 'I like Big Steve. He's better than Scoopy.'

'How would you like me to show you how to

really write your name?' Beezus asked, hoping to divert Ramona from steam shovels.

'OK,' agreed Ramona.

Beezus found pencil and paper and wrote *Ramona* in large, careful letters across the top of the paper.

Ramona studied it critically. 'I don't like it,' she said at last.

'But that's the way your name is spelled,' Beezus explained.

'You didn't make dots and lines,' said Ramona. Seizing the pencil, she wrote,

'But, Ramona, you don't understand.' Beezus took the pencil and wrote her own name on the paper. 'You've seen me write *Beatrice*, which has an *i* and a *t* in it. See, like that. You don't have an *i* or a *t* in your name, because it isn't spelled that way.'

Ramona looked sceptical. She grabbed the pencil again and wrote with a flourish,

'That's my name, because I like it,' she announced. 'I like to make dots and lines.' Lying flat on her stomach on the floor she proceeded to fill the paper with *i*'s and *t*'s.

'But, Ramona, nobody's name is spelled with just . . . ' Beezus stopped. What was the use? Trying to explain spelling and writing to Ramona was too complicated. Everything became difficult when Ramona was around, even an easy thing like taking a book out of the library. Well, if Ramona was happy thinking her name was spelled with *i*'s and *t*'s, she could go ahead and think it.

The next two weeks were fairly peaceful. Mother and father soon tired of tooting and growling and, like Beezus, they looked forward to the day *Big Steve* was due at the library. Father even tried to hide the book behind the radio, but Ramona soon found it. Beezus was happy that one part of her plan had worked—Ramona had forgotten *The Littlest Steam Shovel* now that she had a better book. On Ramona's second trip to the library, perhaps Miss Evans could find a book that would make her forget steam shovels entirely.

As for Ramona, she was perfectly happy. She had three people to read aloud a book she liked, and she spent much of her time covering sheets of paper with *i*'s and *t*'s. Sometimes she wrote in pencil, sometimes she wrote in crayon, and once she wrote in ink until her mother caught her at it.

Finally, to the relief of the rest of the family, the day came when *Big Steve* had to be returned. 'Come on, Ramona,' said Beezus. 'It's time to go to the library for another book.'

'I have a book,' said Ramona, who was lying on her stomach writing her version of her name on a piece of paper with purple crayon.

'No, it belongs to the library,' Beezus explained, glad that for once Ramona couldn't possibly get her own way.

'It's my book,' said Ramona, crossing several *t*'s with a flourish.

'Beezus is right, dear,' observed mother. 'Run along and get *Big Steve*.'

Ramona looked sulky, but she went into the bedroom. In a few minutes she appeared with *Big Steve* in her hand and a satisfied expression on her face. 'It's my book,' she announced. 'I wrote my name in it.'

Mother looked alarmed. 'What do you mean, Ramona? Let me see.' She took the book and opened it. Every page in the book was covered with enormous purple *i*'s and *t*'s in Ramona's very best handwriting.

'Mother!' cried Beezus. 'Look what she's done! And in crayon so it won't erase.'

'Ramona Quimby,' said mother. 'You're a very naughty girl! Why did you do a thing like that?'

'It's my book,' said Ramona stubbornly. 'I like it.'

'Mother, what am I going to do?' Beezus demanded. 'It's checked out on my card and I'm responsible. They won't let me take any more books out of the library, and I won't have anything to read, and it will all be Ramona's fault. She's always spoiling my fun and it isn't fair!' Beezus didn't know what she would do without her library card. She couldn't get along without library books. She just couldn't, that was all.

'I do *not* spoil your fun,' stormed Ramona. 'You have all the fun. I can't read and it isn't fair.' Ramona's words ended in a howl as she buried her face in her mother's skirt.

'I couldn't read when I was your age and I didn't have someone to read to me all the time, so it is too fair,' argued Beezus. 'You always get your own way, because you're the youngest.'

'I do not!' shouted Ramona. 'And you don't read all the time. You're mean!'

'I am *not* mean,' Beezus shouted back.

'Children!' cried mother. 'Stop it, both of you! Ramona, you were a very naughty girl!' A loud sniff came from Ramona. 'And, Beezus,' her mother continued, 'the library won't take your card away from you. If you'll get my purse I'll give you some money to pay for the damage to the book. Take Ramona along with you, explain what happened, and the librarian will tell you how much to pay.'

This made Beezus feel better. Ramona sulked all the way to the library, but when they got there Beezus was pleased to see that Miss Evans, the children's librarian, was sitting behind the desk. Miss Evans was the kind of librarian who would understand about little sisters.

'Hello, Beatrice,' said Miss Evans. 'Is this your little sister I've heard so much about?'

Beezus wondered what Miss Evans had heard about Ramona. 'Yes, this is Ramona,' she said and went on hesitantly, 'and, Miss Evans, she—'

'I'm a bad girl,' interrupted Ramona, smiling winningly at the librarian.

'Oh, you are?' said Miss Evans. 'What did you do?'

'I wrote in a book,' said Ramona, not the least ashamed. 'I wrote in purple crayon and it will never, never erase. Never, never, never.'

Embarrassed, Beezus handed Miss Evans *Big Steve the Steam Shovel*. 'Mother gave me the money to pay for the damage,' she explained.

The librarian turned the pages of the book. 'Well, you didn't miss a page, did you?' she finally said to Ramona.

'No,' said Ramona, pleased with herself. 'And it will never, never—'

'I'm awfully sorry,' interrupted Beezus. 'After this I'll try to keep our library books where she can't reach them.'

Miss Evans consulted a file of little cards in a drawer. 'Since every page in the book was damaged and the library can no longer use it, I'll have to ask you to pay for the whole book. I'm sorry, but this is the rule. It will cost two dollars and fifty cents.'

Two dollars and fifty cents! What a lot of things that would have bought, Beezus reflected, as she pulled three folded dollar bills out of her pocket and handed them to the librarian. Miss Evans put the money in a drawer and gave Beezus fifty cents in change.

Then Miss Evans took a rubber stamp and stamped something inside the book. By twisting her head around, Beezus could see that the word was *Discarded*. 'There!' Miss Evans said, pushing the book across the desk. 'You have paid for it, so now it's yours.'

Beezus stared at the librarian. 'You mean . . . to keep?'

'That's right,' answered Miss Evans.

Ramona grabbed the book. 'It's mine. I told you it was mine!' Then she turned to Beezus and said triumphantly, 'You said people didn't buy books at the library and now you just bought one!'

'Buying a book and paying for damage are not the same thing,' Miss Evans pointed out to Ramona.

Beezus could see that Ramona didn't care. The book was hers, wasn't it? It was paid for and she could keep it. And that's not fair, thought Beezus. Ramona shouldn't get her own way when she had been naughty.

'But, Miss Evans,' protested Beezus, 'if she spoils a book she shouldn't get to keep it. Now every time she finds a book she likes she will . . . ' Beezus did not go on. She knew very well what Ramona would do, but she wasn't going to say it out loud in front of her.

'I see what you mean.' Miss Evans looked thoughtful. 'Give me the book, Ramona,' she said.

Doubtfully Ramona handed her the book.

'Ramona, do you have a library card?' Miss Evans asked.

Ramona shook her head.

'Then Beezus must have taken the book out on her card,' said Miss Evans. 'So the book belongs to Beezus.'

Why, of course! Why hadn't she thought of that before? It was her book, not Ramona's. 'Oh, thank you,' said Beezus gratefully, as Miss Evans handed the book to her. She could do anything she wanted with it.

For once Ramona didn't know what to say. She scowled and looked as if she were building up to a tantrum. 'You've got to read it to me,' she said at last.

'Not unless I feel like it,' said Beezus. 'After all, it's my book,' she couldn't resist adding.

'That's not fair!' Ramona looked as if she were about to howl.

'It is too fair,' said Beezus calmly. 'And if you have a tantrum I won't read to you at all.'

Suddenly, as if she had decided Beezus meant what she said, Ramona stopped scowling. 'OK,' she said cheerfully.

Beezus watched her carefully for a minute. Yes, she really was being agreeable, thought Beezus with a great feeling of relief. And now that she did not have to read *Big Steve* unless she wanted to, Beezus felt she would not mind reading it once in a while. 'Come on, Ramona,' she said. 'Maybe

I'll have time to read to you before father comes home.'

'OK,' said Ramona happily, as she took Beezus's hand.

Miss Evans smiled at the girls as they started to leave. 'Good luck, Beatrice,' she said.

2

BEEZUS AND HER IMAGINATION

Beezus and Ramona both looked forward to Friday afternoons after school—Beezus because she attended the art class in the recreation centre in Glenwood Park, Ramona because she was allowed to go to the park with Beezus and play in the sand pile until the class was over. This Friday while Beezus held Ramona by the hand and waited for the traffic light to change from red to green, she thought how wonderful it would be to have an imagination like Ramona's.

'Oh, you know Ramona. Her imagination runs away with her,' mother said, when Ramona made up a story about seeing a fire engine crash into a garbage truck.

'That child has an imagination a mile long,' the Quimbys' grown-up friends remarked when Ramona sat in the middle of the living-room floor in a plastic wading pool she had dragged up from the basement and pretended she was in a boat in the middle of a lake.

'Did you ever see so much imagination in such a

little girl?' the neighbours asked one another when Ramona hopped around the yard pretending she was the Easter bunny.

One spring day Ramona had got lost, because she started out to find the pot of gold at the end of the rainbow. The rainbow had appeared to end in the park until she reached the park, but then it looked as if it ended behind the supermarket. When the police brought Ramona home, father said, 'Sometimes I think Ramona has too much imagination.'

Nobody, reflected Beezus, ever says anything about my imagination. Nobody at all. And she wished, more than anything, that she had imagination. How pleased Miss Robbins, the art teacher, would be with her if she had an imagination like Ramona's!

Unfortunately, Beezus was not very good at painting—at least not the way Miss Robbins wanted boys and girls to paint. She wanted them to use their imagination and to feel free. Beezus still squirmed with embarrassment when she thought of her first painting, a picture of a dog with *bowwow* coming out of his mouth in a balloon. Miss Robbins pointed out that only in the funny papers did dogs have *bowwow* coming out of their mouths in balloons. *Bowwow* in a balloon was not art. When Miss Robbins did think one of

Beezus's paintings was good enough to put up on the wall, she always pinned it way down at the end, never in the centre. Beezus wished she could have a painting in the centre of the wall.

'Hurry up, Ramona,' Beezus coaxed. Then she noticed that her sister was dragging a string along behind her. 'Oh, Ramona,' she protested, 'why did you have to bring Ralph with you?' Ralph was an imaginary green lizard Ramona liked to pretend she was leading by a string.

'I love Ralph,' said Ramona firmly, 'and Ralph likes to go to the park.'

Beezus knew it was easier to pretend along with Ramona than to try to make her stop. Anyway, it was better to have her pretend to lead a lizard than to pretend to be a lizard herself. 'Can't you carry him?' she suggested.

'No,' said Ramona. 'He's slimy.'

When the girls came to the shopping district, Ramona had to stop at the chemist's scales and pretend to weigh herself while Beezus held Ralph's string. 'I weigh fifty-eleven pounds,' she announced, while Beezus smiled at Ramona's idea of her weight. It just goes to show how much imagination Ramona has, she thought.

At the radio-and-record player store Ramona insisted on petting His Master's Voice, the black-and-white plaster dog, bigger than Ramona, that always sat with one ear cocked in front of the door. Beezus thought admiringly about the amount of imagination it took to pretend that a scarred and chipped plaster dog was real. If only she had an imagination like Ramona's, maybe Miss Robbins would say her paintings were free and imaginative and would pin them on the middle of the wall.

When they reached the park, Beezus left Ramona and Ralph at the sand pile and, feeling more and more discouraged at her own lack of imagination, hurried to the recreation centre. The class had already poured paints into their muffin tins and were painting on paper pinned to drawing boards. The room hummed with activity. Miss Robbins, wearing a gay paint-smeared smock, flew from one artist to another, praising, correcting, suggesting.

Beezus waited until Miss Robbins finished explaining to a boy that he should not outline a mouth with black paint. Her mouth wasn't outlined in black, was it? Then Beezus said, 'I'm sorry I'm late, Miss Robbins.' She stared in fascination at Miss Robbins's earrings. They came almost to her shoulders and were made of silver wire twisted and bent into interesting shapes—not the shape of anything in particular, just interesting shapes.

'That's all right.' Miss Robbins, her earrings

swinging, smiled at Beezus. 'Get your paints and paper. Today everyone is painting an imaginary animal.'

'An imaginary animal?' Beezus repeated blankly. How could she possibly think of an imaginary animal? As Beezus poured paints into her muffin tin and pinned a sheet of paper to her drawing board, she tried to think of an imaginary animal, but all the animals she could think of—cats and dogs, cows and horses, lions and giraffes—were discouragingly real.

Reluctantly Beezus took the only vacant seat, which was beside a boy named Wayne who came to the class only because his mother made him. Once Beezus had hung her sweater on the back of a chair, and Wayne had printed 'Post No Bills' on it in chalk. Beezus had worn it all the way home before she discovered it. Since then she did not care to sit beside Wayne. Today she noticed he had parked a grape-flavoured lollipop on a paper towel beside his muffin tin of paints.

'Hi, Beez,' he greeted her. 'No fair licking my lolly.'

'I don't want your old lolly,' answered Beezus. 'And don't call me Beez.'

'OK, Beez,' said Wayne.

At that moment the door opened and Ramona walked into the room. She was still dragging the string behind her and she looked angry.

'Why, hello,' said Miss Robbins pleasantly.

'Oh, Ramona, you're supposed to be playing in the sand pile,' said Beezus, going over to her.

'No,' said Ramona flatly. 'Howie threw sand on Ralph.' Her dark eyes were busy taking in the paints, the brushes, the drawing boards. 'I'm going to paint,' she announced.

'Mother said you were supposed to play in the sand pile,' protested Beezus. 'You're too little for this class.'

'You say that about everything,' complained Ramona. Then she turned to Miss Robbins. 'Don't step on Ralph,' she said.

'Ralph is a make-believe green lizard she pretends she leads around on a string.' Beezus was embarrassed at having to explain such a silly thing.

Miss Robbins laughed. 'Well, here is a little girl with lots of imagination. How would you like to paint a picture of Ralph for us, Ramona?'

Beezus could not help feeling annoyed. Miss Robbins was letting Ramona stay in the class— the one place where she was never allowed to tag along! Miss Robbins would probably like her painting, because it would be so full of imagination. Ramona's pictures, in fact, were so full of imagination that it took even more imagination to tell what they were.

Ramona beamed at Miss Robbins, who found a drawing board for her and a stool, which she placed between Beezus and Wayne. She lifted Ramona onto the stool. 'There. Now you can share your sister's paints,' she said.

Ramona looked impressed at being allowed to paint with such big boys and girls. She sat quietly on her stool, watching everything around her.

Maybe she'll behave herself after all, thought Beezus as she dipped her brush into blue paint, and now I don't have to sit next to Wayne. Since Beezus still had not thought of an imaginary animal, she decided to start with the sky.

'Do the sky first,' Beezus whispered to Ramona, who looked as if she did not know how to begin. Then Beezus faced her own work, determined to be free and imaginative. To be free on a piece of paper was not as easy as it sounded, she thought. Miss Robbins always said to start with the big areas of a picture and paint them bravely and boldly, so Beezus spread the sky on her paper with brave, bold strokes. Back and forth across the paper she swept her brush. Brave and bold and free—that was the way to do it.

Her sky turned out to be too wet, so while it dried a little, Beezus looked at what the other boys and girls were doing. Celia, who sat on her left, had already filled in a brave, bold background of pink, which she had sprinkled with big purple dots. Now she was painting a long grey line that wound all over the paper, in and out around the dots.

'What's that supposed to be?' whispered Beezus.

'I'm not sure yet,' answered Celia.

Beezus felt better, because Celia was the kind of girl who usually knew exactly what she was doing and whose pictures were often pinned in the centre of the wall. The boy on the other side of Celia, who always wanted to paint aeroplanes, was painting what looked like a giraffe made of pieces of machinery, and another boy was painting a thing that had two heads.

Beezus looked across Ramona to Wayne. He had not bothered with a sky at all. He had painted a hen. Beezus knew it was a hen, because he had printed in big letters, 'This is a real hen,' with an arrow pointing to it. Wayne always tried to do just the opposite of what Miss Robbins wanted.

'Hey, quit peeking,' said Wayne in a loud voice.

'I'm not peeking,' said Beezus, hastily trying to look as if she had been interested in Ramona's paper all the time.

Ramona had dipped her brush into blue paint and had painted a stripe across the top of her paper. 'That's the sky,' she said happily.

'But that's not the way the sky is.' Beezus was

trying to be helpful. She felt better, because Ramona had not plunged in and painted a picture full of imagination. 'Skies should come further down on the paper.'

'The sky is up,' said Ramona firmly.

Beezus decided she couldn't waste time explaining about skies, not when she still hadn't thought of an imaginary animal. Maybe she could take a real animal and sort of change it around. Let's see, she thought, I could take a horse and put feathers on it. No, all those feathers would be too hard to paint. Wings? That was it! A horse with wings was an imaginary animal—a real imaginary animal—because mother had once read aloud a story about Pegasus, the winged horse, out of a library book. In the story Pegasus had been white, which was a real horse colour. Beezus decided to be extra-imaginative. She would make her horse green—a green horse against a blue sky. Miss Robbins ought to like that. Beezus did not think blue and green looked very pretty together, but Miss Robbins often liked colours that Beezus thought did not really go together.

Beezus dipped her brush into green paint and outlined a wing against the sky. Next she outlined the body of the horse and a long tail that hung down. It was a magnificent horse. At least, Beezus hoped it would look magnificent when she finished it. Anyway, it was big, because Miss Robbins liked her artists to cover the whole paper. Quickly and neatly Beezus filled in the outline of the horse, because Miss Robbins, who was looking at Celia's picture, would look at hers next. Somehow the horse was not exactly what Beezus had in her mind's eye, but even so, compared to whatever Celia was painting, a green horse with wings was really a very good imaginary animal. And except for a couple of soggy places in the sky, her work was much neater than Celia's. Beezus waited for Miss Robbins to point this out.

Instead, Miss Robbins said, 'Celia, your picture is work to be proud of. It is a difficult thing to get to be as free as this.'

Then Miss Robbins moved on to Beezus, her long earrings swinging forward as she leaned over the drawing board. Beezus waited anxiously. Maybe her picture wasn't so good, after all. If Miss Robbins liked a grey line winding around a lot of purple dots, maybe she wouldn't like a flying horse. Maybe she liked things with no special shape, like those earrings.

'You have a good sky even if it is a little wet,' said Miss Robbins.

Beezus was disappointed. Anybody could have a good sky.

Miss Robbins continued to study the picture.

'Try to think how a horse would look if it were really flying.'

Beezus tried to think.

'What about the tail?' asked Miss Robbins. 'Wouldn't the tail fly out behind instead of hanging down?'

'Especially if the wind blew real hard,' said Wayne.

'Can't you make the horse look rounder?' asked Miss Robbins. 'Think how a horse looks with the sun shining on him. Part of him would be in shadow.'

'Not that horse,' said Wayne. 'She just copied it off a petrol station billboard, only she made it green instead of red.'

'I did not!' said Beezus indignantly. Then she stared at her painting again. Now that Wayne pointed it out, she could see her horse did look like the one on the billboard at the service station where her father bought petrol. He was a flat cardboard horse, not a magnificent horse at all. Her horse wasn't even as good as the horse on the billboard, because instead of a flying tail he had a tail that hung down like . . . well, like a mop.

'All right, Wayne,' said Miss Robbins. 'I'm sure Beezus did not mean to copy anything from a billboard.'

'No, I didn't,' said Beezus mournfully. 'I was only trying to change a real animal around to make it imaginary, but I just don't have imagination, is all.'

'Why, Beezus, of course you have imagination!' Miss Robbins sounded shocked at the idea of anyone's not having imagination.

'My little sister has lots of imagination,' said Beezus. 'Everybody says so.'

Miss Robbins smiled reassuringly. 'That doesn't mean that you don't have any. I think your trouble is that you work too hard. You don't have to be so neat. Why don't you start another painting and just try to have a good time with your paints?'

Beezus looked uncertain. It was a nice change to have a grown-up tell her she didn't have to be neat, but she didn't understand how she could paint a good picture unless she worked at it. If only she had some imagination, like Ramona—but no, Miss Robbins said everybody had imagination. Well, if she had imagination, where was it? Why wasn't it helping her with her imaginary animal? All she could think of was that cardboard horse on the billboard.

Beezus glanced at Ramona, who had been surprisingly quiet for a long time, to see how she was coming along with her picture of Ralph.

Except for the stripe of sky at the top, Ramona's paper was blank. Now she dipped her brush in yellow paint, divided the hairs of the brush into three tufts, and pressed them on the paper, leaving a mark like the track of a bird.

'That's not the way to use a paint brush,' said Beezus. 'Besides, you're getting paint on your fingers.'

'Look—Ralph's feet marks,' exclaimed Ramona, paying no attention to Beezus.

'You mean footprints,' corrected Beezus. 'Now go on and paint the rest of Ralph.'

'Feet marks,' said Ramona stubbornly, making more footprints across the paper. 'And I can't paint him, because he's just pretend.'

Oh, well, thought Beezus, maybe making foot-prints isn't good for the brush, but it keeps her quiet. She dabbled her own brush in green paint and tried to stir up her imagination. She felt a little encouraged because Ramona was having trouble too.

'Hey!' interrupted Wayne in a loud voice. 'She's licking my lolly!'

'Ramona!' Beezus was horrified to see Ramona, no longer interested in footprints, calmly sucking Wayne's grape-flavoured lollipop. 'Ramona, put that down this instant! You're not supposed to lick other people's lollies.'

'You give me that!' Wayne made a grab for his lollipop.

'No!' screamed Ramona, trying to hold it out of his reach. 'I want it!'

'Ramona, give it to him,' ordered Beezus. 'It's all germy.'

'You mean she's getting germs on it,' said Wayne. 'Give it to me!'

The rest of the class stopped painting to watch. Wayne made another grab for his lollipop. This time he grabbed Ramona by the wrist.

'Let go of her!' said Beezus angrily.

Ramona howled as Wayne tried to prise her fingers loose from the lollipop stick. He knocked against his muffin tin, which flipped into the air spattering paint over the table, the drawing boards, and the floor. Ramona was splashed with red and yellow paint. Blue and green ran down Wayne's jeans onto his sneakers. A pool of brown paint dripped off the table onto the floor.

'Now see what you did,' said Wayne, after he had prised his lollipop out of Ramona's fist.

'See what *you* did,' contradicted Beezus. 'Picking on my little sister like that!' She picked up the paper towel the lollipop had been resting on and began to wipe the spatters off Ramona, who continued to howl.

'Boys and girls!' Miss Robbins raised her voice.

'Let's be quiet. When the room is quiet I know you are thinking. Lots of people don't know you have to think while you paint.' Then she turned to Wayne. 'All right, Wayne, you may get a damp cloth and wipe up that paint.'

'I'm sorry, Miss Robbins,' said Beezus.

'I want the lolly!' screamed Ramona.

Suddenly Beezus decided she had had enough. This art class was one place where Ramona was not supposed to be. She was supposed to play in the sand pile. Mother had said so. She was not supposed to upset the class and spoil everything with one of her tantrums. Beezus made up her mind she was going to do something about it and right now, too, though she didn't know what.

'Ramona, stop that this instant,' Beezus ordered. 'Go out and play in the sand pile, where you belong, or I'll . . . I'll . . . ' Frantically Beezus tried to think what she could do. Then she had an inspiration. 'Or I'll tickle you!' she finished. I guess I do have some imagination, after all, she thought triumphantly.

Instantly Ramona stopped crying. She hugged herself and stared at Beezus. 'Don't tickle, Beezus,' she begged. 'Please don't tickle.'

'Then go out and play in the sand pile, like mother says you're supposed to,' said Beezus.

'Don't tickle,' shrieked Ramona, as she scrambled down from her stool and ran out of the door.

Well! thought Beezus. It worked! It really worked!

Feeling suddenly lighthearted, she pinned a fresh sheet of paper to her drawing board and sat staring at it. Maybe Ramona didn't have so much imagination after all, if she couldn't draw a picture of an imaginary green lizard. Well, if Ramona couldn't paint a picture of Ralph, *she* could. Ramona was not the only one in the family with imagination. So there!

Beezus seized her brush and painted in another sky with bold, free strokes. Then she dipped her brush into green paint and started to outline a lizard on her paper. Let's see, what did a lizard look like? She could not remember. It didn't matter much, anyway—not for an imaginary animal. She had started the lizard with such brave, bold strokes that it took up most of the paper and looked more like a dragon.

Beezus promptly decided the animal was a dragon. Dragons breathed fire, but she did not have any orange paint, and she was so late in starting this picture that she didn't want to take time to mix any. She dipped her brush into pink paint instead and made flames come out of the dragon's mouth. Only they didn't look like flames.

They looked more like the candyfloss Beezus had once eaten at the circus. And a dragon breathing clouds of pink candyfloss was more fun than an ordinary flame-breathing dragon.

Forgetting everyone around her, Beezus made the pink clouds bigger and fluffier. Dragons had pointed things down their backs, so Beezus made a row of spines down the back. They did not look quite right—more like slanting sticks than spines. Lollipop sticks, of course!

At that Beezus laughed to herself. Naturally a dragon that breathed pink candyfloss would have lollipops down its back. Eagerly she dipped her brush into red paint and put a strawberry lollipop on one of the sticks. She painted a different flavour on each stick, finishing with a grape-flavoured lollipop like the one Wayne and Ramona had shared.

Then she held her drawing board at arm's length. She was pleased with her dragon. It was funny and colourful and really imaginary. Beezus wondered what she should do next. Then she remembered that Miss Robbins often said it was important for an artist to know when to stop painting. Maybe she'd spoil her picture if she added anything. No, just one more touch. She dipped her brush in yellow paint and gave the dragon an eye—a lemon-drop eye. There! Her imaginary animal was finished!

By that time it was four-thirty and most of the boys and girls had put away their drawing boards and washed their muffin tins. Several mothers who had come for their children were wandering around the room looking at the paintings.

'Those who have finished, wash your hands clean,' said Miss Robbins. 'And I mean clean.' Then she came across the room to Beezus. 'Why, Beezus!' she exclaimed. 'This is a picture to be proud of!'

'I didn't know whether a dragon should have lollipops down his back or not, but they were fun to paint,' said Beezus.

'Of course he can have lollipops down his back. It's a splendid idea. After all, no one has ever seen a dragon, so no one knows how one should look.' Miss Robbins turned to several of the mothers and said, with admiration in her voice, 'Here's a girl with real imagination.'

Beezus smiled modestly at her toes while the mothers admired her picture.

'We'll pin this in the very centre of the wall for next week's classes to see,' said Miss Robbins.

'It was fun to paint,' confided Beezus, her face flushed with pleasure.

'Of course it was,' said Miss Robbins, as she carefully placed the picture in the centre of the wall. 'Didn't I tell you you worked too hard at painting before?'

Beezus nodded. That was the wonderful thing about it, she thought, as she scrubbed out her muffin tins. Her dragon had been fun, while her flying horse had been work. And she had imagination. Maybe not as much as Ramona, but real imagination just the same. 'Here's a girl with real imagination,' Miss Robbins had said.

A girl with real imagination, a girl with real imagination, Beezus thought as she left the building and ran across the park to the sand pile. 'Come on, Ramona, it's time to go home,' she called to her little sister, who was happily sprinkling sand on a sleeping dog. 'And let's not forget Ralph!' Good old Ralph!

3

Ramona and Ribsy

One day after school Henry Huggins, who lived in the next block, came over to play checkers with Beezus. His dog Ribsy came with him, because Henry never went anywhere without Ribsy. Beezus liked Henry, because she knew he thought she had more sense than most girls, and the two often played checkers together. So far Beezus had won forty-eight games and Henry had won forty-nine, not counting the games Ramona had spoiled by tipping over the checkerboard.

This afternoon Beezus and Henry knelt on either side of the coffee table with the checkerboard between them. Ribsy lay on the rug near Henry and warily watched Ramona, who was wearing her rabbit ears and riding her tricycle around the living room.

'Your move,' said Henry to Beezus.

'I want to play,' said Ramona, riding her tricycle up to the coffee table and shaking her head to make her ears flop. Ribsy got up and moved to a corner, where he lay down with his nose on his paws to watch Ramona.

'You're too little,' said Beezus, as she moved a checker. 'Besides, only two can play checkers.'

'We could play tiddlywinks,' said Ramona. 'I know how to play tiddlywinks.'

Beezus did not answer. Her mind was on the game as she watched Henry's move very carefully.

'I said we could play tiddlywinks,' yelled Ramona.

Beezus looked up from the checkerboard. 'Ramona, you stop bothering us,' she said in her severest voice.

Ramona scowled and pedalled backwards away from the coffee table while Beezus returned to her game and studied the board. She had to be careful, because Henry had already captured half of her checkers. Let's see, she thought, I could move from here to there—no, that wouldn't work, because then he could—but if I move from there to there—yes, that was it! Beezus lifted her hand to pick up the checker.

At that instant Ramona pedalled as fast as she could towards the coffee table. Crash! The front wheel of Ramona's tricycle rammed into the table. Checkers bounced into the air and showered over the table, falling to the floor and rolling across the rug.

'There!' said Ramona, and calmly pedalled away.

'Hey!' protested Henry.

'Mother!' Beezus called. 'Ramona's bothering us!'

Wiping her hands on her apron, mother came out of the kitchen. 'Ramona, you know you're not supposed to bother Henry and Beezus when they're playing checkers. Now go to your room and stay there until you are able to behave yourself.'

'No,' said Ramona. 'I don't have anybody to play with me and I want Beezus and Henry to play with me.'

'You heard me.' Mother lifted Ramona off the tricycle.

I'll bet she has a tantrum, thought Beezus, as she picked up the checkers.

'No!' screamed Ramona.

'Ramona,' said mother in a warning voice, 'I'm going to count to ten.'

Ramona threw herself on the floor and kicked and screamed.

'One . . . two . . . ' began mother.

Ramona went on kicking and screaming until mother counted to seven. Then she lay still on the floor, watching to see if mother really meant what she said.

'Eight . . . nine,' said mother.

Ramona got to her feet, ran into the bedroom,

and slammed the door. Mother returned to the kitchen, and Beezus and Henry started a new game as if nothing had happened. Tantrums were not unusual in the Quimby household. Even Henry knew that.

In a few minutes Beezus heard Ramona open the bedroom door. 'Now can I come out?' she called.

'Can you stop bothering Beezus and Henry?' mother asked from the kitchen.

'No,' said Ramona, and shut the door.

Not more than one minute later Ramona opened the door again and came into the living room. 'I can stop bothering,' she said with a sulky look on her face, and Beezus could see she was still cross because she had been punished.

'That's good,' called mother. 'Come here, and I'll give you a cookie.'

Seeing Ramona go into the kitchen, Ribsy sat up, scratched, and trotted after her. Although Ribsy did not trust Ramona, he was always interested in what went on in a kitchen.

I hope she stays in the kitchen, thought Beezus, as she picked up a checker and skipped from here to there to there and captured two of Henry's men. The game became so exciting that Beezus almost forgot about Ramona. At the same time she was vaguely aware of scuffling sounds in the hall. Then she heard the jingle of Ribsy's licence tags and the click of his claws on the hardwood floor. Ribsy gave a short bark. Then the bathroom door slammed. I wonder what Ramona is doing, thought Beezus, as she captured another checker, but she did not much care so long as Ramona did not interrupt the game.

'Let me in!' screamed Ramona from the hall. 'Let me in the bathroom.'

'Ramona, who are you talking to?' asked mother as she went into the hall.

'Ribsy,' said Ramona, and beat on the door with her fists.

Ribsy began to bark. From behind the bathroom door his barks made a hollow, echoing sound. Puzzled, Henry looked at Beezus. Ribsy in the bathroom? Henry decided he had better investigate. Reluctantly Beezus left the game and followed him into the hall.

'Open the door and let him out,' said mother.

'I can't,' shouted Ramona angrily, above Ribsy's furious barks. 'The bad old dog went and locked the door.'

'Oh, stop pretending.' Beezus was exasperated with Ramona for interrupting the game a second time. It was too bad that a girl couldn't have a friend over for a game of checkers without her little sister spoiling all her fun.

'I'm not pretending,' screamed Ramona, clinging

to the doorknob while Ribsy barked and scratched at the other side of the door.

'Ramona!' mother's voice was stern. 'Let that dog out.'

'I can't,' cried Ramona, rattling the bathroom door. 'The bad old dog locked me out.'

'Nonsense. Dogs can't lock doors,' scolded mother. 'Now open that door and let him out.'

Ramona began to sob and Ribsy barked louder. Ramona gave the door a good hard kick.

'Oh, for Pete's sake,' muttered Henry.

'Ramona, I am very cross with you,' said mother. She prised Ramona's fingers loose and started to open the door. The knob would not turn. 'That's strange,' she remarked, and rattled the door herself. Then she hit the door with her fist to see if it might be stuck. The door did not budge. There was no doubt about it. The bathroom door was locked.

'But how could it be locked?' Henry asked.

'I told you Ribsy locked it,' Ramona shouted.

'Don't be silly,' said Beezus impatiently.

'Now how on earth—' began mother in a puzzled voice and then she interrupted herself. 'Do you suppose when Ribsy was pawing at the door he bumped against the button in the centre of the knob and really did lock the door? Of course! That's exactly what must have happened.'

A dog that locked the bathroom door! That

Ribsy, thought Beezus. He's always getting into trouble, and now he's locked the Quimbys out of their bathroom.

'I told you he locked the door,' Ramona said.

'Yes, but what was my dog doing in the bathroom in the first place?' Henry demanded.

'I put him there,' said Ramona.

'Ramona Quimby!' Even mother sounded exasperated. 'Sometimes I don't know what gets into you. You know dogs don't belong in the bathroom. Now go to your room and stay there until I tell you to come out.'

'Yes, but—' Ramona began.

'I don't want to have to speak to you again.' It was unusual for mother to be as stern as this.

Still crying, Ramona went to her room, which was next to the bathroom. Since mother had not told her to close the door, Ramona stood just inside it and waited to see what would happen next.

'Where is the key?' Beezus asked.

'I don't know,' answered mother. 'I don't remember that we ever had a key.'

'But there's a keyhole,' said Beezus. 'There must be a key.'

'Ribsy, be quiet,' ordered Henry. 'We'll get you out.' But Ribsy only barked harder, and his barks echoed and re-echoed around the small room.

'No one gave us a key to the bathroom when

we rented the house,' explained mother. 'And when Ramona first learned to walk we fastened the button down with Scotch tape so she couldn't lock herself in.'

'You did?' Ramona, fascinated with this bit of information about herself, stopped crying and leaned out into the hall. 'How big was I then?' No one bothered to answer her.

'We've got to get Ribsy out of the bathroom,' said Beezus.

'Yes,' agreed mother, 'but how?'

'If you have a ladder I'll climb in the bathroom window and unlock the door,' Henry offered.

'The window is locked too,' said mother, bending over to examine the knob on the door.

'Maybe we could call the fire department.' Henry tried another suggestion. 'They're always rescuing cats and things.'

'They couldn't do anything with the bathroom window locked,' Beezus pointed out.

'I guess that's right.' Henry sounded disappointed. It would have been exciting to have the fire department rescue Ribsy.

'Well, I just can't see any way to take the knob off,' said mother. 'There aren't any screws on this side of the door.'

'We've got to get him out some way,' said Henry. 'We can't leave him in there. He'll get hungry.'

Beezus did not think this remark of Henry's was very thoughtful. Of course Ribsy would get hungry if he stayed in the bathroom long enough, but on the other hand they would need their bathroom and it was Henry's dog who had locked them out. Then Beezus made a suggestion. 'Maybe if we pushed some glue under the door so Ribsy would get his paws in it, and then called to him so he would scratch the door, maybe his paws would stick to the button in the knob and he could unlock it himself.' Beezus thought her idea was a good one until she saw the disgusted look on Henry's face. 'I just thought it might work,' she said apologetically.

'Mother—' began Ramona, leaning out into the hall.

Mother paid no attention to her. 'I just don't see what we can do—'

'*Mother*,' said Ramona urgently. This time she stepped into the hall.

'Unless we get a ladder (Go back to your room, Ramona) and break the window so we can unlock it,' mother continued, speaking with one sentence inside another, the way grown-ups so often did with Ramona around.

'But, *mother*,' insisted Ramona even more urgently, 'I have to—'

'Oh, dear, I might have known,' sighed mother. 'Well, come on. I'll take you next door.'

Leave it to Ramona, thought Beezus, embarrassed to have her little sister behave this way in front of Henry.

'Don't worry, Ribsy,' said Henry. 'We'll get you out somehow.' He turned to Beezus and said gloomily, 'If we don't get him out by dinnertime, maybe we could cut some meat up in real little pieces and shove it under the door to him. I don't see how we could get a drink of water to him, though.'

'We have to get him out before then,' said Beezus. 'Father wouldn't like it if he came home and found Ribsy had locked him out of the bathroom.'

'Ribsy couldn't have locked the door if Ramona hadn't put him in the bathroom in the first place,' Henry pointed out. 'What a dumb thing to do!'

Beezus had nothing to say to this. What could she say when it really had been Ramona's fault?

Mother and Ramona soon returned. 'I think we'll get Ribsy out now,' said mother cheerfully. 'The lady next door says her little grandson locks himself in the bathroom every time he comes to visit her, and she always unlocks the door with a nail file. She told me how to do it.' Mother found a nail file, which she inserted in the keyhole. She wiggled it around, the doorknob clicked, and mother opened the door. It was as easy as that!

With a joyous bark Ribsy bounded out and jumped up on Henry. 'Good old Ribsy,' said Henry. 'Did you think we were going to leave you in there?' Ribsy wriggled and wagged his tail happily because he was free at last.

'Now maybe he'll be a good dog,' said Ramona sulkily.

'He is a good dog, aren't you, Ribsy?' Henry patted him.

'He is *not* a good dog,' contradicted Ramona. 'He took my cookie away from me and gobbled it right up.'

'Oh,' said Henry uncomfortably. 'I didn't know he ate your cookie.'

'Well, he did,' said Ramona, 'and I made him go in the bathroom until he could be a good dog.'

From the way Henry looked at Ramona, Beezus could tell he didn't think much of her reason for shutting Ribsy in the bathroom.

'Oh, Ramona.' Mother looked amused and exasperated at the same time. 'Just because you were sent to your room is no reason for you to try to punish Henry's dog.'

'It is too,' said Ramona defiantly. 'He was bad.'

'Well, I guess I better be going,' said Henry. 'Come on, Ribsy.'

'Don't go, Henry,' begged Beezus. 'Maybe we could go out on the porch or someplace and play a game.'

'Some other time maybe,' answered Henry. 'I've got things to do.'

'All right,' agreed Beezus reluctantly. Henry probably knew they wouldn't be safe from Ramona anywhere, the way she was behaving today.

When Henry had gone, Ramona gave a hop to make her rabbit ears flop. '*Now* we can play tiddlywinks!' she announced, as if she had been waiting for this moment all afternoon.

'No, we can't,' snapped Beezus, who could not remember when she had been so annoyed with Ramona.

'Yes, we can,' said Ramona. 'Henry's gone now.'

'We can't, because I won't play. So there!' answered Beezus. It wasn't as though Henry came over every day to play checkers. He came only once in a while, and then they couldn't play because Ramona was so awful.

Just then the telephone rang and mother answered it. 'Oh, hello, Beatrice,' Beezus heard her say. 'I was hoping you'd call.'

'Tiddlywinks, tiddlywinks, I want to play tiddlywinks,' chanted Ramona, shaking her head back and forth.

'Not after the way you spoiled our checker

game,' said Beezus. 'I wouldn't play tiddlywinks with you for a million dollars.'

'Yes!' shouted Ramona.

'Children!' Mother put her hand over the mouthpiece of the telephone. 'I'm trying to talk to your Aunt Beatrice.'

For a moment Beezus forgot her quarrel with Ramona. 'Is she coming over today?' she asked eagerly.

'Not today.' Mother smiled at Beezus. 'But I'll tell her you wish she'd come.'

'Tell her she hasn't been here for two whole weeks,' said Beezus.

'Tiddlywinks, tiddlywinks,' chanted Ramona, more quietly this time. 'We're going to play tiddlywinks.'

'We are not!' whispered Beezus furiously. And as she looked at Ramona a terrible thought came to her. Right that very instant she was so exasperated with Ramona that she did not like her at all. Not one little bit. Crashing her tricycle into the checkerboard, throwing a tantrum, and shoving a dog into the bathroom—how could one four-year-old be such a pest all in one afternoon? And Ramona wasn't one bit sorry about it, either. She was glad she had driven Henry home with her naughtiness. Just look at her, thought Beezus. Cookie crumbs sticking to the front of her overalls, her hands and face dirty, and those silly paper ears. She's just awful, that's what she is, perfectly awful—and she looks so cheerful. To look at her you wouldn't know she'd done a thing. She's spoiled my whole afternoon and she's happy. She even thinks she'll get me to play tiddlywinks with her. Well, I won't. I won't, because I don't like her *one little bit*!

To get away from Ramona, Beezus stalked into the living room and threw herself into her father's big chair. Not one little bit, she thought fiercely. But as Beezus sat listening to her mother chatting and laughing over the telephone, she began to feel uncomfortable. She ought to like Ramona. Sisters always liked each other. They were supposed to. Like mother and Aunt Beatrice. But that was different, Beezus thought quickly. Aunt Beatrice wasn't like Ramona. She was—well, she was Aunt Beatrice, loving and understanding and full of fun. Ramona was noisy and grubby and exasperating.

I feel so mixed up, thought Beezus. Sometimes I don't like Ramona at all, and I'm supposed to like her because she's my sister, and . . . Oh, dear, even if she's little, can't she ever be more like other people's sisters?

4

RaMONa aND THe APPLeS

'Mother, I'm home,' Beezus called, as she burst into the house one afternoon after school.

Mother appeared, wearing her hat and coat and carrying a shopping list in her hand. She kissed Beezus. 'How was school today?' she asked.

'All right. We studied about Christopher Columbus,' said Beezus.

'Did you, dear?' said mother absent-mindedly. 'I wonder if you'd mind keeping an eye on Ramona for half an hour or so while I do the shopping. She was up so late last night I let her have a long nap this afternoon, and I wasn't able to go out until she woke up.'

'All right, I'll look after her,' agreed Beezus.

'I told her she could have two marshmallows,' said mother, as she left the house.

Ramona came out of the kitchen with a marshmallow in each hand. Her nose was covered with white powder. 'What's Christopher Colummus?' she asked.

'Christopher Columbus,' Beezus corrected.

'Come here, Ramona. Let me wipe off your nose.'

'No,' said Ramona, backing away. 'I just powdered it.' Closing her eyes, Ramona pounded one of the marshmallows against her nose. Powdered sugar flew all over her face. 'These are my powder puffs,' she explained.

Beezus started to tell Ramona not to be silly, she'd get all sticky, but then decided it would be useless. Ramona never minded being sticky. Instead, she said, 'Christopher Columbus is the man who discovered America. He was trying to prove that the world is round.'

'Is it?' Ramona sounded puzzled. She beat the other marshmallow against her chin.

'Why, Ramona, don't you know the world is round?' Beezus asked.

Ramona shook her head and powdered her forehead with a marshmallow.

'Well, the world is round just like an orange,' Beezus told her. 'If you could start out and travel in a perfectly straight line you would come right back where you started from.'

'I would?' Ramona looked as if she didn't understand this at all. She also looked as if she didn't care much, because she went right on powdering her face with the marshmallows.

Oh, well, thought Beezus, there's no use

64

trying to explain it to her. She went into the bedroom to change from her school clothes into her play clothes. As usual, she found Ramona's doll, Bendix, lying on her bed, and with a feeling of annoyance she tossed it across the room to Ramona's bed. When she had changed her clothes she went into the kitchen, ate some crackers and peanut butter, and helped herself to two marshmallows. If Ramona could have two, it was only fair that she should have two also.

After eating the marshmallows and licking the powdered sugar from her fingers, Beezus decided that reading about Big Steve would be the easiest way to keep Ramona from thinking up some mischief to get into while mother was away. 'Come here, Ramona,' she said as she went into the living room. 'I'll read to you.'

There was no answer. Ramona was not there.

That's funny, thought Beezus, and went into the bedroom. The room was empty. I wonder where she can be, said Beezus to herself. She looked in mother and father's room. No one was there. 'Ramona!' she called. No answer. 'Ramona, where are you?' Still no answer.

Beezus was worried. She did not think Ramona had left the house, because she had not heard any doors open and close. Still, with Ramona you never knew. Maybe she was hiding. Beezus looked under the beds. No Ramona. She looked in the bedroom closets, the hall closet, the linen closet, even the broom closet. Still no Ramona. She ran upstairs to the attic and looked behind the trunks.

Then she ran downstairs to the basement. 'Ramona!' she called anxiously, as she peered around in the dim light. The basement was an eerie place with its grey cement walls and the grotesque white arms of the furnace reaching out in all directions. Except for a faint sound from the pilot light everything was silent. Suddenly the furnace lit itself with such a whoosh that Beezus, her heart pounding, turned and ran upstairs. Even though she knew it was only the furnace, she could not help being frightened. The house seemed so empty when no one answered her calls.

Uneasily Beezus sat down in the living room to try to think while she listened to the silence. She must not get panicky. Ramona couldn't be far away. And if she didn't turn up soon, she would telephone the police, the way mother did the time Ramona got lost because she started out to find the pot of gold at the end of the rainbow.

Thinking of the rainbow reminded Beezus of her attempt to explain to Ramona that the world is round like an orange. Ramona hadn't looked as if she understood, but sometimes it was hard to tell about Ramona. Maybe she just understood the part about coming back where she started from. If Ramona set out to walk to the end of the rainbow, she could easily decide to try walking around the world. That was exactly what she must have done.

The idea frightened Beezus. How would she ever find Ramona? And what would mother say when she came home and found Ramona gone? To think of Ramona walking in a straight line, hoping to go straight around the world and come back where she started from, trying to cross busy streets alone, honked at by trucks, barked at by strange dogs, tired, hungry . . . But I can't just sit here, thought Beezus. I've got to do something. I'll run out and look up and down the street. She can't have gone far.

At that moment Beezus heard a noise. She thought it came from the basement, but she was not certain. Tiptoeing to the cold-air intake in the hall, she bent over and listened. Sure enough, a noise so faint she could scarcely hear it came up through the furnace pipe. So the house wasn't empty after all! Just wait until she got hold of Ramona!

Beezus snapped on the basement light and ran down the steps. 'Ramona, come out,' she ordered. 'I know you're here.'

The only answer was a chomping sound from the corner of the basement. Beezus ran around the furnace and there, in the dimly lit corner, sat Ramona, eating an apple.

Beezus was so relieved to see Ramona safe, and at the same time so angry with her for hiding, that she couldn't say anything. She just stood there filled with the exasperated mixed-up feeling that Ramona so often gave her.

'Hello,' said Ramona through a bite of apple.

'Ramona Geraldine Quimby!' exclaimed Beezus, when she had found her voice. 'What do you think you're doing?'

'Playing hide-and-seek,' answered Ramona.

'Well, I'm not!' snapped Beezus. 'It takes two to play hide-and-seek.'

'You found me,' Ramona pointed out.

'Oh . . . ' Once again Beezus couldn't find any words. To think she had worried so, when all the time Ramona was sitting in the basement listening to her call. And eating an apple, too!

As she stood in front of Ramona, Beezus's eyes began to grow accustomed to the dim light and she realized what Ramona was doing. She stared, horrified at what she saw. As if hiding were not enough! What would mother say when she came home and found what Ramona had been up to this time?

Ramona was sitting on the floor beside a box of apples. Lying around her on the cement floor were a number of apples—each with one bite out of it. While Beezus stared, Ramona reached into the box, selected an apple, took one big bite out of the reddest part, and tossed the rest of the apple onto the floor. While she noisily chewed that bite, she reached into the apple box again.

'Ramona!' cried Beezus, horrified. 'You can't do that.'

'I can, too,' said Ramona through her mouthful.

'Stop it,' ordered Beezus. 'Stop it this instant! You can't eat one bite and then throw the rest away.'

'But the first bite tastes best,' explained Ramona reasonably, as she reached into the box again.

Beezus had to admit that Ramona was right. The first bite of an apple always did taste best. Ramona's sharp little teeth were about to sink into another apple when Beezus snatched it from her.

'That's my apple,' screamed Ramona.

'It is not!' said Beezus angrily, stamping her foot. 'One apple is all you're supposed to have. Just wait till mother finds out!'

Ramona stopped screaming and watched Beezus. Then, seeing how angry Beezus was, she smiled and offered her an apple. 'I want to share the apples,' she said sweetly.

'Oh, no, you don't,' said Beezus. 'And don't try to work that sharing business on me!' That was one of the difficult things about Ramona. When she had done something wrong, she often tried to get out of it by offering to share something. She heard a lot about sharing at nursery school.

Now what am I going to do, Beezus wondered. I promised mother I would keep an eye on Ramona, and look what she's gone and done. How am I going to explain this to mother? I'll get scolded too. And all the apples. What can we do with them?

Beezus was sure about one thing. She no longer felt mixed up about Ramona. Ramona was perfectly impossible. She snatched Ramona's hand. 'You come upstairs with me and be good until mother gets back,' she ordered, pulling her sister up the basement stairs.

Ramona broke away from her and ran into the living room. She climbed onto a chair, where she sat with her legs sticking straight out in front of her. She folded her hands in her lap and said in a little voice, 'Don't bother me. This is my quiet time. I'm supposed to be resting.'

Quiet times were something else Ramona had learned about at nursery school. When she didn't want to do something, she often insisted she was supposed to be having a quiet time. Beezus was

about to say that Ramona didn't need a quiet
time, because she hadn't been playing hard and
mother had said she had already had a nap, but
then she thought better of it. If Ramona wanted
to sit in a chair and be quiet, let her. She might
stay out of mischief until mother came home.

Beezus had no sooner sat down to work on her
pot holders, planning to keep an eye on Ramona
at the same time, when the telephone rang. It
must be Aunt Beatrice, she thought, before she
answered. Mother and Aunt Beatrice almost
always talked to each other about this time of day.

'Hello, darling, how are you?' asked Aunt
Beatrice.

'Oh, Aunt Beatrice,' cried Beezus, 'Ramona has
just done something awful, and I was supposed
to be looking after her. I don't know what to do.'
She told about Ramona's hiding in the cellar and
biting into half a box of apples.

Aunt Beatrice laughed. 'Leave it to Ramona to
think up something new,' she said. 'Do you know
what I'd do if I were you?'

'What?' asked Beezus eagerly, already feeling
better because she had confided her troubles to
her aunt.

'I wouldn't say anything more about it,' said
Aunt Beatrice. 'Lots of times little children are
naughty because they want to attract attention.

I have an idea that saying nothing about her naughtiness will worry Ramona more than a scolding.'

Beezus thought this over and decided her aunt was right. If there was one thing Ramona couldn't stand, it was being ignored. 'I'll try it,' she said.

'And about the apples,' Aunt Beatrice went on. 'All I can suggest is that your mother might make apple sauce.'

This struck Beezus as being funny, and as she and her aunt laughed together over the telephone she felt much better.

'Tell your mother I phoned,' said Aunt Beatrice.

'I will,' promised Beezus. 'And please come over soon.'

When Beezus heard her mother drive up, she rushed out to meet her and tell her the story of what Ramona had done. She also told her Aunt Beatrice's suggestion.

'Oh, dear, leave it to Ramona,' sighed mother. 'Your aunt is right. We won't say a word about it.'

Beezus helped her mother carry the groceries into the house. Ramona came into the kitchen to see if there were any animal crackers among the packages. She waited a few minutes for her sister to tattle on her. Then, when Beezus did not say anything, she announced, 'I was bad this afternoon.' She sounded pleased with herself.

'Were you?' remarked mother calmly. 'Beezus, I think apple sauce would be good for dessert tonight. Will you run down and bring up some apples?'

When Ramona looked disappointed at having failed to arouse any interest, Beezus and her mother exchanged smiles. 'I want to help,' said Ramona, rather than be left out.

Beezus and Ramona made four trips to the basement to bring up all the bitten apples. Mother said nothing about their appearance, but spent the rest of the afternoon peeling and cooking apples. After she had finished, she filled her two largest mixing bowls, a casserole, and the bowl of her electric mixer with apple sauce. It took her quite a while to rearrange the contents of the refrigerator to make room for all the apple sauce.

When Beezus saw her father coming home she ran out on the front walk to tell him what had happened. He, too, agreed that Aunt Beatrice's suggestion was a good one.

'Daddy!' shrieked Ramona when her father came in.

'How's my girl?' asked father as he picked Ramona up and kissed her.

'Oh, I was bad today,' said Ramona.

'Were you?' said father as he put her down.
'Was there any mail today?'

Ramona looked crestfallen. 'I was very bad,' she persisted. 'I was awful.'

Father sat down and picked up the evening paper.

'I hid from Beezus and I bit lots and lots of apples,' Ramona went on insistently.

'Mmm,' remarked father from behind the paper. 'I see they're going to raise bus fares again.'

'Lots and lots of apples,' repeated Ramona in a loud voice.

'They raised bus fares last year,' father went on, winking at Beezus from behind the paper. 'The public isn't going to stand for this.'

Ramona looked puzzled and then disappointed, but she did not say anything.

Father dropped his paper. 'Something certainly smells good,' he said. 'It smells like apple sauce. I hope so. There's nothing I like better than a big dish of apple sauce for dessert.'

Because mother had been so busy making apple sauce, dinner was a little late that night. At the table Ramona was unusually well behaved. She did not interrupt and she did not try to share her carrots, the way she usually did because she did not like carrots.

As Beezus cleared the table and mother served dessert—which was fig rolls and, of course, apple sauce—Ramona's good behaviour continued. Beezus found she was not very hungry for apple sauce, but the rest of the family appeared to enjoy it. After Beezus had wiped the dishes for mother she sat down to embroider her pot holders. She had decided to give Aunt Beatrice the pot holder with the dancing knife and fork on it instead of the one with the laughing teakettle.

Ramona approached her with *Big Steve the Steam Shovel* in her hand. 'Beezus, will you read to me?' she asked.

She thinks I'll say no and then she can make a fuss, thought Beezus. Well, I won't give her a chance. 'All right,' she said, putting down her pot holder and taking the book, while Ramona climbed into the chair beside her.

'Big Steve was a steam shovel. He was the biggest steam shovel in the whole city,' Beezus read. '"Gr-r-r," growled Big Steve when he moved the earth to make way for the new highway.'

Father dropped his newspaper and looked at his two daughters sitting side by side. 'I wonder,' he said, 'exactly how long this is going to last.'

'Just enjoy it while it does,' said mother, who was basting patches on the knees of a pair of Ramona's overalls.

'Gr-r-r-,' growled Ramona. 'Gr-r-r-.'

Beezus also wondered just how long this would go on. She didn't enjoy growling like a steam shovel and she felt that perhaps Ramona was getting her own way after all. I'm trying to like her like I'm supposed to, anyhow, Beezus thought, and I do like her more than I did this afternoon when I found her in the basement. But what on earth will mother ever do with all that apple sauce?

5

A Party at the Quimbys'

Saturday morning turned out to be cold and rainy. Beezus wiped the breakfast dishes for her mother and listened to Ramona, who was riding her tricycle around the house, singing, 'Copycat, cappycot, copycat, cappycot,' over and over at the top of her voice, because she liked the sound of the words.

Beezus and her mother finished the dishes and went into the bedroom to put clean sheets on the beds. 'Copycat, cappycot,' droned Ramona's singsong.

'Ramona, why don't you sing something else?' mother asked at last. 'We've been listening to that for a long time.'

'OK,' agreed Ramona. 'I'm going to have a par-tee,' she sang. 'I'm going to have a par-tee.'

'Thank you, Ramona. That's better.' Mother held one end of a pillow under her chin while she slipped the other end into a fresh case. 'You know, that reminds me,' she said to Beezus. 'What would you like to do to celebrate your birthday next week?'

Beezus thought a minute. 'Well . . . I'd like to have Aunt Beatrice over for dinner. She hasn't been here for such a long time. And I'd like to have a birthday cake with pink frosting.' Beezus smoothed a fresh sheet over the bed. She almost enjoyed helping mother when they could talk without Ramona's interrupting all the time. The rain beating on the windows and Ramona's happy singsong made the day seem cosy and peaceful.

'All right, that's exactly what we'll do.' Mother seemed really pleased with Beezus's suggestions. 'It's a long time since we've seen Aunt Beatrice, but of course teachers always have a lot to do when school starts.' Beezus noticed that mother gave a little sigh as she smoothed her side of the sheet. 'She'll probably have more time now that the semester has started and it really isn't long before Thanksgiving and Christmas vacations. We'll see a lot of her then.'

Why, mother misses Aunt Beatrice too, thought Beezus. I believe she misses her as much as I do, even though she never says so.

Leaving Beezus with the new and surprising thought that grown-ups sometimes missed each other, mother gathered up the sheets and pillowcases that had been removed from the beds and carried them to the basement. While she was downstairs the telephone rang. 'Answer it, will you, Beezus,' mother called.

When Beezus picked up the telephone, a hurried voice said, 'This is Mrs Kemp. Do you mind if I leave Willa Jean when I bring Howie over this afternoon?'

'Just a minute. I'll ask mother.' Beezus called down the basement stairs, repeating the question.

'Why, no, I guess not,' mother replied.

'Mother says it's all right,' Beezus said into the telephone.

'Thank you,' said Mrs Kemp. 'Now I'll (Howie, stop banging!) have a chance to do some shopping.'

Well, thought Beezus when she had hung up, things won't be quiet around here much longer. Howie, who was in Ramona's class at nursery school, was the noisiest little boy she knew, and he and Ramona often quarrelled. Willa Jean was at the awkward age—too big to be a baby and not big enough to be out of nappies.

'You know,' said mother, when she came up from the basement, 'I don't remember telling Mrs Kemp that Howie could come over this afternoon, but maybe I did. I've had so much on my mind lately, trying to get the nursery-school rummage sale organized.'

After an early lunch mother decided there would be enough time to wash everybody's hair before Howie and Willa Jean arrived. She put on her oldest dress, because Ramona always squirmed and got soap all over her. Then she stood Ramona on a chair, made her lean over the kitchen sink, and went to work. Ramona howled, as she always did when her hair was washed. When mother finished she rubbed Ramona's hair with a bath towel, turned up the furnace thermostat so the house would be extra-warm, and gave Ramona two crackers to make up for the indignity of having her hair washed.

Then Beezus stepped onto the stool and bent over the sink for her turn. After mother had washed her own hair and before she went into the bathroom to put it up in pin curls, she said to Beezus, 'Would you mind getting out the vacuum cleaner and picking up those cracker crumbs Ramona spilled on the rug?'

Beezus did not mind. She rather liked running the vacuum cleaner if her mother didn't make a regular chore of it.

'I'm going to have a par-tee,' sang Ramona above the roar of the vacuum cleaner. Then she changed her song. 'Here comes my par-tee!' she chanted.

Beezus glanced out of the window and quickly switched off the vacuum cleaner. Four small children were coming up the front path through the rain. A car stopped in front of the house and three children climbed out. Two more were splashing across the street.

'Mother!' cried Beezus. 'Come here, quick. Ramona wasn't pretending!'

Mother appeared in the living room just as the doorbell rang. One side of her hair was up in pin curls and the other side hung wet and dripping on the towel around her neck. 'Oh, my goodness!' she exclaimed when she understood the situation. 'That explains Mrs Kemp's phone call. Ramona, how could you?'

'I wanted to have a party,' explained Ramona. 'I invited everybody yesterday.'

The doorbell rang again, this time long and hard. There was the sound of many rubber boots jumping up and down on the porch.

'Mother, we just can't have a party with our hair wet,' wailed Beezus.

'What else can we do?' Mother sounded desperate. 'They're here and we can't very well send them home. Their mothers have probably planned to shop or something while we look after them.'

Ramona struggled with the doorknob and managed to open the heavy front door. Mrs Kemp stopped her car in front of the Quimbys', and Howie and Willa Jean hopped out. 'I'll pick them up at four,' she called gaily. 'I'm so glad to have a chance to get out and do some shopping.'

Mother smiled weakly and looked at all the children on the porch.

'Where do you suppose she found them all?' whispered Beezus. 'I don't even know some of them.'

'All right, children.' Mother spoke firmly. 'Leave your wet boots and raincoats on the porch.'

'I've got a par-tee,' sang Ramona happily.

Beezus, who had had plenty of experience with Ramona and her boots, knew where she was needed. She started pulling off boots and unbuttoning raincoats.

'What on earth shall we do with them on a day like this?' whispered mother.

Beezus grabbed a muddy boot. 'Hold still,' she said firmly to its owner. 'They'll expect refreshments,' she said.

'I know,' sighed mother. 'You'll have to put on your coat and run down to the market—Oh, no, you can't go out in this rain with your hair wet.' Mother tugged at another boot. 'I'll have to see what I can find in the kitchen.'

Beezus and her mother herded the wiggling, squealing crowd into the front bedroom and went to work removing sweaters, jackets, caps, and mittens. In between Beezus pulled three children out of the closet, dragged one out from under the bed, and snatched her mother's bottle of best perfume from another.

'All right, everybody out of here,' Beezus ordered, when the last mitten was removed and her mother had hurried into the kitchen. 'We'll go into the living room and . . . and do something,' she finished lamely. 'Ramona, bring some of your toys out of your room.'

'Bingle-bongle-by!' shouted Howie, just to make some noise.

'Bingle-bongle-by!' The others joined in with great delight. It was such a nice noisy thing to yell. 'Bingle-bongle-by,' they screamed at the tops of their voices as they scampered into the living room. 'Bingle-bongle-by.'

Howie grabbed the vacuum cleaner, turned on the switch, and charged across the room. 'I'll suck you up!' he shouted. 'I'll suck everybody up in the vacuum cleaner!'

'Bingle-bongle-by!' shouted the others above the roar of the vacuum cleaner.

One little girl began to cry. 'I don't want to be sucked up in the vacuum cleaner,' she sobbed. Willa Jean, looking bulgy because of the nappy and plastic pants under her overalls, clung to a chair and wept.

Ramona appeared with her arms full of toys, but

no one paid any attention to them. The vacuum cleaner was much more fun.

'I want to push the vacuum cleaner,' screamed Susan, who lived in the next block.

Ramona offered Susan her panda bear, but Susan did not want it. Ramona hit Susan with the panda. 'You take my bear,' she ordered. 'This is my party and you're supposed to do what I say.'

'I don't want your old bear,' answered Susan.

Beezus tried to grab the vacuum cleaner, but Howie was too quick for her. The room was getting uncomfortably hot, so Beezus darted to the thermostat to turn down the heat. Then she dashed to the other side of the room and disconnected the vacuum cleaner at the wall. It died with a noisy groan. Suddenly everyone was quiet, waiting to see what would happen.

'Hey,' protested Howie, 'you can't do that.'

Beezus frantically tried to think of some way to keep fifteen small children busy and out of mischief. At least, she thought there were fifteen. They didn't stand still long enough to be counted.

'Where's the party?' one little boy asked.

Ramona appeared with more toys, which she dumped on the floor. This time she brought a drum. Howie quickly lost interest in the vacuum cleaner and grabbed the drum. Beezus seized the vacuum cleaner and shoved it into the hall closet, while Howie began to beat the drum. 'I'm leading a parade,' he said.

'You are not,' contradicted Ramona. 'This is my party.'

Susan snatched a pink plastic horn and tooted it. 'I'm in the parade too,' she said.

'I want to be in the parade! I want to be in the parade!' cried the others.

That was it! They could play parade! Beezus ran to the bedroom and found a whistle and a couple of horns left over from a Hallowe'en party. What else could be used in a parade? Flags, of course! But what could she use for flags? Beezus thought fast. She gathered up two yardsticks and several rulers; then she ran to the front bedroom and snatched some of her father's handkerchiefs from a drawer. She had to move fast before the children grew tired of the idea.

'I want to be in the parade!' screamed the children.

'Mother, help me,' cried Beezus.

Somehow Beezus and her mother got father's handkerchiefs tied to the sticks and distributed to the children who did not have noisemakers.

Howie banged the drum. 'Follow me,' he ordered, beginning to march. The others followed, blowing whistles, tooting horns, waving flags.

'No!' screamed Ramona, who wanted to boss her own party.

'You wanted a party,' mother reminded her. 'If your guests want to play parade, you'd better join them.'

Ramona scowled, but she took a flag and joined the parade rather than be left out entirely at her own party.

'Playing parade was a wonderful idea.' Mother smiled at Beezus. 'I hope it lasts.'

'So do I,' Beezus agreed.

'Bingle-bongle-by,' yelled the flag wavers.

Howie led the parade, including a sulky Ramona, out of the living room, down the hall, through the kitchen and dining room, and back into the living room again. Willa Jean toddled along at the end of the procession. Beezus was afraid the parade might break up, but all the children appeared delighted with the game. Into the bedroom they marched and out again. Beezus opened the basement door. Down the steps Howie led the parade. Willa Jean had to go down the steps backwards on her hands and knees. Three times around the furnace marched the parade and up the steps again before Willa Jean was halfway down.

Beezus opened the door to the attic. Up the steps marched the parade. Stamp, stamp, stamp went their feet overhead. Stamp, stamp, stamp.

Beezus remembered something Ramona had enjoyed when she was still in nappies. She lugged Willa Jean up the basement steps, sat her in the middle of the kitchen floor, and handed her the egg beater. 'There. Don't step on her,' she said to her mother.

'Thank goodness,' sighed mother. 'Maybe they'll play parade long enough for us to fix something for them to eat.'

'What'll we give them?' Beezus asked.

Mother laughed. 'This is a wonderful chance to get rid of all that apple sauce. Let's hurry and get it ready before they get tired of their game. Get the coloured paper napkins out of the cupboard and—oh, dear, what shall we do for chairs?'

'They can sit on the floor,' suggested Beezus, looking through the cupboard for napkins.

'I guess they'll have to.' Mother took the apple sauce out of the refrigerator. 'If we put a couple of sheets down for them to sit on, maybe they won't get apple sauce on the rug.'

The parade tramped down the attic stairs and through the kitchen. 'But, mother,' said Beezus, when the drum and horns had disappeared into the basement again, 'the only napkins I can find are for St Valentine's Day and Hallowe'en. They won't do.'

'They'll have to do,' said mother.

Beezus spread two sheets in the middle of the living room floor. Then she went into the kitchen to help mother, who was tearing open three boxes of fig rolls. 'It's a good thing I bought these at that sale last week,' she remarked.

'Are we going to give them lemonade or anything to drink?' Beezus asked.

'Not on my living room rug.' Mother rapidly spooned apple sauce into dishes. 'Apple sauce and fig rolls are bad enough.'

'Maybe if we feed them right away some of them will think the party is over and go home.' Beezus piled fig rolls on two plates.

'I hope so. This many small children in the house on a rainy day is too much.' The parade stamped across the attic floor again, and mother had to raise her voice to make herself heard. 'It sounds as if they were coming through the ceiling.'

'Let's catch them the next time they come through the kitchen and hand out the apple sauce,' Beezus shouted back. 'Then maybe we can get them to march into the living room.'

It was not long before Howie led the parade into the kitchen again. He stopped so suddenly that the children bumped into one another. 'When do we eat?' he demanded.

'Now.' Beezus thrust a dish of apple sauce and a spoon into his hands.

'I want some,' cried the others.

Mother handed a second child some apple sauce. 'Forward march!' she ordered.

Beezus led Howie into the living room, and the rest of the parade followed with their apple sauce. 'You sit there,' she said to Howie, pointing to a place on the sheet. She was relieved to see the others seat themselves around the edge of the sheet. Quickly she handed around paper napkins.

'I want one with witches on it,' demanded a boy who had a Valentine napkin.

'I want one with hearts on it,' wailed a girl who had a Hallowe'en napkin.

Beezus hastily counted the napkins. Yes, there were enough of each kind to go around. Two napkins apiece would be safer anyway. She handed each child a second napkin and they all began to eat their apple sauce, except one little girl who didn't like apple sauce. Ramona was beaming, because refreshments were the most important part of any party and now at last her guests were behaving the way she wanted them to.

Mother came out of the kitchen with the plates of fig rolls, which she handed to Beezus. 'Here, pass these around,' she said. 'I think I'd better help Willa Jean.' Willa Jean knew how to eat with a spoon. The trouble was, she had to pick up the food with her left hand and put it into the spoon, which she held in her right hand. Then, most of the time, she was able to get it into her mouth.

Ramona, her face shining with happiness, looked at her friends sharing the apple sauce. 'Those cookies are filled with worms. Chopped-up worms!' she gleefully told everyone.

'Why, Ramona!' Beezus was shocked. 'They aren't either. They're filled with ground-up figs. You know that.'

Ramona did not answer. Her mouth was full of fig rolls.

Beezus passed the plate to a boy named Joey. 'I don't like worms,' he said.

'I don't like worms,' said the next little girl, who had apple sauce all over her chin.

Beezus noticed that Ramona was beginning to scowl. When Howie refused a cookie, it was too much for Ramona. 'You eat that!' she shouted.

'I won't,' yelled Howie. 'You can't make me.'

Ramona jumped up, spilling her apple sauce on the sheet. She thrust a nibbled fig roll at Howie. 'You eat that,' she repeated as she stepped into the apple sauce. 'It's my party and I want you to eat it!'

Howie knocked the cookie out of her hand. Ramona grabbed a handful of fig rolls and thrust them at Susan. 'Eat these,' she shouted.

Susan began to cry. 'They're full of worms,' she sobbed. 'I don't like worms.'

'They're *pretend* worms,' yelled Ramona.

'No, they're not,' cried Susan. 'They're real!'

'You eat these,' Ramona yelled, thrusting her handful of cookies at the children, who backed away. Ramona stamped her feet and screamed. Then she threw the fig rolls at her guests as hard as she could.

'My mother won't let me eat worms!' shouted a little boy.

Ramona threw herself on the floor and kicked.

'Ramona, stop that!' Mother appeared from the kitchen with Willa Jean balanced on one hip. She grabbed Ramona by one arm and tried to drag her to her feet, but Ramona's legs were like rubber.

'All right, Howie, forward march!' Beezus ordered, hoping to draw attention from Ramona. No one moved. It was much more fun to see what was going to happen to Ramona.

'This is my party! They're supposed to eat the refreshments!' Ramona howled, banging her heels on the floor.

'Ramona, you're acting like a two-year-old. You may go to your room and close the door until you can behave yourself,' said mother quietly.

Ramona kicked harder to show that she was not going to mind unless she felt like it.

'Ramona,' said mother even more quietly. 'Don't make me count to ten.'

Gasping with sobs, Ramona got up from the floor and ran into the bedroom, where she slammed the door as hard as she could.

'All right, parade,' said mother wearily. 'Forward march.'

Up and down, whistling, banging, tooting, marched the parade. Mother sat Willa Jean down and was just beginning to gather up the dishes and sheets when a car stopped in front of the house and Mrs Kemp got out. 'At last,' sighed mother, hurrying to the door.

'I've come for Howie and Willa Jean,' said Mrs Kemp, as several other cars stopped in front of the Quimbys'. The parade marched into the living room.

'I don't want to go home,' protested Howie, when he saw his mother.

'The party must have been a success,' Mrs Kemp observed.

'It certainly was.' Mother tried to push the uncurled side of her hair behind her ear and to smooth out her rumpled old dress.

'I like to play parade,' said Howie, 'but I didn't like what they had to eat.'

'Why, Howie,' scolded Mrs Kemp. 'We must remember our manners.'

Ramona, her face streaked with tears, came out of her room, and stood staring unhappily at her departing guests. When the last child had struggled into his boots, she looked tearfully at her mother. 'I'm behaving myself now,' she said meekly.

Mother dropped wearily into a chair. 'Ramona, if you wanted a party, why didn't you ask me to have one?'

'Because when I ask you don't let me do things,' explained Ramona, sniffing.

Beezus couldn't help feeling there was some truth in Ramona's remark. She had often felt that way herself, especially when she was younger. 'Mother, did I do things like Ramona when I was four?' she asked.

'You did some of the things Ramona does now,' said mother thoughtfully, 'but you were really very different. You were quieter, for one thing.'

This pleased Beezus. One of the reasons she sometimes disliked Ramona was that she was never quiet when she could manage to be noisy.

'Of course there are some things that all four-year-olds do,' mother continued, 'but even sisters are usually different. Just the way your Aunt Beatrice and I were different when we were girls. I was a bookworm and went to the library two or three times a week. She was the best hopscotch player and the fastest rope jumper in the neighbourhood. And she was better at jacks than anybody in our whole school.'

This surprised Beezus. She had never thought about her mother and aunt as children before. She tried to picture her schoolteacher aunt jumping rope and found to her surprise that it was not very hard to do. Of course mother and Aunt Beatrice must have been different when they were girls, because they were so different now that they were grown-up. And she was glad they were different. She loved them both.

'Did I have tantrums, too?' Beezus asked.

'Once in a while,' said mother. 'I always dreaded cutting your fingernails, because you kicked and screamed.'

Beezus could not help feeling silly. Imagine having a tantrum over a little thing like having her fingernails cut!

Then Ramona spoke up. 'I don't cry when you cut my fingernails,' she boasted.

'Yes, but you scream when you have your hair washed,' Beezus could not help reminding her.

'Ramona,' said mother, 'you were a very naughty girl this afternoon. What are we going to do with you?'

Ramona stopped sniffing and looked interested. 'Lock me in a closet for a million years?' she suggested cheerfully.

Mother and Beezus exchanged glances. How quickly Ramona recovered!

'Make me sleep outdoors in the rain?' Obviously Ramona was enjoying herself. 'Not let me have anything to eat but carrots?'

Mother laughed and looked at Beezus. 'I'm afraid all we can do is wait for her to grow up,' she said.

And when mother said *we* like that, Beezus almost felt sorry for Ramona, because she would have to wait such a long time to be grown-up.

6

Beezus's Birthday

When Beezus came home from school on the afternoon of her tenth birthday, she felt that so far the day had been perfect—packages by her plate at breakfast, a new dress to wear to school, the whole class singing 'Happy Birthday' just for her. But the best part was still to come. Aunt Beatrice was coming for dinner.

Beezus could hardly wait to tell her aunt about acting the part of Sacajawea leading Lewis and Clark across the plains to Oregon at a PTA meeting. And of course Aunt Beatrice would bring more presents—very special presents, because she was Aunt Beatrice's namesake. And at dinner there would be a beautiful birthday cake with ten candles. Mother had probably worked all afternoon baking and decorating the cake and now had it hidden away in a cupboard.

When mother kissed Beezus she had said, 'I'm sorry, Beezus, but I'll have to ask you to keep Ramona out of the kitchen for a while.'

'Why?' asked Beezus, thinking her mother was planning a surprise.

'So I can bake your birthday cake,' mother explained.

'Isn't it baked yet?' exclaimed Beezus. 'Oh, mother.'

'This has been one of those days when I couldn't seem to get anything done,' said mother. 'It was my morning for the nursery-school car pool. After I picked up all the children and drove them to nursery school and came home and did the breakfast dishes and made the beds, it was time to pick up the children and take them all home again. And after lunch I started the cake and had just creamed the sugar and butter in the electric mixer when I was called to the telephone. When I came back, what do you think had happened?'

'What?' asked Beezus, pretty sure Ramona had something to do with it.

'Ramona had dropped all the eggs in the house into the batter and had started the mixer,' said mother.

'Shells and all?' asked Beezus, horrified.

'Shells and all,' repeated mother wearily. 'And so I had to get out the car again and drive to market and buy more eggs.'

'Ramona, what did you have to go and do a

thing like that for?' Beezus demanded of her little sister, who was playing with her doll Bendix.

'To see what would happen,' answered Ramona.

She doesn't look a bit sorry, thought Beezus crossly. Spoiling my birthday cake like that!

'Don't worry, dear. There's still plenty of time to bake another,' said mother. 'If you'll just keep Ramona out of the kitchen, I can get it into the oven in no time at all.'

That made Beezus feel better. At least she would have a birthday cake, even if it did mean looking after Ramona for a while.

'Read to me,' Ramona demanded. 'Read about Big Steve.'

'I'll read to you, but I won't read that book,' said Beezus, going to the bookcase. She really wanted to read one of her birthday books, called *202 Things to Do on a Rainy Afternoon*, but she knew Ramona would insist on a story. 'How about Hansel and Gretel?' she asked. Next to stories with lots of noise, Ramona liked stories about witches, goblins, or ogres.

'Yes, I like Hansel and Gretel,' agreed Ramona, as she climbed on the couch and sat Bendix beside her. 'OK, I'm ready. Now you can begin.'

Beezus curled up at the other end of the couch with *Grimm's Fairy Tales*. 'Once upon a time . . . ' she began, and Ramona listened contentedly.

When she did not have to make noises like machinery Beezus enjoyed reading to Ramona, and this afternoon reading aloud was particularly pleasant, with mother in the kitchen baking a birthday cake. As Beezus read she listened to the whirr of the mixer and the sound of eggs being cracked against a bowl.

Beezus read about Hansel's leaving a trail of crumbs behind him as he and Gretel went into the woods. She read the part Ramona liked best, about the witch's trying to fatten Hansel. Ramona listened wide-eyed until Beezus came to the end of the story, where Gretel pushed the witch into the oven and escaped through the woods with her brother.

'That's a good story,' said Ramona, as she jumped down from the couch.

Surprised that Ramona didn't demand another story, Beezus picked up *202 Things to Do on a Rainy Afternoon* and began to read. She was learning how to make a necklace out of beans and pumpkin seeds painted with fingernail polish when a lovely sweet vanilla fragrance began to fill the house, and Beezus knew her birthday cake was safely in the oven at last.

Ramona's unusual silence made Beezus glance up from her book. 'Ramona!' she cried, when she saw what her little sister was doing. 'Stop that right away!'

Ramona was busy pulling cracker crumbs out of the pocket of her overalls and sprinkling them across the rug. 'I'm Hansel leaving a trail of crumbs through the woods,' she said, digging more crumbs out of her pocket. 'My father is a poor woodcutter.'

'Oh, Ramona,' said Beezus, but she had to giggle at the picture of father as a poor woodcutter.

Ramona sprinkled more crumbs on the rug, and Beezus knew she had to do something about it. 'Why don't you pretend you're Gretel?' she suggested, because Gretel would not leave crumbs on the rug.

'OK,' agreed Ramona.

That was easy, thought Beezus, and went on reading about making a complete set of doll furniture out of old milk cartons. How good her birthday cake smelled! She hoped mother would remember she had asked for pink icing. She heard the oven door open and close. Mother must be peeking into the oven to see how my cake is coming along, she thought.

Beezus read on, absorbed in the directions for making a vase out of an old tomato-juice can. Something smells funny, she thought as she turned a page. Then she stopped and sniffed. The air was no longer filled with the lovely warm fragrance of a baking cake. It was filled with a horrid rubbery smell. That's funny, thought Beezus. I wonder what it can be. She sniffed again. Maybe somebody was burning trash outside and the smell was coming in through the window.

Mother came into the living room from the bedroom. 'Beezus, do you smell something rubbery?' she asked anxiously.

'Yes, and it smells awful,' said Beezus. Ramona held her nose.

Mother sniffed again. 'It smells as if something is scorching, too.'

Beezus went into the kitchen, where she found the smell so strong that it made her cough. 'It's worse in here, mother,' she called, as she looked to see if anything was burning on the stove. Then Beezus remembered the oven. 'Mother,' she said in a worried voice, 'you don't suppose something has happened to my birthday cake again?'

'Of course not,' said mother, coming into the kitchen and opening the window. 'What could happen to it?'

Just to be sure, Beezus cautiously opened the oven door. 'Mother!' she cried, horrified at what she saw. 'Look!' Ramona's rubber doll, Bendix, leaned over the edge of the cake pan, her head and arms buried in the batter. Her dress was scorched to a golden tan. 'Oh, mother!' repeated Beezus. Her birthday cake, her beautiful, fragrant birthday cake, was ruined.

'Is the witch done yet?' Ramona asked.

'Ramona—' began mother and stopped. She couldn't think of anything to say. Silently she turned off the oven and, with a pot holder, pulled out the doll and the remains of the cake.

'Ramona Geraldine Quimby!' said Beezus angrily. 'You're just awful, that's what you are! Just plain awful. Spoiling your own sister's birthday cake!'

'You told me to pretend I was Gretel,' protested Ramona. 'And Gretel pushed the witch into the oven.'

Beezus looked at the cake and burst into tears. Ramona promptly began to cry too. This made Beezus even angrier. 'You stop crying,' she ordered Ramona furiously. 'It was my birthday cake and I'm the one that's supposed to be crying.'

'Girls!' said mother in a tired voice. 'Ramona, you have been very naughty. You know better than to put anything into the oven. Now go to your room and stay there until I say you can come out.'

Sniffling, Ramona started towards the bedroom.

'And don't you dare put your toys on my bed,' said Beezus. 'Mother, can you fix the cake?'

'I'm afraid not.' Mother poked at the cake with her finger. 'It's fallen, and anyway it would probably taste like burnt rubber.'

Beezus tried to brush the tears out of her eyes. 'Ramona always spoils everything. Now I won't have any birthday cake, and Aunt Beatrice is coming and it won't be like a birthday at all.'

'I know Ramona is a problem but we'll just have to be patient, because she's little,' said mother, as she scraped the cake into the garbage can. 'And you will still have a cake. I'll phone your Aunt Beatrice and have her bring one from the bakery.'

'Oh, mother, will you?' asked Beezus.

'That's what I'll do,' said mother. 'Now run along and wash your face and you'll feel better.'

But as Beezus held her face cloth under the tap she was not at all sure she would feel better. For Ramona to spoil one birthday cake was bad enough, but *two* . . . Probably nobody else in the whole world had a little sister who had spoiled two birthday cakes on the same day.

Beezus scrubbed away the tear stains, feeling more and more sorry for herself for having such a little sister. If Ramona were only bigger, things might be different; but since she was so much younger, she would always be . . . well, a pest. Then the terrible thought came to Beezus again—the thought she had had the time Ramona bit into all the apples and the time she shoved the dog into the bathroom. She tried not to think the thought, but she couldn't help it. There were times when she did not love Ramona. This was one of them. Everyone knew sisters were supposed to love each other. Look how much mother and Aunt Beatrice loved each other. Beezus felt very gloomy indeed as she dried her face. She was a terrible girl who did not love her little sister. Like a wicked sister in a fairy tale. And on her birthday, too, a day that was supposed to be happy.

When Beezus went into the living room, mother switched off the vacuum cleaner, which had been sucking up the crumbs Ramona had sprinkled on the rug. 'Aunt Beatrice said she would be delighted to bring a cake. She knows a bakery that makes very special birthday cakes,' she said, smiling at Beezus. 'You mustn't let Ramona spoil your birthday.'

Beezus felt a little better. She curled up on the couch again with *202 Things to Do on a Rainy Afternoon* and read about making Christmas tree ornaments out of cellophane straws, until she heard her aunt's car turn into the driveway. Then she flung her book aside and ran out to greet her.

'Happy birthday, darling!' cried Aunt Beatrice, as she set the brake and opened the door of her yellow convertible.

Joyfully Beezus ran over to the car and kissed her aunt. 'Did you bring the cake?' she asked.

'I certainly did,' answered Aunt Beatrice. 'The best birthday cake I could find. And that isn't all I brought. Here, help me carry these packages while I carry the cake. We mustn't let anything happen to *this* cake!'

And the way Aunt Beatrice laughed made Beezus laugh too. Her aunt gave her three packages, two large and one small, to carry.

'The little package is for Ramona,' explained Aunt Beatrice. 'So she won't feel left out.'

Mother came out of the house and hugged her sister. 'Hello, Bea,' she said. 'I'm so glad you could come. What would I ever do without you?'

'It's good to see you, Dorothy,' answered Aunt Beatrice. 'And what's an aunt for if she can't come to the rescue with a birthday cake once in a while?'

As Beezus watched her mother and her aunt arm in arm, go into the house, she thought how different they were—mother so tall and comfortable-looking and Aunt Beatrice so small and gay—and yet how happy they looked together. Smiling, Beezus carried the gifts into the house. Aunt Beatrice always brought such beautiful packages, wrapped in fancy paper and tied with big, fluffy bows.

Aunt Beatrice handed the cake box to mother. 'Be sure you put it in a safe place,' she said, and laughed again.

'May I open the packages now?' Beezus asked eagerly, although she felt it was almost too bad to untie such beautiful bows.

'Of course you may,' answered Aunt Beatrice. 'Where's Ramona?'

A subdued Ramona came out of the bedroom to receive her present. She tore off the wrapping, but Beezus painstakingly untied the ribbon on one of her presents and removed the paper carefully so she wouldn't tear it. Her new book, *202 Things to Do on a Rainy Afternoon*, suggested pasting pretty paper on a gallon ice-cream carton to make a wastebasket.

'Oh, Aunt Beatrice,' exclaimed Beezus, as she opened her first package. It was a real grown-up sewing box. It had two sizes of scissors, a fat red pincushion that looked like a tomato, an emery bag that looked like a ripe strawberry, and a tape measure that pulled out of a shiny box. When Beezus pushed the button on the box, the tape measure snapped back inside. The box also had needles, pins, and a thimble. Beezus never wore a thimble, but she thought it would be nice to have one in case she ever wanted to use one. 'Oh, Aunt Beatrice,' she said, 'it's the most wonderful sewing box in the whole world. I'll make you two pot holders for Christmas!' Then, as Aunt Beatrice laughed, Beezus clapped her hand over her mouth. The pot holder was supposed to be a surprise.

Ramona had unwrapped a little steam shovel made of red and yellow plastic, which she was now pushing happily around the rug.

Breathlessly Beezus lifted the lid of the second box. 'Oh, Aunt Beatrice!' she exclaimed, as she lifted out a dress that was a lovely shade of blue.

'It's just the right shade of blue to match your eyes,' explained Aunt Beatrice.

'Is it really?' asked Beezus, delighted that her pretty young aunt liked blue eyes. She was about to tell her about being Sacajawea for the PTA when father came home from work, and before long dinner was on the table. Mother lit the candles and turned off the dining room light. How pretty everything looks, thought Beezus. I wish we had candles on the table every night.

After father had served the chicken and mashed potatoes and peas and mother had passed the hot rolls, Beezus decided the time had come to tell Aunt Beatrice about being Sacajawea. 'Do you know what I did last week?' she began.

'I want some jelly,' said Ramona.

'You mean, "Please pass the jelly,"' corrected mother, while Beezus waited patiently.

'No, what did you do last week?' asked Aunt Beatrice.

'Well, last week I—' Beezus began again.

'I like purple jelly better than red jelly,' said Ramona.

'Ramona, stop interrupting your sister,' said father.

'Well, I *do* like purple jelly better than red jelly,' insisted Ramona.

'Never mind,' said mother. 'Go on, Beezus.'

'Last week—' said Beezus, looking at her aunt, who smiled as if she understood.

'Excuse me, Beezus,' mother cut in. 'Ramona, we do not put jelly on our mashed potatoes.'

'I like jelly on my mashed potatoes.' Ramona stirred potato and jelly around with her fork.

'Ramona, you heard what your mother said.' Father looked stern.

'If I can put butter on my mashed potatoes, why can't I put jelly? I put butter and jelly on toast,' said Ramona.

Father couldn't help laughing. 'That's a hard question to answer.'

'But, mother—' Beezus began.

'I *like* jelly on my mashed potatoes,' interrupted Ramona, looking sulky.

'You can't have jelly on your mashed potatoes, because you aren't supposed to,' said Beezus crossly, forgetting Sacajawea for the moment.

'That's as good an answer as any,' agreed father.

'There are some things we don't do, because we aren't supposed to.'

Ramona looked even more sulky.

'Where is my Merry Sunshine?' mother asked.

Ramona scowled. 'I am *too* a Merry Sunshine!' she shouted angrily.

'Ramona,' said mother quietly, 'you may go to your room until you can behave yourself.'

And serves you right, too, thought Beezus.

'I am *too* a Merry Sunshine,' insisted Ramona, but she got down from the table and ran out of the room.

Everyone was silent for a moment. 'Beezus, what was it you were trying to tell me?' Aunt Beatrice asked.

And finally Beezus got to tell about leading Lewis and Clark to Oregon, with a doll tied to mother's breadboard for a papoose, and how her teacher told her what a clever girl she was to think of using a breadboard for a papoose board. Somehow she did not feel the same about telling the story after all Ramona's interruptions. Being Sacajawea for the PTA did not seem very important now. No matter what she did, Ramona always managed to spoil it. Unhappily, Beezus went on eating her chicken and peas. It was another one of those terrible times when she did not love her little sister.

'You mustn't let Ramona get you down,' whispered mother.

Beezus did not answer. What a terrible girl she was not to love her little sister! How shocked and surprised mother would be if she knew.

'Beezus, you look as if something is bothering you,' remarked Aunt Beatrice.

Beezus looked down at her plate. How could she ever tell such an awful thing?

'Why don't you tell us what is wrong?' Aunt Beatrice suggested. 'Perhaps we could help.'

She sounded so interested and so understanding that Beezus discovered she really wanted to tell what was on her mind. 'Sometimes I just don't love Ramona!' she blurted out, to get it over with. There! She had said it right out loud. And on her birthday, too. Now everyone would know what a terrible girl she was.

'My goodness, is that all that bothers you?' Mother sounded surprised.

Beezus nodded miserably.

'Why, there's no reason why you *should* love Ramona all the time,' mother went on. 'After all, there are probably lots of times when she doesn't love you.'

Now it was Beezus's turn to be surprised—surprised and relieved at the same time. She wondered why she hadn't thought of it that way before.

III

Aunt Beatrice smiled. 'Dorothy,' she said to mother, 'do you remember the time I—' She began to laugh so hard she couldn't finish the sentence.

'You took my doll with the beautiful yellow curls and dyed her hair with black shoe dye,' finished mother, and the two grown-up sisters went into gales of laughter. 'I didn't love you a bit that time,' admitted mother. 'I was mad at you for days.'

'And you were always so bossy, because you were older,' said Aunt Beatrice. 'I'm sure I didn't love you at all when you were supposed to take me to school and made me walk about six feet behind you, because you didn't want people to know you had to look after me.'

'Mother!' exclaimed Beezus in shocked delight.

'Did I do that?' laughed mother. 'I had forgotten all about it.'

'What else did mother do?' Beezus asked eagerly.

'She was terribly fussy,' said Aunt Beatrice. 'We had to share a room and she used to get mad because I was untidy. Once she threw all my paper dolls into the wastebasket, because I had left them on her side of the dresser. That was another time we didn't love each other.'

Fascinated, Beezus hoped this interesting conversation would continue. Imagine mother and Aunt Beatrice quarrelling!

'Oh, but the worst thing of all!' said mother. 'Remember—'

'I'll never forget!' exclaimed Aunt Beatrice, as if she knew what mother was talking about. 'Wasn't I awful?'

'Perfectly terrible,' agreed mother, wiping her eyes because she was laughing so hard.

'What happened?' begged Beezus, who could not wait to find out what dreadful thing Aunt Beatrice had done when she was a girl. 'Mother, tell what happened.'

'It all began when the girls began to take autograph albums to school,' began mother and then went off into another fit of laughter. 'Oh, Beatrice, you tell it.'

'Of course I wanted an autograph album too,' continued Aunt Beatrice. Beezus nodded, because she, too, had an autograph album. 'Well, your mother, who was always very sensible, saved her allowance and bought a beautiful album with a red cover stamped in gold. How I envied her!'

'As soon as your Aunt Beatrice got her allowance she always ran right over to the school store and spent it,' added mother.

'Yes, and on the most awful junk,' agreed Aunt Beatrice. 'Liquorice whips, and pencils that were square instead of round, and I don't know what all.'

'Yes, hut what about the autograph album?' Beezus asked.

'Well, when I—oh, I'm almost ashamed to tell it,' said Aunt Beatrice.

'Oh, go on,' urged mother. 'It's priceless.'

'Well, when I saw your mother with that brand-new autograph album that she bought, because she was so sensible, I was annoyed, because I wanted one too and I hadn't saved my allowance. And then she asked me if I'd like to sign my name in it.'

'It was my night to set the table,' added mother. 'I never should have left her alone with it.'

'But what happened?' Beezus could hardly wait to find out.

'I sat down at the desk and picked up a pen, planning to write on the last page, "By hook or by crook I'll be last in your book,"' said Aunt Beatrice.

'Oh, did people write that in those days, too?

Beezus was surprised, because she had thought this was something very new to write in an autograph album.

'But I didn't write it,' continued Aunt Beatrice.

'I just sat there wishing I had an autograph album, and then I took the pen and wrote my name on every single page in the book!'

'Aunt Beatrice! You didn't! Not in mother's brand-new autograph album!' Beezus was horrified and delighted at the same time. What a terrible thing to do!

'She certainly did,' said mother, 'and not just plain Beatrice Haswell, either. She wrote Beatrice Ann Haswell, Miss Bea Haswell, B. A. Haswell, Esquire, and everything she could think of. When she couldn't think of any more ways to write her name she started all over again.'

'Oh, Aunt Beatrice, how perfectly awful,' exclaimed Beezus, with a touch of admiration in her voice.

'Yes, wasn't it?' agreed Aunt Beatrice. 'I don't know what got into me.'

'And what did mother do?' enquired Beezus, eager for the whole story.

'We had a dreadful quarrel and I got spanked,' said Aunt Beatrice. 'Your mother didn't love me one little bit for a long, long time. And I wouldn't admit it, but I felt terrible because I had spoiled her autograph album. Fortunately Christmas came along about that time and we were both given albums and that put an end to the whole thing.'

Why, thought Beezus, Aunt Beatrice used to be every bit as awful as Ramona. And yet look how nice she is now. Beezus could scarcely believe it. And now mother and Aunt Beatrice, who had quarrelled when they were girls, loved each other and thought the things they had done were funny! They actually laughed about it. Well, maybe when she was grown-up she would think it was funny that Ramona had put eggshells in one birthday cake and baked her rubber doll with another. Maybe she wouldn't think Ramona was so exasperating, after all. Maybe that was just the way things were with sisters. A lovely feeling of relief came over Beezus. What if she *didn't* love Ramona all the time? It didn't matter at all. She was just like any other sister.

'Mother,' whispered Beezus, happier than she had felt in a long time, 'I hope Ramona comes back before we have my birthday cake.'

'Don't worry,' mother said, smiling. 'I'm sure she wouldn't miss it for anything.'

And sure enough, in a few minutes Ramona appeared from the bedroom and took her place at the table. 'I can behave myself,' she said.

'It's about time,' observed father.

Beezus watched Ramona eating her cold mashed potatoes and jelly and thought how much easier things would be now that she could look at her sister when she was exasperating and think, Ha-ha, Ramona, this is one of those times when I don't have to love you.

'Girls with birthdays don't have to help clear the table,' said mother, beginning to carry out the dishes.

Beezus waited expectantly for the most important moment of the day. She heard her mother take the cake out of its box and strike a match to light the candles. 'Oh,' she breathed happily, when mother appeared in the doorway with the cake in her hands. It was the most beautiful cake she had ever seen—pink with a wreath of white roses made of icing, and ten pink candles that threw a soft glowing light on mother's face.

'"Happy birthday to you,"' sang mother and father and Aunt Beatrice and Ramona. '"Happy birthday, dear Beezus, happy birthday to you."'

'Make a wish,' said father.

Beezus paused a minute. Then she closed her eyes and thought, I wish all my birthdays would turn out to be as wonderful as this one finally did. She opened her eyes and blew as hard as she could.

'Your wish is granted!' cried Aunt Beatrice, smiling across the ten smoking candles.

'"Happy birthday, dear Beezus, happy birthday to you!"' sang Ramona at the top of her voice.

'All right, Ramona,' said mother with a touch of exasperation in her voice. 'Once is enough.'

But at that moment Beezus did not think her little sister was exasperating at all.

RaMoNa
THe PeST

CONTENTS

1

Ramona's Great Day

'I am *not* a pest,' Ramona Quimby told her big sister Beezus.

'Then stop acting like a pest,' said Beezus, whose real name was Beatrice. She was standing by the front window waiting for her friend Mary Jane to walk to school with her.

'I'm not acting like a pest. I'm singing and skipping,' said Ramona, who had only recently learned to skip with both feet. Ramona did not think she was a pest. No matter what others said, she never thought she was a pest. The people who called her a pest were always bigger and so they could be unfair.

Ramona went on with her singing and skipping. 'This is a great day, a great day, a great day!' she sang, and to Ramona, who was feeling grown-up in a dress instead of play clothes, this was a great day, the greatest day of her whole life. No longer would she have to sit on her tricycle watching Beezus and Henry Huggins and the rest of the boys and girls in the neighbourhood go off to school. Today she was going to school, too. Today she was going to learn to read and write and do all the things that would help her catch up with Beezus.

'Come *on*, Mama!' urged Ramona, pausing in her singing and skipping. 'We don't want to be late for school.'

'Don't pester, Ramona,' said Mrs Quimby. 'I'll get you there in plenty of time.'

'I'm *not* pestering,' protested Ramona, who never meant to pester. She was not a slowcoach grown-up. She was a girl who could not wait. Life was so interesting she had to find out what happened next.

Then Mary Jane arrived. 'Mrs Quimby, would it be all right if Beezus and I take Ramona to kindergarten?' she asked.

'No!' said Ramona instantly. Mary Jane was one of those girls who always wanted to pretend she was a mother and who always wanted Ramona to be the baby. Nobody was going to catch Ramona being a baby on her first day of school.

'Why not?' Mrs Quimby asked Ramona. 'You could walk to school with Beezus and Mary Jane just like a big girl.'

'No, I couldn't.' Ramona was not fooled for an instant. Mary Jane would talk in that silly voice she used when she was being a mother and take her by the hand and help her across the street, and everyone would think she really was a baby.

'Please, Ramona,' coaxed Beezus. 'It would be lots of fun to take you in and introduce you to the kindergarten teacher.'

'No!' said Ramona, and stamped her foot. Beezus and Mary Jane might have fun, but she wouldn't. Nobody but a genuine grown-up was going to take her to school. If she had to, she would make a great big noisy fuss, and when Ramona made a great big noisy fuss, she usually got her own way. Great big noisy fusses were often necessary when a girl was the youngest member of the family and the youngest person on her block.

'All right, Ramona,' said Mrs Quimby. 'Don't make a great big noisy fuss. If that's the way you feel about it, you don't have to walk with the girls. I'll take you.'

'Hurry, Mama,' said Ramona happily, as she watched Beezus and Mary Jane go out the door. But when Ramona finally got her mother out of the house, she was disappointed to see one of her mother's friends, Mrs Kemp, approaching with her son Howie and his little sister Willa Jean, who was riding in a stroller. 'Hurry, Mama,' urged Ramona, not wanting to wait for the Kemps. Because their mothers were friends, she and Howie were expected to get along with one another.

'Hi, there!' Mrs Kemp called out, so of course Ramona's mother had to wait.

Howie stared at Ramona. He did not like having to get along with her any more than she liked having to get along with him.

Ramona stared back. Howie was a solid-looking boy with curly blond hair. ('Such a waste on a boy,' his mother often remarked.) The legs of his new jeans were turned up, and he was wearing a new shirt with long sleeves. He did not look the least bit excited about starting kindergarten. That was the trouble with Howie, Ramona felt. He never got excited. Straight-haired Willa Jean, who was interesting to Ramona because she was so sloppy, blew out a mouthful of wet crumbs and laughed at her cleverness.

'Today my baby leaves me,' remarked Mrs Quimby with a smile, as the little group proceeded down Klickitat Street towards Glenwood School.

Ramona, who enjoyed being her mother's baby, did not enjoy being called her mother's baby, especially in front of Howie.

'They grow up quickly,' observed Mrs Kemp.

Ramona could not understand why grown-ups always talked about how quickly children grew up. Ramona thought growing up was the slowest thing there was, slower even than waiting for Christmas to come. She had been waiting years just to get to kindergarten, and the last half hour was the slowest part of all.

When the group reached the intersection nearest Glenwood School, Ramona was pleased to see that Beezus's friend Henry Huggins was the traffic boy in charge of that particular corner. After Henry had led them across the street, Ramona ran off towards the kindergarten, which was a temporary wooden building with its own playground. Mothers and children were already entering the open door. Some of the children looked frightened, and one girl was crying.

'We're late!' cried Ramona. 'Hurry!'

Howie was not a boy to be hurried. 'I don't see any tricycles,' he said critically. 'I don't see any dirt to dig in.'

Ramona was scornful. 'This isn't nursery school. Tricycles and dirt are for nursery school.' Her own tricycle was hidden in the garage, because it was too babyish for her now that she was going to school.

Some big first-grade boys ran past yelling, 'Kindergarten babies! Kindergarten babies!'

'We are *not* babies!' Ramona yelled back, as she led her mother into the kindergarten. Once inside she stayed close to her. Everything was so strange, and there was so much to see: the little tables and chairs; the row of cupboards, each with a different picture on the door; the play stove; and the wooden blocks big enough to stand on.

The teacher, who was new to Glenwood School, turned out to be so young and pretty she could not have been a grown-up very long. It was rumoured she had never taught at school before. 'Hello, Ramona. My name is Miss Binney,' she said, speaking each syllable distinctly as she pinned Ramona's name to her dress. 'I am so glad you have come to kindergarten.' Then she took Ramona by the hand and led her to one of the little tables and chairs. 'Sit here for the present,' she said with a smile.

A present! thought Ramona, and knew at once she was going to like Miss Binney.

'Goodbye, Ramona,' said Mrs Quimby. 'Be a good girl.'

As she watched her mother walk out of the door, Ramona decided school was going to be even better than she had hoped. Nobody had told her she was going to get a present the very first day. What kind of present could it be, she wondered, trying to remember if Beezus had ever been given a present by her teacher.

Ramona listened carefully while Miss Binney showed Howie to a table, but all her teacher said was, 'Howie, I would like you to sit here.' Well! thought Ramona. Not everyone is going to get a present so Miss Binney must like me best. Ramona watched and listened as the other boys and girls arrived, but Miss Binney did not tell anyone else he was going to get a present if he sat in a certain chair. Ramona wondered if her present would be wrapped in fancy paper and tied with a ribbon like a birthday present. She hoped so.

As Ramona sat waiting for her present she watched the other children being introduced to Miss Binney by their mothers. She found two members of the morning kindergarten especially interesting. One was a boy named Davy, who was small, thin, and eager. He was the only boy in the class in short pants, and Ramona liked him at once. She liked him so much she decided she would like to kiss him.

The other interesting person was a big girl named Susan. Susan's hair looked like the hair on the girls in the pictures of the old-fashioned stories Beezus liked to read. It was reddish-brown and hung in curls like springs that touched her shoulders and bounced as she walked. Ramona had never seen such curls before. All the curly-haired girls she knew wore their hair short. Ramona put her hand to her own short straight hair, which was an ordinary brown, and longed to touch that bright springy hair. She longed to stretch one of those curls and watch it spring back. *Boing!* thought Ramona, making a mental noise like a spring on a television cartoon and wishing for thick, springy *boing-boing* hair like Susan's.

Howie interrupted Ramona's admiration of Susan's hair. 'How soon do you think we get to go out and play?' he asked.

'Maybe after Miss Binney gives me the present,' Ramona answered. 'She said she was going to give me one.'

'How come she's going to give you a present?' Howie wanted to know. 'She didn't say anything about giving me a present.'

'Maybe she likes me best,' said Ramona.

This news did not make Howie happy. He turned to the next boy, and said, '*She's* going to get a present.'

Ramona wondered how long she would have to sit there to get the present. If only Miss Binney understood how hard waiting was for her! When the last child had been welcomed and the last tearful mother had departed, Miss Binney gave a little talk about the rules of the kindergarten and showed the class the door that led to the bathroom. Next she assigned each person a little cupboard. Ramona's cupboard had a picture of a yellow duck on the door, and Howie's had a green frog. Miss Binney explained that their hooks in the cloakroom were marked with the same pictures. Then she asked the class to follow her quietly into the cloakroom to find their hooks.

Difficult though waiting was for her, Ramona did not budge. Miss Binney had not told her to get up and go into the cloakroom for her present. She had told her to sit for the present, and Ramona was going to sit until she got it. She would sit as if she were glued to the chair.

Howie scowled at Ramona as he returned from the cloakroom, and said to another boy, 'The teacher is going to give *her* a present.'

Naturally the boy wanted to know why. 'I don't know,' admitted Ramona. 'She told me that if I sat here I would get a present. I guess she likes me best.'

By the time Miss Binney returned from the cloakroom, word had spread around the classroom that Ramona was going to get a present.

Next Miss Binney taught the class the words of a puzzling song about 'the dawnzer lee light,' which Ramona did not understand because she did not know what a dawnzer was. 'Oh, say, can you see by the dawnzer lee light,' sang Miss Binney, and Ramona decided that a dawnzer was another word for a lamp.

When Miss Binney had gone over the song several times, she asked the class to stand and sing it with her. Ramona did not budge. Neither did Howie and some of the others, and Ramona knew they were hoping for a present, too. Copycats, she thought.

'Stand up straight like good Americans,' said Miss Binney so firmly that Howie and the others reluctantly stood up.

Ramona decided she would have to be a good American sitting down.

'Ramona,' said Miss Binney, 'aren't you going to stand with the rest of us?'

Ramona thought quickly. Maybe the question was some kind of test, like a test in a fairy tale. Maybe Miss Binney was testing her to see if she could get her out of her seat. If she failed the test, she would not get the present.

'I can't,' said Ramona.

Miss Binney looked puzzled, but she did not insist that Ramona stand while she led the class through the dawnzer song. Ramona sang along with the others and hoped that her present came next, but when the song ended, Miss Binney made no mention of the present. Instead she picked up a book. Ramona decided that at last the time had come to learn to read.

Miss Binney stood in front of her class and began to read aloud from *Mike Mulligan and His Steam Shovel*, a book that was a favourite of

Ramona's because, unlike so many books for her age, it was neither quiet and sleepy nor sweet and pretty. Ramona, pretending she was glued to her chair, enjoyed hearing the story again and listened quietly with the rest of the kindergarten to the story of Mike Mulligan's old-fashioned steam shovel, which proved its worth by digging the basement for the new town hall of Poppersville in a single day beginning at dawn and ending as the sun went down.

As Ramona listened a question came into her mind, a question that had often puzzled her about the books that were read to her. Somehow books always left out one of the most important things anyone would want to know. Now that Ramona was in school, and school was a place for learning, perhaps Miss Binney could answer the question. Ramona waited quietly until her teacher had finished the story, and then she raised her hand the way Miss Binney had told the class they should raise their hands when they wanted to speak in school.

Joey, who did not remember to raise his hand, spoke out. 'That's a good book.'

Miss Binney smiled at Ramona, and said, 'I like the way Ramona remembers to raise her hand when she has something to say. Yes, Ramona?'

Ramona's hopes soared. Her teacher had smiled

at her. 'Miss Binney, I want to know—how did Mike Mulligan go to the bathroom when he was digging the basement of the town hall?'

Miss Binney's smile seemed to last longer than smiles usually last. Ramona glanced uneasily around and saw that others were waiting with interest for the answer. Everybody wanted to know how Mike Mulligan went to the bathroom.

'Well—' said Miss Binney at last. 'I don't really know, Ramona. The book doesn't tell us.'

'I always wanted to know, too,' said Howie, without raising his hand, and others murmured in agreement. The whole class, it seemed, had been wondering how Mike Mulligan went to the bathroom.

'Maybe he stopped the steam shovel and climbed out of the hole he was digging and went to a service station,' suggested a boy named Eric.

'He couldn't. The book says he had to work as fast as he could all day,' Howie pointed out. 'It doesn't say he stopped.'

Miss Binney faced the twenty-nine earnest members of the kindergarten, all of whom wanted to know how Mike Mulligan went to the bathroom.

'Boys and girls,' she began, and spoke in her clear, distinct way. 'The reason the book does not tell us how Mike Mulligan went to the bathroom is that it is not an important part of the story. The story is about digging the basement of the town hall, and that is what the book tells us.'

Miss Binney spoke as if this explanation ended the matter, but the kindergarten was not convinced. Ramona knew and the rest of the class knew that knowing how to go to the bathroom *was* important. They were surprised that Miss Binney did not understand, because she had showed them the bathroom the very first thing. Ramona could see there were some things she was not going to learn in school, and along with the rest of the class she stared reproachfully at Miss Binney.

The teacher looked embarrassed, as if she knew she had disappointed her kindergarten. She recovered quickly, closed the book, and told the class that if they would walk quietly out to the playground she would teach them a game called Grey Duck.

Ramona did not budge. She watched the rest of the class leave the room and admired Susan's *boing-boing* curls as they bounced about her shoulders, but she did not stir from her seat. Only Miss Binney could unstick the imaginary glue that held her there.

'Don't you want to learn to play Grey Duck, Ramona?' Miss Binney asked.

Ramona nodded. 'Yes, but I can't.'

'Why not?' asked Miss Binney.

'I can't leave my seat,' said Ramona. When Miss Binney looked blank, she added, 'Because of the present.'

'What present?' Miss Binney seemed so genuinely puzzled that Ramona became uneasy. The teacher sat down in the little chair next to Ramona's, and said, 'Tell me why you can't play Grey Duck.'

Ramona squirmed, worn out with waiting. She had an uneasy feeling that something had gone wrong someplace. 'I want to play Grey Duck, but you—' she stopped, feeling that she might be about to say the wrong thing.

'But I what?' asked Miss Binney.

'Well . . . uh . . . you said if I sat here I would get a present,' said Ramona at last, 'but you didn't say how long I had to sit here.'

If Miss Binney had looked puzzled before, she now looked baffled. 'Ramona, I don't understand—' she began.

'Yes, you did,' said Ramona, nodding. 'You told me to sit here for the present, and I have been sitting here ever since school started and you haven't given me a present.'

Miss Binney's face turned red and she looked so embarrassed that Ramona felt completely confused. Teachers were not supposed to look that way.

Miss Binney spoke gently. 'Ramona, I'm afraid we've had a misunderstanding.'

Ramona was blunt. 'You mean I don't get a present?'

'I'm afraid not,' admitted Miss Binney. 'You see "for the present" means for now. I meant that I wanted you to sit here for now, because later I may have the children sit at different desks.'

'Oh.' Ramona was so disappointed she had nothing to say. Words were so puzzling. *Present* should mean a present just as *attack* should mean to stick tacks in people.

By now all the children were crowding around the door to see what had happened to their teacher. 'I'm so sorry,' said Miss Binney. 'It's all my fault. I should have used different words.'

'That's all right,' said Ramona, ashamed to have the class see that she was not going to get a present after all.

'All right, class,' said Miss Binney briskly. 'Let's go outside and play Grey Duck. You, too, Ramona.'

Grey Duck turned out to be an easy game, and Ramona's spirits recovered quickly from her disappointment. The class formed a circle, and the person who was 'it' tagged someone who had to chase him around the circle. If 'it' was caught before he got back to the empty space in the circle, he had to go into the centre of the circle, which was called the mush pot, and the person who caught him became 'it'.

Ramona tried to stand next to the girl with the springy curls, but instead she found herself beside Howie. 'I thought you were going to get a present,' gloated Howie.

Ramona merely scowled and made a face at Howie, who was 'it', but quickly landed in the mush pot because his new jeans were so stiff they slowed him down. 'Look at Howie in the mush pot!' crowed Ramona.

Howie looked as if he were about to cry, which Ramona thought was silly of him. Only a baby would cry in the mush pot. Me, me, somebody tag me, thought Ramona, jumping up and down. She longed for a turn to run around the circle. Susan was jumping up and down, too, and her curls bobbed enticingly.

At last Ramona felt a tap on her shoulder. Her turn had come to run around the circle! She ran as fast as she could to catch up with the sneakers pounding on the asphalt ahead of her. The *boing-boing* curls were on the other side of the circle. Ramona was coming closer to them. She put out her hand. She took hold of a curl, a thick springy curl—

'*Yow!*' screamed the owner of the curls.

Startled, Ramona let go. She was so surprised by the scream that she forgot to watch Susan's curl spring back.

Susan clutched her curls with one hand and pointed at Ramona with the other. 'That girl pulled my hair! That girl pulled my hair! Ow-ow-ow.' Ramona felt that Susan did not have to be so touchy. She had not meant to hurt her. She only wanted to touch that beautiful, springy hair that was so different from her own straight brown hair.

'Ow-ow-ow!' shrieked Susan, the centre of everyone's attention.

'Baby,' said Ramona.

'Ramona,' said Miss Binney, 'in our kindergarten we do not pull hair.'

'Susan doesn't have to be such a baby,' said Ramona.

'You may go sit on the bench outside the door while the rest of us play our game,' Miss Binney told Ramona.

Ramona did not want to sit on any bench. She wanted to play Grey Duck with the rest of the class. 'No,' said Ramona, preparing to make a great big noisy fuss. 'I won't.'

Susan stopped shrieking. A terrible silence fell over the playground. Everyone stared at Ramona in such a way that she almost felt as if she were beginning to shrink. Nothing like this had ever happened to her before.

'Ramona,' said Miss Binney quietly. 'Go sit on the bench.'

Without another word Ramona walked across the playground and sat down on the bench by the door of the kindergarten. The game of Grey Duck continued without her, but the class had not forgotten her. Howie grinned in her direction. Susan continued to look injured. Some laughed and pointed at Ramona. Others, particularly Davy, looked worried, as if they had not known such a terrible punishment could be given in kindergarten.

Ramona swung her feet and pretended to be watching some workmen who were building a new market across the street. In spite of the misunderstanding about the present, she wanted so much to be loved by her pretty new teacher. Tears came into Ramona's eyes, but she would not cry. Nobody was going to call Ramona Quimby a crybaby. Never.

Next door to the kindergarten two little girls, about two and four years old, peered solemnly through the fence at Ramona. 'See that girl,' said the older girl to her little sister. 'She's sitting there because she's been bad.' The two-year-old looked awed to be in the presence of such wickedness. Ramona stared at the ground, she felt so ashamed.

When the game ended, the class filed past Ramona into the kindergarten. 'You may come in now, Ramona,' said Miss Binney pleasantly.

Ramona slid off the bench and followed the others. Even though she was not loved, she was forgiven, and that helped. She hoped that learning to read and write came next.

Inside Miss Binney announced that the time had come to rest. This news was another disappointment to Ramona, who felt that anyone who went to kindergarten was too old to rest. Miss Binney gave each child a mat on which there was a picture that matched the picture on his cupboard door and told him where to spread his mat on the floor. When all twenty-nine children were lying down they did not rest. They popped up to see what others were doing. They wiggled. They whispered. They coughed. They asked, 'How much longer do we have to rest?'

'Sh-h,' said Miss Binney in a soft, quiet, sleepy voice. 'The person who rests most quietly will get to be the wake-up fairy.'

'What's the wake-up fairy?' demanded Howie, bobbing up.

'Sh-h,' whispered Miss Binney. 'The wake-up fairy tiptoes around and wakes up the class with a magic wand. Whoever is the fairy wakes up the quietest resters first.'

Ramona made up her mind that she would get to be the wake-up fairy, and then Miss Binney would know she was not so bad after all. She lay flat on her back with her hands tight to her sides. The mat was thin and the floor was hard, but Ramona did not wiggle. She was sure she must be the best rester in the class, because she could hear others squirming around on their mats. Just to show Miss Binney she really and truly was resting she gave one little snore, not a loud snore but a delicate snore, to prove what a good rester she was.

A scatter of giggles rose from the class, followed by several snores, less delicate than Ramona's. They led to more and more, less and less delicate snores until everyone was snoring except the few who did not know how to snore. They were giggling.

Miss Binney clapped her hands and spoke in a voice that was no longer soft, quiet, and sleepy. 'All right, boys and girls!' she said. 'This is enough! We do not snore or giggle during rest time.'

'Ramona started it,' said Howie.

Ramona sat up and scowled at Howie. 'Tattletale,' she said in a voice of scorn. Across Howie she saw that Susan was lying quietly with her beautiful curls spread out on her mat and eyes screwed tight shut.

'Well, you did,' said Howie.

'Children!' Miss Binney's voice was sharp. 'We must rest so that we will not be tired when our mothers come to take us home.'

'Is your mother coming to take you home?' Howie asked Miss Binney. Ramona had been wondering the same thing.

'That's enough, Howie!' Miss Binney spoke the way mothers sometimes speak just before dinnertime. In a moment she was back to her soft, sleepy voice. 'I like the way Susan is resting so quietly,' she said. 'Susan, you may be the wake-up fairy and tap the boys and girls with this wand to wake them up.'

The magic wand turned out to be nothing but an everyday yardstick. Ramona lay quietly, but her efforts were of no use. Susan with her curls bouncing about her shoulders tapped Ramona last. It's not fair, Ramona thought. She was not the worst rester in the class. Howie was much worse.

The rest of the morning went quickly. The class was allowed to explore the paints and the toys, and those who wanted to were allowed to draw with their new crayons. They did not, however, learn to read and write, but Ramona cheered up when Miss Binney explained that anyone who had anything to share with the class could bring it to school the next day for Show and Tell. Ramona was glad when the bell finally rang and she saw her mother waiting for her outside the fence. Mrs Kemp and Willa Jean were waiting for Howie, too, and the five started home together.

Right away Howie said, 'Ramona got benched, and she's the worst rester in the class.'

After all that had happened that morning, Ramona found this too much. 'Why don't you shut up?' she yelled at Howie just before she hit him.

Mrs Quimby seized Ramona by the hand and dragged her away from Howie. 'Now, Ramona,' she said, and her voice was firm, 'this is no way to behave on your first day of school.'

'Poor little girl,' said Mrs Kemp. 'She's worn out.'

Nothing infuriated Ramona more than having a grown-up say, as if she could not hear, that she was worn out. 'I'm *not* worn out!' she shrieked.

'She got plenty of rest while she was benched,' said Howie.

'Now, Howie, you stay out of this,' said Mrs Kemp. Then to change the subject, she asked her son, 'How do you like kindergarten?'

'Oh—I guess it's all right,' said Howie without enthusiasm. 'They don't have any dirt to dig in or tricycles to ride.'

'And what about you, Ramona?' asked Mrs Quimby. 'Did you like kindergarten?'

Ramona considered. Kindergarten had not turned out as she had expected. Still, even though she had not been given a present and Miss Binney did not love her, she had liked being with boys and girls her own age. She liked singing the song about the dawnzer and having her own little cupboard. 'I didn't like it as much as I thought I would,' she answered honestly, 'but maybe it will get better when we have Show and Tell.'

2

SHOW aND TeLL

Ramona looked forward to many things—her first loose tooth, riding a bicycle instead of a tricycle, wearing lipstick like her mother—but most of all she looked forward to Show and Tell. For years Ramona had watched her sister Beezus leave for school with a doll, a book, or a pretty leaf to share with her class. She had watched Beezus's friend Henry Huggins carry mysterious, lumpy packages past her house on his way to school. She had listened to Beezus talk about the interesting things her class brought to school—turtles, ballpoint pens that wrote in three different colours, a live clam in a jar of sand and seawater.

Now at last the time had come for Ramona to show and tell. 'What are you going to take to show your class?' she asked Beezus, hoping for an idea for herself.

'Nothing,' said Beezus, and went on to explain. 'Along about the third grade you begin to outgrow Show and Tell. By the fifth grade it's all right to take something really unusual like somebody's pickled appendix or something to do with social studies. An old piece of fur when you study fur traders would be all right. Or if something really exciting happened like your house burning down, it would be all right to tell about that. But in the fifth grade you don't take an old doll or a toy fire engine to school. And you don't call it Show and Tell by then. You just let the teacher know you have something interesting.'

Ramona was not discouraged. She was used to Beezus's growing out of things as she grew into them. She rummaged around in her toy box and finally dragged out her favourite doll, the doll with the hair that could really be washed. 'I'm going to take Chevrolet,' she told Beezus.

'Nobody names a doll Chevrolet,' said Beezus, whose dolls had names like Sandra or Patty.

'I do,' Ramona answered. 'I think Chevrolet is the most beautiful name in the world.'

'Well, she's a horrid-looking doll,' said Beezus. 'Her hair is green. Besides, you don't play with her.'

'I wash her hair,' said Ramona loyally, 'and the only reason what's left of her hair looks sort of green is that I tried to blue it like Howie's grandmother, who has her hair blued at the beauty shop. Mama said putting bluing on yellow hair turned it green. Anyway, I think it's pretty.'

When the time finally came to start to school,

Ramona was disappointed once more to see Mrs Kemp approaching with Howie and little Willa Jean. 'Mama, come *on*,' begged Ramona, dragging at her mother's hand, but her mother waited until the Kemps had caught up. Willa Jean was even sloppier this morning. There were crumbs on the front of her sweater, and she was drinking apple juice out of a nursing bottle. Willa Jean dropped the bottle when she saw Chevrolet and sat there with apple juice dribbling down her chin while she stared at Ramona's doll.

'Ramona is taking her doll to school for Show and Tell,' said Mrs Quimby.

Howie looked worried. 'I don't have anything for Show and Tell,' he said.

'That's all right, Howie,' said Mrs Quimby. 'Miss Binney doesn't expect you to take something every day.'

'I *want* to take something,' said Howie.

'My goodness, Howie,' said his mother. 'What if twenty-nine children each brought something. Miss Binney wouldn't have time to teach you anything.'

'*She's* taking something.' Howie pointed to Ramona.

There was something familiar about the way Howie was behaving. Ramona pulled at her mother's hand. 'Come *on*, Mama.'

'Ramona, I think it would be nice if you ran in the house and found something to lend Howie to take to school,' said Mrs Quimby.

Ramona did not think this idea was nice at all, but she recognized that lending Howie something might be faster than arguing with him. She ran into the house where she snatched up the first thing she saw—a stuffed rabbit that had already been given hard wear before the cat had adopted it as a sort of practice gopher. The cat liked to chew the rabbit's tail, carry it around in his mouth, or lie down and kick it with his hind feet.

When Ramona thrust the rabbit into Howie's hand, Mrs Kemp said, 'Say thank you, Howie.'

'It's just an old beat-up bunny,' said Howie scornfully. When his mother wasn't looking, he handed the rabbit to Willa Jean, who dropped her apple juice, seized the rabbit, and began to chew its tail.

Just like our cat, thought Ramona, as the group proceeded towards school.

'Don't forget Ramona's bunny,' said Mrs Kemp, when they reached the kindergarten playground.

'I don't want her old bunny,' said Howie.

'Now, Howie,' said his mother. 'Ramona was kind enough to share her bunny so you be nice.' To Mrs Quimby she said, as if Howie could not hear, 'Howie needs to learn manners.'

Share! Ramona had learned about sharing in nursery school, where she either had to share something of her own that she did not want to share or she had to share something that belonged to someone else that she did not want to share either. 'That's all right, Howie,' she said. 'You don't have to share my rabbit.'

Howie looked grateful, but his mother thrust the rabbit into his hands anyway.

At the beginning, on that second day of kindergarten, Ramona felt shy because she was not sure what Miss Binney would think about a girl who had been made to sit on the bench. But Miss Binney smiled, and said, 'Good morning, Ramona,' and seemed to have forgotten all about the day before. Ramona sat Chevrolet in her little cupboard with the duck on the door and waited for Show and Tell.

'Did anyone bring something to show the class?' asked Miss Binney, after the class had sung the dawnzer song.

Ramona remembered to raise her hand, and Miss Binney invited her to come to the front of the room to show the class what she had brought. Ramona took Chevrolet from her cupboard and stood beside Miss Binney's desk, where she discovered she did not know what to say. She looked to Miss Binney for help.

Miss Binney smiled encouragingly. 'Is there something you would like to tell us about your doll?'

'I can really wash her hair,' said Ramona. 'It's sort of green because I gave her a blue rinse.'

'And what do you wash it with?' asked Miss Binney.

'Lots of things,' said Ramona, beginning to enjoy speaking in front of the class. 'Soap, shampoo, detergent, bubble bath. I tried Dutch Cleanser once, but it didn't work.'

'What is your doll's name?' asked Miss Binney.

'Chevrolet,' answered Ramona. 'I named her after my aunt's car.'

The class began to laugh, especially the boys. Ramona felt confused, standing there in front of twenty-eight boys and girls who were all laughing at her. 'Well, I did!' she said angrily, almost tearfully. Chevrolet was a beautiful name, and there was no reason to laugh.

Miss Binney ignored the giggles and snickers. 'I think Chevrolet is a lovely name,' she said. Then she repeated, 'Chev-ro-let.' The way Miss Binney pronounced the word made it sound like music. 'Say it, class.'

'Chev-ro-let,' said the class obediently, and this time no one laughed. Ramona's heart was filled with love for her teacher. Miss Binney was not like most grown-ups. Miss Binney understood.

The teacher smiled at Ramona. 'Thank you, Ramona, for sharing Chevrolet with us.'

After a girl had showed her doll that talked when she pulled a cord in its back and a boy had told the class about his family's new refrigerator, Miss Binney asked, 'Does anyone else have anything to show us or tell us about?'

'That boy brought something,' said Susan of the springy curls, pointing at Howie.

Boing, thought Ramona, as she always did when those curls caught her attention. She was beginning to see that Susan was a girl who liked to take charge.

'Howie, did you bring something?' asked Miss Binney.

Howie looked embarrassed.

'Come on, Howie,' encouraged Miss Binney. 'Show us what you brought.'

Reluctantly Howie went to his cupboard and brought out the shabby blue rabbit with the damp tail. He carried it to Miss Binney's desk, faced the class, and said in a flat voice, 'It's just an old bunny.' The class showed very little interest.

'Is there something you would like to tell us about your bunny?' asked Miss Binney.

'No,' said Howie. 'I just brought it because my mother made me.'

'I can tell you something about your bunny,' said Miss Binney. 'It has had lots of love. That's why it's so worn.'

Ramona was fascinated. In her imagination she could see the cat lying on the carpet with the rabbit gripped in his teeth while he battered it with his hind feet. The look that Howie gave the rabbit was somehow lacking in love. Ramona waited for him to say that it wasn't his rabbit, but he did not. He just stood there.

Miss Binney, seeing that Howie could not be encouraged to speak in front of the class, opened a drawer in her desk, and as she reached inside she said, 'I have a present for your bunny.' She pulled out a red ribbon, took the rabbit from Howie, and tied the ribbon around its neck in a bright bow. 'There you are, Howie,' she said. 'A nice new bow for your bunny.'

Howie mumbled, 'Thank you,' and as quickly as possible hid the rabbit in his cupboard.

Ramona was delighted. She felt that the red ribbon Miss Binney had given her old rabbit took the place of the present she had not been given the day before. All morning she thought about the things she could do with that red ribbon. She could use it to tie up what was left of Chevrolet's hair. She could trade it to Beezus for something valuable, an empty perfume bottle or some coloured paper that wasn't scribbled on. During rest time Ramona had the best idea of all. She would save the ribbon until she got a two-wheeled bicycle. Then she would weave it in and out of the spokes and ride so fast the ribbon would be a red blur as the wheels went around. Yes. That was exactly what she would do with her red ribbon.

When the noon bell rang. Mrs Quimby, Mrs Kemp, and little Willa Jean were waiting by the fence. 'Howie,' Mrs Kemp called out, 'don't forget Ramona's bunny.'

'Oh, that old thing,' muttered Howie, but he returned to his cupboard while Ramona walked along behind the mothers.

'Howie needs to learn responsibility,' Mrs Kemp was saying.

When Howie had caught up, he untied the ribbon and shoved the rabbit at Ramona. 'Here. Take your old rabbit,' he said.

Ramona took it and said, 'Give me my ribbon.'

'It's not your ribbon,' said Howie. 'It's my ribbon.'

The two mothers were so busy talking about their children needing to learn responsibility they paid no attention to the argument.

'It is not!' said Ramona. 'It's my ribbon!'

'Miss Binney gave it to me.' Howie was so calm and so sure that he was right that Ramona was infuriated. She grabbed for the ribbon, but Howie held it away from her.

'Miss Binney tied it around my rabbit's neck, so it's my ribbon!' she said, her voice rising.

'No,' said Howie flatly and calmly.

'Ribbons aren't for boys,' Ramona reminded him. 'Now give it to me!'

'It isn't yours.' Howie showed no excitement, only stubbornness.

Howie's behaviour drove Ramona wild. She wanted him to get excited. She wanted him to get angry. 'It is too mine!' she shrieked, and at last the mothers turned around.

'What's going on?' asked Mrs Quimby.

'Howie has my ribbon and won't give it back,' said Ramona, so angry she was near tears.

'It isn't hers,' said Howie.

The two mothers exchanged glances. 'Howie, where did you get that ribbon?' asked Mrs Kemp.

'Miss Binney gave it to me,' said Howie.

'She gave it to *me*,' corrected Ramona, as she fought back tears. 'She tied it on my rabbit's neck, so it's my ribbon.' Anybody should be able to understand that. Anybody who was not stupid.

'Now, Howie,' said his mother. 'What does a big boy like you want with a ribbon?'

Howie considered this question as if his mother really expected an answer. 'Well . . . I could tie it on the tail of a kite if I had a kite.'

'He just doesn't want me to have it,' explained Ramona. 'He's selfish.'

'I am not selfish,' said Howie. 'You want something that doesn't belong to you.'

'I do *not*!' yelled Ramona.

'Now, Ramona,' said her mother. 'A piece of ribbon isn't worth all this fuss. We have other ribbons at home that you can have.'

Ramona did not know how to make her mother understand. No other ribbon could possibly take the place of this one. Miss Binney had given her the ribbon, and she wanted it because she loved Miss Binney so much. She wished Miss Binney were here now because her teacher, unlike the mothers, would understand. All Ramona could say was, 'It's mine.'

'I know!' said Mrs Kemp, as if a brilliant idea had come to her. 'You can share the ribbon.'

Ramona and Howie exchanged a look in which they agreed that nothing would be worse than sharing the ribbon. They both knew there were some things that could never be shared, and Miss Binney's ribbon was one of them. Ramona wanted that ribbon, and she wanted it all to herself. She knew that a grubby boy like

Howie would probably let Willa Jean drool on it and ruin it.

'That's a good idea,' agreed Mrs Quimby. 'Ramona, you let Howie carry it halfway home, and then you can carry it the rest of the way.'

'Then who gets it?' asked Howie, voicing the question that had risen in Ramona's thoughts.

'We can cut it in two so you each may have half,' said Mrs Kemp. 'We're having lunch at Ramona's house, and as soon as we get there we'll divide the ribbon.'

Miss Binney's beautiful ribbon chopped in two! This was too much. Ramona burst into tears. Her half would not be long enough for anything. If she ever got a two-wheeled bicycle, there would not be enough ribbon to weave through the spokes of a wheel. There would not even be enough to tie up Chevrolet's hair.

'I'm tired of sharing,' said Howie. 'Share, share, share. That's all grown-ups ever talk about.'

Ramona could not understand why both mothers were amused by Howie's words. She understood exactly what Howie meant, and she liked him a little better for saying so. She had always had a guilty feeling she was the only person who felt that way.

'Now, Howie, it isn't as bad as all that,' said his mother.

'It is too,' said Howie, and Ramona nodded through her tears.

'Give me the ribbon,' said Mrs Kemp. 'Maybe after lunch we'll all feel better.'

Reluctantly Howie surrendered the precious ribbon, and said, 'I suppose we're having tuna-fish sandwiches again.'

'Howie, that's not polite,' said his mother.

At the Quimbys' house, Ramona's mother said, 'Why don't you and Howie play with your tricycle while I prepare lunch?'

'Sure, Ramona,' said Howie, as the two mothers boosted Willa Jean's stroller up the steps, and he and Ramona were left together whether they wanted to be or not. Ramona sat down on the steps and tried to think of a name to call Howie. Pieface wasn't bad enough. If she used some of the names she had heard big boys use at school, her mother would come out and scold her. Perhaps 'little booby boy' would do.

'Where's your trike?' asked Howie.

'In the garage,' answered Ramona. 'I don't ride it any more now that I'm in kindergarten.'

'How come?' asked Howie.

'I'm too big,' said Ramona. 'Everybody else on the block rides two-wheelers. Only babies ride tricycles.' She made this remark because she knew Howie still rode his tricycle, and she was so angry about the ribbon she wanted to hurt his feelings.

If Howie's feelings were hurt, he did not show it. He seemed to be considering Ramona's remarks in his usual deliberate way. 'I could take off one of the wheels if I had some pliers and a screwdriver,' he said at last.

Ramona was indignant. 'And wreck my tricycle?' Howie just wanted to get her into trouble.

'It wouldn't wreck it,' said Howie. 'I take the wheels off my tricycle all the time. You can ride on the front wheel and one back wheel. That way you'd have a two-wheeler.'

Ramona was not convinced.

'Come on, Ramona,' coaxed Howie. 'I like to take wheels off tricycles.'

Ramona considered. 'If I let you take off a wheel, do I get to keep the ribbon?'

'Well . . . I guess so.' After all, Howie was a boy. He was more interested in taking a tricycle apart than he was in playing with any ribbon.

Ramona was doubtful about Howie's ability to turn her tricycle into a two-wheeler, but she was determined to have Miss Binney's red ribbon.

She trundled her tricycle out of the garage. Then she found the pliers and a screwdriver, and handed them to Howie, who went to work in a businesslike way. He used the screwdriver to prise off the hub. With the pliers he straightened the cotter pin that held the wheel in place, removed it from the axle, and pulled off the wheel. Next he returned the cotter pin to its hole in the axle and bent the ends out once more so the axle would stay in place. 'There,' he said with satisfaction. For once he looked happy and sure of himself. 'You have to sort of lean to one side when you ride it.'

Ramona was so impressed by Howie's work that her anger began to drain away. Maybe Howie was right. She grasped her tricycle by the handlebars and mounted the seat. By leaning towards the side on which the wheel had been removed, she managed to balance herself and to ride down the driveway in an uncertain and lopsided fashion. 'Hey! It works!' she called out, when she reached the sidewalk. She circled and pedalled back towards Howie, who stood beaming at the success of his alteration.

'I told you it would work,' he bragged.

'I didn't believe you at first,' confessed Ramona, who would never again be seen riding a babyish three-wheeler.

The back door opened, and Mrs Quimby called out, 'Come on, children. Your tuna sandwiches are ready.'

'See my two-wheeler,' cried Ramona, pedalling in a lopsided circle.

'Well, aren't you a big girl!' exclaimed her mother. 'How did you ever manage to do that?'

Ramona came to a halt. 'Howie fixed my trike for me and told me how to ride it.'

'What a clever boy!' said Mrs Quimby. 'You must be very good with tools.'

Howie beamed with pleasure at this compliment.

'And Mama,' said Ramona, 'Howie says I can have Miss Binney's ribbon.'

'Sure,' agreed Howie. 'What do I want with an old ribbon?'

'I'm going to weave it in and out of the front spokes of my two-wheeler and ride so fast it will make a blur,' said Ramona. 'Come on, Howie, let's go eat our tuna-fish sandwiches.'

3

Seat Work

There were two kinds of children who went to kindergarten—those who lined up beside the door before school, as they were supposed to, and those who ran around the playground and scrambled to get into line when they saw Miss Binney approaching. Ramona ran around the playground.

One morning as Ramona was running around the playground she noticed Davy waiting for Henry Huggins to lead him across the intersection. She was interested to see that Davy was wearing a black cape pinned to his shoulders with two big safety pins.

While Henry held up two cars and a cement truck, Ramona watched Davy crossing the street. The more Ramona saw of Davy, the better she liked him. He was such a nice shy boy with blue eyes and soft brown hair. Ramona always tried to choose Davy for her partner in folk dancing, and when the class played Grey Duck Ramona always tagged Davy unless he was already in the mush pot.

When Davy arrived, Ramona marched up to him, and asked, 'Are you Batman?'

'No,' said Davy.

'Are you Superman?' asked Ramona.

'No,' said Davy.

Who else could Davy be in a black cape? Ramona stopped and thought, but was unable to think of anyone else who wore a cape. 'Well, who are you?' she asked at last.

'Mighty Mouse!' crowed Davy, delighted that he had baffled Ramona.

'I'm going to kiss you, Mighty Mouse!' shrieked Ramona.

Davy began to run and Ramona ran after him. Round and round the playground they ran with Davy's cape flying out behind him. Under the travelling bars and around the jungle gym she chased him.

'Run, Davy! Run!' screamed the rest of the class, jumping up and down, until Miss Binney was seen approaching, and everyone scrambled to get into line.

Every morning afterwards when Ramona reached the playground she tried to catch Davy so she could kiss him.

'Here comes Ramona!' the other boys and girls shouted, when they saw Ramona walking down the street. 'Run, Davy! Run!'

And Davy ran with Ramona after him. Round and round the playground they ran while the class cheered Davy on.

'That kid ought to go out for track when he gets a little older,' Ramona heard one of the workmen across the street say one day.

Once Ramona came near enough to grab Davy's clothes, but he jerked away, popping the buttons off his shirt. For once Davy stopped running. 'Now see what you did!' he accused. 'My mother is going to be mad at you.'

Ramona stopped in her tracks. 'I didn't do anything,' she said indignantly. 'I just hung on. You did the pulling.'

'Here comes Miss Binney,' someone called out, and Ramona and Davy scurried to get in line by the door.

After that Davy stayed further away from Ramona than ever, which made Ramona sad because Davy was *such* a nice boy and she did so long to kiss him. However, Ramona was not so sad that she stopped chasing Davy. Round and round they went every morning until Miss Binney arrived.

Miss Binney, by this time, had begun to teach her class something more than games, the rules of the kindergarten and the mysterious dawnzer song. Ramona thought of kindergarten as being divided into two parts. The first part was the running part, which included games, dancing, finger painting, and playing. The second part was called seat work. Seat work was serious. Everyone was expected to work quietly in his own seat without disturbing anyone else. Ramona found it difficult to sit still, because she was always interested in what everyone else was doing. 'Ramona, keep your eyes on your own work,' Miss Binney said, and sometimes Ramona remembered.

For the first seat-work assignment each member of the class was told to draw a picture of his own house. Ramona, who had expected to learn to read and write in school like her sister Beezus, used her new crayons quickly to draw her house with two windows, a door, and a red chimney. With her green crayon she scrubbed in some shrubbery. Anyone familiar with her neighbourhood could tell the picture was of her house, but somehow Ramona was not satisfied. She looked around to see what others were doing.

Susan had drawn a picture of her house and was adding a girl with *boing-boing* curls looking out of the window. Howie, who had drawn his house with the garage door open and a car inside, was adding a motorcycle parked at the kerb. Davy's house looked like a club-house built by some boys who had a few old boards and not enough nails. It leaned to one side in a tired sort of way.

Ramona studied her own drawing and decided she would have to do something to make it more interesting. After considering various colours of crayon, she selected the black and drew big black swirls coming from the windows.

'You aren't supposed to scribble on your picture,' said Howie, who also was inclined to pay attention to other people's work.

Ramona was indignant. 'I didn't scribble. The black is part of my picture.'

When Miss Binney asked the class to set their pictures on the chalk rail so that everyone might see them, the class noticed Ramona's picture at once, because it was drawn with bold, heavy strokes and because of the black swirls.

'Miss Binney, Ramona scribbled all over her house,' said Susan, who by now had revealed herself as the kind of girl who always wanted to play house so she could be the mother and boss everybody.

'I did not!' protested Ramona, beginning to see that her picture was going to be misunderstood by everyone. Maybe she had been wrong to try to make it interesting. Maybe Miss Binney did not want interesting pictures.

'You did, too!' Joey ran up to the chalk rail and pointed to Ramona's black swirls. 'See!'

The class, including Ramona, waited for Miss Binney to say Ramona should not scribble on her picture, but Miss Binney merely smiled and said, 'Remember your seat, Joey. Ramona, suppose you tell us about your picture.'

'I didn't scribble on it,' said Ramona.

'Of course you didn't,' Miss Binney said.

Ramona loved her teacher even more. 'Well,' she began, 'that black isn't scribbling. It's smoke coming out of the windows.'

'And why is smoke coming out of the windows?' gently pressed Miss Binney.

'Because there's a fire in the fireplace and the chimney is stopped up,' explained Ramona. 'It's stopped up with Santa Claus, but he doesn't show in the picture.' Ramona smiled shyly at her teacher. 'I wanted to make my picture interesting.'

Miss Binney returned her smile. 'And you did make it interesting.'

Davy looked worried. 'How does Santa Claus get out?' he asked. 'He doesn't stay in there, does he?'

'Of course he gets out,' said Ramona. 'I just didn't show that part.'

The next day seat work got harder. Miss Binney said that everyone had to learn to print his name.

Ramona saw right away that this business of names was not fair. When Miss Binney handed each member of the class a strip of cardboard with his name printed on it, anyone could see that a girl named Ramona was going to have to work harder than a girl named Ann or a boy named Joe. Not that Ramona minded having to work harder—she was eager to learn to read and write. Having been the youngest member of her family and of the neighbourhood, however, she had learned to watch for unfair situations.

Carefully Ramona printed *R* the way Miss Binney had printed it. *A* was easy. Even a baby could print *A*. Miss Binney said *A* was pointed like a witch's hat, and Ramona was planning to be a witch for the Hallowe'en parade. O was also easy. It was a round balloon. Some people's O's looked like leaky balloons, but Ramona's O's were balloons full of air.

'I like the way Ramona's O's are fat balloons full of air,' Miss Binney said to the class, and Ramona's heart filled with joy. Miss Binney liked her O's best!

Miss Binney walked around the classroom looking over shoulders. 'That's right, boys and girls. Nice pointed *A*'s,' she said. '*A*'s with nice sharp peaks. No, Davy. *D* faces the other way. Splendid, Karen. I like the way Karen's *K* has a nice straight back.'

Ramona wished she had a *K* in her name, so that she could give it a nice straight back. Ramona enjoyed Miss Binney's descriptions of the letters of the alphabet and listened for them while she worked. In front of her Susan played with a curl while she worked. She twisted it around her finger, stretched it out, and let it go. *Boing*, thought Ramona automatically.

'Ramona, let's keep our eyes on our work,' said Miss Binney. 'No, Davy. *D* faces the *other* way.'

Once more Ramona bent over her paper. The hardest part of her name, she soon discovered, was getting the right number of points on the *M* and *N*. Sometimes her name came out RANOMA, but before long she remembered that two points came first. 'Good work, Ramona,' said Miss Binney, the first time Ramona printed her name correctly. Ramona hugged herself with happiness and love for Miss Binney. Soon, she was sure, she would be able to join her letters together and write her name in the same rumply grown-up way that Beezus wrote her name.

Then Ramona discovered that some boys and girls had an extra letter followed by a dot. 'Miss Binney, why don't I have a letter with a dot after it?' she asked.

'Because we have only one Ramona,' said Miss Binney. 'We have two Erics. Eric Jones and Eric

Ryan. We call them Eric J. and Eric R., because we don't want to get our Erics mixed up.'

Ramona did not like to miss anything. 'Could I have another letter with a little dot?' she asked, knowing that Miss Binney would not think she was pestering.

Miss Binney smiled and leaned over Ramona's table. 'Of course you may. This is the way to make a Q. A nice round O with a little tail like a cat. And there is your little dot, which is called a period.' Then Miss Binney walked on, supervising seat work.

Ramona was charmed by her last initial. She drew a nice round O beside the one Miss Binney had drawn, and then she added a tail before she leaned back to admire her work. She had one balloon and two Hallowe'en hats in her first name and a cat in her last name. She doubted if anyone else in the morning kindergarten had such an interesting name.

The next day at seat-work time Ramona practised her Q while Miss Binney walked around helping those with S in their names. All the S's were having trouble. 'No, Susan,' said Miss Binney. 'S stands up straight. It does not lie down as if it were a little worm crawling along the ground.'

Susan pulled out a curl and let it spring back.

Boing, thought Ramona.

'My, how many *S*'s we have that are crawling along like little worms,' remarked Miss Binney.

Ramona was pleased that she had escaped *S*. She drew another Q and admired it a moment before she added two little pointed ears, and then she added two whiskers on each side so that her Q looked the way the cat looked when crouched on a rug in front of the fireplace. How pleased Miss Binney would be! Miss Binney would say to the kindergarten, 'What a splendid Q Ramona has made. It looks exactly like a little cat.'

'No, Davy,' Miss Binney was saying. 'A *D* does not have four corners. It has two corners. One side is curved like a robin redbreast.'

This conversation was so interesting that Ramona was curious to see Davy's *D* for herself. She waited until Miss Binney had moved away before she slipped out of her seat and over to the next table to look at Davy's *D*. It was a great disappointment. 'That *D* doesn't look like a robin,' she whispered. 'It doesn't have any feathers. A robin has to have feathers.' She had watched robins pulling worms out of her front lawn many times. They all had feathers on their breasts, little soft feathers mussed by the wind.

Davy studied his work. Then he scrubbed out half his *D* with his eraser and drew it in a series of little jags. It did not look like Miss Binney's *D*, but it did look, in Ramona's opinion, more like the front of a robin with feathers mussed by the wind, which was what Miss Binney wanted, wasn't it? A *D* like a robin redbreast.

'Good work, Davy,' said Ramona, trying to sound like her teacher. Now maybe Davy would let her kiss him.

'Ramona,' said Miss Binney, 'in your seat, please.' She walked back to look at Davy's seat work. 'No, Davy. Didn't I tell you the curve of a *D* is as smooth as a robin redbreast? Yours is all jagged.'

Davy looked bewildered. 'Those are feathers,' he said. 'Feathers like a robin.'

'Oh, I'm sorry, Davy. I didn't mean . . . ' Miss Binney behaved as if she did not know quite what to say. 'I didn't mean you to show each feather. I meant you to make it smooth and round.'

'Ramona told me to do it this way,' said Davy. 'Ramona said a robin has to have feathers.'

'Ramona is not the kindergarten teacher.' Miss Binney's voice, although not exactly cross, was not her usual gentle voice. 'You make your *D* the way I showed you and never mind what Ramona says.'

Ramona felt confused. Things had such an unexpected way of turning out all wrong. Miss Binney said a *D* should look like a robin redbreast, didn't she? And robins had feathers, didn't they? So why wasn't putting feathers on a *D* all right?

Davy glared at Ramona as he took his eraser and scrubbed out half his *D* a second time. He scrubbed so hard he rumpled his paper. 'Now see what you did,' he said.

Ramona felt terrible. Dear little Davy whom she loved so much was angry with her, and now he would run faster than ever. She never would get to kiss him.

And even worse, Miss Binney did not like *D*'s with feathers, so she probably would not like *Q*'s with ears and whiskers either. Hoping her teacher would not see what she was doing, Ramona quickly and regretfully erased the ears and whiskers from her *Q*. How plain and bare it looked with only its tail left to keep it from being an *O*. Miss Binney, who could understand that Santa Claus in the chimney would make a fireplace smoke, might be disappointed if she knew Ramona had given her *Q* ears and whiskers, because lettering was different from drawing pictures.

Ramona loved Miss Binney so much she did not want to disappoint her. Not ever. Miss Binney was the nicest teacher in the whole world.

4

THe SUBSTITUTE

Before long Mrs Quimby and Mrs Kemp decided the time had come for Ramona and Howie to walk to school by themselves. Mrs Kemp, pushing Willa Jean in her stroller, walked Howie to the Quimby's house where Ramona's mother invited her in for a cup of coffee.

'You better put all your stuff away,' Howie advised Ramona, as his mother lifted his little sister out of the stroller. 'Willa Jean crawls around and chews things.'

Grateful for this advice, Ramona closed the door of her room.

'Now, Howie, you be sure to look both ways before you cross the street,' cautioned his mother.

'You, too, Ramona,' said Mrs Quimby. 'And be sure you walk. And walk on the sidewalk. Don't go running out in the street.'

'And cross between the white lines,' said Mrs Kemp.

'And wait for the traffic boy near the school,' said Mrs Quimby.

'And don't talk to strangers,' said Mrs Kemp.

Ramona and Howie, weighed down by the responsibility of walking themselves to school, trudged off down the street. Howie was even gloomier than usual, because he was the only boy in the morning kindergarten who wore jeans with only one hip pocket. All the other boys had two hip pockets.

'That's silly,' said Ramona, still inclined to be impatient with Howie. If Howie did not like his jeans, why didn't he make a great big noisy fuss about them?

'No, it isn't,' contradicted Howie. 'Jeans with one hip pocket are babyish.'

At the cross street Ramona and Howie stopped and looked both ways. They saw a car coming a block away so they waited. They waited and waited. When the car finally passed, they saw another car coming a block away in the opposite direction. They waited some more. At last the coast was clear, and they walked, stiff-legged in their haste, across the street. 'Whew!' said Howie, relieved that they were safely across.

The next intersection was easier because Henry Huggins, in his red traffic sweater and yellow cap, was the traffic boy on duty. Ramona was not awed by Henry even though he often got to hold up cement and lumber trucks delivering material for the market that was being built across from the school. She had known Henry and his dog Ribsy as long as she could remember, and she admired Henry because not only was he a traffic boy, he also delivered papers.

Now Ramona looked at Henry, who was standing with his feet apart and his hands clasped behind his back. Ribsy was sitting beside him as if he were watching traffic, too. Just to see what Henry would do, Ramona stepped off the kerb.

'You get back on the kerb, Ramona,' Henry ordered above the noise of the construction on the corner.

Ramona set one foot back on the kerb.

'All the way, Ramona,' said Henry.

Ramona stood with both heels on the kerb, but her toes out over the gutter. Henry could not say she was not standing on the kerb, so he merely glared. When several boys and girls were waiting to cross the street, Henry marched across with Ribsy prancing along beside him.

'Beat it, Ribsy,' said Henry between his teeth. Ribsy paid no attention.

Directly in front of Ramona Henry executed a sharp about-face like a real soldier. Ramona marched behind Henry, stepping as close to his sneakers as she could. The other children laughed.

On the opposite kerb Henry tried to execute

another military about-face, but instead he tripped over Ramona. 'Doggone you, Ramona,' he said angrily. 'If you don't cut that out I'm going to report you.'

'Nobody reports kindergarteners,' scoffed an older boy.

'Well, I'm going to report Ramona if she doesn't cut it out,' said Henry. Obviously Henry felt it was his bad luck that he had to guard an intersection where Ramona crossed the street.

Between crossing the street without a grown-up and getting so much attention from Henry, Ramona felt that her day was off to a good start. However, as she and Howie approached the kindergarten building, she saw at once that something was wrong. The door to the kindergarten was already open. No one was playing on the jungle gym. No one was running around the playground. No one was even waiting in line by the door. Instead the boys and girls were huddled in groups like frightened mice. They all looked worried and once in a while someone who appeared to be acting brave would run to the open door, peer inside, and come running back to one of the groups to report something.

'What's the matter?' asked Ramona.

'Miss Binney isn't there,' whispered Susan. 'It's a different lady.'

'A substitute,' said Eric R.

Miss Binney not there! Susan must be wrong. Miss Binney had to be there. Kindergarten would not be kindergarten without Miss Binney. Ramona ran to the door to see for herself. Susan was right. Miss Binney was not there. The woman who was busy at Miss Binney's desk was taller and older. She was as old as a mother. Her dress was brown and her shoes were sensible.

Ramona did not like what she saw at all, so she ran back to a cluster of boys and girls. 'What are we going to do?' she asked, feeling as if she had been deserted by Miss Binney. For her teacher to go home and not come back was not right.

'I think I'll go home,' said Susan.

Ramona thought this idea was babyish of Susan. She had seen what happened to boys and girls who ran home from kindergarten. Their mothers marched them right straight back again, that's what happened. No, going home would not do.

'I bet the substitute won't even know the rules of our kindergarten,' said Howie.

The children agreed. Miss Binney said following the rules of their kindergarten was important. How could this stranger know what the rules were? A stranger would not even know the names of the boys and girls. She might get them mixed up.

Still feeling that Miss Binney was disloyal to stay

away from school, Ramona made up her mind she was not going into that kindergarten room with that strange teacher. Nobody could make her go in there. But where could she go? She could not go home, because her mother would march her back. She could not go into the main building of Glenwood School, because everyone would know a girl her size belonged out in the kindergarten. She had to hide, but where?

When the first bell rang, Ramona knew she did not have much time. There was no place to hide on the kindergarten playground, so she slipped around behind the little building and joined the boys and girls who were streaming into the red-brick building.

'Kindergarten baby!' a first grader shouted at Ramona.

'Pieface!' answered Ramona with spirit. She could see only two places to hide—behind the bicycle racks or behind a row of trash cans. Ramona chose the trash cans. As the last children entered the building she got down on her hands and knees and crawled into the space between the cans and the red-brick wall.

The second bell rang. 'Hup, two, three, four! Hup, two, three four!' The traffic boys were marching back from their posts at the intersections near the school. Ramona crouched motionless on the asphalt. 'Hup, two, three, four!' The traffic boys, heads up, eyes front, marched past the trash cans and into the building. The playground was quiet, and Ramona was alone.

Henry's dog Ribsy, who had followed the traffic boys as far as the door of the school, came trotting over to check the odours of the trash cans. He put his nose down to the ground and whiffled around the cans while Ramona crouched motionless with the rough asphalt digging into her knees. Ribsy's busy nose led him around the can face to face with Ramona.

'Wuf!' said Ribsy.

'Ribsy, go away!' ordered Ramona in a whisper.

'R-r-r-wuf!' Ribsy knew Ramona was not supposed to be behind the trash cans.

'You be quiet!' Ramona's whisper was as ferocious as she could make it. Over in the kindergarten the class began to sing the song about the dawnzer. At least the strange woman knew that much about kindergarten. After the dawnzer song the kindergarten was quiet. Ramona wondered if the teacher knew that Show and Tell was supposed to come next. She strained her ears, but she could not hear any activity in the little building.

The space between the brick wall and the trash cans began to feel as cold as a refrigerator to Ramona in her thin sweater. The asphalt dug into her knees, so she sat down with her feet straight out towards Ribsy's nose. The minutes dragged by.

Except for Ribsy, Ramona was lonely. She leaned against the chill red bricks and felt sorry for herself. Poor little Ramona, all alone except for Ribsy, behind the trash cans. Miss Binney would be sorry if she knew what she had made Ramona do. She would be sorry if she knew how cold and lonesome Ramona was. Ramona felt so sorry for the poor shivering little child behind the trash cans that one tear and then another slid down her cheeks. She sniffed pitifully. Ribsy opened one eye and looked at her before he closed it again. Not even Henry's dog cared what happened to her.

After a while Ramona heard the kindergarten running and laughing outside. How disloyal everyone was to have so much fun when Miss Binney had deserted her class. Ramona wondered if the kindergarten missed her and if anyone else would chase Davy and try to kiss him. Then Ramona must have dozed off, because the next thing she knew recess time had come and the playground was swarming with shouting, yelling, ball-throwing older boys and girls. Ribsy was gone. Stiff with cold, Ramona hunched down as low as she could. A ball bounced with a bang against a trash can. Ramona shut her eyes and hoped that if she could not see anyone, no one could see her.

Footsteps came running towards the ball. 'Hey!' exclaimed a boy's voice. 'There's a little kid hiding back here!'

Ramona's eyes flew open. 'Go away!' she said fiercely to the strange boy, who was peering over the cans at her.

'What are you hiding back there for?' asked the boy.

'Go *away*!' ordered Ramona.

'Hey, Huggins!' yelled the boy. 'There's a little kid back here who lives over near you!'

In a moment Henry was peering over the trash cans at Ramona. 'What are you doing there?' he demanded. 'You're supposed to be in kindergarten.'

'You mind your own business,' said Ramona.

Naturally when two boys peered behind the trash cans, practically the whole school had to join them to see what was so interesting. 'What's she doing?' people asked. 'How come she's hiding?'

'Does her teacher know she's here?'

In the midst of all the excitement, Ramona felt a new discomfort.

'Find her sister,' someone said. 'Get Beatrice. She'll know what to do.'

No one had to find Beezus. She was already there. 'Ramona Geraldine Quimby!' she said. 'You come out of there this minute!'

'I won't,' said Ramona, even though she knew she could not stay there much longer.

'Ramona, you just wait until mother hears about this!' stormed Beezus. 'You're really going to catch it!'

Ramona knew that Beezus was right, but catching it from her mother was not what was worrying her at the moment.

'Here comes the yard teacher,' someone said.

Ramona had to admit defeat. She got to her hands and knees and then to her feet and faced the crowd across the trash-can lids as the yard teacher came to investigate the commotion.

'Don't you belong in kindergarten?' the yard teacher asked.

'I'm not going to go to kindergarten,' said Ramona stubbornly, and cast an anguished glance at Beezus.

'She's supposed to be in kindergarten,' said Beezus, 'but she needs to go to the bathroom.' The older boys and girls thought this remark was funny, which made Ramona so angry she wanted to cry. There was nothing funny about it at all, and if she didn't hurry—

The yard teacher turned to Beezus. 'Take her to the bathroom and then to the principal's office. She'll find out what the trouble is.'

The first words were a relief to Ramona, but

the second a shock. No one in the morning kindergarten had ever been sent to Miss Mullen's office in the big building, except to deliver a note from Miss Binney, and then the children went in pairs, because the errand was such a scary one. 'What will the principal do to me?' Ramona asked, as Beezus led her away to the girls' bathroom in the big building.

'I don't know,' said Beezus. 'Talk to you, I guess, or call mother. Ramona, why did you have to go and do a dumb thing like hiding behind the trash cans?'

'Because.' Ramona was cross since Beezus was so cross. When the girls came out of the bathroom, Ramona reluctantly allowed herself to be led into the principal's office, where she felt small and frightened even though she tried not to show it.

'This is my little sister Ramona,' Beezus explained to Miss Mullen's secretary in the outer office. 'She belongs in kindergarten, but she's been hiding behind the trash cans.'

Miss Mullen must have overheard, because she came out of her office. Frightened though she was, Ramona braced herself to say, I won't go back to kindergarten!

'Why, hello, Ramona,' said Miss Mullen. 'That's all right, Beatrice. You may go back to your class. I'll take over.'

Ramona wanted to stay close to her sister, but Beezus walked out of the office, leaving her alone with the principal, the most important person in the whole school. Ramona felt small and pitiful with her knees still marked where the asphalt had gouged her. Miss Mullen smiled as if Ramona's behaviour was of no particular importance, and said, 'Isn't it too bad Miss Binney had to stay home with a sore throat? I know what a surprise it was for you to find a strange teacher in your kindergarten room.'

Ramona wondered how Miss Mullen knew so much. The principal did not even bother to ask what Ramona was doing behind the trash cans. She did not feel the least bit sorry for the poor little girl with the gouged knees. She simply took Ramona by the hand, and said, 'I'm going to introduce you to Mrs Wilcox. I know you're going to like her,' and started out of the door.

Ramona felt a little indignant, because Miss Mullen did not demand to know why she had been hiding all that time. Miss Mullen did not even notice how forlorn and tearstained Ramona looked. Ramona had been so cold and lonely and miserable that she thought Miss Mullen should show some interest. She had half expected the principal to say, Why you poor little thing! Why were you hiding behind the trash cans?

The looks on the faces of the morning kindergarten, when Ramona walked into the room with the principal, made up for Miss Mullen's lack of concern. Round eyes, open mouths, faces blank with surprise—Ramona was delighted to see the whole class staring at her from their seats. *They* were worried about her. *They* cared what had happened to her.

'Ramona, this is Miss Binney's substitute, Mrs Wilcox,' said Miss Mullen. To the substitute she said, 'Ramona is a little late this morning.' That was all. Not a word about how cold and miserable Ramona had been. Not a word about how brave she had been to hide until recess.

'I'm glad you're here, Ramona,' said Mrs Wilcox, as the principal left. 'The class is drawing with crayons. What would you like to draw?'

Here it was seat-work time, and Mrs Wilcox was not even having the class do real seat work, but was letting them draw pictures as if this day were the first day of kindergarten. Ramona was most disapproving. Things were not supposed to be this way. She looked at Howie scrubbing away with a blue crayon to make a sky across the top of his paper and at Davy, who was drawing a man whose arms seemed to come out of his ears. They were busy and happy drawing whatever they pleased.

'I would like to make Q's,' said Ramona on sudden inspiration.

'Make use of what?' asked Mrs Wilcox, holding out a sheet of drawing paper.

Ramona had been sure all along that the substitute could not be as smart as Miss Binney, but at least she expected her to know what the letter Q was. All grown-ups were supposed to know Q. 'Nothing,' Ramona said, as she accepted the paper and, pleasantly self-conscious under the awed stares of the kindergarten, went to her seat.

At last Ramona was free to draw her Q her own way. Forgetting the loneliness and discomfort of the morning, she drew a most satisfying row of Q's, Ramona-style, and decided that having a substitute teacher was not so bad after all.

Mrs Wilcox wandered up and down the aisle looking at pictures. 'Why, Ramona,' she said, pausing by Ramona's desk, 'what charming little cats you've drawn! Do you have kittens at home?'

Ramona felt sorry for poor Mrs Wilcox, a grown-up lady teacher who did not know Q. 'No,' she answered. 'Our cat is a boy cat.'

5

RAMONA'S ENGAGEMENT RING

'No!' said Ramona on the first rainy morning after she had started kindergarten.

'Yes,' said Mrs Quimby.

'No!' said Ramona. 'I won't!'

'Ramona, be sensible,' said Mrs Quimby.

'I don't want to be sensible,' said Ramona. 'I hate being sensible!'

'Now, Ramona,' said her mother, and Ramona knew she was about to be reasoned with. 'You have a new raincoat. Boots cost money, and Howie's old boots are perfectly good. The soles are scarcely worn.'

'The tops aren't shiny,' Ramona told her mother. 'And they're brown boots. Brown boots are for boys.'

'They keep your feet dry,' said Mrs Quimby, 'and that is what boots are for.'

Ramona realized she looked sulky, but she could not help herself. Only grown-ups would say boots were for keeping feet dry. Anyone in kindergarten knew that a girl should wear shiny red or white boots on the first rainy day, not to keep her feet dry, but to show off. That's what boots were for—showing off, wading, splashing, stamping.

'Ramona,' said Mrs Quimby sternly. 'Get that look off your face this instant. Either you wear these boots or you stay home from school.'

Ramona recognized that her mother meant what she said, and so, because she loved kindergarten, she sat down on the floor and dragged on the hated brown boots, which did not go with her new flowered plastic raincoat and hat.

Howie arrived in a yellow slicker that was long enough for him to grow into for at least two years and a yellow rain hat that almost hid his face. Beneath the raincoat Ramona glimpsed a pair of shiny brown boots, which she supposed she would have to wear someday when they were old and dull and dirty.

'Those are my old boots,' said Howie, looking at Ramona's feet as they started off to school.

'You better not tell anybody.' Ramona plodded along on feet almost too heavy to lift. It was a perfect morning for anyone with new boots. Enough rain had fallen in the night to fill the gutters with muddy streams and to bring worms squirming out of the lawns onto the sidewalks.

The intersection by the school was unusually quiet that morning, because rain had halted construction on the new market. Ramona was so downhearted that she did not even tease Henry Huggins when he led her across the street. The kindergarten playground, as she had expected, was swarming with boys and girls in raincoats, most of them too big, and boots, most of them new. The girls wore various sorts of raincoats and red or white boots—all except Susan, who carried her new white boots so she would not get them muddy. The boys looked alike, because they all wore yellow raincoats and hats and brown boots. Ramona was not even sure which boy was Davy, not that he mattered to her this morning. Her feet felt too heavy for chasing anyone.

Part of the class had lined up properly by the door, waiting for Miss Binney, while the rest ran about clomping, splashing, and stamping. 'Those are boy's boots you're wearing,' said Susan to Ramona.

Ramona did not answer. Instead she picked up a smooth pink worm that lay wiggling on the playground and, without really thinking, wound it around her finger.

'Look!' yelled Davy from beneath his big rain hat. 'Ramona's wearing a ring made out of a *worm*!'

Ramona had not thought of the worm as a ring until now, but she saw at once that the idea was interesting. 'See my ring!' she shouted, thrusting her fist towards the nearest face.

Boots were temporarily forgotten. Everyone ran screaming from Ramona to avoid being shown her ring.

'See my ring! See my ring!' shouted Ramona, racing around the playground on feet that were suddenly much lighter.

When Miss Binney appeared around the corner, the class scrambled to line up by the door. 'Miss Binney! Miss Binney!' Everyone wanted to be the first to tell. 'Ramona is wearing a worm for a ring!'

'It's a pink worm,' said Ramona, thrusting out her hand. 'Not an old dead white worm.'

'Oh . . . what a pretty worm,' said Miss Binney bravely. 'It's so smooth and . . . pink.'

Ramona elaborated. 'It's my engagement ring.'

'Who are you engaged to?' asked Ann.

'I haven't decided,' answered Ramona.

'Not me,' Davy piped up.

'Not me,' said Howie.

'Not me,' said Eric R.

'Well . . . a . . . Ramona . . . ' Miss Binney was searching for words. 'I don't think you should wear your . . . ring during kindergarten. Why don't you put it down on the playground in a puddle so that it will . . . stay fresh.'

Ramona was happy to do anything Miss Binney

wanted her to. She unwound the worm from her finger and placed it carefully in a puddle, where it lay limp and still.

After that Ramona raced around the playground with a worm around her finger whenever her mother made her wear Howie's old boots to school, and when everyone asked who she was engaged to, she always answered, 'I haven't decided.'

'Not me!' Davy always said, followed by Howie, Eric R., and any other boy who happened to be near.

Then one Saturday Mrs Quimby examined Ramona's scuffed shoes and discovered that not only were the heels worn down, the leather of the toes was worn through because Ramona stopped her lopsided two-wheeled tricycle by dragging her toes on the concrete. Mrs Quimby had Ramona stand up while she felt her feet through the leather.

'It's time for new shoes,' Mrs Quimby decided. 'Get your jacket and your boots, and we'll drive down to the shopping centre.'

'It isn't raining today,' said Ramona. 'Why do I have to take boots?'

'To see if they will fit over your new shoes,' answered her mother. 'Hurry along, Ramona.'

When they reached the shoe store, Ramona's favourite shoe salesman said, as Ramona and her mother sat down, 'What's the matter with my little Petunia today? Don't you have a smile for me?'

Ramona shook her head and looked sadly and longingly at a row of beautiful shiny girls' boots displayed on one side of the store. There she sat with Howie's dingy old brown boots beside her. How could she smile? A babyish nursery-school girl, who was wearing new red boots, was rocking joyously on the shoe store's rocking horse while her mother paid for the boots.

'Well, we'll see what we can do for you,' said the salesman briskly, as he pulled off Ramona's shoes and made her stand with her foot on the measuring stick. Finding the right pair of oxfords for her did not take him long.

'Now try on the boots,' said Mrs Quimby in her no-nonsense voice, when Ramona had walked across the shoe store and back in her new shoes.

For a moment, as Ramona sat down on the floor and grasped one of the hated boots, she considered pretending she could not get it on. However, she knew she could not get away with this trick, because the shoe-store man understood both children and shoes. She pulled and yanked and tugged and managed to get her foot most of the way in. When she stood up she was on tiptoe inside the boot. Her mother tugged some more, and her shoe went all the way into the boot.

'There,' said Mrs Quimby. Ramona sighed.

The babyish nursery-school girl stopped rocking long enough to announce to the world, 'I have new boots.'

'Tell me, Petunia,' said the shoe man. 'How many boys and girls in your kindergarten?'

'Twenty-nine,' said Ramona with a long face. Twenty-nine, most of them with new boots. The happy booted nursery-school baby climbed off the rocking horse, collected her free balloon, and left with her mother.

The shoe man spoke to Mrs Quimby. 'Kindergarten teachers like boots to fit loosely so the children can manage by themselves. I doubt if Petunia's teacher has time to help with fifty-eight boots.'

'I hadn't thought of that,' said Mrs Quimby. 'Perhaps we had better look at boots after all.'

'I'll bet Petunia here would like red boots,' said the shoe man. When Ramona beamed, he added, 'I had a hunch that would get a smile out of you.'

When Ramona left the shoe store with her beautiful red boots, *girl's* boots, in a box, which she carried herself, she was so filled with joy she set her balloon free just to watch it sail over the parking lot and up, up into the sky until it was a tiny red dot against the grey clouds. The stiff soles of her new shoes made such a pleasant noise on the pavement that she began to prance. She was a pony. No, she was one of the three Billy Goats Gruff, the littlest one, trip-trapping over the bridge that the troll was hiding under. Ramona trip-trapped joyfully all the way to the parked car, and when she reached home she trip-trapped up and down the hall and all around the house.

'For goodness' sake, Ramona,' said Mrs Quimby, while she was marking Ramona's name in the new boots, 'can't you just walk?'

'Not when I'm the littlest Billy Goat Gruff,' answered Ramona, and trip-trapped down the hall to her room.

Unfortunately, there was no rain the next morning so Ramona left her new boots at home and trip-trapped to school, where she did not have much chance of catching Davy because he could run faster than she could trip-trap in her stiff new shoes. She trip-trapped to her seat, and later, because she was art monitor who got to pass out drawing paper, she trip-trapped to the supply cupboard and trip-trapped up and down the aisles passing out paper.

'Ramona, I would like it if you walked quietly,' said Miss Binney.

'I am the littlest Billy Goat Gruff,' explained Ramona. 'I have to trip-trap.'

'You may trip-trap when we go outdoors.' Miss Binney's voice was firm. 'You may not trip-trap in the classroom.'

At playtime the whole class turned into Billy Goats Gruff and trip-trapped around the playground, but none so joyfully or so noisily as Ramona. The gathering clouds, Ramona noticed, were dark and threatening.

Sure enough, that evening rain began to fall, and all night long it beat against the south side of the Quimby's house. The next morning Ramona, in her boots and raincoat, was out long before Howie arrived to walk to school with her. She waded through the wet lawn, and her boots became even shinier when they were wet. She stamped in all the little puddles on the driveway. She stood in the gutter and let muddy water run over the toes of her beautiful new boots. She gathered wet leaves to dam the gutter, so she could stand in deeper water. Howie, as she might have expected, was used to his boots and not a bit excited. He did enjoy stamping in puddles, however, and together they stamped and splashed on the way to school.

Ramona came to a halt at the intersection guarded by Henry Huggins in his yellow slicker, rain hat, and brown boots. 'Look at all that nice mud,' she said, pointing to the area that was to be the parking lot for the new market. It was such nice mud, rich and brown with puddles and little rivers in the tyre tracks left by the construction trucks. It was the best mud, the muddiest mud, the most tempting mud Ramona had ever seen. Best of all, the day was so rainy there were no construction workers around to tell anyone to stay out of the mud.

'Come on, Howie,' said Ramona. 'I'm going to see how my boots work in the mud.' Of course, she would get her shiny boots muddy, but then she could have the fun of turning the hose on them that afternoon after kindergarten.

Howie was already following Henry across the street.

When Henry executed his sharp about-face on the opposite kerb, he saw that Ramona had been left behind. 'You were supposed to cross with me,' he told her. 'Now you have to wait until some more kids come.'

'I don't care,' said Ramona happily, and marched off to the muddy mud.

'Ramona, you come back here!' yelled Henry. 'You're going to get into trouble.'

'Traffic boys aren't supposed to talk on duty,' Ramona reminded him, and marched straight into the mud. Surprisingly her feet started to slide out from under her. She had not realized that mud was so slippery. Managing to regain her balance, she set each boot down slowly and carefully before she pulled her other boot from the sucking mud. She waved happily to Henry, who seemed to be going through some sort of struggle within himself. He kept opening his mouth, as if he wanted to say something, and then closing it again. Ramona also waved at the members of the morning kindergarten, who were watching her through the playground fence.

More mud clung to her boots with each step. 'Look at my elephant feet!' she called out. Her boots were becoming heavier and heavier.

Henry gave up his struggle. 'You're going to get stuck!' he yelled.

'No, I'm not!' insisted Ramona, and discovered she was unable to raise her right boot. She tried to raise her left boot, but it was stuck fast. She grasped the top of one of her boots with both hands and tried to lift her foot, but she could not budge it. She tried to lift the other foot, but she could not budge it either. Henry was right. Miss Binney was not going to like what had happened, but Ramona was stuck.

'I told you so!' yelled Henry against the traffic rules.

Ramona was becoming warmer and warmer

inside her raincoat. She pulled and lifted. She could raise her feet, one at a time, inside her boots, but no matter how she tugged and yanked with her hands she could not lift her precious boots from the mud.

Ramona grew warmer and warmer. She could never get out of this mud. Kindergarten would start without her, and she would be left all alone in the mud. Miss Binney would not like her being out here in the mud, when she was supposed to be inside singing the dawnzer song and doing seat work. Ramona's chin began to quiver.

'Look at Ramona! Look at Ramona!' shrieked the kindergarten, as Miss Binney, in a raincoat and with a plastic hood over her hair, appeared on the playground.

'Oh dear!' Ramona heard Miss Binney say.

Drivers of cars paused to stare and smile as tears mingled with the rain on Ramona's cheeks. Miss Binney came splashing across the street. 'My goodness, Ramona, how are we going to get you out?'

'I d-don't know,' sobbed Ramona. Miss Binney could not get stuck in the mud, too. The morning kindergarten needed her.

A man called out from a car, 'What you need is a few boards.'

'Boards would only sink into the muck,' said a passerby on the sidewalk.

The first bell rang. Ramona sobbed harder. Now Miss Binney would have to go into school and leave her out here alone in the mud and the rain and the cold. By now some of the older boys and girls were staring at her from the windows of the big school.

'Now don't worry, Ramona,' said Miss Binney. 'We'll get you out somehow.'

Ramona, who wanted to be helpful, knew what happened when a car was stuck in the mud. 'Could you call a t-tow t-truck?' she asked with a big sniff. She could see herself being yanked out of the mud by a heavy chain hooked on the collar of her raincoat. She found this picture so interesting that her sobs subsided, and she waited hopefully for Miss Binney's answer.

The second bell rang. Miss Binney was not looking at Ramona. She was looking thoughtfully at Henry Huggins, who seemed to be staring at something way off in the distance. The traffic sergeant blew his whistle summoning the traffic boys to return from their posts to school.

'Boy!' Miss Binney called out. 'Traffic boy!'

'Who? Me?' asked Henry, even though he was the only traffic boy stationed at that intersection.

'That's Henry Huggins,' said helpful Ramona.

'Henry, come here, please,' said Miss Binney.

'I'm supposed to go in when the whistle blows,' said Henry, as he glanced up at the boys and girls who were watching from the big brick building.

'But this is an emergency,' Miss Binney pointed out. 'You have boots on, and I need your help in getting this little girl out of the mud. I'll explain to the principal.'

Henry did not seem very enthusiastic as he splashed across the street, and when he came to the mud he heaved a big sigh before he stepped into it. Carefully he picked his way through the muck and the puddles to Ramona. 'Now see what you got me into,' he said crossly. 'I told you to keep out of here.'

For once Ramona had nothing to say. Henry was right.

'I guess I'll have to carry you,' he said, and his tone was grudging. 'Hang on.' He stooped and grasped Ramona around the waist, and she obediently put her arms around the wet collar of his raincoat. Henry was big and strong. Then, to Ramona's horror, she found herself being lifted right out of her beautiful new boots.

'My boots!' she wailed. 'You're leaving my boots!'

Henry slipped, slid, and in spite of Ramona's

weight regained his balance. 'You keep quiet,' he ordered. 'I'm getting you out of here, aren't I? Do you want us both to land in the mud?'

Ramona hung on and said no more. Henry lurched and skidded through the mud to the sidewalk, where he set his burden down in front of Miss Binney.

'Yea!' yelled some big boys who had opened a window. 'Yea, Henry!' Henry scowled in their direction.

'Thank you, Henry,' said Miss Binney with real gratitude, as Henry tried to scrape the mud from his boots on the edge of the kerb. 'What do you say, Ramona?'

'My boots,' said Ramona. 'He left my new boots in the mud!' How lonely they looked, two bright spots of red in all that mud. She could not leave her boots behind, not when she had waited so long to get them. Somebody might take them, and she would have to go back to shoving her feet into Howie's ugly old boots.

'Don't worry, Ramona,' said Miss Binney, looking anxiously towards the rest of her morning kindergarten growing wetter by the minute as they watched through the fence. 'Nobody is going to take your boots on a day like this. We'll get them back when it stops raining and the ground dries off.'

'But they'll fill up with rain without my feet in them,' protested Ramona. 'The rain will spoil them.'

Miss Binney was sympathetic but firm. 'I know how you feel, but I'm afraid there isn't anything we can do about it.'

Miss Binney's words were too much for Ramona. After all the times she had been forced to wear Howie's ugly old brown boots she could not leave her beautiful new red boots out in the mud to fill up with rainwater. 'I want my boots,' she howled, and began to cry again.

'Oh, all right,' said Henry crossly. 'I'll get your old boots. Don't start crying again.' And heaving another gusty sigh, he waded back out into the empty lot, yanked the boots out of the mud, and waded back to the sidewalk, where he dropped them at Ramona's feet. 'There,' he said, looking at the mud-covered objects with dislike.

Ramona expected him to add, I hope you're satisfied, but he did not. He just started across the street to school.

'Thank you, Henry,' Ramona called after him without being reminded. There was something very special about being rescued by a big strong traffic boy in a yellow slicker.

Miss Binney picked up the muddy boots, and said, 'What beautiful red boots. We'll wash off the mud in the sink, and they'll be as good as new. And now we must hurry back to the kindergarten.'

Ramona smiled at Miss Binney, who was again, she decided, the nicest most understanding teacher in the world. Not once had Miss Binney scolded or made any tiresome remarks about why on earth did Ramona have to do such a thing. Not once had Miss Binney said she should know better.

Then something on the sidewalk caught Ramona's eye. It was a pink worm that still had some wiggle left in it. She picked it up and wound it around her finger as she looked towards Henry. 'I'm going to marry you, Henry Huggins!' she called out.

Even though traffic boys were supposed to stand up straight, Henry seemed to hunch down inside his raincoat as if he were trying to disappear.

'I've got an engagement ring, and I'm going to marry you!' yelled Ramona after Henry, as the morning kindergarten laughed and cheered.

'Yea, Henry!' yelled the big boys, before their teacher shut the window.

As she followed Miss Binney across the street Ramona heard Davy's joyful shout. 'Boy, I'm glad it isn't me!'

6

The Baddest Witch in the World

When the morning kindergarten cut jack-o'-lanterns from orange paper and pasted them on the windows so that the light shone through the eye and mouth holes, Ramona knew that at last Hallowe'en was not far away. Next to Christmas and her birthday, Ramona liked Hallowe'en best. She liked dressing up and going trick-or-treating after dark with Beezus. She liked those nights when the bare branches of trees waved against the streetlights, and the world was a ghostly place. Ramona liked scaring people, and she liked the shivery feeling of being scared herself.

Ramona had always enjoyed going to school with her mother to watch the boys and girls of Glenwood School parade on the playground in their Hallowe'en costumes. Afterwards she used to eat a doughnut and drink a paper cup of apple juice if there happened to be some left over. This year, after years of sitting on the benches with mothers and little brothers and sisters, Ramona was finally going to get to wear a costume and march around and around the playground. This year she had a doughnut and apple juice coming to her.

'Mama, did you buy my mask?' Ramona asked every day, when she came home from school.

'Not today, dear,' Mrs Quimby answered. 'Don't pester. I'll get it the next time I go down to the shopping centre.'

Ramona, who did not mean to pester her mother, could not see why grown-ups had to be so slow. 'Make it a bad mask, Mama,' she said. 'I want to be the baddest witch in the whole world.'

'You mean the worst witch,' Beezus said, whenever she happened to overhear this conversation.

'I do not,' contradicted Ramona. 'I mean the baddest witch.' 'Baddest witch' sounded much scarier than 'worst witch', and Ramona did enjoy stories about bad witches, the badder the better. She had no patience with books about good witches, because witches were supposed to be bad. Ramona had chosen to be a witch for that very reason.

Then one day when Ramona came home from school she found two paper bags on the foot of her bed. One contained black material and a pattern for a witch costume. The picture on the pattern showed the witch's hat pointed like the letter *A*. Ramona reached into the second bag and pulled out a rubber witch mask so scary that she quickly dropped it on the bed because she was not sure she even wanted to touch it. The flabby thing was the greyish-green colour of mould and had stringy hair, a hooked nose, snaggle teeth, and a wart on its nose. Its empty eyes seemed to stare at Ramona with a look of evil. The face was so ghastly that Ramona had to remind herself that it was only a rubber mask from the dime store before she could summon enough courage to pick it up and slip it over her head.

Ramona peeked cautiously in the mirror, backed away, and then gathered her courage for a longer look. That's really me in there, she told herself and felt better. She ran off to show her mother and discovered that she felt very brave when she was inside the mask and did not have to look at it. 'I'm the baddest witch in the world!' she shouted, her voice muffled by the mask, and was delighted when her mother was so frightened she dropped her sewing.

Ramona waited for Beezus and her father to come home, so she could put on her mask and jump out and scare them. But that night, before she went to bed, she rolled up the mask and hid it behind a cushion of the couch in the living room.

'What are you doing that for?' asked Beezus,

who had nothing to be afraid of. She was planning to be a princess and wear a narrow pink mask.

'Because I want to,' answered Ramona, who did not care to sleep in the same room with that ghastly, leering face.

Afterwards when Ramona wanted to frighten herself she would lift the cushion for a quick glimpse of her scary mask before she clapped the pillow over it again. Scaring herself was such fun.

When Ramona's costume was finished and the day of the Hallowe'en parade arrived, the morning kindergarten had trouble sitting still for seat work. They wiggled so much while resting on their mats that Miss Binney had to wait a long time before she found someone quiet enough to be the wake-up fairy. When kindergarten was finally dismissed, the whole class forgot the rules and went stampeding out of the door. At home Ramona ate only the soft part of her tuna-fish sandwich, because her mother insisted she could not go to the Hallowe'en parade on an empty stomach. She wadded the crusts into her paper napkin and hid them beneath the edge of her plate before she ran to her room to put on her long black dress, her cape, her mask, and her pointed witch hat held on by an elastic under her chin. Ramona had doubts about that elastic— none of the witches whom she met in books seemed to have elastic under their chin— but today she was too happy and excited to bother to make a fuss.

'See, Mama!' she cried. 'I'm the baddest witch in the world!'

Mrs Quimby smiled at Ramona, patted her through the long black dress, and said affection- ately, 'Sometimes I think you are.'

'Come on, Mama! Let's go to the Hallowe'en parade.' Ramona had waited so long that she did not see how she could wait another five minutes.

'I told Howie's mother we would wait for them,' said Mrs Quimby.

'Mama, did you have to?' protested Ramona, running to the front window to watch for Howie. Fortunately, Mrs Kemp and Willa Jean were already approaching with Howie dressed in a black cat costume lagging along behind holding the end of his tail in one hand. Willa Jean in her stroller was wearing a buck-toothed rabbit mask.

Ramona could not wait. She burst out of the front door yelling through her mask, 'Yah! Yah! I'm the baddest witch in the world! Hurry, Howie! I'm going to get you, Howie!'

Howie walked stolidly along, lugging his tail, so Ramona ran out to meet him. He was not wearing a mask, but instead had pipe cleaners Scotch- taped to his face for whiskers.

'I'm the baddest witch in the world,' Ramona informed him, 'and you can be my cat.'

'I don't want to be your cat,' said Howie. 'I don't want to be a cat at all.'

'Why not, Howie?' asked Mrs Quimby, who had joined Ramona and the Kemps. 'I think you make a very nice cat.'

'My tail is busted,' complained Howie. 'I don't want to be a cat with a busted tail.'

Mrs Kemp sighed. 'Now, Howie, if you'll just hold up the end of your tail nobody will notice.' Then she said to Mrs Quimby, 'I promised him a pirate costume, but his older sister was sick and while I was taking her temperature Willa Jean crawled into a cupboard and managed to dump a whole quart of salad oil all over the kitchen floor. If you've ever had to clean oil off a floor, you know what I went through, and then Howie went into the bathroom and climbed up—yes, dear, I understand you wanted to help—to get a sponge, and he accidentally knelt on a tube of toothpaste that someone had left the top off of—now, Howie, I didn't say you left the top off—and toothpaste squirted all over the bathroom, and there was another mess to clean up. Well, I finally had to drag his sister's old cat costume out of a drawer, and when he put it on we discovered the wire in the tail was broken, but there wasn't time to rip it apart and put in a new wire.'

'You have a handsome set of whiskers,' said Mrs Quimby, trying to coax Howie to look on the bright side.

'Scotch tape itches me,' said Howie.

Ramona could see that Howie was not going to be any fun at all, even on Hallowe'en. Never mind. She would have fun all by herself. 'I'm the baddest witch in the world,' she sang in her muffled voice, skipping with both feet. 'I'm the baddest witch in the world.'

When they were in sight of the playground, Ramona saw that it was already swarming with both the morning and the afternoon kindergartens in their Hallowe'en costumes. Poor Miss Binney, dressed like Mother Goose, now had the responsibility of sixty-eight boys and girls. 'Run along, Ramona,' said Mrs Quimby, when they had crossed the street. 'Howie's mother and I will go around to the big playground and try to find a seat on a bench before they are all taken.'

Ramona ran screaming onto the playground. 'Yah! Yah! I'm the baddest witch in the world!' Nobody paid any attention, because everyone else was screaming, too. The noise was glorious. Ramona yelled and screamed and shrieked and chased anyone who would run. She chased tramps and ghosts and ballerinas. Sometimes other witches in masks exactly like hers chased

her, and then she would turn around and chase
the witches right back. She tried to chase Howie,
but he would not run. He just stood beside the
fence holding his broken tail and missing all the
fun.

Ramona discovered dear little Davy in a
skimpy pirate costume from the dime store. She
could tell he was Davy by his thin legs. At last!
She pounced and kissed him through her rubber
mask. Davy looked startled, but he had the
presence of mind to make a gagging noise while
Ramona raced away, satisfied that she finally had
managed to catch and kiss Davy.

Then Ramona saw Susan getting out of her
mother's car. As she might have guessed, Susan
was dressed as an old-fashioned girl with a long
skirt, an apron, and pantalettes. 'I'm the baddest
witch in the world!' yelled Ramona, and ran after
Susan whose curls bobbed daintily about her
shoulders in a way that could not be disguised.
Ramona was unable to resist. After weeks of
longing, she tweaked one of Susan's curls, and
yelled, 'Boing!' through her rubber mask.

'You stop that,' said Susan, and smoothed her
curls.

'Yah! Yah! I'm the baddest witch in the world!'
Ramona was carried away. She tweaked another
curl and yelled a muffled, 'Boing!'

A clown laughed and joined Ramona. He too tweaked a curl and yelled, '*Boing!*'

The old-fashioned girl stamped her foot. 'You stop that!' she said angrily.

'*Boing! Boing!*' Others joined the game. Susan tried to run away, but no matter which way she ran there was someone eager to stretch a curl and yell, '*Boing!*' Susan ran to Miss Binney. 'Miss Binney! Miss Binney!' she cried. 'They're teasing me! They're pulling my hair and boinging me!'

'Who's teasing you?' asked Miss Binney.

'Everybody,' said Susan tearfully. 'A witch started it.'

'Which witch?' asked Miss Binney.

Susan looked around. 'I don't know which witch,' she said, 'but it was a bad witch.'

That's me, the baddest witch in the world, thought Ramona. At the same time she was a little surprised. That others really would not know that she was behind her mask had never occurred to her.

'Never mind, Susan,' said Miss Binney. 'You stay near me, and no one will tease you.'

Which witch, thought Ramona, liking the sound of the words. Which witch, which witch. As the words ran through her thoughts Ramona began to wonder if Miss Binney could guess who she was. She ran up to her teacher and shouted in her muffled voice, 'Hello, Miss Binney! I'm going to get you, Miss Binney!'

'Ooh, what a scary witch!' said Miss Binney, rather absentmindedly, Ramona thought. Plainly Miss Binney was not really frightened, and with so many witches running around she had not recognized Ramona.

No, Miss Binney was not the one who was frightened. Ramona was. Miss Binney did not know who this witch was. Nobody knew who Ramona was, and if nobody knew who she was, she wasn't anybody.

'Get out of the way, old witch!' Eric R. yelled at Ramona. He did not say, Get out of the way, Ramona.

Ramona could not remember a time when there was not someone near who knew who she was. Even last Hallowe'en, when she dressed up as a ghost and went trick-or-treating with Beezus and the older boys and girls, everyone seemed to know who she was. 'I can guess who this little ghost is,' the neighbours said, as they dropped a miniature candy bar or a handful of peanuts into her paper bag. And now, with so many witches running around and still more witches on the big playground, no one knew who she was.

'Davy, guess who I am!' yelled Ramona. Surely Davy would know.

'You're just another old witch,' answered Davy.

The feeling was the scariest one Ramona had ever experienced. She felt lost inside her costume. She wondered if her mother would know which witch was which, and the thought that her own mother might not know her frightened Ramona even more. What if her mother forgot her? What if everyone in the whole world forgot her? With that terrifying thought Ramona snatched off her mask, and although its ugliness was no longer the most frightening thing about it, she rolled it up so she would not have to look at it.

How cool the air felt outside that dreadful mask! Ramona no longer wanted to be the baddest witch in the world. She wanted to be Ramona Geraldine Quimby and be sure that Miss Binney and everyone on the playground knew her. Around her the ghosts and tramps and pirates raced and shouted, but Ramona stood near the door of the kindergarten quietly watching.

Davy raced up to her and yelled. 'Yah! You can't catch me!'

'I don't want to catch you,' Ramona informed him.

Davy looked surprised and a little disappointed, but he ran off on his thin little legs, shouting, 'Yo-ho-ho and a bottle of rum!'

Joey yelled after him, 'You're not really a pirate. You're just Mush Pot Davy!'

Miss Binney was trying to herd her sixty-eight charges into a double line. Two mothers who felt sorry for the teacher were helping round up the kindergarten to start the Hallowe'en parade, but as always there were some children who would rather run around than do what they were supposed to do. For once Ramona was not one of them. On the big playground someone started to play a marching record through a loudspeaker. The Hallowe'en parade that Ramona had looked forward to since she was in nursery school was about to begin.

'Come along, children,' said Miss Binney. Seeing Ramona standing alone, she said, 'Come on, Ramona.'

It was a great relief to Ramona to hear Miss Binney speak her name, to hear her teacher say 'Ramona' when she was looking at her. But as much as Ramona longed to prance along to the marching music with the rest of her class, she did not move to join them.

'Put on your mask, Ramona, and get in line,' said Miss Binney, guiding a ghost and a gypsy into place.

Ramona wanted to obey her teacher, but at the same time she was afraid of losing herself behind that scary mask. The line of kindergarteners, all of them wearing masks except Howie with his pipe-cleaner whiskers, was less straggly now, and everyone was eager to start the parade. If Ramona did not do something quickly she would be left behind, and she could not let such a thing happen, not when she had waited so many years to be in a Hallowe'en parade.

Ramona took only a moment to decide what to do. She ran to her cupboard inside the kindergarten building and snatched a crayon from her box. Then she grabbed a piece of paper from the supply cupboard. Outside she could hear the many feet of the morning and afternoon kindergartens marching off to the big playground. There was no time for Ramona's best printing, but that was all right. This job was not seat work to be supervised by Miss Binney. As fast as she could Ramona printed her name, and then she could not resist adding with a flourish her last initial complete with ears and whiskers.

RAMONA ⚛

Now the whole world would know who she was! She was Ramona Quimby, the only girl in the world with ears and whiskers on her last initial. Ramona pulled on her rubber mask, clapped her pointed hat on top of it, snapped the elastic under her chin, and ran after her class as it marched onto the big playground. She did not care if she was last in line and had to march beside gloomy old Howie still lugging his broken tail.

Around the playground marched the kindergarten followed by the first grade and all the other grades while mothers and little brothers and sisters watched. Ramona felt very grown-up remembering how last year she had been a little sister sitting on a bench watching for her big sister Beezus to march by and hoping for a left-over doughnut.

'Yah! Yah! I'm the baddest witch in the world!' Ramona chanted, as she held up her sign for all to see. Around the playground she marched towards her mother, who was waiting on the bench. Her mother saw her, pointed her out to Mrs Kemp, and waved. Ramona beamed inside her stuffy mask. Her mother recognized her!

Poor little Willa Jean in her stroller could not read, so Ramona called out to her, 'It's me, Willa Jean. I'm Ramona, the baddest witch in the world!'

Willa Jean in her rabbit mask understood. She laughed and slapped her hands on the tray of her stroller.

Ramona saw Henry's dog Ribsy trotting along, supervising the parade. 'Yah! Ribsy! I'm going to get you, Ribsy!' she threatened, as she marched past.

Ribsy gave a short bark, and Ramona was sure that even Ribsy knew who she was as she marched off to collect her doughnut and apple juice.

7

The Day Things Went Wrong

Ramona's day was off to a promising start for two reasons, both of which proved she was growing up. First of all, she had a loose tooth, a very loose tooth, a tooth that waggled back and forth with only a little help from her tongue. It was probably the loosest tooth in the morning kindergarten, which meant that the tooth fairy would finally pay a visit to Ramona before long.

Ramona had her suspicions about the tooth fairy. She had seen Beezus search under her pillow in the morning, after losing a tooth, and then call out, 'Daddy, my tooth is still here. The tooth fairy forgot to come!'

'That's funny,' Mr Quimby would answer. 'Are you sure?'

'Positive. I looked everyplace for the dime.'

'Let me look,' was always Mr Quimby's suggestion. Somehow he could always find the tooth fairy's dime when Beezus could not.

Now Ramona's turn would soon come. She

planned to stay awake and trap the tooth fairy to make sure it really was her father.

Not only did Ramona have a loose tooth to make her feel that she was finally beginning to grow up, she was going to get to walk to school all by herself. At last! Howie was home with a cold, and her mother had to drive Beezus downtown for an early dental appointment.

'Now, Ramona,' said Mrs Quimby, as she put on her coat, 'I'm going to trust you to stay all by yourself for a little while before you start to school. Do you think you can be a good girl?'

'Of course, Mama,' said Ramona, who felt that she was always a good girl.

'Now be sure you watch the clock,' said Mrs Quimby, 'and leave for school at exactly quarter past eight.'

'Yes, Mama.'

'And look both ways before you cross the street.'

'Yes, Mama.'

Mrs Quimby kissed Ramona goodbye. 'And be sure to close the door behind you when you leave.'

'Yes, Mama,' was Ramona's tolerant answer. She could not see why her mother was anxious.

When Mrs Quimby and Beezus had gone, Ramona sat down at the kitchen table to wiggle her tooth and watch the clock. The little hand was at eight, and the big hand was at one. Ramona wiggled her tooth with her finger. Then she wiggled it with her tongue, back and forth, back and forth. The big hand crept to two. Ramona took hold of her tooth with her fingers, but as much as she longed to surprise her mother with an empty space in her mouth, actually pulling the tooth was too scary. She went back to wiggling.

The big hand moved slowly to three. Ramona continued to sit on the chair wiggling her tooth and being a very good girl as she had promised. The big hand crawled along to four. When it reached five, Ramona knew that it would be quarter after eight and time to go to school. A quarter was twenty-five cents. Therefore, a quarter past eight was twenty-five minutes after eight. She had figured the answer out all by herself.

At last the big hand crawled to five. Ramona slid off the chair and slammed the door behind her as she started off to school alone. So far, so good, but as soon as Ramona reached the sidewalk, she realized that something was wrong. In a moment she understood what it was. The street was too quiet. No one else was walking to school. Ramona stopped in confusion. Maybe she was mixed up. Maybe today was really Saturday. Maybe her mother forgot to look at the calendar.

No, it could not be Saturday because yesterday was Sunday. Besides, there was Henry Huggins' dog Ribsy, trotting along the street on his way home from escorting Henry to school. Today really was a school day, because Ribsy followed Henry to school every morning. Maybe the clock was wrong. In a panic Ramona began to run. Miss Binney would not want her to be late for school. She did manage to slow down and look both ways before she walked across the streets, but when she saw that Henry was not guarding his usual intersection, she knew that the traffic boys had gone in and she was even later than she had thought. She ran across the kindergarten playground, and then stopped. The door of the kindergarten was shut. Miss Binney had started school without her.

Ramona stood puffing a moment trying to catch her breath. Of course, she could not expect Miss Binney to wait for her when she was late, but she could not help wishing that her teacher had missed her so much she had said, 'Class, let's wait for Ramona. Kindergarten isn't any fun without Ramona.'

When Ramona caught her breath, she knew what she should do. She knocked and waited for the door monitor to open the door. The monitor turned out to be Susan, who said accusingly, 'You're late.'

'Never mind, Susan,' said Miss Binney, who was standing in front of the class holding up a brown paper sack with a big *T* printed on it. 'What happened, Ramona?'

'I don't know,' Ramona was forced to admit. 'I left at a quarter after eight like my mother told me.'

Miss Binney smiled, and said, 'Next time try to walk a little faster,' before she continued where she had left off. 'Now who can guess what I have in this bag with the letter *T* printed on it? Remember, it is something that begins with *T*. Who can tell me how *T* sounds?'

'T-t-t-t-t,' ticked the kindergarten.

'Good,' said Miss Binney. 'Davy, what do you think is in the *b*ag?' Miss Binney was inclined to bear down on the first letters of words now that the class was working on the sounds letters make.

' 'Taterpillars?' said Davy hopefully. He rarely got anything right, but he kept trying.

'No, Davy. Caterpillar begins with C. C-c-c-c-c. What I have in the bag begins with *T*. T-t-t-t-t.'

Davy was crestfallen. He had been so sure caterpillar began with *T*.

T-t-t-t-t. The class ticked quietly while it thought. 'TV?' someone suggested. TV began with *T*, but was not in the bag.

'T-t-t-t-tadpoles?' Wrong.

'Teeter-totter?' Wrong again. How could anyone have a teeter-totter in a paper bag?

T-t-t-t, Ramona ticked to herself as she wiggled her tooth with her fingers. 'Tooth?' she suggested.

'*Tooth* is a good *T* word, Ramona,' said Miss Binney, 'but it is not what I have in the bag.'

Ramona was so pleased by Miss Binney's compliment that she wiggled her tooth even harder and suddenly found it in her hand. A strange taste filled her mouth. Ramona stared at her little tooth and was astonished to discover that one end was bloody. 'Miss Binney!' she cried without raising her hand. 'My tooth came out!'

Someone had lost a tooth! The kindergarten began to crowd around Ramona. 'Seats, please, boys and girls,' said Miss Binney. 'Ramona, you may go rinse your mouth, and then you may show us your *tooth*.'

Ramona did as she was told, and when she held up her tooth for all to admire, Miss Binney said, '*Tooth. T-t-t-t.*' When Ramona pulled down her lip to show the hole where her tooth had been, Miss Binney did not say anything because the class was working on *T* and hole did not begin with *T*. It turned out that Miss Binney had a t-t-t-t-tiger, stuffed, of course, in the *bag*.

Before the class started seat work, Ramona

went to her teacher with her precious bloody tooth, and asked, 'Would you keep this for me?' Ramona wanted to be sure she did not lose her tooth, because she needed it for bait to catch the tooth fairy. She planned to pile a lot of clattery things like saucepans and pie tins and old broken toys beside her bed so the tooth fairy would trip and wake her up.

Miss Binney smiled as she opened a drawer of her desk. 'Your first tooth! Of course, I'll keep it safe so you can take it home for the tooth fairy. You're a brave girl.'

Ramona loved Miss Binney for understanding. She loved Miss Binney for not being cross when she was late for school. She loved Miss Binney for telling her she was a brave girl.

Ramona was so happy that the morning went quickly. Seat work was unusually interesting. The kindergarten now had sheets of pictures, three to a row, printed in purple ink by a ditto machine. One row showed a top, a girl, and a toe. The kindergarten was supposed to circle the top and the toe, because they both began with *T*, and cross out the girl, because girl began with a different sound. Ramona dearly loved to circle and cross out, and was sorry when recess time came.

'Want to see where my tooth was?' Ramona asked Eric J., when the class had finished with *T* for the day and had gone out to the playground. She opened her mouth and pulled down her lower lip.

Eric J. was filled with admiration. 'Where your tooth was is all bloody,' he told her.

The glory of losing a tooth! Ramona ran over to Susan. 'Want to see where my tooth was?' she asked.

'No,' said Susan, 'and I'm glad you were late, because I got to open the door my very first day as door monitor.'

Ramona was indignant that Susan had refused to admire the bloody hole in her mouth. No one else bravely had lost a tooth during kindergarten. Ramona seized one of Susan's curls, and, careful not to pull hard enough to hurt Susan, she stretched it out and let it spring back. '*Boing!*' she cried and ran off, circling the jungle gym and coming back to Susan, who was about to climb the steps to the travelling bars. She stretched another curl and yelled, '*Boing!*'

'Ramona Quimby!' shrieked Susan. 'You stop boinging me!'

Ramona was filled with the glory of losing her first tooth and love for her teacher. Miss Binney had said she was brave! This day was the most wonderful day in the world! The sun shone, the sky was blue, and Miss Binney loved her. Ramona flung out her arms and circled the jungle gym once more on feet light with joy. She swooped towards Susan, stretched a curl, and uttered a long drawn-out, '*Boi-i-ing!*'

'Miss Binney!' cried Susan on the verge of tears. 'Ramona is boinging me, and I bet she was the witch who boinged me at the Hallowe'en parade!'

Tattletale, thought Ramona scornfully, as she circled the jungle gym on feet of joy. Circle Ramona, cross out Susan!

'Ramona,' said Miss Binney, as Ramona flew past. 'Come here. I want to talk to you.'

Ramona turned back and looked expectantly at her teacher.

'Ramona, you must stop pulling Susan's hair,' said Miss Binney.

'Yes, Miss Binney,' said Ramona, and skipped off to the travelling bars.

Ramona intended to stop pulling Susan's curls, she truly did, but unfortunately Susan would not co-operate. When recess was over and the class was filing back into the room, Susan turned to Ramona, and said, 'You're a big pest.'

Susan could not have chosen a word that Ramona would resent more. Beezus was always saying she was a pest. The big boys and girls on Ramona's street called her a pest, but Ramona did not consider herself a pest. People who called her a pest did not understand that a littler person sometimes had to be a little bit noisier and a little bit more stubborn in order to be noticed at all. Ramona had to put up with being called a pest by older boys and girls, but she did not have to put up with being called a pest by a girl her own age.

'I'm not a pest,' said Ramona indignantly, and to get even she stretched one of Susan's curls and whispered, '*Boing!*'

Ramona's luck was bad, however, for Miss Binney happened to be watching. 'Come here, Ramona,' said her teacher.

Ramona had a terrible feeling that this time Miss Binney was not going to understand.

'Ramona, I'm disappointed in you.' Miss Binney's voice was serious.

Ramona had never seen her teacher look so serious. 'Susan called me a pest,' she said in a small voice.

'That is no excuse for pulling hair,' said Miss Binney. 'I told you to stop pulling Susan's hair, and I meant it. If you cannot stop pulling Susan's hair, you will have to go home and stay there until you can.'

Ramona was shocked. Miss Binney did not love her any more. The class was suddenly quiet, and Ramona could almost feel their stares against her back as she stood there looking at the floor.

'Do you think you can stop pulling Susan's hair?' asked Miss Binney.

Ramona thought. Could she really stop pulling Susan's curls? She thought about those thick, springy locks that were so tempting. She thought about Susan, who always acted big. In kindergarten there was no worse crime than acting big. In the eyes of the children acting big was worse than being a pest. Ramona finally looked up at Miss Binney and gave her an honest answer. 'No,' she said. 'I can't.'

Miss Binney looked a little surprised. 'Very well, Ramona. You will have to go home and stay there until you can make up your mind not to pull Susan's curls.'

'Now?' asked Ramona in a small voice.

'You may sit outside on the bench until it's time to go home,' said Miss Binney. 'I'm sorry, Ramona, but we cannot have a hair puller in our kindergarten.'

No one said a word as Ramona turned and walked out of the kindergarten and sat down on the bench. The little children next door stared at her through the fence. The workmen across the street looked at her in amusement. Ramona gave a long shuddering sigh, but she just managed to hold back the tears. Nobody was going to see Ramona Quimby acting like a baby.

'That girl has been bad again,' Ramona heard the four-year-old next door say to her little sister.

When the bell rang, Miss Binney opened the door to see her class out, and said to Ramona, 'I hope you'll decide you can stop pulling Susan's hair so you can come back to kindergarten.'

Ramona did not answer. Her feet, no longer light with joy, carried her slowly towards home. She could never go to kindergarten, because Miss Binney did not love her any more. She would never get to show-and-tell or play Grey Duck again. She wouldn't get to work on the paper turkey Miss Binney was going to teach the class to make for Thanksgiving. Ramona sniffed and wiped the sleeve of her sweater across her eyes. She did love kindergarten, but it was all over now. Cross out Ramona.

Not until she was halfway home did Ramona remember her precious tooth in Miss Binney's desk.

8

KiNDeRGaRTeN DROPOUT

'Why, Ramona, whatever is the matter?' Mrs Quimby wanted to know, when Ramona opened the back door.

'Oh . . . nothing.' Ramona had no trouble hiding the gap in her teeth. She did not feel like smiling, and not having a tooth to leave for the tooth fairy was only a small part of her trouble.

Mrs Quimby laid her hand on Ramona's forehead. 'Are you feeling all right?' she asked.

'Yes, I feel all right,' answered Ramona, meaning that she did not have a broken leg, a skinned knee, or a sore throat.

'Then something must be wrong,' insisted Mrs Quimby. 'I can tell by your face.'

Ramona sighed. 'Miss Binney doesn't like me any more,' she confessed.

'Of course, Miss Binney likes you,' said Mrs Quimby. 'She may not like some of the things you do, but she likes you.'

'No, she doesn't,' contradicted Ramona. 'She doesn't want me there any more.' Ramona felt sad thinking about the recesses and the new seat work she was going to miss.

'Why, what do you mean?' Mrs Quimby was puzzled. 'Of course, Miss Binney wants you there.'

'No, she doesn't,' insisted Ramona. 'She told me not to come back.'

'But why?'

'She doesn't like me,' was Ramona's answer.

Mrs Quimby was exasperated. 'Then something must have happened. There is only one thing to do, and that is to go to school and find out. Eat your lunch, and we'll go to school before afternoon kindergarten starts and see what this is all about.'

After Ramona had picked at her sandwich awhile, Mrs Quimby said briskly, 'Put on your sweater Ramona, and come along.'

'No,' said Ramona. 'I'm not going.'

'Oh yes, you are, young lady,' said her mother, and took her daughter by the hand.

Ramona knew she had no choice when her mother started calling her young lady. She dragged her feet as much as she could on the way to school, where the afternoon kindergarten was behaving like the morning kindergarten. Half the class was lined up by the door waiting for Miss Binney while the other half raced around the playground. Ramona stared at the ground, because she did not want anyone to see her, and when Miss Binney arrived, Mrs Quimby asked to talk to her for a moment.

Ramona did not look up. Her mother led her to the bench beside the kindergarten door. 'You sit there and don't budge while I have a little talk with Miss Binney,' she told Ramona.

Ramona sat on the bench swinging her feet thinking about her tooth in Miss Binney's drawer and wondering what her teacher and her mother were saying about her. Finally she could stand the suspense no longer. She had to budge so she slipped over to the door, as close as she could without being seen, and listened. The afternoon kindergarten and the workmen across the street were making so much noise she could catch only a few phrases such as 'bright and imaginative', 'ability to get along with her peer group', and 'negative desire for attention'. Ramona felt awed and frightened to be discussed in such strange big words, which must mean Miss Binney thought she was very bad indeed. She scuttled back to the bench when at last she heard her mother walk to the door.

'What did she say?' Ramona's curiosity was almost more than she could endure.

Mrs Quimby looked stern. 'She said she will be glad to have you back when you are ready to come back.'

'Then I'm not going back,' announced Ramona. She would never go to kindergarten at all if her teacher did not like her. Never.

'Oh yes, you are,' said Mrs Quimby wearily.

Ramona knew better.

Thus began a difficult time in the Quimby household. 'But, Ramona, you have to go to kindergarten,' protested Beezus, when she came home from school that afternoon. 'Everybody goes to kindergarten.'

'I don't,' said Ramona. 'I used to, but I don't now.'

When Mr Quimby came home from work, Mrs Quimby took him aside and talked quietly to him. Ramona was not fooled for a minute. She knew exactly what those whispers were about.

'Well, Ramona, suppose you tell me all about what went on at school today,' said Mr Quimby with that false cheerfulness grown-ups use when they are trying to persuade children to tell something they don't want to tell.

Ramona, who longed to run to her father and show him where her tooth used to be, thought awhile before she said, 'We guessed what Miss Binney had in a paper bag that began with a *T*, and Davy guessed 'taterpillars.'

'And what else happened?' asked Mr Quimby, all set to be patient.

Ramona could not tell her father about her tooth, and she was not going to tell about pulling Susan's curls. Nothing much was left to talk about. 'We learned *T*,' she said at last.

Mr Quimby gave his daughter a long look, but said nothing.

After dinner Beezus talked to Mary Jane on the telephone, and Ramona heard her say, 'Guess what! Ramona is a kindergarten dropout!' She seemed to think this remark was very funny, because she giggled into the telephone. Ramona was not amused.

Later Beezus settled down to read a book while Ramona got out her crayons and some paper.

'Beezus, you don't have a very good light for reading,' said Mrs Quimby. And she added as she always did, 'You have only one pair of eyes, you know.'

Here was an opportunity for Ramona to show off her new kindergarten knowledge. 'Why don't you turn on the dawnzer?' she asked, proud of her new word.

Beezus looked up from her book. 'What are you talking about?' she asked Ramona. 'What's a dawnzer?'

Ramona was scornful. 'Silly. Everybody knows what a dawnzer is.'

'I don't,' said Mr Quimby, who had been reading the evening paper. 'What is a dawnzer?'

'A lamp,' said Ramona. 'It gives a lee light. We sing about it every morning in kindergarten.'

A puzzled silence fell over the room until Beezus suddenly shouted with laughter. 'She-she means—' she gasped, '*The Star-Spangled B-banner!*' Her laughter dwindled to giggles. 'She means the *dawn's early light.*' She pronounced each word with exaggerated distinctness, and then she began to laugh again.

Ramona looked at her mother and father, who had the straight mouths and laughing eyes of grown-ups who were trying not to laugh out loud. Beezus was right and she was wrong. She was nothing but a girl who used to go to kindergarten and who got everything wrong and made everyone laugh. She was a stupid little sister. A dumb stupid little sister, who never did anything right.

Suddenly everything that had happened that day was too much for Ramona. She glared at her sister, made a big crisscross motion in the air with her hand, and shouted, 'Cross out Beezus!' Then she threw her crayons on the floor, stamped her feet, burst into tears, and ran into the room she shared with her sister.

'Ramona Quimby!' her father said sternly, and Ramona knew that she was about to be ordered back to pick up her crayons. Well, her father could order all he wanted to. She was not going to pick up her crayons. Nobody could make her pick up her crayons. Nobody. Not her father nor her mother. Not even the principal. Not even God.

'Now, never mind,' Ramona heard her mother say. 'Poor little girl. She's upset. She's had a difficult day.'

Sympathy made things worse. 'I am *not* upset!' yelled Ramona, and yelling made her feel so much better that she continued. 'I am *not* upset, and I'm not a *little* girl, and everybody is *mean* to laugh at me!' She threw herself on her bed and pounded her heels on the bedspread, but pounding on the bedclothes was not bad enough. Far from it.

Ramona wanted to be wicked, really wicked, so she swung around and beat her heels on the wall. Bang! Bang! Bang! That noise ought to make everybody good and mad. 'Mean, mean, mean!' she yelled, in time to her drumming heels. She wanted to make her whole family feel as angry as she felt. 'Mean, mean, mean!' She was glad her heels left marks on the wallpaper. Glad! Glad! Glad!

'Mother, Ramona's kicking the wall,' cried tattletale Beezus, as if her mother did not know what Ramona was doing. 'It's my wall, too!'

Ramona did not care if Beezus tattled. She

wanted her to tattle. Ramona wanted the whole world to know she was so bad she kicked the wall and left heel marks on the wallpaper.

'Ramona, if you're going to do that you had better take off your shoes.' Mrs Quimby's voice from the living room was tired but calm.

Ramona drummed harder to show everyone how bad she was. She would *not* take off her shoes. She was a terrible, wicked girl! Being such a bad, terrible, horrid, wicked girl made her feel *good*! She brought both heels against the wall at the same time. Thump! Thump! Thump! She was not the least bit sorry for what she was doing. She would *never* be sorry. Never! Never! Never!

'Ramona!' Mr Quimby's voice held a warning note. 'Do you want me to come in there?'

Ramona paused and considered. Did she want her father to come in? No, she did not. Her father, her mother, nobody could understand how hard it was to be a little sister. She drummed her heels a few more times to prove that her spirit was not broken. Then she lay on her bed and thought wild fierce thoughts until her mother came and silently helped her undress and get into bed. When the light had been turned out, Ramona felt so limp and tired that she soon fell asleep. After all she had no reason to try to stay awake, because the tooth fairy was not going to come to her house that night.

The next morning Mrs Quimby walked into the girls' room, and said briskly to Ramona, 'Which dress do you want to wear to school today?'

The empty space in her mouth and the heel marks on the wall above her bed reminded Ramona of all that had happened the day before. 'I'm not going to school,' she said, and reached for her playclothes while Beezus put on a fresh school dress.

A terrible day had begun. No one said much at breakfast. Howie, who had recovered from his cold, stopped for Ramona on his way to school, and then went on without her. Ramona watched all the children in the neighbourhood go to school, and when the street was quiet, she turned on the television set.

Her mother turned it off, saying, 'Little girls who don't go to school can't watch television.'

Ramona felt that her mother did not understand. She wanted to go to school. She wanted to go to school more than anything in the world, but she could not go back when her teacher did not like her. Ramona got out her crayons and paper, which someone had put away for her, and settled down to draw. She drew a bird, a cat, and a ball in a row, and then with her red crayon she crossed out the cat, because it did not begin with the same sound as bird and ball. Afterwards she covered a whole sheet of paper with Q's, Ramona-style, with ears and whiskers.

Ramona's mother did not feel sorry for Ramona. She merely said, 'Get your sweater, Ramona. I have to drive down to the shopping centre.' Ramona wished she had a dime from the tooth fairy to spend.

There followed the most boring morning of Ramona's entire life. She trailed along after her mother in the shopping centre while Mrs Quimby bought socks for Beezus, some buttons and thread, pillowcases that were on sale, a new electric cord for the toaster, a package of paper for Ramona to draw on, and a pattern. Looking at patterns was the worst part. Ramona's mother seemed to sit for hours looking at pictures of boring dresses.

At the beginning of the shopping trip, Mrs Quimby said, 'Ramona, you mustn't put your hands on things in stores.' Later she said, 'Ramona, please don't touch things.' By the time they reached the pattern counter, she said, 'Ramona, how many times do I have to tell you to keep your hands to yourself?'

When Mrs Quimby had finally selected a pattern and they were leaving the store, who should they run into but Mrs Wisser, a neighbour. 'Why, hello!' exclaimed Mrs Wisser. 'And there's Ramona! I thought a big girl like you would be going to kindergarten.'

Ramona had nothing to say.

'How old are you, dear?' asked Mrs Wisser.

Ramona still had nothing to say to Mrs Wisser, but she did hold up five fingers for the neighbour to count.

'Five!' exclaimed Mrs Wisser. 'What's the matter, dear? Has the cat got your tongue?'

Ramona stuck out her tongue just enough to show Mrs Wisser that the cat had not got it.

Mrs Wisser gasped.

'Ramona!' Mrs Quimby was thoroughly exasperated. 'I'm sorry, Mrs Wisser. Ramona seems to have forgotten her manners.' After this apology she said angrily, 'Ramona Geraldine Quimby, don't you ever let me catch you doing such a thing again!'

'But, Mama,' protested Ramona, as she was dragged towards the parking lot, 'she *asked* me, and I was just showing—' There was no use in finishing the sentence, because Mrs Quimby was not listening and she probably would not have understood if she had listened.

Mrs Quimby and Ramona returned home in time to pass the morning kindergarten straggling along the sidewalk with their seat-work papers to show their mothers. Ramona got down on the floor of the car so she would not be seen.

Later that afternoon Beezus brought Mary Jane

home from school to play. 'How did you like kindergarten today, Ramona?' asked Mary Jane in a bright, false tone. It told Ramona all too clearly that she already knew Ramona had not gone to kindergarten.

'Why don't you shut up?' asked Ramona.

'I'll bet Henry Huggins isn't going to want to marry a girl who hasn't even finished kindergarten,' said Mary Jane.

'Oh, don't tease her,' said Beezus, who might laugh at her sister herself, but was quick to protect her from others. Ramona went outside and rode her two-wheeled, lopsided tricycle up and down the sidewalk for a while before she sadly removed Miss Binney's red ribbon, which she had woven through the spokes of her front wheel.

On the second morning, Mrs Quimby took a dress out of Ramona's closet without a word.

Ramona spoke. 'I'm not going to school,' she said.

'Ramona, aren't you ever going back to kindergarten?' Mrs Quimby asked wearily.

'Yes,' said Ramona.

Mrs Quimby smiled. 'Good. Let's make it today.'

Ramona reached for her playclothes. 'No. I'm going to stay away until Miss Binney forgets all about me, and then when I go back she'll think I'm somebody else.'

Mrs Quimby sighed and shook her head. 'Ramona, Miss Binney is not going to forget you.'

'Yes, she will,' insisted Ramona. 'She will if I stay away long enough.'

Some older children on the way to school shouted, 'Dropout!' as they passed the Quimbys' house. The day was a long, long one for Ramona. She drew some more seat work for herself, and afterwards there was nothing to do but wander around the house poking her tongue in the hole where her tooth was while she kept her lips shut tight.

That evening her father said, 'I miss my little girl's smiles.' Ramona managed a tight-lipped smile that did not show the gap in her teeth. Later she heard her father say something to her mother about 'this nonsense has gone on long enough,' and her mother answered with something about 'Ramona has to make up her own mind she wants to behave herself.'

Ramona despaired. Nobody understood. She wanted to behave herself. Except when banging her heels on the bedroom wall, she had always wanted to behave herself. Why couldn't people understand how she felt? She had only touched Susan's hair in the first place because it was so beautiful, and the last time—well, Susan had been so bossy she deserved to have her hair pulled.

Ramona soon discovered the other children in the neighbourhood were fascinated by her predicament. 'How come you get to stay out of school?' they asked.

'Miss Binney doesn't want me,' Ramona answered.

'Did you have fun in kindergarten today?' Mary Jane asked each day, pretending she did not know Ramona had stayed home. Ramona, who was not fooled for an instant, disdained to answer.

Henry Huggins was the one, quite unintentionally, who really frightened Ramona. One afternoon when she was pedalling her lopsided, two-wheeled tricycle up and down in front of her house, Henry came riding down the street delivering the *Journal*. He paused with one foot on the kerb in front of the Quimbys' house while he rolled a paper.

'Hi,' said Henry. 'That's quite a trike you're riding.'

'This isn't a trike,' said Ramona with dignity. 'This is my two-wheeler.'

Henry grinned and threw the paper onto the Quimbys' front steps. 'How come the truant officer doesn't make you go to school?' he asked.

'What's a truant officer?' asked Ramona.

'A man who gets after kids who don't go

248

to school,' was Henry's careless answer, as he pedalled on down the street.

A truant officer, Ramona decided, must be something like the dog catcher who sometimes came to Glenwood School when there were too many dogs on the playground. He tried to lasso the dogs, and once when he did manage to catch an elderly overweight Bassett hound, he shut the dog in the back of his truck and drove away with it. Ramona did not want any truant officer to catch her and drive away with her, so she put her lopsided, two-wheeled tricycle into the garage and went into the house and stayed there, looking out from behind the curtains at the other children and poking her tongue into the space where her tooth used to be.

'Ramona, why do you keep making such faces?' asked Mrs Quimby in that tired voice she had been using the last day or so.

Ramona took her tongue out of the space. 'I'm not making faces,' she said. Pretty soon her grown-up tooth would come in without the tooth fairy paying a visit, and no one would ever know she had lost a tooth. She wondered what Miss Binney had done with her tooth. Thrown it away, most likely.

The next morning Ramona continued to draw rows of three pictures, circle two and cross out one, but the morning was long and lonely. Ramona was so lonely she even considered going back to kindergarten, but then she thought about Miss Binney, who did not like her any more and who might not be glad to see her. She decided she would have to wait much, much longer for Miss Binney to forget her.

'When do you think Miss Binney will forget me?' Ramona asked her mother.

Mrs Quimby kissed the top of Ramona's head. 'I doubt if she will ever forget you,' she said. 'Not ever, as long as she lives.'

The situation was hopeless. That noon Ramona was not at all hungry when she sat down to soup, a sandwich, and some carrot sticks. She bit into a carrot stick, but somehow chewing it took a long time. She stopped chewing altogether when she heard the doorbell chime. Her heart began to thump. Maybe the truant officer had finally come to get her and carry her off in the back of his truck. Maybe she should run and hide.

'Why, Howie!' Ramona heard her mother say. Feeling that she had had a close call, she went on chewing away at the carrot stick. She was safe. It was only Howie.

'Come on in, Howie,' said Mrs Quimby. 'Ramona is having her lunch. Would you like to stay for some soup and a sandwich? I can phone your mother and ask her if it's all right.'

Ramona hoped Howie would stay. She was that lonely.

'I just brought Ramona a letter.'

Ramona jumped up from the table. 'A letter for me? Who's it from?' Here was the first interesting thing that had happened in days.

'I don't know,' said Howie. 'Miss Binney told me to give it to you.'

Ramona snatched the envelope from Howie, and, sure enough, there was RAMONA printed on the envelope.

'Let me read it to you,' said Mrs Quimby.

'It's *my* letter,' said Ramona, and tore open the envelope. When she pulled out the letter, two things caught her eye at once—her tooth Scotch-taped to the top of the paper and the first line, which Ramona could read because she knew how all letters began. 'DEAR RAMONA ' was followed by two lines of printing, which Ramona was not able to read.

'Mama!' cried Ramona, filled with joy. Miss Binney had not thrown away her tooth, and Miss Binney had drawn ears and whiskers on her Q. The teacher liked the way Ramona made Q, so she must like Ramona, too. There was hope after all.

'Why, Ramona!' Mrs Quimby was astonished. 'You've lost a tooth! When did that happen?'

'At school,' said Ramona, 'and here it is!' She waved the letter at her mother, and then she studied it carefully, because she wanted so much to be able to read Miss Binney's words herself. 'It says, "Dear Ramona Q. Here is your tooth. I hope the tooth fairy brings you a dollar. I miss you and want you to come back to kindergarten. Love and kisses, Miss Binney."'

Mrs Quimby smiled and held out her hand. 'Why don't you let me read the letter?'

Ramona handed over the letter. Maybe the words did not say exactly what she had pretended to read, but she was sure they must mean the same.

'"Dear Ramona Q,"' began Mrs Quimby. And she remarked, 'Why, she makes her Q the same way you do.'

'Go on, Mama,' urged Ramona, eager to hear what the letter really said.

Mrs Quimby read, '"I am sorry I forgot to give you your tooth, but I am sure the tooth fairy will understand. When are you coming back to kindergarten?"'

Ramona did not care if the tooth fairy understood or not. Miss Binney understood and nothing else mattered. 'Tomorrow, Mama!' she cried. 'I'm going to kindergarten tomorrow!'

'Good girl!' said Mrs Quimby and hugged Ramona.

'She can't,' said matter-of-fact Howie. 'Tomorrow is Saturday.'

Ramona gave Howie a look of pity, but she said, 'Please stay for lunch, Howie. It isn't tuna fish. It's peanut butter and jelly.'

RaMoNa THe BRaVe

CONTENTS

1

TROUBLE IN THE PARK

Ramona Quimby, brave and fearless, was half-running, half-skipping to keep up with her big sister Beatrice on their way home from the park. She had never seen her sister's cheeks so flushed with anger as they were this August afternoon. Ramona was sticky from heat and grubby from landing in the sawdust at the foot of the slides, but she was proud of herself. When Mrs Quimby had sent the girls to the park for an hour, because she had an errand to do—an important errand, she hinted—she told Beezus, as Beatrice was called, to look after Ramona.

And what had happened? For the first time in her six years Ramona had looked after Beezus, who was supposed to be the responsible one. *Bossy* was a better word, Ramona sometimes thought. But not today. Ramona had stepped forward and defended her sister for a change.

'Beezus,' said Ramona, panting, 'slow down.'

Beezus, clutching her library book in her sweaty hand, paid no attention. The clang of rings, the steady pop of tennis balls against asphalt, and the shouts of children grew fainter as the girls approached their house on Klickitat Street.

Ramona hoped their mother would be home from her errand, whatever it was. She couldn't wait to tell her what had happened and how she had defended her big sister. Her mother would be so proud, and so would her father when he came home from work and heard the story. 'Good for you, Ramona,' he would say. 'That's the old fight!' Brave little Ramona.

Fortunately, the car was in the garage and Mrs Quimby was in the living room when the girls burst into the house. 'Why, Beezus,' said their mother, when she saw the flushed and sweaty faces of her daughters, one angry and one triumphant.

Beezus blinked to hold back the tears in her eyes.

'Ramona, what happened to Beezus?' Mrs Quimby was alarmed.

'Don't *ever* call me Beezus again!' Beezus's voice was fierce.

Mrs Quimby looked at Ramona for the explanation, and Ramona was eager to give it. Usually Beezus was the one who explained what had happened to Ramona, how she had dropped her ice-cream cone on the sidewalk and cried when Beezus would not let her pick it up, or how she tried, in spite of the rules, to go down a slide head first and had landed on her face in the sawdust. Now Ramona was going to have a turn. She took a deep breath and prepared to tell her tale. 'Well, when we went to the park, I slid on the slides awhile and Beezus sat on a bench reading her library book. Then I saw an empty swing. A big swing, not a baby swing over the wading pool, and I thought since I'm going to be in the first grade next month I should swing on the big swings. Shouldn't I, Mama?'

'Yes, of course.' Mrs Quimby was impatient. 'Please, go on with the story. What happened to Beezus?'

'Well, I climbed up in the swing,' Ramona continued, 'only my feet wouldn't touch the ground because there was this big hollow under the swing.' Ramona recalled how she had longed to swing until the chains went slack in her hands and her toes pointed to the tops of the fir trees, but she sensed that she had better hurry up with her story or her mother would ask Beezus to tell it. Ramona never liked to lose an audience. 'And I said, "Beezus, push me," and some big boys, big bad boys, heard me and one of them said—' Ramona, eager to be the one to tell the story but reluctant to repeat the words, hesitated.

'Said what?' Mrs Quimby was baffled. 'Said what, Ramona? Beezus, what did he say?'

Beezus wiped the back of her wrist across her eyes and tried. 'He said, "J-j-j—"'

Eagerness to beat her sister at telling what had happened overcame Ramona's reluctance. 'He said, "Jesus, Beezus!"' Ramona looked up at her mother, waiting for her to be shocked. Instead she merely looked surprised and—could it be?—amused.

'And that is why I never, never, *never* want to be called Beezus again!' said Beezus.

'And all the other boys began to say it, too,' said Ramona, warming to her story now that she was past the bad part. 'Oh, Mama, it was just awful. It was *terrible*. All those big awful boys! They kept saying, "Jesus, Beezus" and "Beezus, Jesus." I jumped out of the swing, and I told them—'

Here Beezus interrupted. Anger once more replaced tears. 'And then Ramona had to get into the act. Do you know what she did? She jumped out of the swing and preached a sermon! Nobody wants a little sister tagging around preaching sermons to a bunch of boys. And they weren't that big either. They were just trying to act big.'

Ramona was stunned by this view of her behaviour. How unfair of Beezus when she had been so brave. And the boys *had* seemed big to her.

Mrs Quimby spoke to Beezus as if Ramona were not present. 'A sermon! You must be joking.'

Ramona tried again. 'Mama, I—'

Beezus was not going to give her little sister a chance to speak. 'No, I'm not joking. And then Ramona stuck her thumbs in her ears, waggled her fingers, and stuck out her tongue. I just about died, I was so embarrassed.'

Ramona was suddenly subdued. She had thought Beezus was angry at the boys, but now it turned out she was angry with her little sister, too. Maybe angrier. Ramona was used to being considered a little pest, and she knew she sometimes was a pest, but this was something different. She felt as if she were standing aside looking at herself. She saw a stranger, a funny little six-year-old girl with straight brown hair, wearing grubby shorts and an old T-shirt, inherited from Beezus, which had Camp Namanu printed across the front. A silly little girl embarrassing her sister so much that Beezus was ashamed of her. And she had been proud of herself because she thought she was being brave. Now it turned out that she was not brave. She was silly and embarrassing. Ramona's confidence in herself was badly shaken. She tried again. 'Mama, I—'

Mrs Quimby felt her older daughter deserved all her attention. 'Were they boys you know?' she asked.

'Sort of,' said Beezus with a sniff. 'They go to our school, and now when school starts all the boys in the sixth grade will be saying it. Sixth-grade boys are *awful*.'

'They will have forgotten by then.' Mrs Quimby tried to be reassuring. Beezus sniffed again.

'Mama, I think we *should* stop calling her Beezus.' Even though her feelings were hurt, and her confidence shaken, Ramona had a reason of her own for trying to help Beezus. Whenever someone asked Beezus where she got such an unusual nickname, Beezus always answered that it came from Ramona. When she was little she couldn't say Beatrice. Now that Ramona was about to enter first grade, she did not like to remember there was a time when she could not pronounce her sister's name.

'Just because I have an Aunt Beatrice, I don't see why I have to be named Beatrice, too,' said Beezus. 'Nobody else has a name like Beatrice.'

'You wouldn't want a name like everyone else's,' Mrs Quimby pointed out.

'I know,' agreed Beezus, 'but *Beatrice*.'

'Yuck,' said Ramona, trying to be helpful, but

her mother frowned at her. 'How about Trissy?' she suggested hastily.

Beezus was rude. 'Don't be dumb. Then they would call me Sissy Trissy or something. Boys in the sixth grade think up *awful* names.'

'Nobody ever calls me anything but Ramona Kimona.' Ramona could not help thinking that an awful nickname might be interesting to have. 'Why not just be Beatrice? Nobody can think up a bad nickname for Beatrice.'

'Yes, I guess you're right,' agreed Beezus. 'I'll have to be plain old Beatrice with her plain old brown hair.'

'I think Beatrice is fancy,' said Ramona, who also had plain old brown hair but did not take it so hard. Agreeing with Beezus—Beatrice—gave Ramona a cosy feeling, as if something unusually pleasant had taken place. Beezus honoured Ramona with a watery smile, forgiving her, at least for the moment, for preaching a sermon.

Ramona felt secure and happy. Agreeing was so pleasant she wished she and her sister could agree more often. Unfortunately, there were many things to disagree about—whose turn it was to feed Picky-picky, the old yellow cat, who should change the paper under Picky-picky's dish, whose washcloth had been left sopping in the bathtub because someone had not wrung it out, and whose dirty underwear had been left in whose half of the room. Ramona always said Beezus—Beatrice— was bossy, because she was older. Beatrice said Ramona always got her own way, because she was the baby and because she always made a fuss. For the moment all this was forgotten.

Mrs Quimby smiled to see her girls at peace with one another. 'Don't worry, Beatrice. If the boys tease you, just hold your head high and ignore them. When they see they can't tease you, they will stop.'

The two sisters exchanged a look of complete understanding. They both knew this was the sort of advice easy for adults to give but difficult for children to follow. If the boys remembered, Beezus might have to listen to 'Jesus, Beezus' for months before they gave up.

'By the way, Ramona,' said Mrs Quimby, as Beatrice went off to the bathroom to splash cold water on her face, 'what did you say to the boys in the park?'

Ramona, who had flopped back on the couch, sat up straight. 'I told them they were not supposed to take the name of the Lord in vain,' she said in her most proper Sunday School voice. 'That's what my Sunday School teacher said.'

'Oh, I see,' said Mrs Quimby. 'And what did they say to that?'

Ramona was chagrined because she knew her mother was amused, and Ramona did not like anyone to be amused when she was serious. 'Wasn't I right? That's what I learned in Sunday School.' She was filled with uncertainty by her mother's amusement, as well as by her sister's anger over the incident.

'Of course, you were right, dear, although I don't suppose a bunch of boys would pay much attention.' Mrs Quimby's lips were not smiling, but amusement lingered in her eyes. 'How did the boys answer?'

Ramona's confidence wilted completely. She was seeing that little girl in the park who was not the heroine she thought she was after all. 'They laughed,' Ramona admitted in a small voice, feeling sorry for herself. Poor little Ramona, laughed at and picked on. Nobody understood how she felt. Nobody understood what it was like to be six years old and the littlest one in the family unless you counted old Picky-picky, and even he was ten years old.

Mrs Quimby gave Ramona a big hug. 'Well, it's all over now,' she said. 'Run along and play, but *please* don't play Brick Factory this afternoon.'

'Don't worry, mother. I don't have any bricks left.'

Ramona felt that her mother should be

able to see that running along and playing was impossible on a hot summer afternoon when everyone Ramona's age had gone to the beach or the mountains or to visit a grandmother. The two weeks the Quimbys had spent in a borrowed mountain cabin in July now seemed a long time away. Who was she supposed to play with?

Summer was boring. Long and boring. No bricks left for the game of Brick Factory, which she and her friend Howie had invented, nobody to play with, and Beezus with her nose in a book all day.

Not having any place to run along to, Ramona sat looking at her mother, thinking that her fresh haircut and touch of eye shadow made her look unusually nice this afternoon. She wondered if her mother would tell her father about the incident in the park and if they would have a good laugh over it when they thought Ramona could not hear. She hoped not. She did not want her father to laugh at her.

Seeing her mother looking so nice made Ramona recall the reason for the trip to the park. 'What was your errand that you didn't want to drag us along on?' she asked.

Mrs Quimby smiled a different smile, exasperating and mysterious. 'Sh-h-h,' she said, her finger on her lips. 'It's a secret, and wild horses couldn't drag it out of me.'

Ramona found secrets hard to bear. 'Tell me, Mama! Mama, *please* tell me.' She threw her arms around her mother, who had a good smell of clean clothes and perfumed soap. 'Please, please, *please!*' Learning a big juicy secret would help make up for Ramona's unhappy afternoon.

Mrs Quimby shook her head.

'Pretty please with a lump of sugar on it?' Ramona felt she could not bear not knowing this very minute.

'If I told you, it wouldn't be a secret any more,' said Mrs Quimby.

That, Ramona felt, was just about the most exasperating sentence ever spoken by a grown-up.

2

MRS QUIMBY'S SECRET

Mrs Quimby, wearing a dress instead of old slacks, had gone off on another mysterious errand. She promised not to be away long, and Beezus and Ramona promised to stay out of trouble while she was out, a promise easier for Beezus to keep than for Ramona. Beezus disappeared with a book into the room the girls shared. Ramona settled herself at the kitchen table with paper and crayons to draw a picture of the cat on the label of a can of Puss'n Boots cat food. Ramona loved that jaunty booted cat, so different from old Picky-picky, who spent most of his time napping on Beezus's bed.

The house was quiet. Ramona worked happily, humming a tune from a television commercial. She used a pencil to draw cat fur, because she could draw finer lines with it than she could with a crayon. She used her crayons for Puss'n Boots's clothes, but when she came to his boots, she discovered her red crayon was missing. Most likely she had left it in her room.

'Beezus, have you seen my red crayon?' The

girls had made an agreement that Ramona could call her sister Beezus at home, but in public she had better remember to call her Beatrice or look out!

'Um-hm.' Without looking up from her book, Beezus waved her hand in the direction of Ramona's bed.

Peace between the sisters could not last. Ramona saw the broken remains of her red crayon lying in the middle of her bed. 'Who broke my crayon?' she demanded.

'You shouldn't leave your crayon on other people's beds where it can get sat on.' Beezus did not even bother to look up from her book.

Ramona found this answer most annoying. 'You should look where you sit,' she said, 'and you don't have to be so bossy.'

'This is my bed.' Beezus glanced at her sister. 'You have your own half of the room.'

'I don't have anywhere to put anything.'

'Pooh,' said Beezus. 'You're just careless and messy.'

Ramona was indignant. 'I am not careless and messy!' Picky-picky woke up, leaped from Beezus's bed, and departed, tail held straight. Picky-picky often made it plain he did not care for Ramona.

'Yes, you are,' said Beezus. 'You don't hang up your clothes, and you leave your toys all over.'

'Just because the clothes rail is easy for you to reach,' said Ramona, 'and you think you're too big for toys.' To show her sister that she did pick up her things, she laid the pieces of her broken crayon in her drawer on top of her underwear. She had lost interest in crayoning. She did not want to colour boots with the rough ends of a broken crayon.

'Besides,' said Beezus, who did not like to be interrupted when she was deep in a good book, 'you're a pest.'

Pest was a fighting word to Ramona, because it was unfair. She was not a pest, at least not all the time. She was only littler than anyone else in the family, and no matter how hard she tried, she could not catch up. 'Don't you call me a pest,' she shouted, 'or I'll tell Mama you have a lipstick hidden in your drawer.'

Beezus finally laid down her book. 'Ramona Geraldine Quimby!' Her voice and manner were fierce. 'You're nothing but a snoop and a tattletale!'

Ramona had gone too far. 'I wasn't snooping. I was looking for a safety pin,' she explained, adding, as if she were a very good girl, 'and anyway I haven't told Mama *yet*.'

Beezus gave her sister a look of disgust. 'Ramona, grow up!'

Ramona lost all patience. *'Can't you see I'm trying?'* she yelled at the top of her voice. People were always telling her to grow up. What did they think she was trying to do?

'Try harder,' was Beezus's heartless answer. 'And stop bothering me when I've come to the good part in my book.'

Ramona shoved aside her stuffed animals and threw herself on her bed with *Wild Animals of Africa*, a book with interesting pictures but without the three grown-up words, *petrol*, *motel*, and *burger*, which she had taught herself from signs but was unable to find in books. The book fell open to the page that she had looked at most often, a full-page colour photograph of a gorilla. Ramona stared briefly and intensely at the gorilla, taking in his mighty body covered with blue-black hair, his tiny eyes, the dark caves of his nostrils, his long and powerful arms with hands like leather that hung almost to the ground. With a satisfying shiver, Ramona slammed the book shut. She wouldn't want to meet that old gorilla coming down the street or swinging through the trees of the park. She let the book fall open again. The gorilla was still there, staring out of the page with fierce little eyes. Ramona slammed the gorilla in again. When Ramona was bored, she enjoyed scaring herself.

'Ramona, do you have to keep slamming that book?' asked Beezus.

Ramona slammed the book a few more times to show her sister she could slam the book all she wanted to.

'Pest,' said Beezus, to show Ramona she could call her a pest if she wanted to.

'I am not a pest!' yelled Ramona.

'You are too a pest!' Beezus yelled back.

Ha, thought Ramona, at least I got you away from your old book. 'I'm not a pest, and you're just bossy!' she shouted.

'Silence, varlet,' commanded Beezus. 'Yonder car approacheth. Our noble mother cometh.' People talked like that in the books Beezus was reading lately.

Ramona thought Beezus was showing off. 'Don't you call me a bad name!' she shouted, half hoping her mother would hear.

In a moment Mrs Quimby appeared in the doorway. She looked angry. Beezus shot Ramona an it's-all-your-fault look.

'Girls, you can be heard all over the neighbourhood,' said Mrs Quimby.

Ramona sat up and looked virtuous. 'Beezus called me a bad name.'

'How do you know?' asked Beezus. 'You don't even know what *varlet* means.'

Mrs Quimby took in the two girls on their rumpled beds, Ramona's toys heaped in the corner, the overflowing dresser. Then, when she spoke, she said an astonishing thing. 'I don't blame you girls one little bit for bickering so much. This room is much too small for two growing girls, so of course you get on one another's nerves.'

The sisters looked at each other and relaxed. Their mother understood.

'Well, we're going to do something about it,' Mrs Quimby continued. 'We're going to go ahead and build that extra bedroom onto the house.'

Beezus sat up, and this time she was the one to slam her book shut. 'Oh, mother!' she cried. 'Are we *really*?'

Ramona understood the stress on that last word. The extra room had been talked about for so long that neither sister believed it would actually be built. Mr Quimby had drawn plans for knocking out the back of the closet where the vacuum cleaner was kept and extending the house into the backyard just enough to add a small bedroom with the closet-turned-into-a-hall leading to it. Ramona had heard a lot of uninteresting grown-up talk about borrowing money from a bank to pay for it, but nothing had ever come of it. All she understood was that her father worked at something that sounded boring in an office downtown, and there was never quite enough money in the Quimby family. They were certainly not poor, but her parents worried a lot about taxes and college educations.

'Where will we get the money to pay back the bank?' asked Beezus, who understood these things better than Ramona.

Mrs Quimby smiled, about to make an important announcement. 'I have a job that begins as soon as school starts.'

'A job!' cried the sisters.

'Yes,' said their mother. 'I am going to work from nine in the morning till two in the afternoon in Dr Perry's office. That way I can be here when Ramona gets home from school. And on my way home from talking to Dr Perry, I stopped at the bank and arranged to borrow the money to pay for the room.'

'Oh, mother!' Beezus was all enthusiasm. Dr Perry was the woman who had given the girls their check-ups and their shots ever since they were born. 'Just think! You're going to be liberated!'

Ramona was pleased by the look of amusement that flickered across her mother's face. Ramona wasn't the only one who said things grown-ups thought funny.

'That remains to be seen,' said Mrs Quimby,

'and depends on how much help I get from you girls.'

'And you'll get to see all the darling babies!' Beezus loved babies and could hardly wait until she was old enough to baby sit. 'Oh, mother, you're so lucky!'

Mrs Quimby smiled. 'I'm going to be Dr Perry's bookkeeper. I won't be taking care of babies.'

Ramona was less enthusiastic than Beezus. 'Who will take care of me if I get sick?' she wanted to know.

'Howie's grandmother,' said Mrs Quimby. 'She's always glad to earn a little extra money.'

Ramona, who knew all about Howie's grandmother, made up her mind to stay well. 'Who will bake cookies?' she asked.

'Oh, cookies.' Mrs Quimby dismissed cookies as unimportant. 'We can buy them at the store, or you can bake them from a mix. You're old enough now.'

'I might burn myself,' said Ramona darkly.

'Not if you are careful.' Mrs Quimby's good spirits could not be budged.

Suddenly Ramona and her sister exchanged an anxious glance, and each tried to speak faster than the other. 'Who gets the new room?' they both wanted to know.

Ramona began to feel unhappy and left out

before her mother had a chance to answer. Beezus always got everything, because she was older. Beezus got to stay up later. She got to spend the night at Mary Jane's house and go away to camp. She got most of the new clothes, and when she had outgrown them, they were put away for Ramona. There was no hope.

'Now, girls,' said Mrs Quimby, 'don't get all worked up. Your father and I talked it over a long time ago and decided you will take turns. Every six months you will trade.'

Ramona had a quick word with God. 'Who gets it first?' she asked, anxious again.

Mrs Quimby smiled. 'You do.'

'Moth-ther!' wailed Beezus. 'Couldn't we at least draw straws?'

Mrs Quimby shook her head. 'Ramona has a point when she says she never gets anything first because she is younger. We thought this time Ramona could be first for a change. Don't you agree that's fair?'

'Yes!' shouted Ramona.

'I guess so,' said Beezus.

'Good,' said Mrs Quimby, the matter settled.

'Is a man going to come and really chop a hole in the house?' asked Ramona.

'Next week,' said her mother.

Ramona could hardly wait. The summer was

no longer boring. Something was going to happen after all. And when school started, she would have something exciting to share with her class for Show and Tell. A hole chopped in the house!

3

The Hole in The House

Although Ramona was standing with her nose pressed against the front window, she was wild with impatience. She was impatient for school to start. She was impatient because no matter how many times her mother telephoned, the workmen had not come to start the new room, and if they did not start the new room, how was Ramona going to astound the first grade by telling them about the hole chopped in the house? She was impatient because she had nothing to do.

'Ramona, how many times do I have to tell you not to rub your nose against the window? You smudge the glass.' Mrs Quimby sounded as if she too looked forward to the beginning of school.

Ramona's answer was, 'Mother! Here comes Howie. With bricks!'

'Oh, dear,' said Mrs Quimby.

Ramona ran out to meet Howie, who was trudging down Klickitat Street pulling his little red wagon full of old bricks, the very best kind for playing Brick Factory, because they were old and broken with the corners crumbled away. 'Where did you get them?' asked Ramona, who knew how scarce old bricks were in their neighbourhood.

'At my other grandmother's,' said Howie. 'A bulldozer was smashing some old houses so somebody could build a shopping centre, and the man told me I could pick up broken bricks.'

'Let's get started,' said Ramona, running to the garage and returning with two big rocks she and Howie used in playing Brick Factory, a simple but satisfying game. Each grasped a rock in both hands and with it pounded a brick into pieces and the pieces into smithereens. The pounding was hard, tiring work. *Pow! Pow! Pow!* Then they reduced the smithereens to dust. *Crunch, crunch, crunch.* They were no longer six year olds. They were the strongest people in the world. They were giants.

When the driveway was thick with red dust, Ramona dragged out the hose and pretended that a terrible flood was washing away the Brick Factory in a stream of red mud. 'Run, Howie! Run before it gets you!' screamed Ramona. She was mighty Ramona, brave and strong. Howie's sneakers left red footprints, but he did not really run away. He only ran to the next driveway and back. Then the two began the game all over again. Howie's short blond hair turned rusty red. Ramona's brown hair only looked dingy.

Ramona, who was usually impatient with Howie because he always took his time and refused to get excited, found him an excellent Brick Factory player. He was strong, and his pounding was hard and steady. They met each day on the Quimbys' driveway to play their game. Their arms and shoulders ached. They had Band-Aids on their blisters, but they pounded on.

Mrs Quimby decided that when Ramona was playing Brick Factory she was staying out of trouble. However, she did ask several times why the game could not be played on Howie's driveway once in a while. Howie always explained that his mother had a headache or that his little sister Willa Jean was taking a nap.

'That is the dumbest game in the world,' said Beezus, who spent her time playing jacks with Mary Jane when she was not reading. 'Why do you call your game Brick Factory? You aren't making bricks. You're wrecking them.'

'We just do,' said Ramona, who left rusty footprints on the kitchen floor, rusty fingerprints on the doors, and rusty streaks in the bathtub. Picky-picky spent a lot of time washing brick dust off his paws. Mrs Quimby had to wash separate loads of Ramona's clothes in the washing machine to prevent them from staining the rest of the laundry.

'Let the kids have their fun,' said Mr Quimby, when he came home tired from work. 'At least, they're out in the sunshine.'

He was not so tired he could not run when Ramona chased him with her rusty hands. 'I'm going to get you, Daddy!' she shouted. 'I'm going to get you!' He could run fast for a man who was thirty-three years old, but Ramona always caught him and threw her arms around him. He was not a father to worry about a little brick dust on his clothes. The neighbours all said Ramona was her father's girl. There was no doubt about that.

'Oh, well, school will soon be starting,' said Mrs Quimby with a sigh.

And then one morning, before Ramona and Howie could remove their bricks from the garage, their game was ended by the arrival of two workmen in an old truck. The new room was actually going to be built! Summer was suddenly worthwhile. Brick Factory was forgotten as the two elderly workmen unloaded tools and marked foundation with string. *Chunk! Chunk!* Picks tore into the lawn while Mrs Quimby rushed out to pick the zinnias before the plants were yanked out of the ground.

'That's where my new room is going to be,' Ramona boasted to Howie.

'For six months, don't forget.' Beezus still felt

they should have drawn straws to see who would get it first.

Howie, who liked tools, spent all his time at the Quimbys' watching. A trench was dug for the foundation, forms were built, concrete mixed and poured. Howie knew the name of every tool and how it was used. Howie was a great one for thinking things over and figuring things out. The workmen even let him try their tools. Ramona was not interested in tools or in thinking things over and figuring things out. She was interested in results. Fast.

When the workmen had gone home for the day and no one was looking, Ramona, who had been told not to touch the wet concrete, marked it with her special initial, a Q with ears and whiskers: 🐱. She had invented her own Q in kindergarten after Miss Binney, the teacher, had told the class the letter Q had a tail. Why stop there? Ramona had thought. Now her 🐱 in the concrete would make the room hers, even when Beezus's turn to use it came.

Mrs Quimby watched advertisements in the newspaper and found a second-hand dresser and bookcase for Ramona and a desk for Beezus, which she stored in the garage where she worked with sandpaper and paint to make them look like new. Neighbours dropped by to see what was going

on. Howie's mother came with his messy little
sister Willa Jean, who was the sort of child known
as a toddler. Mrs Kemp and Mrs Quimby sat in
the kitchen drinking coffee and discussing their
children while Beezus and Ramona defended
their possessions from Willa Jean. This was what
grown-ups called playing with Willa Jean.

When the concrete was dry, the workmen
returned for the exciting part. They took crowbars
from their truck, and with a screeching of nails
being pulled from wood, they prised siding off
the house and knocked out the lath and plaster
at the back of the vacuum-cleaner closet. There
it was, a hole in the house! Ramona and Howie
ran in through the back door, down the hall, and
jumped out of the hole, round and round, until
the workmen said, 'Get lost, kids, before you get
hurt.'

Ramona felt light with joy. A real hole in the
house that was going to lead to her very-own-for-
six-months room! She could hardly wait to go to
school, because now, for the first time in her life,
she had something really important to share with
her class for Show and Tell! 'My room, *boom*! My
room, *boom*!' she sang.

'Be quiet, Ramona,' said Beezus. 'Can't you see
I'm trying to read?'

Before the workmen left for the day, they nailed

a sheet of plastic over the hole in the house. That night, after the sisters had gone to bed, Beezus whispered, 'It's sort of scary, having a hole in the house.' The edges of the plastic rustled and flapped in the night breeze.

'Really scary.' Ramona had been thinking the same thing. 'Spooky.' She planned to tell the first grade that she not only had a hole in her house, she had a spooky hole in her house.

'A ghost could ooze in between the nails,' whispered Beezus.

'A cold clammy ghost,' agreed Ramona with a delicious shiver.

'A cold clammy ghost that sobbed in the night,' elaborated Beezus, 'and had icy fingers that—'

Ramona burrowed deeper into her bed and pulled her pillow over her ears. In a moment she emerged. 'I know what would be better,' she said. 'A gorilla. A gorilla without bones that could ooze around the plastic—'

'Girls!' called Mrs Quimby from the living room. 'It's time to go to sleep.'

Ramona's whisper could barely be heard. '— and reached out with his cold, cold hands—'

'And grabbed us!' finished Beezus in her softest whisper. The sisters shivered with pleasure and were silent while Ramona's imagination continued. The boneless gorilla ghost could ooze under

the closet door . . . let's see . . . and he could swing
on the clothes rail . . . and in the morning when
they opened the closet door to get their school
clothes he would . . . Ramona fell asleep before
she could decide what the ghost would do.

4

THE FIRST DAY OF SCHOOL

When the first day of school finally arrived, Ramona made her own bed so her mother would be liberated. She hid the lumps under stuffed animals.

'That's cheating,' said Beezus, who was pulling up her own blankets smooth and tight.

'Pooh, who cares?' This morning Ramona did not care what her sister said. She was now in the first grade and eager to leave for school all by herself before old slowpoke Howie could catch up with her. She clattered down the hall in her stiff new sandals, grabbed her new blue lunch box from the kitchen counter, kissed her mother goodbye, and was on her way before her mother could tell her she must try to be a good girl now that she was in the first grade. She crunched through the fallen leaves on the sidewalk and held her head high. She wanted people to think, How grown up Ramona Quimby is. Last year she was a little kindergartener in the temporary building and look at her now, a big girl on her way to school in the big brick building.

289

A neighbour who had come out to move her lawn sprinkler actually did say, 'Hello, Ramona. My, aren't you a big girl!'

'Yes,' said Ramona, but she spoke modestly. She did not want people to think that being in the first grade had gone to her head. She was tempted to try going to school a new way, by another street, but decided she wasn't quite that brave yet.

How little the new members of the morning kindergarten looked! Some of them were clinging to their mother's hands. One was actually crying. Babies! Ramona called out to her old kindergarten teacher crossing the playground, 'Miss Binney! Miss Binney! It's me, Ramona!'

Miss Binney waved and smiled. 'Ramona Q.! How nice to see you!' Miss Binney understood that Ramona used her last initial because she wanted to be different, and when Miss Binney printed Ramona's name, she always added ears and whiskers to the Q. That was the kind of teacher Miss Binney was.

Ramona saw Beezus and Mary Jane. 'Hi, Beatrice,' she called, to let her sister know she would remember not to call her Beezus at school. 'How are you, Beatrice?'

Little Davy jumped at Ramona. 'Ho-*hah*!' he shouted.

Ramona knew first graders could not really use

karate. 'You mean, "Hah-*yah*!"' she said. Davy never got anything right.

Ramona felt much smaller and less sure of herself as she made her way up the steps of the big brick building with the older boys and girls. She felt smaller still as they jostled her in the hall on her way to the room she had looked forward to for so long. Room One, at the foot of the stairs that led to the classrooms of the upper grades, was the classroom for Ramona and the other morning kindergarteners of last year. Last year's afternoon kindergarten was entering the first grade in Room Two.

Many of Ramona's old kindergarten class, taller now and with more teeth missing, were already in their seats behind desks neatly labelled with their names. Like place cards at a party, thought Ramona. Eric J. and Eric R., little Davy with the legs of his new jeans turned up further than the legs of any other boy's jeans, Susan with her fat curls like springs touching her shoulders. *Boing*, thought Ramona as always, at the sight of those curls. This year she promised herself she would not pull those curls no matter how much they tempted her.

Mrs Griggs was seated at her desk. 'And what is your name?' she asked Ramona. Mrs Griggs, older than Miss Binney, looked pleasant enough, but of course she was not Miss Binney. Her hair, which was no special colour, was parted in the middle and held at the back of her neck with a plastic clasp.

'Ramona. Ramona Q.'

'Good morning, Ramona,' said Mrs Griggs. 'Take the fourth desk in the second row,' she said.

The desk, which had *Ramona*, taped to the front where Mrs Griggs could see it, turned out to be across the aisle from Susan. 'Hi, Ramona Kimona,' said Susan.

'Hi, Susan Snoozin',' answered Ramona, as she opened her desk and took out a pencil. She untaped her label, printed her special Q, with ears and whiskers on it, and retaped it. Next she explored her reader to see if she could find the grown-up words she knew: *petrol, motel, burger.* She could not.

The bell rang and after Mrs Griggs chose Joey to lead the flag salute, she made a little speech about how grown-up they were now that they were in the first grade and how the first grade was not a place to play like kindergarten. The class was here to work. They had much to learn, and she was here to help them. And now did anyone have anything to share with the class for Show and Tell?

Hands waved. Stevie showed the horse

chestnuts he had picked up on the way to school. The class was not impressed. Everyone who passed a horse-chestnut tree on the way to school picked up chestnuts, but no one ever found a use for them. Ramona waved her hand harder.

'Yes, Ramona. What do you have to share with the class?' asked Mrs Griggs. Then, seeing the initial on the label on Ramona's desk, she smiled and asked, 'Or should I call you Ramona Kitty Cat?'

Much to Ramona's annoyance, the class tittered at Mrs Griggs's joke. They knew she always added ears and whiskers to her Q's. There was no need to laugh at this grown-up question that she was not expected to answer. Mrs Griggs knew her name was not Ramona Kitty Cat.

'Meow,' said one of the boys. Room One giggled. Some meowed, others purred, until the cat noises dwindled under the disapproving look of the teacher.

Ramona faced the class, took a deep breath, and said, 'Some men came and chopped a great big hole in the back of our house!' She paused dramatically to give the class time to be surprised, astonished, perhaps a little envious of such excitement. Then she would tell them how spooky the hole was.

Instead, Room One, still in the mood for amusement, laughed. Everyone in the room except Howie laughed. Ramona was startled, then embarrassed. Once more she felt as if she were standing aside, seeing herself as someone else, a strange first grader at the front of the room, laughed at by her class. What was the matter with them? She could not see anything funny about herself. Her cheeks began to feel hot. 'They did,' Ramona insisted. 'They did too chop a hole in our house.' She turned to Mrs Griggs for help.

The teacher looked puzzled, as if she could not understand a hole chopped in a house. As if, perhaps, she did not believe a hole chopped in a house. Maybe that was why the class laughed. They thought she was making the whole thing up. 'Tell us about it, Ramona,' said Mrs Griggs.

'They did,' Ramona insisted. 'I'm not making it up.' At least Howie, sitting there looking so serious, was still her friend. 'Howie knows,' Ramona said. 'Howie came over to my house and jumped through the hole.'

The class found this very funny. Howie jumping out of a hole in Ramona's house. Ramona's ears began to burn. She turned to her friend for support. 'Howie, didn't they chop a hole in my house?'

'No,' said Howie.

Ramona was outraged. She could not believe her ears. 'They did, too!' she shouted. 'You were there. You saw them. You jumped through the hole like I said.'

'Ramona,' said Mrs Griggs, in a quiet voice that was neither cross nor angry, 'you may take your seat. We do not shout in the classroom in the first grade.'

Ramona obeyed. Tears of humiliation stung her eyes, but she was too proud to let them fall. Mrs Griggs wasn't even going to give her a chance to explain. And what was the matter with Howie? He knew she was telling the truth. I'll get you for this, Howie Kemp, Ramona thought bitterly, and after they had had such a good time playing Brick Factory, too. Ramona wanted to run home when recess came, but her house was locked, and her mother had gone off to work in that office near all those darling babies.

Ramona was unable to keep her mind on Jack and Becky, their dog Pal, and their cat Fluff in her stiff new reader. She could only sit and think, *I was telling the truth. I was telling the truth.*

At recess one of the Erics yelled at Ramona, 'Liar, liar, pants on fire, sitting on a telephone wire!'

Ramona pointed to Howie. 'He's the fibber!' she yelled.

Howie remained calm. 'No, I'm not.'

As usual, Howie's refusal to get excited

infuriated Ramona. She wanted him to get excited. She wanted him to yell back. 'You did too see the hole,' she shouted. 'You did too jump through it!'

'Sure I jumped through it, but nobody chopped a hole in your house,' Howie told Ramona.

'But they did!' cried Ramona, burning with fury. 'They did, and you know it! You're a fibber, Howie Kemp!'

'You're just making that up,' said Howie. 'Two men prised some siding off your house with crowbars. Nobody chopped a hole at all.'

Ramona was suddenly subdued. 'What's the difference?' she asked, even though she knew in her heart that Howie was right.

'Lots,' said Howie. 'You chop with an axe, not a crowbar.'

'Howie Kemp! You make me so mad!' shouted Ramona. 'You knew what I meant!' She wanted to hit. She wanted to kick, but she did not, because now she was in the first grade. Still, she had to punish Howie, so she said, 'I am never going to play Brick Factory with you again! So there!'

'OK,' said Howie. 'I guess I'll have to come and take back my bricks.'

Ramona was sorry she had spoken so hastily. She would miss Howie's bricks. She turned and kicked the side of the school. She had not fibbed. Not really. She had only meant to make the story exciting, and since tools did not interest her, she felt that a hole really had been chopped in her house. That was the trouble with Howie. If she offered him a glass of bug juice, he said, 'That's Kool-Aid.' If she said, 'It's been a million years since I had an ice lolly,' he said, 'You had an ice lolly last week. I saw you.'

Ramona began to feel heavy with guilt. Now the whole class and Mrs Griggs thought Ramona was a fibber. Here it was, the first half of the first morning of the first day of school, and already the first grade was spoiled for her. When the class returned to Room One, Ramona did not raise her hand the rest of the day, even though she ached to give answers. She wanted to go to Mrs Griggs and explain the whole thing, but Mrs Griggs seemed so busy she did not know how to approach her.

The class forgot the incident. By lunchtime no one called her a liar with pants on fire, but Ramona remembered and, as it turned out, so did Howie.

That afternoon Ramona had to go shopping with her mother. Ramona could see that having to make her own bed and maybe even bake her own cookies were not the only disadvantages of her mother's new job. Ramona was going to be dragged around on boring errands after school, because her mother could no longer do them in the

morning. When they returned and Mrs Quimby
was unloading groceries on the driveway, the first
thing that Ramona noticed was that Howie had
come and taken away all of his bricks. She looked
to see if he had left her one little piece of a brick,
but he had taken them all, even the smithereens.
And just when she most felt like some good hard
pounding, too.

5

OWL TROUBLE

One afternoon late in September, when the air was hazy with smoke from distant forest fires and the sun hung in the sky like an orange volleyball, Ramona was sharpening her pencil as an excuse to look out of the window at Miss Binney's afternoon kindergarten class, busy drawing butterflies with coloured chalk on the asphalt of the playground. This had been a disappointing day for Ramona, who had come to school eager to tell about her new room, which was almost completed. Mrs Griggs said they did not have time for Show and Tell that morning. Ramona had sat up as tall as she could, but Mrs Griggs chose Patty to lead the flag salute.

How happy the kindergarteners looked out in the smoky autumn sunshine! Ramona turned the handle of the pencil sharpener more and more slowly while she admired the butterflies with pink wings and yellow spots and butterflies with green wings and orange spots. She longed to be outside drawing with those bright chalks.

At the same time Ramona wondered what Beezus was doing upstairs in Mr Cardoza's room. Beezus was enjoying school. The boys, as Mrs Quimby had predicted, had forgotten the Beezus-Jesus episode. Every time Beezus opened her mouth at home it was Mr Cardoza this or Mr Cardoza that. Mr Cardoza let his class push their desks around any way they wanted. Mr Cardoza— guess what!—drove a red sports car. Mr Cardoza let his class bring mice to school. Mr Cardoza said funny things that made his class laugh. When his class grew too noisy, he said, 'All right, let's quiet down to a dull roar.' Mr Cardoza expected his class to have good manners . . .

Mrs Griggs's calm voice interrupted Ramona's thoughts. 'Ramona, remember your seat.'

Ramona, who discovered she had ground her pencil in half, remembered her seat. She sat quietly as Mrs Griggs pushed a lock of hair behind her ear and said, as she had said every day since first grade had started, 'We are not in kindergarten any longer. We are in the first grade, and people in the first grade must learn to be good workers.'

What Mrs Griggs did not seem to understand was that Ramona was a good worker. She had learned *bunny* and *apple* and *airplane* and all the other words in her new reader. When Mrs Griggs read out, 'Toys', Ramona could circle *toys* in her workbook. She was not like poor little Davy, who was still stuck on *saw* and *was*. If the book said *saw*, Davy read *was*. If the book said *dog*, Davy read *god*. Ramona felt so sorry for Davy that whenever she could she tried to help him circle the right pictures in his workbook. Mrs Griggs did not understand that Ramona wanted to help Davy. She always told Ramona to keep her eyes on her own work. 'Keep your eyes on your own work,' was a favourite saying of Mrs Griggs. Another was, 'Nobody likes a tattletale.' If Joey complained that Eric J. hit him, Mrs Griggs answered, 'Joey, nobody likes a tattletale.'

Now Mrs Griggs was saying, 'If Susan and Howie and Davy were eating apples and gave apples to Eric J. and Patty, how many people would have apples?' Ramona sat quietly while half the class waved their hands.

'Ramona,' said Mrs Griggs, in a voice that hinted she had caught Ramona napping.

'Five,' answered Ramona. She was bored, not napping. She had learned to think about school work, and at the same time think about other things in a private corner of her mind. 'Mrs Griggs, when do we get to make paper-bag owls?'

Susan spoke without raising her hand. 'Yes, Mrs Griggs. You said we would get to make wise old owls for Parents' Night.' Parents' Night was not the same as Open House. On Parents' Night the children stayed home while parents came to school to listen to teachers explain what the children were going to learn during the school year.

'Yes,' said Howie. 'We remembered to bring our paper bags from home.'

Mrs Griggs looked tired. She glanced at the clock.

'Whoo-whoo!' hooted Davy, which was brave of him and, as Ramona could not help thinking, rather kindergartenish. Others must not have agreed with this thought, for Mrs Griggs's room was filled with a hubbub of hoots.

Mrs Griggs tucked the wisp of hair behind her ear and gave up. 'All right, class. Since the afternoon is so warm, we will postpone our seat work and work on our owls.

Instantly Room One was wide awake. Paper bags and crayons came out of desks. The scissors monitor passed out scissors. The paper monitor passed out squares of orange, black, and yellow paper. Mrs Griggs got out the pastepots and paper bags for those who had forgotten to bring theirs from home. The class would make owls, print their names on them, and set them up on their desks for their parents to admire.

The minutes on the electric clock clicked by

with an astonishing speed. Mrs Griggs showed the class how to make orange triangles for beaks and big yellow circles with smaller black circles on top for eyes. She told Patty not to worry if her bag had *Frosty Ice Cream Bag* printed on one side. Just turn it over and use the other side. Most people tried to make their owls look straight ahead, but Eric R. made his owl cross-eyed. Ramona tried her eyes in several positions and finally decided to have them looking off to the right. Then she noticed Susan's owl was looking off to the right, too.

Ramona frowned and picked up her black crayon. Since the owl was supposed to look wise, she drew spectacles around his eyes, and out of the corner of her eye, she noticed Susan doing the same thing. Susan was copying Ramona's owl! 'Copycat!' whispered Ramona, but Susan ignored her by going over her crayon lines to make them blacker.

'Ramona, pay attention to your own work,' said Mrs Griggs. 'Howie, it is not necessary to pound your eyes down with your fist. The paste will make them stick.'

Ramona pulled her owl closer to her chest and tried to hide it in the circle of her arm, so that old copycat Susan could not see. With her brown crayon she drew wings and began to cover her owl with *V*s, which represented feathers.

By now Mrs Griggs was walking up and down between the desks admiring and commenting on the owls. Karen's owl was such a nice, neat owl. My, what big eyes Patty's owl had! George wasted paste. So had several others. 'Class, when we waste paste,' said Mrs Griggs, 'and then pound our eyes down with our fists, our eyes skid.' Ramona congratulated herself on her owl's non-skid eyes.

Mrs Griggs paused between Ramona's and Susan's desks. Ramona bent over her owl, because she wanted to surprise Mrs Griggs when it was finished. 'What a wise old owl Susan has made!' Mrs Griggs held up Susan's owl for the class to see while Susan tried to look modest and pleased at the same time. Ramona was furious. Susan's owl had wings and feathers exactly like her owl. Susan had peeked! Susan had copied! She scowled at Susan and thought, Copycat, copycat! She longed to tell Mrs Griggs that Susan had copied, but she knew what the answer would be. 'Ramona, nobody likes a tattletale.'

Mrs Griggs continued to admire Susan's owl. 'Susan, your owl is looking at something. What do you think he's looking at?'

'Um-m.' Susan was taken by surprise. 'Um-m. Another owl?'

How dumb, thought Ramona. He's looking at

a bat, a mouse, a witch riding on a broomstick, Superman, anything but another owl.

Mrs Griggs suspended Susan's owl with two paper clips to the wire across the top of the blackboard for all to admire. 'Class, it is time to clean up our desks. Scissors monitor, collect the scissors,' said Mrs Griggs. 'Leave your owls on your desks for me to hang up after the paste dries.'

Ramona stuffed her crayons into the box so hard that she broke several, but she did not care. She refused to look at Susan. She looked at her own owl, which no longer seemed like her own. Suddenly she hated it. Now everyone would think Ramona had copied Susan's owl, when it was the other way around. They would call her Ramona Copycat instead of Ramona Kitty Cat. With both hands she crushed her owl, her beautiful wise owl, into a wad and squashed it down as hard as she could. Then, with her head held high, she marched to the front of the room and flung it into the wastebasket. As the bell rang, she marched out of the room without looking back.

All that week Ramona stared at the owls above the blackboard. Cross-eyed owls, paste-waster's owls with eyes that had skidded off in all directions, one-eyed owls made by those so anxious not to waste paste that they had not used enough, and right in the centre Susan's wise and handsome owl copied from Ramona's owl.

If Mrs Griggs noticed that Ramona's owl was missing, she said nothing. The afternoon of Parents' Night she unclipped the owls from the wire and passed them out to their owners along with sheets of old newspaper for wadding up and stuffing inside the owls to make them stand up. Miserable because she had no owl to stand upon her desk, Ramona pretended to be busy making her desk tidy.

'Ramona, what happened to your owl?' asked Susan, who knew very well what had happened to Ramona's owl.

'You shut up,' said Ramona.

'Mrs Griggs, Ramona doesn't have an owl,' said Howie, who was the kind of boy who always looked around the classroom to make sure everything was in order.

Ramona scowled.

'Why, Ramona,' said Mrs Griggs. 'What happened to your owl?'

Ramona spoke with all the dignity she could muster. 'I do not care for owls.' She did care. She cared so much it hurt, but Mrs Griggs was not going to call her a tattletale.

Mrs Griggs looked at Ramona as if she were trying to understand something. All she said was, 'All right, Ramona, if that's the way you feel.'

That was not the way Ramona felt, but she was relieved to have Mrs Griggs's permission to remain owlless on Parents' Night. She felt unhappy and confused. Which was worse, a copycat or a tattletale? Ramona thought a copycat was worse. She half-heartedly joined the class in cleaning up the room for their parents, and every time she passed Susan's desk, she grew more angry. Susan was a copycat and a cheater. Ramona longed to seize one of those curls, stretch it out as far as she could, and then let it go. *Boing*, she thought, but she kept her hands to herself, which was not easy even though she was in the first grade.

Susan sat her owl up on her desk and gave it a little pat. Fury made Ramona's chest feel tight. Susan was pretending not to notice Ramona.

At last the room was in order for Parents' Night. Twenty-five owls stood up straight looking in all directions. The bell rang. Mrs Griggs took her place by the door as the class began to leave the room.

Ramona slid out of her seat. Her chest felt tighter. Her head told her to keep her hands to herself, but her hands did not obey. They seized Susan's owl. They crushed the owl with a sound of crackling paper.

Susan gasped. Ramona twisted the owl as hard as she could until it looked like nothing but an old paper bag scribbled with crayon. Without meaning to, Ramona had done a terrible thing.

'Mrs Griggs!' cried Susan. 'Ramona scrunched my owl!'

'Tattletale.' Ramona threw the twisted bag on the floor, and as Mrs Griggs approached to see what had happened, she dodged past her teacher, out of the door and down the hall, running as fast as she could, even though running in the halls was forbidden. She wove through the upper classes, who had come down the stairs. She ploughed through the other first grade coming out of Room Two. She jumped down the steps and was out of the building on her way home, running as hard as she could, her sandals pounding on the sidewalk and crackling through fallen leaves. She ran as if she were pursued by Susan, Mrs Griggs, the principal, all of Room One, the whole school. She ran from her conscience and from God, who, as they said in Sunday School, was everywhere. She ran as if Something was coming to get her. She ran until her lungs felt as if they were bursting with the smoky air. She ran until her sandals slipped on dry leaves and she fell sprawling on the sidewalk. Ignoring the pain, she scrambled to her feet and fled home with blood trickling from her knees.

Ramona burst through the back door, safe from Something. 'Mama! Mama! I fell down!' she managed between gasps.

'Oh, poor baby!' Mrs Quimby took one look at Ramona's bloody legs and led her into the bathroom, where she knelt and cleaned the wounds, dabbed them with antiseptic, and covered them with Band-Aids. Her mother's sympathy made Ramona feel very sorry for herself. Poor little misunderstood first grader.

Mrs Quimby wiped Ramona's sweaty tear-stained face with a damp washcloth, kissed Ramona for comfort, and said, 'That's my brave girl.'

Ramona wanted to say, But I'm not brave, Mama. I'm scared because I did something bad. Yet she could not bring herself to admit the truth. Poor little Ramona with her wounded knees. It was all mean old Susan's fault for being such a copycat.

Mrs Quimby sat back on her heels. 'Guess what?' she said.

'What?' Ramona hoped for a glorious surprise to make up for her unhappy day. Ramona always longed for glorious surprises. That was the way she was.

'The workmen finished the new room, and before they left they moved your bed and the dresser and bookcase we had stored in the garage, and tonight you are going to sleep in your very own room!'

'*Really?*' This actually was a glorious surprise. There had been days when the workmen had not come at all, and the whole Quimby family had despaired of the room ever being completed. Ramona's knees hurt, but who cared? She ran down the hall to see the room for herself.

Yes, there was her bed in one corner, the bookcase filled with more toys than books in another, and against the wall, the dresser.

For the first time Ramona looked into her very own mirror in her very own room. She saw a stranger, a girl with red eyes and a puffy, tear-stained face, who did not look at all the way Ramona pictured herself. Ramona thought of herself as the kind of girl everyone should like, but this girl . . .

Ramona scowled, and the girl scowled back. Ramona managed a small smile. So did the girl. Ramona felt better. She wanted the girl in the mirror to like her.

6

PaReNTs' NiGHT

Ramona stood inside her new closet, pretending she was in an elevator. She slid open the door and stepped into her new room, which she pretended was on the tenth floor. There she drew a deep breath, inhaling the fragrance of new wood and the flat smell of sheet rock, which her father was going to paint when he found time. Her mother had been too busy to find curtains for the windows or to clean the smudges of putty from the glass, but Ramona did not mind. Tonight she was going to sleep for the first time in her very-own-for-six-months room, the only room in the house with a sliding closet door and windows that opened out instead of up and down.

'Ramona, Howie's grandmother is here,' called Mrs Quimby. 'We re going now.'

Ramona stepped back into her closet, slid the door shut, pressed an imaginary button, and when her imaginary elevator had made its imaginary descent, stepped out onto the real first floor and faced a real problem. Her mother and father were leaving for Parents' Night.

After Ramona said hello to Howie's grandmother ('Say hello to Howie's grandmother, Ramona'), she flopped down in a chair and peeled off one end of a Band-Aid to examine her sore knee. She was disappointed when Howie's grandmother did not notice. 'I don't see why you have to go to Parents' Night,' Ramona said to her mother and father. 'It's probably boring.'

'We want to hear what Mrs Griggs has to say,' said Mrs Quimby.

This was what worried Ramona.

'And I want to meet the famous Mr Cardoza,' said Mr Quimby. 'We've been hearing so much about him.'

'Daddy, you're really going to like him,' said Beezus. 'Do you know what he said when I got five wrong on my maths test? He said, "Good. Now I can see what it is you don't understand." And then he said he was there to help me understand, and he did!'

'We're going over to Howie's house after Parents' Night,' said Mrs Quimby, 'but we won't be late.'

Beezus made a face and said to Ramona, 'That means they'll talk about their children. They always do.' Ramona knew her sister spoke the truth.

Mr Quimby smiled as he went out of the door. 'Don't worry. We won't reveal the family secrets.'

Beezus went off to her room, eager to do her homework on the new-to-her desk. Ramona pulled off the other Band-Aid and examined her other knee. She wondered if what Mrs Griggs was sure to say about Susan's owl would be considered a family secret. She poked her sore knee and said, 'Ouch!' so Howie's grandmother could not help hearing. When Mrs Kemp failed to ask, Why, Ramona, how did you hurt your knee?, Ramona stuck the Band-Aid back in place and studied her sitter.

Mrs Kemp, who wore glasses with purple frames, was not the sort of sitter who played games with children. When she came to sit, she sat. She was sitting on the couch knitting something out of green wool while she looked at an old movie on television, some boring thing about grown-ups who talked a lot and didn't do much of anything. Ramona liked good lively comedies with lots of children and animals and grown-ups doing silly things. Next to that she liked cat-food commercials.

Ramona picked up the evening paper from the floor beside her chair. 'Well, I guess I'll read the paper,' she said, showing off for Howie's grandmother. She studied the headlines, making a sort of mental buzz when she came to words she could not read. Z-z-z-z to run for z-z-z-z, she read. Z-z-z-z of z-z-z-z-ing to go up. She turned a page. Z-z-z-z to play z-z-z-z at z-z-z-z. Play what, she wondered, and with a little feeling of triumph discovered that the Z-z-z-z-s were going to play z-z-z-z-ball.

'And what is the news tonight?' asked Mrs Kemp, her eyes on the television set.

Attention at last. 'Somebody is going to play some kind of ball,' answered Ramona, proud to have actually read something in the newspaper. She hoped Mrs Kemp would say, Why, Ramona, I had no idea you were such a good reader.

'Oh, I see,' said Mrs Kemp, a remark Ramona knew grown-ups made when they were not interested in conversation with children.

Ramona tried again. 'I know how to set the table,' she boasted.

Instead of saying, You must be a big help to your mother, Mrs Kemp only murmured, 'Mm-hm' with her eyes on the television set.

Ramona said, 'I have a room of my own, and tonight I'm going to sleep in it all by myself.'

'That's nice,' said Mrs Kemp absently.

Ramona gave up. Mrs Kemp did not know the right answers. The clock said seven thirty. Even though Ramona had fought long and hard for the right to stay up until eight fifteen and was now working on eight thirty, she decided that since her parents were not there, she would not lose ground in her battle for a later bedtime by going to bed early to try out her new room. She said goodnight and took her bath without using her washcloth, so she would not have to waste time wringing it out and hanging it up. Then she got into bed, turned out her light, said her prayers asking God to bless her family including Picky-picky, and there she lay, a big girl, alone in her bed in a room of her own.

Unfortunately, in spite of pretending bedtime had come, Ramona was wide awake with nothing to do but think. She lay there wondering what was happening at school. Guilt over Susan's owl grew heavy within her. What would happen when her mother and father heard the whole terrible story? They would be disappointed in Ramona, that's what they'd be, and nothing made Ramona feel worse than knowing that her parents were disappointed in her.

In spite of Howie's grandmother knitting on the couch, the house seemed empty. Ramona thought about how bad she was. She thought about the gorilla in the book in her bookcase and wished she had not. The sound of gunfire and a woman's scream came from the television set. Nothing to be scared about, Ramona told herself, just the TV. She wished her window had curtains.

Although Ramona dreaded knowing what Mrs Griggs would say, she felt she had to know. As Beezus had predicted, her parents were sure to talk on and on with Howie's parents about their children. Mrs Kemp would say Howie needed to learn to be creative, and Ramona's mother would say Ramona needed to learn to be responsible like Beezus. There was no telling what the fathers would say, although fathers, Ramona knew, did not spend as much time as mothers thinking up ways to improve their children.

Ramona decided to act. She got out of bed and pattered down the hall in her bare feet.

Howie's grandmother looked up from her knitting. 'It's past your bedtime, Ramona,' she said.

So time had passed after all. 'I know,' said Ramona and could not resist boasting a little. 'I have to leave a note for my mother.' On the note pad by the telephone she carefully printed:

Come here Moth
er. Come here
to me.

No need to sign the note. Her mother would know who it was from, because Beezus wrote joined-up. Ramona left her note on the table beside the front door, where the family always looked for mail and messages. She sidled closer to Howie's grandmother, pretending interest in her knitting, which appeared to be a small sweater of strange shape.

'Is that for a doll?' asked Ramona.

Mrs Kemp's eyes were on the television screen, where two boring grown-ups were saying goodbye for ever to one another. 'It's a sweater for my little dachshund,' she answered. 'When I finish I'm going to make a little beret to match. Now run along to bed.'

For a moment Ramona had enjoyed relief from her troubles. Reluctantly she returned to bed. She heard Beezus take her bath, get into bed, and turn out her light without being told. That was the kind of girl Beezus was. Beezus would never get herself into the sort of mess Ramona faced. Ramona's conscience hurt, and a hurting conscience was the worst feeling in the world. Ramona thought of the ghost and the boneless gorilla that she and Beezus had scared themselves with the night of the hole in the house, but she quickly squashed the thoughts by thinking how surprised her mother would be when she discovered what a grown-up note Ramona had written. Ramona must have fallen asleep, because the next thing she knew, her mother was whispering, 'Ramona?'

'I'm awake, Mama. Did you get my note?'

'Yes, Ramona. I had no idea you were old enough to leave a note.' Mrs Quimby's words gave Ramona a good feeling. Her mother knew the right answers to questions.

Beezus called out from her room. 'What did you talk about at the Kemps'?'

'Your mother's new job,' answered Mr Quimby.

'Oh,' said Beezus. 'What else?'

'The high cost of living. Football. Things like that,' said Mr Quimby. 'No family secrets.'

Mrs Quimby bumped against Ramona's bed in the dark.

'Mama?'

'Yes, Ramona.'

'What did Mrs Griggs say about me?'

Mrs Quimby's answer was honest and direct. 'She said you refused to make an owl like the rest of the class and that for no reason you crumpled up the owl Susan worked so hard to make.'

Beezus was standing in the hall. 'Oh, owls,' she said, remembering. 'Next you make Thanksgiving things.'

Tears filled Ramona's eyes. Mrs Griggs was so unfair. Turkeys came next, and trouble would start all over again.

'I was sorry to hear it, Ramona,' said Mrs Quimby. 'What on earth got into you?'

Ramona's stiff lips quivered. 'She's wrong, Mama,' she managed to get out. 'Mama, she's wrong.' Ramona struggled for control. Now Mr Quimby and Beezus were listening shadows in the doorway. 'Mama, I did make an owl. A good owl.' Ramona drew a long shuddering breath and described what had happened: how Mrs Griggs had praised Susan's owl and said she hadn't wasted paste, and how she had thrown away her own owl because she did not want people to think she had copied from Susan. 'And so I scrunched her owl,' she concluded, relieved to have told the whole story.

'But what difference did it make?' asked Mrs Quimby. 'The class was making owls for fun. It wasn't the same as copying arithmetic or spelling papers.'

'But it does make a difference.' Beezus spoke with the wisdom of a higher grade. 'It makes a lot of difference.'

Ramona was grateful for this support. 'I wanted my owl to be my very own.'

'Of course, you did,' said Mr Quimby, who had once drawn cartoons for his high school paper. 'Every artist wants his work to be his very own, but that does not excuse you from trying to destroy Susan's owl.'

Ramona let out a long shuddering sigh. 'I just got mad. Old copycat Susan thought she was so big.'

Mrs Quimby smoothed Ramona's blankets. 'Susan is the one I feel sorry for. You are the lucky one. You can think up your own ideas because you have imagination.'

Ramona was silent while she thought this over. 'But that doesn't help now,' she said at last.

'Someday it will.' Mrs Quimby rose from the bed. 'And Ramona, Mrs Griggs expects you to apologize to Susan for destroying her owl.'

'Mama!' cried Ramona. 'Do I *have* to?'

'Yes, Ramona, you do.' Mrs Quimby leaned over and kissed Ramona goodnight.

'But, Mama, it isn't fair! Susan is a copycat and a tattletale.'

Mrs Quimby sighed again. 'Maybe so, but that does not give you the right to destroy her property.'

Mr Quimby kissed Ramona goodnight. 'Chin up, old girl,' he said. 'It will all come out in the wash.'

As her family left her room, Ramona heard Beezus say, 'Mrs Griggs always was big on apologies.'

Ramona lay in bed with her thoughts as jumbled as a bag of jacks. Susan's property was just an old paper bag, and who cared about an old paper bag.

Susan cared, that's who cared. Ramona could not escape the truth. Why was everything so mixed up? When school had started, Ramona was friends with Susan, and now look at what happened. Ramona had spoiled everything. Ramona always spoiled everything. Ramona, finding gloomy comfort in thinking how bad she was, fell asleep.

The next morning as Ramona left for school, she asked her mother what she could say to Susan.

'Just say "I'm sorry I spoiled your owl,"' said Mrs Quimby. 'And Ramona—try to stay out of mix-ups after this.'

The wind had changed in the night, some rain had fallen, and the air was clean and cool. Ramona's feet felt heavy as she walked through soggy leaves. How could she stay out of mix-ups when she never knew what would suddenly turn into a mix-up? She plodded on, as if she were wading through glue, and when she reached the schoolyard, she stood quietly watching Miss Binney's carefree kindergarteners chase one another. How young and light-hearted she had been a year ago! Miss Binney waved, and Ramona waved back without smiling.

When the bell rang, Ramona walked in dread to Room One, where she took her seat without looking at Susan. Perhaps Mrs Griggs was so busy with her plans for seatwork that she would forget about the owl.

Ramona should have known better. Quite unexpectedly, in the midst of Show and Tell, Mrs Griggs said, 'Ramona has something to say to us.'

Ramona was startled. 'But I didn't bring anything to show today,' she said.

'You have something to say to Susan,' Mrs Griggs reminded her. 'Come to the front of the room.'

Ramona was horrified. Now? In front of the whole class? Room One turned and looked at Ramona.

'We're waiting,' said Mrs Griggs.

Ramona felt as if she were walking on someone else's feet. They carried her to the front of the room, even though she did not want them to. There she stood thinking, I won't! I won't! while trapped by twenty-five pairs of eyes. Twenty-six, counting Mrs Griggs. Her cheeks were hot. Her eyes were too dry for tears, and her mouth too dry for words. The silence was terrible. The click of the electric clock finishing off a minute. Ramona looked desperately at Mrs Griggs, who smiled an encouraging but unyielding smile. There was no way out.

Ramona looked at the toes of her sandals, noticed that the new had worn off, and after swallowing managed to speak in a small, unhappy voice. 'I'm sorry I scrunched Susan's owl.'

'Thank you, Ramona,' said Mrs Griggs gently.

Ramona returned to her seat. The look on Susan's face was too much to bear. Old goody-goody Susan. Ramona glared and added to her apology in a furious whisper, 'Even if you are a copycat who—*stinks*!'

Mrs Griggs did not notice because she was saying, 'Class, open your arithmetic workbooks to page ten. Who can tell me how many mittens are in the picture at the top of the page?'

The room hummed with whispers as mittens were counted. Susan's cheeks were red beneath her *boing-boing* curls. She was not counting mittens.

Ramona was fiercely glad she had upset Susan so much she was unable to count mittens.

'Seven mittens.' Several people spoke at the same time.

'Seven is correct,' said Mrs Griggs. 'But let's remember to raise our hands. Now pretend three mittens are lost. How many are left?'

Ramona was not counting mittens either. She looked at Mrs Griggs, standing there in her pale green sweater with a wisp of hair hanging in front of each ear. She was always so calm. Ramona liked people who got excited. She would rather have a teacher angry with her than one who stood there being calm.

Mrs Griggs, finished with mittens, had the class counting balloons. Unexcited Mrs Griggs. Mrs Griggs who did not understand. Mrs Griggs who went on and on about counting and adding and taking away, and on and on about Tom and Becky and their dog Pal and their cat Fluff, who could run, run, run and come, come, come. Mrs Griggs, always calm, never raising her voice, everything neat, everything orderly with no paste wasted.

Ramona wished she could run, run, run out of that classroom as she had the day before and never come back.

7

ALONE iN THE DARK

Ramona did not run away. Where could she run to? She had no place to go. Each of her days seemed to plod along more slowly than the day before. Every morning Mrs Quimby looked out of the window at the rain dripping from the trees and said, 'Rain, rain, go away. Come again some other day.' The weather paid no attention. Ramona, who could not wear sandals in such weather, now had to wear oxfords and a pair of Beezus's old boots to school, because she had outgrown her red boots during the summer. Mrs Griggs wore the same sweater, the colour of split-pea soup, day after day. Ramona did not like split-pea soup. Ramona never got to lead the flag salute or be scissors monitor. Number combinations. Reading circles. Bologna sandwiches and chocolate-chip cookies from the store in her lunch three times in one week.

One day the reading workbook showed a picture of a chair with a wrinkled slipcover. Beneath the picture were two sentences. 'This is for Pal.' 'This is not for Pal.' Ramona circled 'This is for Pal', because she decided Tom and Becky's mother had put a slipcover on the chair so that Pal could lie on it without getting the chair dirty. Mrs Griggs came along and put a big red check mark over her answer. 'Read every word, Ramona,' she said, which Ramona thought was unfair. She *had* read every word.

Ramona dreaded school because she felt Mrs Griggs did not like her, and she did not enjoy spending the whole day in a room with someone who did not like her, especially when that person was in charge.

Ramona's days were bad, but her nights were worse. At eight o'clock she sat very, very still on a chair in the corner of the living room with an open book, one that Beezus had read, on her lap. If she did not move, if she did not make a sound, her mother might forget to tell her to go to bed, and more than anything in the world Ramona did not want to go to bed. She pretended to read, she even tried to read, but she could not understand the story, because she had to skip some of the most important words. She was bored and uncomfortable from sitting so still, but anything was better than going off alone to her new room. The nights her father went bowling were worst of all, and this was one of those nights.

'Isn't it time for Ramona to go to bed?' asked Beezus.

Ramona would not allow herself to say, Shut-up, Beezus, because doing so would call attention to herself. She lifted her eyes to the clock on the mantel. Eight sixteen. Eight seventeen.

Beezus, always her mother's girl, went into the kitchen to help prepare lunches for the next day. Ramona wanted something besides a bologna sandwich in her lunch, but she knew that if she spoke, she risked being sent to bed. Eight eighteen.

'Ramona, it's past your bedtime,' Mrs Quimby called from the kitchen. Ramona did not budge. Eight nineteen. 'Ramona!'

'As soon as I finish this chapter.'

'Now!'

What worked for Beezus would not work for Ramona. She closed her book and walked down the hall to the bathroom, where she drew her bath, undressed, and climbed into the tub. There she sat until Mrs Quimby called out, 'Ramona! No dawdling!'

Ramona got out, dried herself, and put on her pyjamas. She remembered to dip her washcloth in the bathwater and wring it out before she let the water out of the tub. She brushed and brushed her teeth until her mother called through the door, 'That's enough, Ramona!'

Ramona ran back to the living room and seized the unsuspecting Picky-picky asleep on Mr Quimby's chair. 'Picky-picky wants to sleep with me,' she said, lugging the cat in the direction of her room. Picky-picky did not agree. He struggled out of her arms and ran back to the chair, where he began to wash away the taint of Ramona's hands. Mean old Picky-picky. Ramona longed for a soft, comfortable, purring cat that would snuggle against her and make her feel safe. She wished Picky-picky would behave more like Fluff in her reader. Fluff was always willing to chase a ball of yarn or ride in a doll carriage.

'What time will Daddy be home?' asked Ramona.

'Around eleven,' answered her mother. 'Now scoot.'

Hours and hours away. Ramona walked slowly down the hall and into her room, which smelled of fresh paint. She closed her new curtains, shutting out the dark eye of the night. She looked inside her closet to make sure Something was not hiding in the shadows before she slid the doors shut tight. She pushed her bed out from the wall so that Something reaching out from under the curtains or slithering around the wall might not find her. She picked up Pandy, her battered old panda bear, and tucked it into bed with its head on her pillow. Then she climbed into bed beside Pandy and pulled the blankets up under her chin.

In a moment Mrs Quimby came to say good-night. 'Why do you always push your bed out from the wall?' she asked and pushed it back.

'What do we do tomorrow?' asked Ramona, ashamed to admit she was afraid of the dark, ashamed to let her mother know she was no longer her brave girl, ashamed to confess she was afraid to sleep alone in the room she had wanted so much. If she told her mother how she felt, she would probably be given the old room, which would be the same as saying she was failing at the job of growing up.

'We are doing the usual,' answered Mrs Quimby. 'School for you and Beezus, work for Daddy and me.'

Ramona hoped to hold her mother a little longer. 'Mama, why doesn't Picky-picky like me?'

'Because he has grown grouchy in his old age and because you were rough with him when you were little. Now go to sleep.' Mrs Quimby kissed Ramona and snapped off the light.

'Mama?'

'Yes, Ramona?'

'I—I forgot what I was going to say.'

'Goodnight, dear.'

'Mama, kiss Pandy too.'

Mrs Quimby did as she was told. 'Now that's enough stalling.'

Ramona was left alone in the dark. She said her prayers and then repeated them in case God was not listening the first time.

I will think good things, Ramona told herself, and in spite of her troubles she had good things to think about. After Ramona had to apologize to Susan, some members of Room One were especially nice to her because they felt Mrs Griggs should not have made her apologize in front of the class. Howie had brought some of his bricks back, so they could play Brick Factory if it ever stopped raining. Linda, whose mother baked fancier cookies than any other Room One mother, shared butterscotch-fudge-nut cookies with Ramona. Even little Davy, who usually tried to avoid Ramona because she had tried to kiss him in kindergarten, tagged her when the class played games. Best of all, Ramona was actually learning to read. Words leaped out at her from the newspaper, signs, and cartons. *Crash, highway, salt, tyres*. The world was suddenly full of words that Ramona could read.

Ramona had run out of good thoughts. She heard Beezus take her bath, get into bed, and turn out her light. She heard her mother set the table for breakfast, shut Picky-picky in the basement, and go to bed. If only her father would come home.

Ramona knew she could get away with going to the bathroom at least once. She stood up on her bed, and even though she knew it was not a safe thing to do, she leaped into the centre of her room and ran into the hall before Something hiding under the bed could reach out and grab her ankles. On her way back she reversed her flying leap and landed on her bed, where she quickly pulled her covers up to her chin.

The moment Ramona dreaded had come. There was no one awake to protect her. Ramona tried to lie as flat and as still as a paper doll so that Something slithering under the curtains and slinking around the walls would not know she was there. She kept her eyes wide open. She longed for her father to come home; she was determined to stay awake until morning.

Ramona thought of Beezus safely asleep in the friendly dark of the room they had once shared. She thought of the way they used to whisper and giggle and sometimes scare themselves. Even their quarrels were better than being alone in the dark. She ached to move, to ease her muscles rigid from lying still so long, but she dared not. She thought of the black gorilla with fierce little eyes in the book in her bookcase and tried to shove the thought out of her mind. She listened for cars on the wet street and strained her ears for the sound of a familiar motor. After what seemed like hours and hours, Ramona caught the sound of the Quimby car turning into the driveway. She went limp with relief. She heard her father unlock the back door and enter. She heard him pause by the thermostat to turn off the furnace. She heard him turn off the living room light and tiptoe down the hall.

'Daddy!' whispered Ramona.

Her father stopped by her door. 'You're supposed to be asleep.'

'Come here for just a minute.' Mr Quimby stepped into Ramona's room. 'Daddy, turn on the light a minute. Please.'

'It's late.' Mr Quimby did as he was told.

The light, which made Ramona squint, was a relief. She held up her hand to shield her eyes. She was so glad to see her father standing there in his bowling clothes. He looked so good and so familiar and made her feel so safe. 'Daddy, see that big book in my bookcase?'

'Yes.'

'Take it out of my room,' said Ramona. To herself, she thought, Please, Daddy, don't ask me why. She added, to protect herself from any questions, 'It's a good book. I think you might like it.'

Mr Quimby pulled the book from the bookcase, glanced at it, and then bent over and kissed Ramona on the forehead. 'No more stalling, young lady,' he said. 'You were supposed to be asleep hours ago.' He turned out the light and left, taking *Wild Animals of Africa* with him and leaving Ramona alone in the dark to worry about the mysterious noises made by an old house cooling off for the night. She wondered how much of the six months was left before she could return to her old room. She lay as flat and as still as a paper doll while she listened to her father splashing in the shower. Ramona had to think about her eyelids to force them to stay open. Her father got into bed. Her parents were whispering, probably talking about her, saying, What are we going to do about Ramona, always getting into trouble! Even her teacher doesn't like her. Everyone was asleep but Ramona, whose eyelids grew heavier and heavier. She was afraid of the dark, but she would not give up the new room. Only babies were afraid to sleep alone.

The next morning, as Ramona took her sandwiches out of the refrigerator and put them in her lunch box, Mrs Quimby asked, 'Does your throat feel all right?'

'Yes,' answered Ramona crossly.

'Sore throats are going around,' said Mrs Quimby. Since she had gone to work in the paediatrician's office, she looked for symptoms in her daughters. Last week it had been chicken-pox spots, and the week before swollen glands.

'Mama, I had a bad dream last night.'

'What did you dream?'

'Something was chasing me, and I couldn't run.' The dream was still vivid in Ramona's mind. She had been standing at the corner of the house where the zinnias used to be. She knew something terrible was about to come around the corner of the house to get her. She stood as if frozen, unable to lift her feet from the grass. She had been terrified in her dream and yet the yard had looked clear and bright. The grass was green, the zinnias blooming in shades of pink and orange and scarlet, so real Ramona felt she could have touched them.

Beezus was rinsing her cereal bowl under the kitchen tap. 'Ugh, that old dream,' she remarked. 'I've had it several times, and it's awful.'

'You did not!' Ramona was indignant. Her dream was her own, not something passed down from Beezus like an old dress or old rain boots. 'You're just saying that.'

'I did too have it.' Beezus shrugged off the

dream as of little importance. 'Everybody has that dream.'

'Ramona, are you sure you feel all right?' asked Mrs Quimby. 'You seem a little cranky this morning.'

Ramona scowled. 'I am *not* cranky.'

'Another dream I don't like,' said Beezus, 'is the one where I'm standing in my underwear in the hall at school and everybody is staring at me. That is just about the worst dream there is.'

This, too, was a familiar dream to Ramona, not that she was going to admit it. Beezus needn't think she dreamed all the dreams first.

Mrs Quimby looked at Ramona scowling by the refrigerator with her lunch box in her hand. She laid her hand on Ramona's head to see if she was feverish.

Ramona jerked away. 'I'm not sick, and I'm not cranky,' she told her mother and flounced out of the door on her way to another day in Room One.

When Ramona reached Glenwood School, she trudged into the building where she sat huddled at the foot of the staircase that led to the upper grades. She wondered what it would be like to spend her days in one of the upstairs classrooms. Anything would be better than the first grade. What if I don't go into Room One? she thought.

What if I hide in the girls' bathroom until school is out? Before she found the answer to her question, Mr Cardoza came striding down the hall on his way to the stairs. He stopped directly in front of Ramona.

Mr Cardoza was a tall thin man with dark hair and eyes, and he made Ramona, sitting there on the bottom steps, feel very small. Mr Cardoza frowned and pulled down the corners of his mouth in a way that made Ramona understand that he was poking fun at the expression on her face. Suddenly he smiled and pointed at her as if he had made an exciting discovery.

Startled, Ramona drew back.

'I know who you are!' Mr Cardoza spoke as if identifying Ramona was the most interesting thing that could happen.

'You do?' Ramona forgot to scowl.

'You are Ramona Quimby. Also known as Ramona Q.'

Ramona was astonished. She had expected him to tell her, if he knew who she was at all, that she was Beatrice's little sister. 'How do you know?' she asked.

'Oh, I get around,' he said and, whistling softly through his teeth, started up the stairs.

Ramona watched him take the steps two at a time with his long legs and suddenly felt more cheerful, cheerful enough to face Room One once more. A teacher from the upper grades knew the name of a little first grader. Maybe someday Mr Cardoza would be her teacher too.

8

RaMONa SaYs a BaD WoRD

The more Ramona dreaded school, the more enthusiastic Beezus became, or so it seemed to Ramona. Mr Cardoza had his class illustrate their spelling papers, and guess what! It was easy. Beezus, who always had trouble drawing because she felt she had no imagination, had no trouble drawing pictures of *ghost* and *laundry*.

One day Beezus came home waving a paper and looking especially happy. For language arts Mr Cardoza had asked his class to list five examples of several different words. For *pleasant* Beezus had listed *picnics*, our *classroom*, *Mr Cardoza*, *reading*, and *school*. When Mr Cardoza had corrected her paper, he had written 'Thanks' beside his name. For a joke she had also included his name as an example under *frightening*, and his red-pencilled comment was 'Well!' Beezus received an *A* on her paper. Nothing that pleasant ever happened to Ramona, who spent her days circling sentences in workbooks, changing first letters of words to make different words, and trying to help Davy when she could, even though he was in a different reading circle.

Then one afternoon Mrs Griggs handed each member of Room One a long sealed envelope. 'These are your progress reports for you to take home to your parents,' she said.

Ramona made up her mind then and there that she was not going to show any progress report to her mother and father if she could get out of it. As soon as she reached home, she hid her envelope at the bottom of a drawer under her summer playclothes. Then she got out paper and crayons and went to work on the kitchen table. On each sheet of paper she drew in black crayon a careful outline of an animal: a mouse on one sheet, a bear on another, a turtle on a third. Ramona loved to crayon and crayoning made her troubles fade away. When she had filled ten pages with outlines of animals, she found her father's stapler and fastened the paper together to make a book. Ramona could make an amazing number of things with paper, crayons, staples, and Scotch tape. Bee's wings to wear on her wrists, a crown to wear on her head, a paper catcher's mask to cover her face.

'What are you making?' asked her mother.

'A colouring book,' said Ramona. 'You won't buy me one.'

'That's because the art teacher who talked to the PTA said colouring books were not creative. She said children needed to be free and creative and draw their own pictures.'

'I am,' said Ramona. 'I am drawing a colouring book. Howie has a colouring book, and I want one too.'

'I guess Howie's mother missed that meeting.' Mrs Quimby picked up Ramona's colouring book and studied it. 'Why, Ramona,' she said, sounding pleased, 'you must take after your father. You draw unusually well for a girl your age.'

'I know.' Ramona was not bragging. She was being honest. She knew her drawing was better than most of the baby work done in Room One. So was her printing. She went to work colouring her turtle green, her mouse brown. Filling in outlines was not very interesting, but it was soothing. Ramona was so busy that by dinner time she had forgotten her hidden progress report.

Ramona forgot until Beezus laid her long white envelope on the table after the dessert of canned peaches and store macaroons. 'Mr Cardoza gave us our progress reports,' she announced.

Mr Quimby tore open the envelope and pulled out the yellow sheet of paper. 'M-m-m. Very good, Beezus. I'm proud of you.'

'What did he say?' Beezus asked. Ramona could

tell that Beezus was eager to have the family hear the nice things Mr Cardoza had to say about her.

'He said, "Beatrice has shown marked improvement in maths. She is willing and a conscientious pupil, who gets along well with her peers. She is a pleasure to have in the classroom."'

'May I please be excused?' asked Ramona and did not wait for an answer.

'Just a minute, young lady,' said Mr Quimby.

'Yes, what about your progress report?' asked Mrs Quimby.

'Oh . . . that old thing,' said Ramona.

'Yes, that old thing.' Mr Quimby looked amused, which annoyed Ramona. 'Bring it here,' he said.

Ramona faced her father. 'I don't want to.'

Mr Quimby was silent. The whole family was silent, waiting. Even Picky-picky, who had been washing his face, paused, one paw in the air, and waited. Ramona turned and walked slowly to her room and slowly returned with the envelope. Scowling, she thrust it at her father who tore it open.

'Does Beezus have to hear?' she asked.

'Beezus, you may be excused,' said Mrs Quimby. 'Run along and do your homework.'

Ramona knew that Beezus was in no hurry to run along and do her homework. Beezus was going to listen, that's what Beezus was going to do. Ramona scowled more ferociously as her father pulled out the sheet of yellow paper.

'If you don't look out, your face might freeze that way,' said Mr Quimby, which did not help. He studied the yellow paper and frowned. He handed it to Mrs Quimby, who read it and frowned.

'Well,' said Ramona, unable to stand the suspense, 'what does it say?' She would have grabbed it and tried to read it herself, but she knew it was written in joined-up writing.

Mrs Quimby read, '"Ramona's letter formation is excellent, and she is developing good word-attacking skills."'

Ramona relaxed. This did not sound so bad, even though she had never thought of reading as attacking words. She rather liked the idea.

Mrs Quimby read on. '"She is learning her numbers readily."'

That mitten counting, thought Ramona with scorn.

'"However, Ramona sometimes shows more interest in the seatwork of others than in her own. She needs to learn to keep her hands to herself. She also needs to work on self-control in the classroom."'

'I do not!' Ramona was angry at the unfairness of her teacher's report. What did Mrs Griggs think she had been working on? She hardly ever raised her hand any more, and she never spoke out the way she used to. And she wasn't really interested in Davy's seatwork. She was trying to help him because he was having such a hard time.

'Now, Ramona.' Mrs Quimby's voice was gentle. 'You must try to grow up.'

Ramona raised her voice. 'What do you think I'm doing?'

'You don't have to be so noisy about it,' said Mr Quimby.

Of course, Beezus had to come butting in to see what all the fuss was about. 'What did Mrs Griggs say?' she wanted to know, and it was easy to see she knew that what Mr Cardoza had said was better.

'You mind your own business,' said Ramona.

'Ramona, don't talk that way.' Mr Quimby's voice was mild.

'I will *too* talk that way,' said Ramona. 'I'll talk any way I want!'

'Ramona!' Mr Quimby's voice held a warning.

Ramona was defiant. 'Well, I will!' Nothing could possibly get any worse. She might as well say anything she pleased.

'Now see here, young lady—' began Mr Quimby.

Ramona had had enough. She had been miserable the whole first grade, and she no longer cared what happened. She wanted to do something bad. She wanted to do something terrible that would shock her whole family, something that would make them sit up and take notice. 'I'm going to say a bad word!' she shouted with a stamp of her foot.

That silenced her family. Picky-picky stopped washing and left the room. Mr Quimby looked surprised and—how could he be so disloyal?—a little amused. This made Ramona even angrier. Beezus looked interested and curious. After a moment Mrs Quimby said quietly, 'Go ahead, Ramona, and say the bad word if it will make you feel any better.'

Ramona clenched her fists and took a deep breath. 'Guts!' she yelled. *'Guts! Guts! Guts!'* There. That should show them.

Unfortunately, Ramona's family was not shocked and horrified as Ramona had expected. They laughed. All three of them laughed. They tried to hide it, but they laughed.

'It isn't funny!' shouted Ramona. 'Don't you dare laugh at me!' Bursting into tears, she threw herself face down on the couch. She kicked and she pounded the cushions with her fists. Everyone was against her. Nobody liked her. Even the cat did not like her. The room was silent, and Ramona had the satisfaction of knowing she had stopped their laughing. She heard responsible old Beezus go to her room to do her responsible old homework. Her parents continued to sit in silence, but Ramona was past caring what anyone did. She cried harder than she ever had cried in her life. She cried until she was limp and exhausted.

Then Ramona felt her mother's hand on her back. 'Ramona,' she said gently, 'what are we going to do with you?'

With red eyes, a swollen face, and a streaming nose, Ramona sat up and glared at her mother. 'Love me!' Her voice was fierce with hurt. Shocked at her own words, she buried her face in the pillow. She had no tears left.

'Dear heart,' said Mrs Quimby. 'We *do* love you.'

Ramona sat up and faced her mother, who looked tired, as if she had been through many scenes with Ramona and knew many more lay ahead. 'You do not. You love Beezus.' There. She had said it right out loud. For years she had wanted to tell her parents how she felt.

Mr Quimby wiped Ramona's nose on a Kleenex, which he then handed to her. She clenched it in her fist and glowered at her parents.

'Of course we love Beezus,' said Mrs Quimby. 'We love you both.'

'You love her more,' said Ramona. 'A whole lot more.' She felt better for having said the words, getting them off her chest, as grown-ups would say.

'Love isn't like a cup of sugar that gets used up,' said Mrs Quimby. 'There is enough to go around. Loving Beezus doesn't mean we don't have enough love left for you.'

'You don't laugh at Beezus all the time,' said Ramona.

'They used to,' said Beezus, who was unable to stay away from this family discussion. 'They always laughed at the funny things I did, and it used to make me mad.'

Ramona sniffed and waited for Beezus to continue.

Beezus was serious. 'Like the time when I was about your age and thought frankincense and myrrh were something the three Wise Men were bringing to the baby Jesus to put on his rash like that stuff Mom used on you when you were a baby. Mom and Dad laughed, and Mom told all her friends, and they laughed too.'

'Oh, dear,' said Mrs Quimby. 'I had no idea I upset you that much.'

'Well, you did,' said Beezus, still grumpy over the memory. 'And there was the time I thought toilet water was water out of the toilet. You practically had hysterics.'

'Now you're exaggerating,' said Mrs Quimby.

Comforted by this unexpected support from her sister, Ramona scrubbed her face with her soggy Kleenex. 'Mama, if you really do love me, why do I have to go to school?' At the same time she wondered how she could find out what frankincense and myrrh were without letting anyone know of her ignorance. She had always thought in a vague sort of way that they were something expensive like perfume and whiskey done up in an extra-fancy Christmas wrapping.

'Ramona, everyone has to go to school,' Mrs Quimby answered. 'Loving you has nothing to do with it.'

'Then why can't I be in the other first grade, the one in Room Two?' Ramona asked. 'Mrs Griggs doesn't like me.'

'Of course she likes you,' contradicted Mrs Quimby.

'No, she doesn't,' said Ramona. 'If she liked me, she wouldn't make me tell Susan in front of the whole class that I was sorry I scrunched her owl, and she would ask me to lead the Pledge Allegiance. And she wouldn't say bad things about me on my progress report.'

'I told you Mrs Griggs was great on apologies,' Beezus reminded her family. 'And she will get around to asking Ramona to lead the flag salute. She asks everybody.'

'But, Beezus, you got along with Mrs Griggs when you had her,' said Mrs Quimby.

'I guess so,' said Beezus. 'She wasn't my favourite teacher, though.'

'What was wrong with her?' asked Mrs Quimby.

'There wasn't anything really wrong with her, I guess,' answered Beezus. 'She just wasn't very exciting is all. She wasn't mean or anything like that. We just seemed to go along doing our work, and that was it.'

'Was she unfair?' asked Mrs Quimby.

Beezus considered the question. 'No, but I was the kind of child she liked. You know . . . neat and dependable.'

'I bet you never wasted paste,' said Ramona, who was not a paste waster herself. Too much paste was likely to spoil a piece of artwork.

'No,' admitted Beezus. 'I wasn't that type.'

Ramona persisted. *'Why* can't I change to Room Two?'

Mr Quimby took over. 'Because Mrs Griggs is teaching you to read and do arithmetic, and because the things she said about you are fair. You do need to learn self-control and to keep your hands to yourself. There are all kinds of teachers in the world just as there are all kinds of other people, and you must learn to get along with them. Maybe Mrs Griggs doesn't understand how you feel, but you aren't always easy to understand. Did you ever think of that?'

'Please, Daddy,' begged Ramona. 'Please don't make me go back to Room One.'

'Buck up, Ramona,' said Mr Quimby. 'Show us your spunk.'

Ramona felt too exhausted to show anyone her spunk, but for some reason her father's order made her feel better. If her mother had said, Poor baby, she would have felt like crying again. Mrs Quimby led her from the room and, skipping her bath, helped her into bed. Before the light was turned out, Ramona noticed that *Wild Animals of Africa* had been returned to her bookcase.

'Stay with me, Mama,' coaxed Ramona, dreading solitude, darkness, and the gorilla in the book. Mrs Quimby turned off the light and sat down on the bed.

'Mama?'

'Yes, Ramona?

'Isn't *guts* a bad word?'

Mrs Quimby thought for a moment. 'I wouldn't say it's exactly a bad word. It isn't the nicest word in the world, but there are much worse words. Now go to sleep.'

Ramona wondered what could be worse than guts.

Out in the kitchen Mr Quimby was rattling dishes and singing, 'Oh, my gal, she am a spunky gal! Sing polly-wolly doodle all the day!'

Ramona always felt safe while her father was awake. Dread of Something was worse after he had gone to bed and the house was dark. No need to turn herself into a paper doll for a while. Crying had left Ramona tired and limp, but somehow she felt better, more at peace with herself, as if trouble and guilt had been washed away by tears. She knew her father was singing about her, and in spite of her troubles Ramona found comfort in being her father's spunky gal. Somehow Something seemed less frightening.

Worn out as she was by anger and tears, Ramona faced the truth. She could no longer go on being afraid of the dark. She was too weary to remain frightened and sleepless. She could no longer fear shadows and spooks and strange little noises. She stepped bravely out of bed and, in the faint light from the hall, pulled the big flat book from her bookcase. She carried it into the living room and shoved it under a cushion. Her parents, busy with supper dishes in the kitchen, did not know she was out of bed.

She walked back to her room, climbed into bed and pulled up the covers. Nothing had grabbed her by the ankles. Nothing slithered out from under the curtains to harm her. Nothing had chased her. She was safe. Gratefully Ramona said her prayers and, exhausted, fell asleep.

9

MR QUIMBY'S SPUNKY GAL

Filled with spirit and pluck, Ramona started off to school with her lunch box in her hand. She was determined that today would be different. She would make it different. She was her father's spunky gal, wasn't she? She twirled around for the pleasure of making her pleated skirt stand out beneath her coat.

Ramona was so filled with spunk she decided to go to school a different way, by the next street over, something she had always wanted to do. The distance to Glenwood School was no greater. There was no reason she should not go to school any way she pleased as long as she looked both ways before she crossed the street and did not talk to strangers.

Slowpoke Howie, half a block behind, called out when he saw her turn the corner, 'Ramona, where are you going?'

'I'm going to school a different way,' Ramona called back, certain that Howie would not follow to spoil her feeling of adventure. Howie was not a boy to change his ways.

Ramona skipped happily down the street, singing to herself, 'Hippity-hop to the barber shop to buy a stick of candy. One for you and one for me and one for sister Mandy.' The sky through the bare branches overhead was clear, the air was crisp, and Ramona's feet in their brown oxfords felt light. Beezus's old boots, which so often weighed her down, were at home in the hall closet. Ramona was happy. The day felt different already.

Ramona turned the second corner, and as she hippity-hopped down the unfamiliar street past three white houses and a tan stucco house, she enjoyed a feeling of freedom and adventure. Then as she passed a grey shingle house in the middle of the block, a large German shepherd dog, licence tags jingling, darted down the driveway towards her. Terrified, Ramona stood rooted to the sidewalk. She felt as if her bad dream had come true. The grass was green, the sky was blue. She could not move; she could not scream.

The dog, head thrust forward, came close. He sniffed with his black nose. Here was a stranger. He growled. This was his territory, and he did not want a stranger to trespass.

This is not a dream, Ramona told herself. This is real. My feet will move if I make them. 'Go 'way!' she ordered, backing away from the dog, which answered with a sharp bark. He had teeth like the wolf in *Little Red Riding Hood*. Oh, Grandmother, what big teeth you have! The better to eat you with, my dear. Ramona took another step back. Growling, the dog advanced. He was a dog, not a wolf, but that was bad enough.

Ramona used the only weapon she had—her lunch box. She slung her lunch box at the dog and missed. The box crashed to the sidewalk, tumbled, and came to rest. The dog stopped to sniff it. Ramona forced her feet to move, to run. Her oxfords pounded on the sidewalk. One shoelace came untied and slapped against her ankle. She looked desperately at a passing car, but the driver did not notice her peril.

Ramona cast a terrified look over her shoulder. The dog had lost interest in her unopened lunch box and was coming towards her again. She could hear his toenails on the sidewalk and could hear him growling deep in his throat. She had to do something, but what?

Ramona's heart was pounding in her ears as she stopped to reach for the only weapon left— her shoe. She had no choice. She yanked off her brown oxford and hurled it at the dog. Again she missed. The dog stopped, sniffed the shoe, and then to Ramona's horror, picked it up, and trotted off in the direction from which he had come.

Ramona stood aghast with the cold from the

concrete sidewalk seeping through her sock. Now what should she do? If she said, You come back here, the dog might obey, and she did not want him any closer. She watched helplessly as he returned to his own lawn, where he settled down with the shoe between his paws like a bone. He began to gnaw.

Her shoe! There was no way Ramona could take her shoe away from the dog by herself. There was no one she could ask for help on this street of strangers. And her blue lunch box, now dented, lying there on the sidewalk. Did she dare try to get it back while the dog was busy chewing her shoe? She took a cautious step towards her lunch box. The dog went on gnawing. She took another step. I really am brave, she told herself. The dog looked up. Ramona froze. The dog began to gnaw again. She darted forward, grabbed her lunch box, and ran towards school, *slap-pat*, *slap-pat*, on the cold concrete.

Ramona refused to cry—she was brave, wasn't she?—but she was worried. Mrs Griggs frowned on tardiness, and Ramona was quite sure she expected everyone in her class to wear two shoes. Ramona would probably catch it from Mrs Griggs at school and from her mother at home for losing a shoe with a lot of wear left in it. Ramona was always catching it.

When Ramona reached Glenwood School, the
bell had rung and the traffic boys were leaving
their posts. The children crowding into the
building did not notice Ramona's predicament.
Ramona *slap-patted* down the hall to Room One,
where she quickly left her lunch box and coat in
the cloakroom before she sat down at her desk
with one foot folded under her. She spread her
pleated skirt to hide her dirty sock.

Susan noticed. 'What happened to your other
shoe?' she asked.

'I lost it, and don't you tell!' If Susan told,
Ramona would have a good excuse to pull Susan's
boing-boing curls.

'I won't,' promised Susan, pleased to share a
secret, 'but how are you going to keep Mrs Griggs
from finding out?'

Ramona cast a desperate look at Susan. 'I don't
know,' she confessed.

'Class,' said Mrs Griggs in a calm voice. This was
her way of saying, All right, everyone quiet down
and come to order because we have work to do, and
we won't accomplish anything if we waste time
talking to one another. Ramona tried to warm her
cold foot by rubbing it through her pleated skirt.

Mrs Griggs looked around her classroom. 'Who
has not had a turn at leading the flag salute?' she
asked.

Ramona stared at her desk while trying to shrink so small Mrs Griggs could not see her.

'Ramona, you have not had a turn,' said Mrs Griggs with a smile. 'You may come to the front of the room.'

Ramona and Susan exchanged a look. Ramona's said, Now what am I going to do? Susan's said, I feel sorry for you.

'Ramona, we're waiting,' said Mrs Griggs.

There was no escape. Ramona slid from her seat and walked to the front of the room where she faced the flag and stood on one foot like a stork to hide her shoeless foot behind her pleated skirt. 'I pledge allegiance,' she began, swaying.

'I pledge allegiance,' said the class.

Mrs Griggs interrupted. 'Both feet on the floor, Ramona.'

Ramona felt a surge of defiance. Mrs Griggs wanted two feet on the floor, so she put two feet on the floor. '—to the flag,' she continued with such determination that Mrs Griggs did not have another chance to interrupt. When Ramona finished, she took her seat. So there, Mrs Griggs, was her spunky thought. What if I am wearing only one shoe?

'Ramona, what happened to your other shoe?' asked Mrs Griggs.

'I lost it,' answered Ramona.

'Tell me about it,' said Mrs Griggs.

Ramona did not want to tell. 'I was chased by a ... ' She wanted to say gorilla, but after a moment's hesitation she said, ' ... dog, and I had to throw my shoe at him, and he ran off with it.' She expected the class to laugh, but instead they listened in silent sympathy. They did not understand about a hole in a house, but they understood about big dogs. They too had faced big dogs and been frightened. Ramona felt better.

'Why, that's too bad,' said Mrs Griggs, which surprised Ramona. Somehow she had not expected her teacher to understand. Mrs Griggs continued. 'I'll call the office and ask the secretary to telephone your mother and have her bring you another pair of shoes.'

'My mother isn't home,' said Ramona. 'She's at work.'

'Well, don't worry, Ramona,' said Mrs Griggs. 'We have some boots without owners in the cloakroom. You may borrow one to wear when we go out for recess.'

Ramona was familiar with those boots, none of them related and all of them a dingy brown, because no one would lose a new red boot. If there was one thing Ramona did not like, it was old brown boots. They were really ugly. She could not run and play kickball in one shoe and one boot.

Spirit and spunk surged back into Ramona. Mrs Griggs meant well, but she did not understand about boots. Miss Binney would never have told Ramona to wear one old boot. Ramona did not want to wear an old brown boot, and she made up her mind she was not going to wear an old brown boot!

Once Ramona had made this decision, it was up to her to decide what to do about it. If only she had some heavy paper and a stapler, she could make a slipper, one that might even be strong enough to last until she reached home. She paid attention to number combinations in one part of her mind, while in that private place in the back of her mind she thought about a paper slipper and how she could make one if she only had a stapler. A stapler, a stapler, where could she find a stapler? Mrs Griggs would want an explanation if she asked to borrow Room One's stapler. To borrow Miss Binney's stapler, Ramona would have to run across the playground to the temporary building, and Mrs Griggs was sure to call her back. There had to be another way. And there was, if only she could make it work.

When recess finally came, Ramona was careful to leave the room with several other members of her class and to slip down to the girls' bathroom in the basement before Mrs Griggs could remind her to put on the boot. She jerked four rough paper towels out of the container by the sinks. She folded three of the paper towels in half, making six layers of rough paper. The fourth towel she folded in thirds, which also made six layers of paper.

Now came the scary part of her plan. Ramona returned to the hall, which was empty because both first grades were out on the playground. The doors of the classrooms were closed. No one would see the brave thing she was about to do. Ramona climbed the stairs to the first landing, where she paused to take a fresh grip on her courage. She had never gone to the upstairs hall alone. First graders rarely ventured there unless accompanied by their parents on Open House night. She felt small and frightened, but she held fast to her courage, as she ran up the second half of the flight of stairs.

Ramona found Mr Cardoza's room. She quietly opened the door a crack. Mr Cardoza was telling his class, 'Spelling *secretary* is easy. Just remember the first part of the word is *secret* and think of a *secretary* as someone who keeps *secrets*. You will never again spell the word with two *a*'s instead of two *e*'s.'

Ramona opened the door a little wider and peeked inside. How big the desks looked compared to her own down in Room One! She heard the whirr of a wheel spinning in a mouse's cage.

Mr Cardoza came to investigate. He opened the door wider and said, 'Hello, Ramona Q. What may we do for you?'

There was Ramona standing on one foot, trying to hide her dirty sock behind her shoe while Beezus's whole class, and especially Beezus, stared at her. Beside her classmates Beezus did not look so big as Ramona had always thought her to be. Ramona was secretly pleased to discover her sister was a little less than medium-sized. Ramona wondered how Beezus would report this scene at home. Mother! The door opened, and there was Ramona standing with one shoe on . . .

Ramona refused to let her courage fail her. She remembered her manners and asked, 'May I please borrow your stapler? I can use it right here in the hall, and it will only take a minute.'

Once again she had that strange feeling of standing aside to look at herself. Was she a funny little girl whom Mr Cardoza would find amusing? Apparently not because Mr Cardoza did not hesitate.

'Certainly,' he said and strode to his desk for the stapler, which he handed to her without question. Mrs Griggs would have said, Tell me why you want it, Ramona. Miss Binney would have said,

Won't you let me help you with it? Mr Cardoza closed the door, leaving Ramona in the privacy of the hall.

Ramona knelt on the floor and went to work. She stapled the three paper towels together. The towel folded in thirds she placed at one end of the other towels and stapled it on three sides to make the toe of a slipper. She had to push down hard with both hands to force the staples through so much paper. Then she turned her slipper over and sent staples through in the other direction to make it stronger. There. Ramona slid her foot into her slipper. With more time and a pair of scissors, she could have made a better slipper with a rounded toe, but this slipper was better than an old boot, and it should last all day, school paper towels being what they were.

Ramona opened the door again and held out the stapler. Mr Cardoza looked up from the book in his hand and walked over to take the stapler from her. 'Thank you, Mr Cardoza,' she said, because she knew he expected good manners.

'You're welcome, Ramona Q,' said Mr Cardoza with a smile that was a friendly smile, not an amused-by-a-funny-little-girl smile. 'We're always glad to be of help.'

Ramona had not felt so happy since she was in Miss Binney's kindergarten. Too bad Beezus had first dibs on Mr Cardoza. Ramona might have married him herself someday if she ever decided to get married. She reached Room One just as the two first grades were returning from recess. She heard someone from Room Two say, 'Ramona must have hurt her foot.'

Someone else said, 'I bet it hurts.'

Ramona began to limp. She was enjoying the attention her slipper attracted.

'Oh, there you are, Ramona,' said Mrs Griggs, who was standing by her door to make sure her class entered the room in an orderly manner. 'Where have you been? We missed you on the playground.'

'I was making a slipper.' Ramona looked up at Mrs Griggs. 'I didn't want to wear a dirty old boot.' She had not felt so brave since the day she started off to the first grade.

'After this you should ask permission to stay in during recess.' Mrs Griggs looked down at the slipper and said, 'You have made a very good slipper.'

Encouraged by this bit of praise, Ramona said, 'I could make a better slipper if I had scissors and crayons. I could draw a bunny face on the toe and make ears like a real bunny slipper.'

Mrs Griggs's expression was thoughtful. She seemed to be studying Ramona, who shrank inside herself, uncertain as to what her teacher might be about to say. Mrs Griggs looked more tired than cross, so Ramona summoned her spunk and said, 'Maybe I could finish my slipper instead of making a Thanksgiving turkey.'

'We always—' began Mrs Griggs and changed her mind. 'I don't see why not,' she said.

Mrs Griggs approved of her! Ramona smiled with relief and pretended to limp to her seat as her teacher closed the door. She no longer had to dread turkeys—or her teacher.

The class took out arithmetic workbooks. While Ramona began to count cowboy boots and butterflies and circled the correct number under the pictures, she was busy and happy in the private corner of her mind planning improvements in her slipper. She would round the heel and toe. She would draw a nose with pink crayon and eyes, too, and cut two ears . . . Ramona's happy thoughts were interrupted by another less happy thought. Her missing brown oxford. What was her mother going to say when she came home without it? Tell her she was careless? Tell her how much shoes cost these days? Ask her why on earth she didn't go to school the usual way? Because I was feeling full of spunk, Ramona answered in her thoughts. Her father would understand. She hoped her mother would, too.

Workbooks were collected. Reading circles were next. Prepared to attack words, Ramona limped to a little chair in the front of the room with the rest of her reading group. She felt so much better towards Mrs Griggs that she was first to raise her hand on almost every question, even though she was worried about her missing oxford. The reader was more interesting now that her group was attacking bigger words. *Fire engine*. Ramona read to herself and thought, Pow! I got you, *fire engine*. *Monkey*. Pow! I got you, *monkey*.

The buzz of the little black telephone beside Mrs Griggs's desk interrupted work in Room One. Everyone wanted to listen to Mrs Griggs talk to the principal's office, because they might hear something important.

'Yes,' said Mrs Griggs to the telephone. 'Yes, we do.' With the receiver pressed to her ear, she turned away from the telephone and looked at Ramona. Everyone else in Room One looked at her, too. Now what? thought Ramona. Now what have I done? 'All right,' said Mrs Griggs to the telephone. 'I'll send her along.' She replaced the receiver. Room One, most of all Ramona, waited.

'Ramona, your shoe is waiting for you in the office,' said the teacher. 'When the dog's owner found it on the lawn, he brought it to school and the secretary guessed it was a first-grade size. You may be excused to go get it.'

Whew! thought Ramona in great relief, as she limped happily off to the office. This day was turning out to be better than she had expected. She accepted her shoe, now interestingly scarred with toothmarks, from Mrs Miller, the school secretary.

'My goodness,' said Mrs Miller, as Ramona shoved her foot into her shoe and tied the lace, still damp from being chewed, in a tight bow. 'It's a good thing your foot came out of your shoe when the dog got hold of it. He must have had pretty big teeth.'

'He did,' Ramona assured the secretary. 'Great big teeth. Like a wolf. He chased me.' Now that Ramona was safe in her two shoes, she was eager for an audience. 'He chased me, but I took off my shoe and threw it at him, and that stopped him.'

'Fancy that!' Mrs Miller was plainly impressed by Ramona's story. 'You took off your shoe and threw it right at him! You must be a very brave girl.'

'I guess maybe I am,' said Ramona, pleased by the compliment. Of course, she was brave. She had scars on her shoe to prove it. She hoped her mother would not be in too much of a hurry to hide the toothmarks with fresh shoe polish. She hippity-hopped, paper slipper in hand, down the hall to show off her scars to Room One. Brave Ramona, that's what they would think, just about the bravest girl in the first grade. And they would be right. This time Ramona was sure.

RaMoNa aND HeR FaTHeR

CONTENTS

1

PaY DaY

'Ye-e-ep!' sang Ramona Quimby one warm September afternoon, as she knelt on a chair at the kitchen table to make out her Christmas list. She had enjoyed a good day in second grade, and she looked forward to working on her list. For Ramona a Christmas list was a list of presents she hoped to receive, not presents she planned to give. 'Ye-e-ep!' she sang again.

'Thank goodness today is pay day,' remarked Mrs Quimby, as she opened the refrigerator to see what she could find for supper.

'Ye-e-ep!' sang Ramona, as she printed *mice or ginny pig* on her list with purple crayon. Next to Christmas and her birthday, her father's pay day was her favourite day. His pay day meant treats. Her mother's pay day from her part-time job in a doctor's office meant they could make payments on the bedroom the Quimbys had added to their house when Ramona was in first grade.

'What's all this yeeping about?' asked Mrs Quimby.

'I'm making a joyful noise until the Lord like they say in Sunday school,' Ramona explained. 'Only they don't tell us what the joyful noise sounds like so I made up my own.' *Hooray* and *wow*, joyful noises to Ramona, had not sounded right, so she had settled on *yeep* because it sounded happy but not rowdy. 'Isn't that all right?' she asked, as she began to add *myna bird that talks* to her list.

'Yeep is fine if that's the way you feel about it,' reassured Mrs Quimby.

Ramona printed *coocoo clock* on her list while she wondered what the treat would be this pay day. Maybe, since this was Friday, they could all go to a movie if her parents could find one suitable. Both Ramona and her big sister, Beezus, christened Beatrice, wondered what went on in all those other movies. They planned to find out the minute they were grown-up. That was one thing they agreed on. Or maybe their father would bring presents, a package of coloured paper for Ramona, a paperback book for Beezus.

'I wish I could think of something interesting to do with leftover pot roast and creamed cauliflower,' remarked Mrs Quimby.

Leftovers—yuck!, thought Ramona. 'Maybe Daddy will take us to the Whopperburger for supper for pay day,' she said. A soft, juicy hamburger spiced with relish, french fries, crisp on the outside and mealy inside, a little paper cup of coleslaw at the Whopperburger Restaurant were Ramona's favourite pay day treat. Eating close together in a booth made Ramona feel snug and cosy. She and Beezus never quarrelled at the Whopperburger.

'Good idea.' Mrs Quimby closed the refrigerator door. 'I'll see what I can do.'

Then Beezus came into the kitchen through the back door, dropped her books on the table, and flopped down on a chair with a gusty sigh.

'What was that all about?' asked Mrs Quimby, not at all worried.

'Nobody is any fun any more,' complained Beezus. 'Henry spends all his time running around the track over at the high school getting ready for the Olympics in eight or twelve years, or he and Robert study a book of world records trying to find a record to break, and Mary Jane practises the piano all the time.' Beezus sighed again. 'And Mrs Mester says we are going to do lots of creative writing, and I hate creative writing. I don't see why I had to get Mrs Mester for seventh grade anyway.'

'Creative writing can't be as bad as all that,' said Mrs Quimby.

'You just don't understand,' complained Beezus.

'I can never think of stories, and my poems are stuff like, "See the bird in the tree. He is singing to me."'

'Tee-hee, tee-hee,' added Ramona without thinking.

'Ramona,' said Mrs Quimby, 'that was not necessary.'

Because Beezus had been so grouchy lately, Ramona could manage to be only medium sorry.

'Pest!' said Beezus. Noticing Ramona's work, she added, 'Making out a Christmas list in September is silly.'

Ramona calmly selected an orange crayon. She was used to being called a pest. 'If I am a pest, you are a rotten dinosaur egg,' she informed her sister.

'Mother, make her stop,' said Beezus.

When Beezus said this, Ramona knew she had won. The time had come to change the subject. 'Today's pay day,' she told her sister. 'Maybe we'll get to go to the Whopperburger for supper.'

'Oh, mother, will we?' Beezus's unhappy mood disappeared as she swooped up Picky-picky, the Quimbys' shabby old cat, who had strolled into the kitchen. He purred a rusty purr as she rubbed her cheek against his yellow fur.

'I'll see what I can do,' said Mrs Quimby.

Smiling, Beezus dropped Picky-picky, gathered

up her books, and went off to her room. Beezus was the kind of girl who did her homework on Friday instead of waiting until the last minute on Sunday.

Ramona asked in a quiet voice, 'Mother, why is Beezus so cross lately?' Letting her sister overhear such a question would lead to real trouble.

'You mustn't mind her,' whispered Mrs Quimby. 'She's reached a difficult age.'

Ramona thought such an all-purpose excuse for bad behaviour would be a handy thing to have. 'So have I,' she confided to her mother.

Mrs Quimby dropped a kiss on the top of Ramona's head. 'Silly girl,' she said. 'It's just a phase Beezus is going through. She'll out-grow it.'

A contented silence fell over the house as three members of the family looked forward to supper at the Whopperburger, where they would eat, close and cosy in a booth, their food brought to them by a friendly waitress who always said, 'There you go,' as she set down their hamburgers and french fries.

Ramona had decided to order a cheese-burger when she heard the sound of her father's key in the front door. 'Daddy, Daddy!' she shrieked, scrambling down from the chair and running to meet her father as he opened the door. 'Guess what?'

Beezus, who had come from her room, answered before her father had a chance to guess. 'Mother said maybe we could go to the Whopperburger for dinner!'

Mr Quimby smiled and kissed his daughters before he held out a small white paper bag. 'Here, I brought you a little present.' Somehow he did not look as happy as usual. Maybe he had had a hard day at the office of the van-and-storage company where he worked.

His daughters pounced and opened the bag together. 'Gummybears!' was their joyful cry. The chewy little bears were the most popular sweet at Glenwood School this fall. Last spring powdered Jell-o eaten from the package had been the fad. Mr Quimby always remembered these things.

'Run along and divide them between you,' said Mr Quimby. 'I want to talk to your mother.'

'Don't spoil your dinner,' said Mrs Quimby.

The girls bore the bag off to Beezus's room, where they dumped the gummybears onto the bedspread. First they divided the cinnamon-flavoured red bears, one for Beezus, one for Ramona. Then they divided the orange bears and the green, and as they were about to divide the yellow bears, both girls were suddenly aware that their mother and father were no longer talking. Silence filled the house. The sisters looked at one another. There was something unnatural about this silence. Uneasy, they waited for some sound, and then their parents began to speak in whispers. Beezus tiptoed to the door to listen.

Ramona bit the head off a red gummybear. She always ate toes last. 'Maybe they're planning a big surprise,' she suggested, refusing to worry.

'I don't think so,' whispered Beezus, 'but I can't hear what they are saying.'

'Try listening through the furnace pipes,' whispered Ramona.

'That won't work here. The living room is too far away.' Beezus strained to catch her parents' words. 'I think something's wrong.'

Ramona divided her gummybears, one heap to eat at home, the other to take to school to share with friends if they were nice to her.

'Something is wrong. Something awful,' whispered Beezus. 'I can tell by the way they are talking.'

Beezus looked so frightened that Ramona became frightened, too. What could be wrong? She tried to think what she might have done to make her parents whisper this way, but she had stayed out of trouble lately.

She could not think of a single thing that could be wrong. This frightened her even more. She no longer felt like eating chewy little bears. She wanted to know why her mother and father were whispering in a way that alarmed Beezus.

Finally the girls heard their father say in a normal voice, 'I think I'll take a shower before supper.' This remark was reassuring to Ramona.

'What'll we do now?' whispered Beezus. 'I'm scared to go out.'

Worry and curiosity, however, urged Beezus and Ramona into the hall.

Trying to pretend they were not concerned about their family, the girls walked into the kitchen where Mrs Quimby was removing leftovers from the refrigerator. 'I think we'll eat at home after all,' she said, looking sad and anxious.

Without being asked, Ramona began to deal four place mats around the dining room table, laying them all right side up. When she was cross with Beezus, she laid her sister's place mat face down.

Mrs Quimby looked at the cold creamed cauliflower with distaste, returned it to the refrigerator, and reached for a can of green beans before she noticed her silent and worried daughters watching her for clues as to what might be wrong.

Mrs Quimby turned and faced Beezus and Ramona. 'Girls, you might as well know. Your father has lost his job.'

something important, because her family was in trouble and there was nothing she could do to help. When she had finished setting the table, she returned to the list she had begun, it now seemed, a long time ago. 'But what about Christmas?' she asked her mother.

'Right now Christmas is the least of our worries.' Mrs Quimby looked sadder than Ramona had ever seen her look. 'Taxes are due in November. And we have to buy groceries and make car payments and a lot of other things.'

'Don't we have any money in the bank?' asked Beezus.

'Not much,' admitted Mrs Quimby, 'but your father was given two weeks' pay.'

Ramona looked at the list she had begun so happily and wondered how much the presents she had listed would cost. Too much, she knew. Mice were free if you knew the right person, the owner of a mother mouse, so she might get some mice.

Slowly Ramona crossed out *ginny pig* and the other presents she had listed. As she made black lines through each item, she thought about her family. She did not want her father to be worried, her mother sad, or her sister cross. She wanted her whole family, including Picky-picky, to be happy.

Ramona studied her crayons, chose a pinky-red

one because it seemed the happiest colour, and printed one more item on her Christmas list to make up for all she had crossed out. *One happy family.* Beside the words she drew four smiling faces and beside them, the face of a yellow cat, also smiling.

2

RaMONa aND The MiLLiON DOLLaRS

Ramona wished she had a million dollars so her father would be fun again. There had been many changes in the Quimby household since Mr Quimby had lost his job, but the biggest change was in Mr Quimby himself.

First of all, Mrs Quimby found a full-time job working for another doctor, which was good news. However, even a second-grader could understand that one pay cheque would not stretch as far as two pay cheques, especially when there was so much talk of taxes, whatever they were. Mrs Quimby's new job meant that Mr Quimby had to be home when Ramona returned from school.

Ramona and her father saw a lot of one another. At first she thought having her father to herself for an hour or two every day would be fun, but when she came home, she found him running the vacuum cleaner, filling out job applications, or sitting on the couch, smoking and staring into space. He could not take her to the park because he had to stay near the telephone. Someone might call to offer him a job. Ramona grew uneasy. Maybe he was too worried to love her any more.

One day Ramona came home to find her father in the living room drinking warmed-over coffee, smoking, and staring at the television set. On the screen a boy a couple of years younger than Ramona was singing:

> Forget your pots, forget your pans.
> It's not too late to change your plans.
> Spend a little, eat a lot,
> Big fat burgers, nice and hot
> At your nearest Whopperburger!

Ramona watched him open his mouth wide to bite into a fat cheeseburger with lettuce and tomato spilling out of the bun and thought wistfully of the good old days when the family used to go to the restaurant on pay day and when her mother used to bring home little treats—stuffed olives, cinnamon buns for Sunday breakfast, a bag of potato chips.

'That kid must be earning a million dollars.' Mr Quimby snuffed out his cigarette in a loaded ashtray. 'He's singing that commercial every time I turn on the television.'

A boy Ramona's age earning a million dollars? Ramona was all interest. 'How's he earning a million dollars?' she asked. She had often thought of all the things they could do if they had a million dollars, beginning with turning up the thermostat so they wouldn't have to wear sweaters in the house to save fuel oil.

Mr Quimby explained. 'They make a movie of him singing the commercial, and every time the movie is shown on television he gets paid. It all adds up.'

Well! This was a new idea to Ramona. She thought it over as she got out her crayons and paper and knelt on a chair at the kitchen table. Singing a song about hamburgers would not be hard to do. She could do it herself. Maybe she could earn a million dollars like that boy so her father would be fun again, and everyone at school would watch her on television and say, 'There's Ramona Quimby. She goes to our school.' A million dollars would buy a cuckoo clock for every room in the house, her father wouldn't need a job, the family could go to Disneyland ...

'Forget your pots, forget your pans,' Ramona began to sing, as she drew a picture of a hamburger and stabbed yellow dots across the top of the bun for sesame seeds. With a million dollars the Quimbys could eat in a restaurant every day if they wanted to.

After that Ramona began to watch for children

on television commercials. She saw a boy eating bread and margarine when a crown suddenly appeared on his head with a fanfare—ta *da*!—of music. She saw a girl who asked, 'Mommy, wouldn't it be nice if caramel apples grew on trees?' and another girl who took a bite of cereal and said, 'It's good, hm-um,' and giggled. There was a boy who asked at the end of a weiner commercial, 'Dad, how do you tell a boy hot dog from a girl hot dog?' and a girl who tipped her head to one side and said, 'Pop-pop-pop,' as she listened to her cereal. Children crunched potato chips, chomped on pickles, gnawed at fried chicken. Ramona grew particularly fond of the curly-haired little girl saying to her mother at the zoo, 'Look, Mommy, the elephant's legs are wrinkled just like your pantyhose.' Ramona could say all those things.

Ramona began to practise. Maybe someone would see her and offer her a million dollars to make a television commercial. On her way to school, if her friend Howie did not walk with her, she tipped her head to one side and said, 'Pop-pop-pop.' She said to herself, 'M-m-m, it's good,' and giggled. Giggling wasn't easy when she didn't have anything to giggle about, but she worked at it. Once she practised on her mother by asking, 'Mommy, wouldn't it be nice if caramel apples grew on trees?' She had taken to calling her mother

Mommy lately, because children on commercials always called their mothers Mommy.

Mrs Quimby's absent-minded answer was, 'Not really. Caramel is bad for your teeth.' She was wearing slacks so Ramona could not say the line about pantyhose.

Since the Quimbys no longer bought potato chips or pickles, Ramona found other foods— toast and apples and carrot sticks—to practise good loud crunching on. When they had chicken for dinner, she smacked and licked her fingers.

'Ramona,' said Mr Quimby, 'your table manners grow worse and worse. Don't eat so noisily. My grandmother used to say, "A smack at the table is worth a smack on the bottom."'

Ramona, who did not think she would have liked her father's grandmother, was embarrassed. She had been practising to be on television, and she had forgotten her family could hear.

Ramona continued to practise until she began to feel as if a television camera was watching her wherever she went. She smiled a lot and skipped, feeling that she was cute and lovable. She felt as if she had fluffy blonde curls, even though in real life her hair was brown and straight.

One morning, smiling prettily, she thought, and swinging her lunch box, Ramona skipped to school. Today someone might notice her because she was wearing her red tights. She was happy because this was a special day, the day of Ramona's parent-teacher conference. Since Mrs Quimby was at work, Mr Quimby was going to meet with Mrs Rogers, her second-grade teacher. Ramona was proud to have a father who would come to school.

Feeling dainty, curly-haired, and adorable, Ramona skipped into her classroom, and what did she see but Mrs Rogers with wrinkles around her ankles. Ramona did not hesitate. She skipped right over to her teacher and, since there did not happen to be an elephant in Room 2, turned the words around and said, 'Mrs Rogers, your pantyhose are wrinkled like an elephant's legs.'

Mrs Rogers looked surprised, and the boys and girls who had already taken their seats giggled. All the teacher said was. 'Thank you, Ramona, for telling me. And remember, we do not skip inside the school building.'

Ramona had an uneasy feeling she had displeased her teacher.

She was sure of it when Howie said, 'Ramona, you sure weren't very polite to Mrs Rogers.' Howie, a serious thinker, was usually right.

Suddenly Ramona was no longer an adorable little fluffy-haired girl on television. She was plain old Ramona, a second-grader whose own red tights bagged at the knee and wrinkled at the ankle. This wasn't the way things turned out on television. On television grown-ups always smiled at everything children said.

During recess Ramona went to the girls' bathroom and rolled her tights up at the waist to stretch them up at the knee and ankle. Mrs Rogers must have done the same thing to her pantyhose, because after recess her ankles were smooth. Ramona felt better.

That afternoon, when the lower grades had been dismissed from their classrooms, Ramona found her father, along with Davy's mother, waiting outside the door of Room 2 for their conferences with Mrs Rogers. Davy's mother's appointment was first, so Mr Quimby sat down on a chair outside the door with a folder of Ramona's schoolwork to look over. Davy stood close to the door, hoping to hear what his teacher was saying about him. Everybody in Room 2 was anxious to learn what the teacher said.

Mr Quimby opened Ramona's folder. 'Run along and play on the playground until I'm through,' he told his daughter.

'Promise you'll tell me what Mrs Rogers says about me,' said Ramona.

Mr Quimby understood. He smiled and gave his promise.

Outside, the playground was chilly and damp. The only children who lingered were those whose parents had conferences, and they were more interested in what was going on inside the building than outside. Bored, Ramona looked around for something to do, and because she could find nothing better, she followed a traffic boy across the street. On the opposite side, near the market that had been built when she was in kindergarten, she decided she had time to explore. In a weedy space at the side of the market building, she discovered several burdock plants that bore a prickly crop of brown burs, each covered with sharp little hooks.

Ramona saw at once that burs had all sorts of interesting possibilities. She picked two and stuck them together. She added another and another. They were better than Tinker-toys. She would have to tell Howie about them. When she had a string of burs, each clinging to the next, she bent it into a circle and stuck the ends together. A crown! She could make a crown. She picked more burs and built up the circle by making peaks all the way around like the crown the boy wore in the margarine commercial. There was only one thing to do with a crown like that. Ramona crowned herself—ta *da!*—like the boy on television.

Prickly though it was, Ramona enjoyed wearing the crown. She practised looking surprised, like the boy who ate the margarine, and pretended she was rich and famous and about to meet her father, who would be driving a big shiny car bought with the million dollars she had earned.

The traffic boys had gone off duty. Ramona remembered to look both ways before she crossed the street, and as she crossed she pretended people were saying, 'There goes that rich girl. She earned a million dollars eating margarine on TV.'

Mr Quimby was standing on the playground, looking for Ramona. Forgetting all she had been pretending, Ramona ran to him. 'What did Mrs Rogers say about me?' she demanded.

'That's some crown you've got there,' Mr Quimby remarked.

'Daddy, what did she *say*?' Ramona could not contain her impatience.

Mr Quimby grinned. 'She said you were impatient.'

Oh, that. People were always telling Ramona not to be so impatient. 'What else?' asked Ramona, as she and her father walked towards home.

'You are a good reader, but you are careless about spelling.'

Ramona knew this. Unlike Beezus, who was an excellent speller, Ramona could not believe spelling was important as long as people could understand what she meant. 'What else?'

'She said you draw unusually well for a second-grader and your printing is the best in the class.'

'What else?'

Mr Quimby raised one eyebrow as he looked down at Ramona. 'She said you were inclined to show off and you sometimes forget your manners.'

Ramona was indignant at this criticism. 'I do not! She's just making that up.' Then she remembered what she had said about her teacher's pantyhose and felt subdued. She hoped her teacher had not repeated her remark to her father.

'I remember my manners most of the time,' said Ramona, wondering what her teacher had meant by showing off. Being first to raise her hand when she knew the answer?

'Of course you do,' agreed Mr Quimby. 'After all, you are my daughter. Now tell me, how are you going to get that crown off?'

Using both hands, Ramona tried to lift her crown but only succeeded in pulling her hair. The tiny hooks clung fast. Ramona tugged. Ow! That hurt. She looked helplessly up at her father.

Mr Quimby appeared amused. 'Who do you think you are? A Rose Festival Queen?'

Ramona pretended to ignore her father's question. How silly to act like someone on television when she was a plain old second-grader whose tights bagged at the knees again.

She hoped her father would not guess. He might. He was good at guessing.

By then Ramona and her father were home. As Mr Quimby unlocked the front door, he said, 'We'll have to see what we can do about getting you uncrowned before your mother gets home. Any ideas?'

Ramona had no answer, although she was eager to part with the crown before her father guessed what she had been doing. In the kitchen, Mr Quimby picked off the top of the crown, the part that did not touch Ramona's hair. That was easy. Now came the hard part.

'Yow!' said Ramona, when her father tried to lift the crown.

'That won't work,' said her father. 'Let's try one bur at a time.' He went to work on one bur, carefully trying to untangle it from Ramona's hair, one strand at a time. To Ramona, who did not like to stand still, this process took forever. Each bur was snarled in a hundred hairs, and each hair had to be pulled before the bur was loosened. After a very long time, Mr Quimby handed a hair-entangled bur to Ramona.

'Yow! Yipe! Leave me some hair,' said Ramona, picturing a bald circle around her head.

'I'm trying,' said Mr Quimby and began on the next bur.

Ramona sighed. Standing still doing nothing was tiresome.

After what seemed like a long time, Beezus came home from school. She took one look at Ramona and began to laugh.

'I don't suppose you ever did anything dumb,' said Ramona, short of patience and anxious lest her sister guess why she was wearing the remains of a crown. 'What about the time you—'

'No arguments,' said Mr Quimby. 'We have a problem to solve, and it might be a good idea if we solved it before your mother comes home from work.'

Much to Ramona's annoyance, her sister sat down to watch. 'How about soaking?' suggested Beezus. 'It might soften all those millions of little hooks.'

'Yow! Yipe!' said Ramona. 'You're pulling too hard.'

Mr Quimby laid another hair-filled bur on the table. 'Maybe we should try. This isn't working.'

'It's about time she washed her hair anyway,' said Beezus, a remark Ramona felt was entirely unnecessary. Nobody could shampoo hair full of burs.

Ramona knelt on a chair with her head in a sinkful of warm water for what seemed like hours until her knees ached and she had a crick in her neck. 'Now, Daddy?' she asked at least once a minute.

'Not yet,' Mr Quimby answered, feeling a bur. 'Nope,' he said at last. 'This isn't going to work.'

Ramona lifted her dripping head from the sink. When her father tried to dry her hair, the bur hooks clung to the towel. He jerked the towel loose and draped it around Ramona's shoulders.

'Well, live and learn,' said Mr Quimby. 'Beezus, scrub some potatoes and throw them in the oven. We can't have your mother come home and find we haven't started supper.'

When Mrs Quimby arrived, she took one look at her husband trying to untangle Ramona's wet hair from the burs, groaned, sank limply onto a kitchen chair, and began to laugh.

By now Ramona was tired, cross, and hungry. 'I don't see anything funny,' she said sullenly.

Mrs Quimby managed to stop laughing. 'What on earth got into you?' she asked.

Ramona considered. Was this a question grown-ups asked just to be asking a question, or did her mother expect an answer? 'Nothing,' was a safe reply. She would never tell her family how she happened to be wearing a crown of burs. Never, not even if they threw her into a dungeon.

'Beezus, bring me the scissors,' said Mrs Quimby.

Ramona clapped her hands over the burs. 'No!' she shrieked and stamped her foot. 'I won't let you cut off my hair! I won't! I won't! I won't!'

Beezus handed her mother the scissors and gave her sister some advice. 'Stop yelling. If you go to bed with burs in your hair, you'll really get messed up.'

Ramona had to face the wisdom of Beezus's words. She stopped yelling to consider the problem once more. 'All right,' she said, as if she were granting a favour, 'but I want Daddy to do it.' Her father would work with care while her mother, always in a hurry since she was working full-time, would go *snip-snip-snip* and be done with it. Besides, supper would be prepared faster and would taste better if her mother did the cooking.

'I am honoured,' said Mr Quimby. 'Deeply honoured.'

Mrs Quimby did not seem sorry to hand over the scissors. 'Why don't you go someplace else to work while Beezus and I get supper on the table?'

Mr Quimby led Ramona into the living room, where he turned on the television set. 'This may take time,' he explained, as he went to work. 'We might as well watch the news.'

Ramona was still anxious. 'Don't cut any more than you have to, Daddy,' she begged, praying the margarine boy would not appear on the screen. 'I don't want everyone at school to make fun of me.' The newscaster was talking about strikes and a lot of things Ramona did not understand.

'The merest smidgin,' promised her father. *Snip. Snip. Snip.* He laid a hair-ensnarled bur in an ashtray. *Snip. Snip. Snip.* He laid another bur beside the first.

'Does it look awful?' asked Ramona.

'As my grandmother would say, "It will never be noticed from a trotting horse."'

Ramona let out a long, shuddery sigh, the closest thing to crying without really crying. *Snip. Snip. Snip.* Ramona touched the side of her head. She still had hair there. More hair than she expected. She felt a little better.

The newscaster disappeared from the television screen, and there was that boy again singing:

> Forget your pots, forget your pans,
> It's not too late to change your plans.

Ramona thought longingly of the days before her father lost his job, when they could forget their pots and pans and change their plans. She watched the boy open his mouth wide and sink his teeth into that fat hamburger with lettuce, tomato, and cheese hanging out of the bun. She swallowed and said, 'I bet that boy has a lot of fun with his million dollars.' She felt so sad. The Quimbys really needed a million dollars. Even one dollar would help.

Snip. Snip. Snip. 'Oh, I don't know,' said Mr Quimby. 'Money is handy, but it isn't everything.'

'I wish I could earn a million dollars like that boy,' said Ramona. This was the closest she would ever come to telling how she happened to set a crown of burs on her head.

'You know something?' said Mr Quimby. 'I don't care how much that kid or any other kid earns. I wouldn't trade you for a million dollars.'

'Really, Daddy?' That remark about any other kid—Ramona wondered if her father had guessed her reason for the crown, but she would never ask. Never. 'Really? Do you mean it?'

'Really.' Mr Quimby continued his careful snipping. 'I'll bet that boy's father wishes he had a little girl who finger-painted and wiped her hands on the cat when she was little and who once cut her own hair so she would be bald like her uncle and who then grew up to be seven years old and crowned herself with burs. Not every father is lucky enough to have a daughter like that.'

Ramona giggled. 'Daddy, you're being silly!' She was happier than she had been in a long time.

3

The Night of The Jack-o'-Lantern

'Please pass the tommy-toes,' said Ramona, hoping to make someone in the family smile. She felt good when her father smiled as he passed her the bowl of stewed tomatoes. He smiled less and less as the days went by and he had not found work. Too often he was just plain cross. Ramona had learned not to rush home from school and ask, 'Did you find a job today, Daddy?' Mrs Quimby always seemed to look anxious these days, either over the cost of groceries or money the family owed. Beezus had turned into a regular old grouch, because she dreaded Creative Writing and perhaps because she had reached that difficult age Mrs Quimby was always talking about, although Ramona found this hard to believe.

Even Picky-picky was not himself. He lashed his tail and stalked angrily away from his dish when Beezus served him Puss-puddy, the cheapest brand of cat food Mrs Quimby could find in the market.

All this worried Ramona. She wanted her father

to smile and joke, her mother to look happy, her sister to be cheerful, and Picky-picky to eat his food, wash his whiskers, and purr the way he used to.

'And so,' Mr Quimby was saying, 'at the end of the interview for the job, the man said he would let me know if anything turned up.'

Mrs Quimby sighed. 'Let's hope you hear from him. Oh, by the way, the car has been making a funny noise. A sort of *tappety-tappety* sound.'

'It's Murphy's Law,' said Mr Quimby. 'Anything that can go wrong will.'

Ramona knew her father was not joking this time. Last week, when the washing machine refused to work, the Quimbys had been horrified by the size of the repair bill.

'I like tommy-toes,' said Ramona, hoping her little joke would work a second time. This was not exactly true, but she was willing to sacrifice truth for a smile.

Since no one paid any attention, Ramona spoke louder as she lifted the bowl of stewed tomatoes. 'Does anybody want any tommy-toes?' she asked. The bowl tipped. Mrs Quimby silently reached over and wiped spilled juice from the table with her napkin. Crestfallen, Ramona set the bowl down. No one had smiled.

'Ramona,' said Mr Quimby, 'my grandmother

used to have a saying. "First time is funny, second time is silly, third time is a spanking."'

Ramona looked down at her place mat. Nothing seemed to go right lately. Picky-picky must have felt the same way. He sat down beside Beezus and meowed his crossest meow.

Mr Quimby lit a cigarette and asked his older daughter, 'Haven't you fed that cat yet?'

Beezus rose to clear the table. 'It wouldn't do any good. He hasn't eaten his breakfast. He won't eat that cheap Puss-puddy.'

'Too bad about him.' Mr Quimby blew a cloud of smoke towards the ceiling.

'He goes next door and mews as if we never give him anything to eat,' said Beezus. 'It's embarrassing.'

'He'll just have to learn to eat what we can afford,' said Mr Quimby. 'Or we will get rid of him.'

This statement shocked Ramona. Picky-picky had been a member of the family since before she was born.

'Well, I don't blame him,' said Beezus, picking up the cat and pressing her cheek against his fur. 'Puss-puddy stinks.'

Mr Quimby ground out his cigarette.

'Guess what?' said Mrs Quimby, as if to change the subject. 'Howie's grandmother drove out to visit her sister, who lives on a farm, and her sister sent in a lot of pumpkins for jack-o'-lanterns for the neighbourhood children. Mrs Kemp gave us a big one, and it's down in the basement now, waiting to be carved.'

'Me! Me!' cried Ramona. 'Let me get it!'

'Let's give it a real scary face,' said Beezus, no longer difficult.

'I'll have to sharpen my knife,' said Mr Quimby.

'Run along and bring it up, Ramona,' said Mrs Quimby with a real smile.

Relief flooded through Ramona. Her family had returned to normal. She snapped on the basement light, thumped down the stairs, and there in the shadow of the furnace pipes, which reached out like ghostly arms, was a big, round pumpkin. Ramona grasped its scratchy stem, found the pumpkin too big to lift that way, bent over, hugged it in both arms, and raised it from the cement floor. The pumpkin was heavier than she had expected, and she must not let it drop and smash all over the concrete floor.

'Need some help, Ramona?' Mrs Quimby called down the stairs.

'I can do it.' Ramona felt for each step with her feet and emerged, victorious, into the kitchen.

'Wow! That *is* a big one.' Mr Quimby was

sharpening his jackknife on a whetstone while Beezus and her mother hurried through the dishes.

'A pumpkin that size would cost a lot at the market,' Mrs Quimby remarked. 'A couple of dollars, at least.'

'Let's give it eyebrows like last year,' said Ramona.

'And ears,' said Beezus.

'And lots of teeth,' added Ramona. There would be no jack-o'-lantern with one tooth and three triangles for eyes and nose in the Quimbys' front window on Hallowe'en. Mr Quimby was the best pumpkin carver on Klickitat Street. Everybody knew that.

'Hmm. Let's see now.' Mr Quimby studied the pumpkin, turning it to find the best side for the face. 'I think the nose should go about here.' With a pencil he sketched a nose-shaped nose, not a triangle, while his daughters leaned on their elbows to watch.

'Shall we have it smile or frown?' he asked.

'Smile!' said Ramona, who had had enough of frowning.

'Frown!' said Beezus.

The mouth turned up on one side and down on the other. Eyes were sketched and eyebrows. 'Very expressive,' said Mr Quimby. 'Something between a leer and a sneer.' He cut a circle around the top of the pumpkin and lifted it off for a lid.

Without being asked, Ramona found a big spoon for scooping out the seeds.

Picky-picky came into the kitchen to see if something besides Puss-puddy had been placed in his dish. When he found that it had not, he paused, sniffed the unfamiliar pumpkin smell, and with his tail twitching angrily stalked out of the kitchen. Ramona was glad Beezus did not notice.

'If we don't let the candle burn the jack-o'-lantern, we can have pumpkin pie,' said Mrs Quimby. 'I can even freeze some of the pumpkin for Thanksgiving.'

Mr Quimby began to whistle as he carved with skill and care, first a mouthful of teeth, each one neat and square, then eyes and jagged ferocious eyebrows. He was working on two ears shaped like question marks, when Mrs Quimby said, 'Bedtime, Ramona.'

'I am going to stay up until Daddy finishes,' Ramona informed her family. 'No ifs, ands, or buts.'

'Run along and take your bath,' said Mrs Quimby, 'and you can watch awhile longer.'

Because her family was happy once more, Ramona did not protest. She returned quickly, however, still damp under her pyjamas, to see what her father had thought of next. Hair, that's what he had thought of, something he could carve because the pumpkin was so big. He cut a few C-shaped curls around the hole in the top of the pumpkin before he reached inside and hollowed out a candle holder in the bottom.

'There,' he said and rinsed his jackknife under the kitchen tap. 'A work of art.'

Mrs Quimby found a candle stub, inserted it in the pumpkin, lit it, and set the lid in place. Ramona switched off the light. The jack-o'-lantern leered and sneered with a flickering flame.

'Oh, Daddy!' Ramona threw her arms around her father. 'It's the wickedest jack-o'-lantern in the whole world.'

Mr Quimby kissed the top of Ramona's head. 'Thank you. I take that as a compliment. Now run along to bed.'

Ramona could tell by the sound of her father's voice that he was smiling. She ran off to her room without thinking up excuses for staying up just five more minutes, added a postscript to her prayers thanking God for the big pumpkin, and another asking him to find her father a job, and fell asleep at once, not bothering to tuck her panda bear in beside her for comfort.

In the middle of the night Ramona found herself

suddenly awake without knowing why she was awake. Had she heard a noise? Yes, she had. Tense, she listened hard. There it was again, a sort of thumping, scuffling noise, not very loud but there just the same. Silence. Then she heard it again. Inside the house. In the kitchen. Something was in the kitchen, and it was moving.

Ramona's mouth was so dry she could barely whisper, 'Daddy!' No answer. More thumping. Someone bumped against the wall. Someone, something was coming to get them. Ramona thought about the leering, sneering face on the kitchen table. All the ghost stories she had ever heard, all the ghostly pictures she had ever seen flew through her mind. Could the jack-o'-lantern have come to life? Of course not. It was only a pumpkin, but still—A bodyless, leering head was too horrifying to think about.

Ramona sat up in bed and shrieked, 'Daddy!'

A light came on in her parents' room, feet thumped to the floor, Ramona's tousled father in rumpled pyjamas was silhouetted in Ramona's doorway, followed by her mother tugging a robe on over her short nightgown.

'What is it, Baby?' asked Mr Quimby. Both Ramona's parents called her Baby when they were worried about her, and tonight Ramona was so relieved to see them she did not mind.

'Was it a bad dream?' asked Mrs Quimby.

'Th-there's something in the kitchen.' Ramona's voice quavered.

Beezus, only half-awake, joined the family. 'What's happening?' she asked. 'What's going on?'

'There's something in the kitchen,' said Ramona, feeling braver. 'Something moving.'

'Sh-h!' commanded Mr Quimby.

Tense, the family listened to silence.

'You just had a bad dream.' Mrs Quimby came into the room, kissed Ramona, and started to tuck her in.

Ramona pushed the blanket away. 'It was *not* a bad dream,' she insisted. 'I did too hear something. Something spooky.'

'All we have to do is look,' said Mr Quimby, reasonably—and bravely, Ramona thought. Nobody would get her into that kitchen.

Ramona waited, scarcely breathing, fearing for her father's safety as he walked down the hall and flipped on the kitchen light. No shout, no yell came from that part of the house. Instead her father laughed, and Ramona felt brave enough to follow the rest of the family to see what was funny.

There was a strong smell of cat food in the kitchen. What Ramona saw, and what Beezus saw, did not strike them as one bit funny. Their jack-o'-lantern, the jack-o'-lantern their father had worked so hard to carve, no longer had a whole face. Part of its forehead, one ferocious eyebrow, one eye, and part of its nose were gone, replaced by a jagged hole edged by little teeth marks. Picky-picky was crouched in guilt under the kitchen table.

The nerve of that cat. 'Bad cat! Bad cat!' shrieked Ramona, stamping her bare foot on the cold linoleum. The old yellow cat fled to the dining room, where he crouched under the table, his eyes glittering out of the darkness.

Mrs Quimby laughed a small rueful laugh. 'I knew he liked canteloupe, but I had no idea he liked pumpkin, too.' With a butcher's knife she began to cut up the remains of the jack-o'-lantern, carefully removing, Ramona noticed, the parts with teeth marks.

'I *told* you he wouldn't eat that awful Puss-puddy.' Beezus was accusing her father of denying their cat. 'Of course he had to eat our jack-o'-lantern. He's starving.'

'Beezus, dear,' said Mrs Quimby. 'We simply cannot afford the brand of food Picky- picky used to eat. Now be reasonable.'

Beezus was in no mood to be reasonable. 'Then how come Daddy can afford to smoke?' she demanded to know.

Ramona was astonished to hear her sister speak this way to her mother.

Mr Quimby looked angry. 'Young lady,' he said, and when he called Beezus young lady, Ramona knew her sister had better watch out. 'Young lady, I've heard enough about that old tom cat and his food. My cigarettes are none of your business.'

Ramona expected Beezus to say she was sorry or maybe burst into tears and run to her room. Instead she pulled Picky-picky out from under the table and held him to her chest as if she was shielding him from danger. 'They are too my business,' she informed her father. 'Cigarettes can kill you. Your lungs will turn black and you'll *die*! We made posters about it at school. And besides, cigarettes pollute the air!'

Ramona was horrified by her sister's daring, and at the same time she was a tiny bit pleased. Beezus was usually well-behaved while Ramona was the one who had tantrums. Then she was struck by the meaning of her sister's angry words and was frightened.

'That's enough out of you,' Mr Quimby told Beezus, 'and let me remind you that if you had shut that cat in the basement as you were supposed to, this would never have happened.'

Mrs Quimby quietly stowed the remains of the jack-o'-lantern in a plastic bag in the refrigerator.

Beezus opened the basement door and gently set Picky-picky on the top step. 'Nighty-night,' she said tenderly.

'Young lady,' began Mr Quimby. Young lady again! Now Beezus was really going to catch it. 'You are getting altogether too big for your britches lately. Just be careful how you talk around this house.'

Still Beezus did not say she was sorry. She did not burst into tears. She simply stalked off to her room.

Ramona was the one who burst into tears. She didn't mind when she and Beezus quarrelled. She even enjoyed a good fight now and then to clear the air, but she could not bear it when anyone else in the family quarrelled, and those awful things Beezus said—were they true?

'Don't cry, Ramona.' Mrs Quimby put her arm around her younger daughter. 'We'll get another pumpkin.'

'B-but it won't be as big,' sobbed Ramona, who wasn't crying about the pumpkin at all. She was crying about important things like her father being cross so much now that he wasn't working and his lungs turning black and Beezus being so disagreeable when before she had always been so polite (to grown-ups) and anxious to do the right thing.

'Come on, let's all go to bed and things will look brighter in the morning,' said Mrs Quimby.

'In a few minutes.' Mr Quimby picked up a package of cigarettes he had left on the kitchen table, shook one out, lit it, and sat down, still looking angry.

Were his lungs turning black this very minute? Ramona wondered. How would anybody know, when his lungs were inside him? She let her mother guide her to her room and tuck her in bed.

'Now don't worry about your jack-o'-lantern. We'll get another pumpkin. It won't be as big, but you'll have your jack-o'-lantern.' Mrs Quimby kissed Ramona goodnight.

'Nighty-night,' said Ramona in a muffled voice. As soon as her mother left, she hopped out of bed and pulled her old panda bear out from under the bed and tucked it under the covers beside her for comfort. The bear must have been dusty because Ramona sneezed.

'*Gesundheit!*' said Mr Quimby, passing by her door. 'We'll carve another jack-o'-lantern tomorrow. Don't worry.' He was not angry with Ramona.

Ramona snuggled down with her dusty bear. Didn't grown-ups think children worried about anything but jack-o'-lanterns? Didn't they know children worried about grown-ups?

4

RaMONa To The Rescue

The Quimbys said very little at breakfast the next morning. Beezus was moody and silent. Mrs Quimby, in her white uniform, was in a hurry to leave for work. Picky-picky resentfully ate a few bites of Puss-puddy. Mr Quimby did not say, 'I told you he would eat it when he was really hungry,' but the whole family was thinking it. He might as well have said it.

Ramona wished her family would cheer up. When they had finished eating, she found herself alone with her father.

'Bring me an ashtray, please,' said Mr Quimby. 'That's a good girl.'

Reluctantly Ramona brought the ashtray and, with her face rigid with disapproval, watched her father light his after-breakfast cigarette.

'Why so solemn?' he asked as he shook out the flame of the match.

'Is it true what Beezus said?' Ramona demanded.

'About what?' asked Mr Quimby.

Ramona had a feeling her father really knew

what she meant. 'About smoking will make your lungs turn black,' she answered.

Mr Quimby blew a puff of smoke towards the ceiling. 'I expect to be one of those old men with a long grey beard who has his picture in the paper on his hundredth birthday and who tells reporters he owes his long life to cigarettes and whisky.'

Ramona was not amused. 'Daddy'—her voice was stern—'you are just being silly again.'

Her father took a deep breath and blew three smoke rings across the table, a most unsatisfactory answer to Ramona.

On the way to school Ramona cut across the lawn for the pleasure of leaving footprints in the dew and then did not bother to look back to see where she had walked. Instead of running or skipping, she trudged. Nothing was much fun any more when her family quarrelled and then was silent at breakfast and her father's lungs were turning black from smoke.

Even though Mrs Rogers announced, 'Today our second grade is going to have fun learning,' as she wrote the date on the blackboard, school turned out to be dreary because the class was having Review again. Review meant boredom for some, like Ramona, because they had to repeat what they already knew, and worry for others, like

Davy, because they had to try again what they could not do in the first place. Review was the worst part of school. Ramona passed the morning looking through her workbook for words with double *o*'s like *book* and *cook*. She carefully drew eyebrows over the *o*'s and dots within, making the *o*'s look like crossed eyes. Then she drew mouths with the ends turned down under the eyes. When she finished, she had a cross-looking workbook that matched her feelings.

She was in no hurry to leave the building at recess, but when she did, Davy yelled, 'Look out! Here comes Ramona!' and began to run, so of course Ramona had to chase him around and around the playground until time to go inside again.

Running until she was hot and panting made Ramona feel so much better that she was filled with sudden determination. Her father's lungs were not going to turn black. She would not let them. Ramona made up her mind, right then and there in the middle of arithmetic, that she was going to save her father's life.

That afternoon after school Ramona gathered up her crayons and papers from the kitchen table, took them into her room, and shut the door. She got down on her hands and knees and went to work on the bedroom floor, printing a sign in big letters. Unfortunately, she did not plan ahead and soon reached the edge of the paper. She could not find the Scotch tape to fasten two pieces of paper together, so she had to continue on another line. When she finished, her sign read:

NO SMO KING

It would do. Ramona found a pin and fastened her sign to the living-room curtains, where her father could not miss it. Then she waited, frightened by her daring.

Mr Quimby, although he must have seen the sign, said nothing until after dinner when he had finished his pumpkin pie. He asked for an ashtray and then enquired, 'Say, who is this Mr King?'

'What Mr King?' asked Ramona, walking into his trap.

'Nosmo King,' answered her father without cracking a smile.

Chagrined, Ramona tore down her sign, crumpled

it, threw it into the fireplace, and stalked out of the room, resolving to do better the next time.

The next day after school Ramona found the Scotch tape and disappeared into her room to continue work on her plan to save her father's life. While she was working, she heard the phone ring and waited, tense, as the whole family now waited whenever the telephone rang. She heard her father clear his throat before he answered. 'Hello?' After a pause he said, 'Just a minute, Howie. I'll call her.' There was disappointment in his voice. No one was calling to offer him a job after all.

'Ramona, can you come over and play?' Howie asked, when Ramona went to the telephone.

Ramona considered. Of course they would have to put up with Howie's messy little sister, Willa Jean, but she and Howie would have fun building things if they could think of something to build. Yes, she would like to play with Howie, but saving her father's life was more important. 'No, thank you. Not today,' she said. 'I have important work to do.'

Just before dinner she taped to the refrigerator door a picture of a cigarette so long she had to fasten three pieces of paper together to draw it. After drawing the cigarette, she had crossed it out with a big black X and under it she had printed in big letters the word *BAD*. Beezus giggled when she saw it and Mrs Quimby smiled as if she were trying not to smile. Ramona was filled with fresh courage. She had allies. Her father had better watch out.

When Mr Quimby saw the picture, he stopped and looked while Ramona waited. 'Hmm,' he said, backing away for a better view. 'An excellent likeness. The artist shows talent.' And that was all he said.

Ramona felt let down, although she was not sure what she had expected. Anger, perhaps? Punishment? A promise to give up smoking?

The next morning the sign was gone, and that afternoon Ramona had to wait until Beezus came home from school to ask, 'How do you spell *pollution?*' When Beezus printed it out on a piece of paper, Ramona went to work making a sign that said, *Stop Air Pollution*.

'Let me help,' said Beezus, and the two girls, kneeling on the floor, printed a dozen signs. *Smoking Stinks. Cigarettes Start Forest Fires. Smoking Is Hazardous to Your Health*. Ramona learned new words that afternoon.

Fortunately Mr Quimby went out to examine the car, which was still making the *tappety-tappety* noise. This gave the girls a chance to tape the signs to the mantel, the refrigerator, the dining-room curtains, the door of the hall closet, and every other conspicuous place they could think of.

This time Mr Quimby simply ignored the signs. Ramona and Beezus might as well have saved themselves a lot of work for all he seemed to notice. But how could he miss so many signs? He must be pretending. He had to be pretending. Obviously the girls would have to step up their campaign. By now they were running out of big pieces of paper, and they knew better than to ask their parents to buy more, not when the family was so short of money.

'We can make little signs on scraps of paper,' said Ramona, and that was what they did. Together they made tiny signs that said, *No Smoking, Stop Air Pollution, Smoking Is Bad for Your Health*, and *Stamp Out Cigarettes*. On some Ramona drew stick figures of people stretched out flat and dead, and on one, a cat on his back with his feet in the air. These they hid wherever their father was sure to find them—in his bathrobe pocket, fastened around the handle of his toothbrush with a rubber band, inside his shoes, under his electric razor.

Then they waited. And waited. Mr Quimby said nothing while he continued to smoke. Ramona held her nose whenever she saw her father with a cigarette. He appeared not to notice. The girls felt discouraged and let down.

Once more Ramona and Beezus devised a plan, the most daring plan of all because they had to get hold of their father's cigarettes just before dinner. Fortunately he had tinkered with the car, still trying to find the reason for the *tappety-tappety-tap*, and had to take a shower before dinner, which gave the girls barely enough time to carry out their plan.

All through dinner the girls exchanged excited glances, and by the time her father asked her to fetch an ashtray, Ramona could hardly sit still she was so excited.

As usual her father pulled his cigarettes out of his shirt pocket. As usual he tapped the package against his hand, and as usual a cigarette, or what appeared to be a cigarette, slid out. Mr Quimby must have sensed that what he thought was a cigarette was lighter than it should be, because he paused to look at it. While Ramona held her breath, he frowned, looked more closely, unrolled the paper, and discovered it was a tiny sign that said, *Smoking Is Bad!* Without a word, he crumpled it and pulled out another—he thought—cigarette, which turned out to be a sign saying, *Stamp Out Cigarettes!* Mr Quimby crumpled it and tossed it onto the table along with the first sign.

'Ramona.' Mr Quimby's voice was stern. 'My grandmother used to say, "First time is funny, second time is silly—"' Mr Quimby's grandmother's wisdom was interrupted by a fit of coughing.

Ramona was frightened. Maybe her father's lungs already had begun to turn black.

Beezus looked triumphant. See, we told you smoking was bad for you, she was clearly thinking.

Mrs Quimby looked both amused and concerned.

Mr Quimby looked embarrassed, pounded himself on the chest with his fist, took a sip of coffee, and said, 'Something must have caught in my throat.' When his family remained silent, he said, 'All right, Ramona. As I was saying, enough is enough.'

Ramona scowled and slid down in her chair. Nothing was ever fair for second-graders. Beezus helped, but Ramona was getting all the blame. She also felt defeated. Nobody ever paid any attention to second-graders except to scold them. No matter how hard she tried to save her father's life, he was not going to let her save it.

Ramona gave up, and soon found she missed the excitement of planning the next step in her campaign against her father's smoking. Her afternoons after school seemed empty. Howie was home with tonsillitis, and she had no one to play with. She wished there were more children her age in her neighbourhood. She was so lonely she picked up the telephone and dialled the

Quimbys' telephone number to see if she could answer herself. All she got was a busy signal and a reprimand from her father for playing with the telephone when someone might be trying to reach him about a job.

On top of all this, the family had pumpkin pie for dinner.

'Not *again*!' protested Beezus. The family had eaten pumpkin pie and pumpkin custard since the night the cat ate part of the jack-o'-lantern. Beezus had once told Ramona that she thought her mother had tried to hide pumpkin in the meat loaf, but she wasn't sure because everything was all ground up together.

'I'm sorry, but there aren't many pumpkin recipes. I can't bear to waste good food,' said Mrs Quimby. 'But I do remember seeing a recipe for pumpkin soup someplace—'

'No!' Her family was unanimous.

Ramona was so disappointed because her father had ignored all her little signs that she did not feel much like eating, and especially not pumpkin pie for what seemed like the hundredth time. She eyed her triangle of pie and knew she could not make it go down. She was sick of pumpkin. 'Are you sure you cut off all the parts with cat spit on them?' she asked her mother.

'Ramona!' Mr Quimby, who had been stirring

his coffee, dropped his spoon. 'Please! We are eating.'

They had been eating, but after Ramona's remark no one ate a bite of pie.

Mr Quimby continued to smoke, and Ramona continued to worry. Then one afternoon, when Ramona came home from school, she found the back door locked. When she pounded on it with her fist, no one answered. She went to the front door, rang the doorbell, and waited. Silence. Lonely silence. She tried the door even though she knew it was locked. More silence. Nothing like this had ever happened to Ramona before. Someone was always waiting when she came home from school.

Ramona was frightened. Tears filled her eyes as she sat down on the cold concrete steps to think. Where could her father be? She thought of her friends at school, Davy and Sharon, who did not have fathers. Where had their fathers gone? Everybody had a father sometime. Where could they go?

Ramona's insides tightened with fear. Maybe her father was angry with her. Maybe he had gone away because she tried to make him stop smoking. She thought she was saving his life, but maybe she was being mean to him. Her mother said she must not annoy her father, because he was worried about being out of work. Maybe she had made him so angry he did not love her any more. Maybe he had gone away because he did not love her. She thought of all the scary things she had seen on television—houses that had fallen down in earthquakes, people shooting people, big hairy men on motorcycles—and knew she needed her father to keep her safe.

The cold from the concrete seeped through Ramona's clothes. She wrapped her arms around her knees to keep warm as she watched a dried leaf scratch along the driveway in the autumn wind. She listened to the honking of a flock of wild geese flying through the grey clouds on their way south for the winter. They came from Canada, her father had once told her, but that was before he had gone away. Raindrops began to dot the driveway, and tears dotted Ramona's skirt. She put her head down on her knees and cried. Why had she been so mean to her father? If he ever came back he could smoke all he wanted, fill the ashtrays and turn the air blue, and she wouldn't say a single word. She just wanted her father back, black lungs and all.

And suddenly there he was, scrunching through the leaves on the driveway with the collar of his windbreaker turned up against the wind and his old fishing hat pulled down over his eyes. 'Sorry

I'm late,' he said, as he got out his key. 'Is that what all this boohooing is about?'

Ramona wiped her sweater sleeve across her nose and stood up. She was so glad to see her father and so relieved that he had not gone away, that anger blazed up. Her tears became angry tears. Fathers were not supposed to worry their little girls. 'Where have you been?' she demanded. 'You're supposed to be here when I come home from school! I thought you had gone away and left me.'

'Take it easy. I wouldn't go off and leave you. Why would I do a thing like that?' Mr Quimby unlocked the door and, with a hand on Ramona's shoulder, guided her into the living room. 'I'm sorry I had to worry you. I was collecting my unemployment insurance, and I had to wait in a long line.'

Ramona's anger faded. She knew all about long lines and understood how difficult they were. She had waited in lines for her turn at the slides in the park, she had waited in lines in the school lunchroom back in the days when her family could spare lunch money once in a while, she had waited in lines with her mother at the check-out counter in the market, when she was little she had waited in long, long lines to see Santa Claus in the department store, and—these were the worst, most boring lines of all—she had waited in lines with her mother in the bank. She felt bad because her father had had to wait in line, and she also understood that collecting unemployment insurance did not make him happy.

'Did somebody try to push ahead of you?' Ramona was wise in the ways of lines.

'No. The line was unusually long today.' Mr Quimby went into the kitchen to make himself a cup of instant coffee. While he waited for the water to heat, he poured Ramona a glass of milk and gave her a graham cracker.

'Feeling better?' he asked.

Ramona looked at her father over the rim of her glass and nodded, spilling milk down her front. Silently he handed her a dish towel to wipe up while he poured hot water over the instant coffee in his mug. Then he reached into his shirt pocket, pulled out a package of cigarettes, looked at it a moment, and tossed it onto the counter. Ramona had never seen her father do this before. Could it be . . .

Mr Quimby leaned against the counter and took a sip of coffee. 'What would you like to do?' he asked Ramona.

Ramona considered before she answered. 'Something big and important.' But what? she wondered. Break a record in that book of records Beezus talked about? Climb Mount Hood?

'Such as?' her father asked.

Ramona finished scrubbing the front of her sweater with the dish towel. 'Well—' she said, thinking. 'You know that big bridge across the Columbia River?'

'Yes. The Interstate Bridge. The one we cross when we drive to Vancouver.'

'I've always wanted to stop on that bridge and get out of the car and stand with one foot in Oregon and one foot in Washington.'

'A good idea, but not practical,' said Mr Quimby. 'Your mother has the car, and I doubt if cars are allowed to stop on the bridge. What else?'

'It's not exactly important, but I always like to crayon,' said Ramona. How long would her father leave his cigarettes on the counter?

Mr Quimby set his cup down. 'I have a great idea! Let's draw the longest picture in the world.' He opened a drawer and pulled out a roll of shelf paper. When he tried to unroll it on the kitchen floor, the paper rolled itself up again. Ramona quickly solved that problem by Scotch-taping the end of the roll to the floor. Together she and her father unrolled the paper across the kitchen and knelt with a box of crayons between them.

'What shall we draw?' she asked.

'How about the state of Oregon?' he suggested. 'That's big enough.'

Ramona's imagination was excited. 'I'll begin with the Interstate Bridge,' she said.

'And I'll tackle Mount Hood,' said her father.

Together they went to work, Ramona on the end of the shelf paper and her father halfway across the kitchen. With crayons Ramona drew a long black bridge with a girl standing astride a line in the centre. She drew blue water under the bridge, even though the Columbia River always looked grey. She added grey clouds, grey dots for raindrops, and all the while she was drawing she was trying to find courage to tell her father something.

Ramona glanced at her father's picture, and sure enough he had drawn Mount Hood peaked with a hump on the south side exactly the way it looked in real life on the days when the clouds lifted.

'I think you draw better than anybody in the whole world,' said Ramona.

Mr Quimby smiled. 'Not quite,' he said.

'Daddy—' Ramona summoned courage. 'I'm sorry I was mean to you.'

'You weren't mean.' Mr Quimby was adding trees at the base of the mountain. 'You're right, you know.'

'Am I?' Ramona wanted to be sure.

'Yes.'

This answer gave Ramona even more courage. 'Is that why you didn't have a cigarette with your coffee? Are you going to stop smoking?'

'I'll try,' answered Mr Quimby, his eyes on his drawing. 'I'll try.'

Ramona was filled with joy, enthusiasm, and relief. 'You can do it, Daddy! I know you can do it.'

Her father seemed less positive. 'I hope so,' he answered, 'but if I succeed, Picky-picky will still have to eat Puss-puddy.'

'He can try, too,' said Ramona and slashed dark V's across her grey sky to represent a flock of geese flying south for the winter.

5

Beezus's Creative Writing

The Quimby women, as Mr Quimby referred to his wife and daughters, were enthusiastic about Mr Quimby's decision to give up smoking. He was less enthusiastic because, after all, he was the one who had to break the habit.

Ramona took charge. She collected all her father's cigarettes and threw them in the garbage, slamming down the lid of the can with a satisfying crash, a crash much less satisfying to her father, who looked as if he wanted those cigarettes back.

'I was planning to cut down gradually,' he said. 'One less cigarette each day.'

'That's not what you said,' Ramona informed him. 'You said you would try to give up smoking, not try to cut down gradually.'

There followed an even more trying time in the Quimby household. Out of habit Mr Quimby frequently reached for cigarettes that were no longer in his pocket. He made repeated trips to the refrigerator, looking for something to nibble on. He thought he was gaining weight. Worst of all, he was even crosser than when he first lost his job.

With a cross father, a tired mother, a sister who worried about creative writing, and a cat who grudgingly ate his Puss-puddy, Ramona felt she was the only happy member of the family left. Even she had run out of ways to amuse herself. She continued to add to the longest picture in the world, but she really wanted to run and yell and make a lot of noise to show how relieved she was that her father was giving up smoking.

One afternoon Ramona was on her knees on the kitchen floor working on her picture when Beezus came home from school, dropped her books on the kitchen table, and said, 'Well, it's come.'

Ramona looked up from the picture of Glenwood School she was drawing on the roll of shelf paper taped to the floor. Mr Quimby, who had a dish towel tucked into his belt for an apron, turned from the kitchen sink. 'What's come?' he asked. Although it was late in the afternoon, he was washing the breakfast dishes. He had been interviewed for two different jobs that morning.

'Creative writing.' Beezus's voice was filled with gloom.

'You make it sound like a calamity,' said her father.

Beezus sighed. 'Well—maybe it won't be so bad this time. We aren't supposed to write stories or poems after all.'

'Then what does Mrs Mester mean by creative?'

'Oh, you know . . . ' Beezus twirled around on one toe to define creative.

'What are you supposed to write if you don't write a story or a poem?' asked Ramona. 'Arithmetic problems?'

Beezus continued to twirl as if spinning might inspire her. 'She said we should interview some old person and ask questions about something they did when they were our age. She said she would run off what we wrote on the copying machine, and we could make a book.' She stopped twirling to catch the dish towel her father tossed to her. 'Do we know anyone who helped build a log cabin or something like that?'

'I'm afraid not,' said Mr Quimby. 'We don't know anybody who skinned buffalo either. How old is old?'

'The older the better,' said Beezus.

'Mrs Swink is pretty old,' volunteered Ramona. Mrs Swink was a widow who lived in the house on the corner and drove an old sedan that Mr Quimby admiringly called a real collector's item.

'Yes, but she wears polyester trouser suits,' said

435

Beezus, who had grown critical of clothing lately. She did not approve of polyester trouser suits, white shoes, or Ramona's T-shirt with Rockaway Beach printed on the front.

'Mrs Swink is old inside the trouser suits,' Ramona pointed out.

Beezus made a face. 'I can't go barging in on her all by myself and ask her a bunch of questions.' Beezus was the kind of girl who never wanted to go next door to borrow an egg and who dreaded having to sell mints for the Campfire Girls.

'I'll come,' said Ramona, who was always eager to go next door to borrow an egg and looked forward to being old enough to sell mints.

'You don't barge in,' said Mr Quimby, wringing out the dishcloth. 'You phone and make an appointment. Go on. Phone her now and get it over.'

Beezus put her hand on the telephone book. 'But what'll I say?' she asked.

'Just explain what you want and see what she says,' said Mr Quimby. 'She can't bite you over the telephone.'

Beezus appeared to be thinking hard. 'OK,' she said with some reluctance, 'but you don't have to listen.'

Ramona and her father went into the living room and turned on the television so they couldn't overhear Beezus. When Ramona noticed her father reached for the cigarettes that were not there, she gave him a stern look.

In a moment Beezus appeared, looking flustered. 'I meant sometime in a day or so, but she said to come right now because in a little while she has to take a moulded salad to her lodge for a potluck supper. Dad, what'll I *say*? I haven't had time to think.'

'Just play it by ear,' he advised. 'Something will come to you.'

'I'm going too,' Ramona said, and Beezus did not object.

Mrs Swink saw the sisters coming and opened the door for them as they climbed the front steps. 'Come on in, girls, and sit down,' she said briskly. 'Now what is it you want to interview me about?'

Beezus seemed unable to say anything, and Ramona could understand how it might be hard to ask someone wearing a polyester trouser suit questions about building a log cabin. Someone had to say something so Ramona spoke up. 'My sister wants to know what you used to do when you were a little girl.'

Beezus found her tongue. 'Like I said over the phone. It's for creative writing.'

Mrs Swink looked thoughtful. 'Let's see.

Nothing very exciting, I'm afraid. I helped with the dishes and read a lot of books from the library. The *Red Fairy Book* and *Blue Fairy Book* and all the rest.'

Beezus looked worried, and Ramona could see that she was trying to figure out what she could write about dishes and library books. Ramona ended another awkward silence by asking, 'Didn't you make anything?' She had noticed that Mrs Swink's living room was decorated with mosaics made of dried peas and beans and with owls made out of pinecones. The dining-room table was strewn with old Christmas cards, scissors, and paste, a sure sign of a craft project.

'Let's see now . . . ' Mrs Swink looked thoughtful. 'We made fudge, and—oh, I know—tin-can stilts.' She smiled to herself. 'I had forgotten all about tin-can stilts until this very minute.'

At last Beezus could ask a question. 'How did you make tin-can stilts?'

Mrs Swink laughed, remembering. 'We took two tall cans. Two-pound coffee cans were best. We turned them upside down and punched two holes near what had once been the bottom of each. The holes had to be opposite one another on each can. Then we poked about four feet of heavy twine through each pair of holes and knotted the ends to make a loop. We set one foot on each can, took hold of a loop of twine in each hand, and began to walk. We had to remember to lift each can by the loop of twine as we raised a foot or we fell off—my knees were always skinned. Little girls wore dresses instead of trousers in those days, and I always had dreadful scabs on my knees.'

Maybe this was why Mrs Swink always wore trouser suits now, thought Ramona. She didn't want scabs on her knees in case she fell down.

'And the noise those hollow tin cans made on the sidewalk!' continued Mrs Swink, enjoying the memory. 'All the kids in the neighbourhood went clanking up and down. Sometimes the cans would cut through the twine, and we would go sprawling on the sidewalk. I became expert at walking on tin-can stilts and used to go clanking around the block yelling, "Pieface!" at all the younger children.'

Ramona and Beezus both giggled. They were surprised that someone as old as Mrs Swink had once called younger children by a name they sometimes called one another.

'There.' Mrs Swink ended the interview. 'Does that help?'

'Yes, thank you.' Beezus stood up, and so did Ramona, although she wanted to ask Mrs Swink about the craft project on the dining-room table.

'Good.' Mrs Swink opened the front door. 'I hope you get an *A* on your composition.'

'Tin-can stilts weren't exactly what I expected,' said Beezus, as the girls started home. 'But I guess I can make them do.'

Do! Ramona couldn't wait to get to Howie's house to tell him about the tin-can stilts. And so, as Beezus went home to labour over her creative writing, Ramona ran over to the Kemps' house. Just as she thought, Howie listened to her excited description and said, 'I could make some of those.' Good old Howie. Ramona and Howie spent the rest of the afternoon finding four two-pound coffee cans. The search involved persuading Howie's mother to empty out her coffee into mayonnaise jars and calling on neighbours to see if they had any empty cans.

The next day after school Howie arrived on the Quimby doorstep with two sets of tin-can stilts. 'I made them!' he announced, proud of his work. 'And Willa Jean wanted some, so I made her a pair out of tuna cans so she wouldn't have far to fall.'

'I knew you could do it!' Ramona, who had already changed to her playclothes, stepped onto two of the cans and pulled the twine loops up tight before she took a cautious step, lifting a can as she lifted her foot. First the left foot, then the right foot. *Clank, clank.* They worked! Howie clanked along beside her. They clanked carefully down the driveway to the sidewalk, where Ramona tried to pick up speed, forgot to lift a can at the same time she lifted her foot, and, as Mrs Swink had recalled, fell off her stilts. She caught herself before she tumbled to the sidewalk and climbed back on.

Clank, clank. Clank, clank. Ramona found deep satisfaction in making so much noise, and so did Howie. Mrs Swink, turning into her driveway in her dignified old sedan, smiled and waved. In a moment of daring, Ramona yelled, 'Pieface!' at her.

'Pieface yourself!' Mrs Swink called back, understanding Ramona's joke.

Howie did not approve. 'You aren't supposed to call grown-ups pieface,' he said. 'Just kids.'

'I can call Mrs Swink pieface,' boasted Ramona. 'I can call her pieface any old time I want to.'
Clank, clank. Clank, clank. Ramona was having such a good time she began to sing at the top of her voice, 'Ninety-nine bottles of beer on the wall, ninety-nine bottles of beer. You take one down and pass it around. Ninety-eight bottles of beer on the wall . . . '

Howie joined the singing. 'Ninety-eight bottles of beer on the wall. You take one down and pass it around. Ninety-seven bottles of beer . . . '

Clank, clank. Clank, clank. Ninety-six bottles of beer, ninety-five bottles of beer on the wall. Sometimes Ramona and Howie tripped, sometimes they stumbled, and once in a while they fell, muddying the knees of their jeans on the wet sidewalk. Progress was slow, but what their stilts lost in speed they made up in noise.

Eighty-nine bottles of beer, eighty-six . . . Ramona was happier than she had been in a long time. She loved making noise, and she was proud of being able to count backwards. Neighbours looked out of their windows to see what all the racket was about while Ramona and Howie clanked determinedly on. 'Eighty-one bottles of beer on the wall . . .' As Mrs Swink had predicted, one of the twine loops broke, tumbling Ramona to the sidewalk. Howie knotted the ends together, and they clanked on until suppertime.

'That was some racket you two made,' remarked Mr Quimby.

Mrs Quimby asked, 'Where on earth did you two pick up that song about bottles of beer?'

'From Beezus,' said Ramona virtuously. 'Howie and I are going to count backwards all the way to one bottle of beer.'

Beezus, doing homework in her room, had not missed out on the conversation. 'We used to sing it at camp when the counsellors weren't around,' she called out.

'When I used to go to camp, we sang about

the teeny-weeny 'pider who went up the water 'pout,' said Mrs Quimby.

The teeny-weeny 'pider song was a favourite of Ramona's too, but it was not so satisfying as 'Ninety-nine Bottles of Beer', which was a much louder song.

'I wonder what the neighbours think,' said Mrs Quimby. 'Wouldn't some other song do?'

'No,' said Ramona. Only a noisy song would do.

'By the way, Ramona,' said Mr Quimby. 'Did you straighten your room today?'

Ramona was not much interested in the question. 'Sort of,' she answered truthfully, because she had shoved a lot of old school artwork and several pairs of dirty socks under the bed.

The next afternoon after school was even better, because Ramona and Howie had mastered walking on the tin-can stilts without falling off. 'Sixty-one bottles of beer on the wall. Take one down and pass it around,' they sang, as they clanked around the block. Ramona grew hot and sweaty, and when rain began to fall, she enjoyed the cold drops against her flushed face. On and on they clanked, singing at the top of their voices. Ramona's hair grew stringy, and Howie's blond curls tightened in the rain. 'Forty-one bottles of beer on the wall . . . ' *Clank, crash, clank.* 'Thirty-seven bottles of beer . . . ' *Clank, crash, clank.* Ramona forgot about her father being out of a job, she forgot about how cross he had been since he gave up smoking, she forgot about her mother coming home tired from work and about Beezus being grouchy lately. She was filled with joy.

The early winter darkness had fallen and the streetlights had come on by the time Ramona and Howie had clanked and crashed and sung their way down to that last bottle of beer. Filled with a proud feeling that they had accomplished something big, they jumped off their stilts and ran home with their coffee cans banging and clashing behind them.

Ramona burst in through the back door, dropped her wet stilts with a crash on the linoleum, and announced hoarsely, 'We did it! We sang all the way down to one bottle of beer!' She waited for her family to share her triumph.

Instead her father said, 'Ramona, you know you are supposed to be home before dark. It was a good thing I could hear where you were, or I would have had to go out after you.'

Mrs Quimby said, 'Ramona, you're sopping wet. Go change quickly before you catch cold.'

Beezus, who was often embarrassed by her

little sister, said, 'The neighbours will think we're a bunch of beer guzzlers.'

Well! thought Ramona. Some family! She stood dripping on the linoleum a moment, expecting hurt feelings to take over, perhaps even to make her cry a little so her family would be sorry they had been mean to her. To her wonder, no heavy feeling weighed her down, no sad expression came to her face, no tears. She simply stood there, cold, dripping, and feeling *good*. She felt good from making a lot of noise, she felt good from the hard work of walking so far on her tin-can stilts, she felt good from calling a grown-up pieface and from the triumph of singing backwards from ninety-nine to one. She felt good from being out after dark with rain on her face and the streetlights shining down on her. Her feelings were not hurt at all.

'Don't just stand there sogging,' said Beezus. 'You're supposed to set the table.'

Bossy old Beezus, thought Ramona. She squelched off to her room in her wet sneakers, and as she left the kitchen she began to sing, 'Ninety-nine bottles of beer on the wall . . . '

'Oh, no!' groaned her father.

6

THE SHEEP SUIT

Ramona did not expect trouble to start in Sunday school of all places, but that was where it was touched off one Sunday early in December. Sunday school began as usual. Ramona sat on a little chair between Davy and Howie with the rest of their class in the basement of the grey stone church. Mrs Russo, the superintendent, clapped her hands for attention.

'Let's have quiet, boys and girls,' she said. 'It's time to make plans for our Christmas carol programme and Nativity scene.'

Bored, Ramona hooked her heels on the rung of her little chair. She knew what her part would be—to put on a white choir robe and walk in singing carols with the rest of the second-grade class, which would follow the kindergarten and first grade. The congregation always murmured and smiled at the kindergarteners in their wobbly line, but nobody paid much attention to second-graders. Ramona knew she would have to wait years to be old enough for a chance at a part in the Nativity scene.

Ramona only half listened until Mrs Russo asked Beezus's friend Henry Huggins if he would like to be Joseph. Ramona expected him to say no, because he was so busy training for the Olympics in about eight or twelve years. He surprised her by saying, 'I guess so.'

'And Beatrice Quimby,' said Mrs Russo, 'would you like to be Mary?'

This question made Ramona unhook her heels and sit up. Her sister, grouchy old Beezus—Mary? Ramona searched out Beezus, who was looking pink, embarrassed, and pleased at the same time.

'Yes,' answered Beezus.

Ramona couldn't get over it. Her sister playing the part of Mary, mother of the baby Jesus, and getting to sit up there on the chancel with that manger they got out every year.

Mrs Russo had to call on a number of older boys before she found three who were willing to be wise men. Shepherds were easier. Three sixth-grade boys were willing to be shepherds.

While the planning was going on, a little voice inside Ramona was saying, 'Me! Me! What about me?' until it could be hushed no longer. Ramona spoke up. 'Mrs Russo, I could be a sheep. If you have shepherds, you need a sheep.'

'Ramona, that's a splendid idea,' said Mrs Russo, getting Ramona's hopes up, 'but I'm afraid the church does not have any sheep costumes.'

Ramona was not a girl to abandon her hopes if she could help it. 'My mother could make me a sheep costume,' she said. 'She's made me lots of costumes.' Maybe 'lots' was stretching the truth a bit. Mrs Quimby had made Ramona a witch costume that had lasted three Hallowe'ens, and when Ramona was in nursery school she had made her a little red devil suit.

Now Mrs Russo was in a difficult position because she had told Ramona her idea was splendid. 'Well . . . yes, Ramona, you may be a sheep if your mother will make you a costume.'

Howie had been thinking things over. 'Mrs Russo,' he said in that serious way of his, 'wouldn't it look silly for three shepherds to herd just one sheep? My grandmother could make me a sheep costume, too.'

'And my mother could make me one,' said Davy.

Sunday school was suddenly full of volunteer sheep, enough for a large flock. Mrs Russo clapped her hands for silence. 'Quiet, boys and girls! There isn't room on the chancel for so many sheep, but I think we can squeeze in one sheep per shepherd. Ramona, Howie, and Davy, since you asked first, you may be sheep if someone will make you costumes.'

Ramona smiled across the room at Beezus. They would be in the Nativity scene together.

When Sunday school was over, Beezus found Ramona and asked, 'Where's mother going to find time to make a sheep costume?'

'After work, I guess.' This problem was something Ramona had not considered.

Beezus looked doubtful. 'I'm glad the church already has my costume,' she said. Ramona began to worry.

Mrs Quimby always washed her hair after church on Sunday morning. Ramona waited until her mother had taken her head out from under the kitchen tap and was rubbing her hair on a bath towel. 'Guess what!' said Ramona. 'I get to be a sheep in the Nativity scene this year.'

'That's nice,' said Mrs Quimby. 'I'm glad they are going to do something a little different this year.'

'And I get to be Mary,' said Beezus.

'Good!' said Mrs Quimby, still rubbing.

'I'll need a sheep costume,' said Ramona.

'The church has my costume,' said Beezus.

Ramona gave her sister a you-shut-up look. Beezus smiled serenely. Ramona hoped she wasn't going to start acting like Mary already.

Mrs Quimby stopped rubbing to look at Ramona. 'And where are you going to get this sheep costume?' she asked.

Ramona felt very small. 'I—I thought you could make me a sheep suit.'

'When?'

Ramona felt even smaller. 'After work?'

Mrs Quimby sighed. 'Ramona, I don't like to disappoint you, but I'm tired when I come home from work. I don't have time to do a lot of sewing. A sheep suit would be a lot of work and mean a lot of little pieces to put together, and I don't even know if I could find a sheep pattern.'

Mr Quimby joined in the conversation. That was the trouble with a father with time on his hands. He always had time for other people's arguments. 'Ramona,' he said, 'you know better than to involve other people in work without asking first.'

Ramona wished her father could sew. He had plenty of time. 'Maybe Howie's grandmother could make me a costume, too,' she suggested.

'We can't ask favours like that,' said Mrs Quimby, 'and besides material costs money, and with Christmas coming and all we don't have a nickel to spare.'

Ramona knew all this. She simply hadn't thought; she had wanted to be a sheep so much.

She gulped and sniffed and tried to wiggle her toes inside her shoes. Her feet were growing and her shoes felt tight. She was glad she had not mentioned this to her mother. She would never get a costume if they had to buy shoes.

Mrs Quimby draped the towel around her shoulders and reached for her comb.

'I can't be a sheep without a costume.' Ramona sniffed again. She would gladly suffer tight shoes if she could have a costume instead.

'It's your own fault,' said Mr Quimby. 'You should have thought.'

Ramona now wished she had waited until after Christmas to persuade her father to give up smoking. Then maybe he would be nice to his little girl when she needed a sheep costume.

Mrs Quimby pulled the comb through her tangled hair. 'I'll see what I can do,' she said. 'We have that old white terry-cloth bathrobe with the sleeve seams that pulled out. It's pretty shabby, but if I bleached it, I might be able to do something with it.'

Ramona stopped sniffing. Her mother would try to make everything all right, but Ramona was not going to risk telling about her tight shoes in case she couldn't make a costume out of the bathrobe and needed to buy material.

That evening, after Ramona had gone to bed,

she heard her mother and father in their bedroom talking in those low, serious voices that so often meant that they were talking about her. She slipped out of bed and knelt on the floor with her ear against the furnace outlet to see if she could catch their words.

Her father's voice, coming through the furnace pipes, sounded hollow and far away. 'Why did you give in to her?' he was asking. 'She had no business saying you would make her a sheep costume without asking first. She has to learn sometime.'

I have learned, thought Ramona indignantly. Her father did not have to talk this way about her behind her back.

'I know,' answered Ramona's mother in a voice also sounding hollow and far away. 'But she's little, and these things are so important to her. I'll manage somehow.'

'We don't want a spoiled brat on our hands,' said Ramona's father.

'But it's Christmas,' said Mrs Quimby, 'and Christmas is going to be slim enough this year.'

Comforted by her mother but angry at her father, Ramona climbed back into bed. Spoiled brat! So that was what her father thought of her.

The days that followed were difficult for Ramona, who was now cross with her cross father.

He was *mean*, talking about her behind her back that way.

'Well, what's eating you?' he finally asked Ramona.

'Nothing.' Ramona scowled. She could not tell him why she was angry without admitting she had eavesdropped.

And then there was Beezus, who went around smiling and looking serene, perhaps because Mrs Mester had given her an A on her creative-writing composition and read it aloud to the class, but more likely because she was practising for her part as Mary. Having a sister who tried to act like the Virgin Mary was not easy for a girl who felt as Ramona did.

And the costume. Mrs Quimby found time to bleach the old bathrobe in the washing machine, but after that nothing happened. The doctor she worked for was so busy because of all the earaches, sore throats, and flu that came with winter weather that she was late coming home every evening.

On top of that, Ramona had to spend two afternoons watching Howie's grandmother sew on his sheep suit, because arrangements had now been made for Ramona to go to Howie's house if Mr Quimby could not be home after school. This week he had to collect unemployment insurance and take a civil-service examination for a job in the post office.

Ramona studied Howie's sheep suit, which was made out of fluffy white acrylic. The ears were lined with pink, and Mrs Kemp was going to put a zipper down the front. The costume was beautiful, soft and furry. Ramona longed to rub her cheek against it, hug it, take it to bed with her.

'And when I finish Howie's costume, I am going to make another for Willa Jean,' said Mrs Kemp. 'Willa Jean wants one, too.'

This was almost too much for Ramona to bear. Besides, her shoes felt tighter than ever. She looked at Willa Jean, who was clomping around the house on her little tuna-can stilts. Messy little Willa Jean in a beautiful sheep suit she didn't even need. She would only spoil the furry cloth by dribbling apple juice down the front and spilling graham-cracker crumbs all over it. People said Willa Jean behaved just the way Ramona used to, but Ramona could not believe them.

A week before the Christmas programme Mrs Quimby managed to find time to buy a pattern during her lunch hour, but she did not find time to sew for Ramona.

Mr Quimby, on the other hand, had plenty of time for Ramona. Too much, she was beginning to think. He nagged. Ramona should sit up closer to the table so she wouldn't spill so much. She should stop making rivers in her mashed potatoes. She should wring out her washcloth instead of leaving it sopping in the tub. Look at the circle of rust her tin-can stilts had left on the kitchen floor. Couldn't she be more careful? She should fold her bath towel in half and hang it up straight. How did she expect it to dry when it was all wadded up, for Pete's sake? She found a sign in her room that said, *A Messy Room Is Hazardous to Your Health*. That was too much.

Ramona marched out to the garage where her father was oiling the lawnmower so it would be ready when spring came and said, 'A messy room is not hazardous to my health. It's not the same as smoking.'

'You could trip and break your arm,' her father pointed out.

Ramona had an answer. 'I always turn on the light or sort of feel along with my feet.'

'You could smother in old school papers, stuffed animals, and hula hoops if the mess gets deep enough,' said her father and added, 'Miss Radar Feet.'

Ramona smiled. 'Daddy, you're just being silly again. Nobody ever smothered in a hula hoop.'

'You never can tell,' said her father. 'There is always a first time.'

Ramona and her father got along better for a while after that, and then came the terrible afternoon when Ramona came home from school to find her father closing the living-room windows, which had been wide open even though the day was raw and windy. There was a faint smell of cigarette smoke in the room.

'Why there's Henry running down the street,' said Mr Quimby, his back to Ramona. 'He may make it to the Olympics, but that old dog of his won't.'

'Daddy,' said Ramona. Her father turned. Ramona looked him in the eye. 'You *cheated*!'

Mr Quimby closed the last window. 'What are you talking about?'

'You smoked and you *promised* you wouldn't!' Ramona felt as if she were the grown-up and he were the child.

Mr Quimby sat down on the couch and leaned back as if he were very, very tired, which made some of the anger drain out of Ramona. 'Ramona,' he said, 'it isn't easy to break a bad habit. I ran across one cigarette, an old stale cigarette, in my raincoat pocket and thought it might help if I smoked just one. I'm trying. I'm really trying.'

Hearing her father speak this way, as if she really was a grown-up, melted the last of Ramona's anger. She turned into a seven year old again and climbed on the couch to lean against her father. After a few moments of silence, she whispered, 'I love you, Daddy.'

He tousled her hair affectionately and said, 'I know you do. That's why you want me to stop smoking, and I love you, too.'

'Even if I'm a brat sometimes?'

'Even if you're a brat sometimes.'

Ramona thought awhile before she sat up and said, 'Then why can't we be a happy family?'

For some reason Mr Quimby smiled. 'I have news for you, Ramona,' he said. 'We *are* a happy family.'

'We are?' Ramona was sceptical.

'Yes, we are.' Mr Quimby was positive. 'No family is perfect. Get that idea out of your head. And nobody is perfect either. All we can do is work at it. And we do.'

Ramona tried to wiggle her toes inside her shoes and considered what her father had said. Lots of fathers wouldn't draw pictures with their little girls. Her father bought her paper and crayons when he could afford them. Lots of mothers wouldn't step over a picture that spread across the kitchen floor while cooking supper. Ramona knew mothers who would scold and say, 'Pick that up. Can't you see I'm trying to get supper?' Lots of big sisters wouldn't let their little sister go along when they interviewed someone for creative writing. They would take more than their fair share of gummybears because they were bigger and . . .

Ramona decided her father was probably right, but she couldn't help feeling they would be a happier family if her mother could find time to sew that sheep costume. There wasn't much time left.

7

RaMONa aND THe THRee Wise PeRSONS

Suddenly, a few days before Christmas when the Quimby family least expected it, the telephone rang for Ramona's father. He had a job! The morning after New Year's Day he was to report for training as a checker in a chain of supermarkets. The pay was good, he would have to work some evenings, and maybe someday he would get to manage a market!

After that telephone call Mr Quimby stopped reaching for cigarettes that were not there and began to whistle as he ran the vacuum cleaner and folded the clothes from the dryer. The worried frown disappeared from Mrs Quimby's forehead. Beezus looked even more calm and serene. Ramona, however, made a mistake. She told her mother about her tight shoes. Mrs Quimby then wasted a Saturday afternoon shopping for shoes when she could have been sewing on Ramona's costume. As a result, when they drove to church the night of the Christmas carol programme, Ramona was the only unhappy member of the family.

Mr Quimby sang as he drove:

'There's a little wheel a-turning in my heart.

There's a little wheel a-turning in my heart.'

Ramona loved that song because it made her think of Howie, who liked machines. Tonight, however, she was determined not to enjoy her father's singing.

Rain blew against the car, headlights shone on the pavement, the windshield wipers *splip-splopped*. Mrs Quimby leaned back, tired but relaxed. Beezus smiled her gentle Virgin Mary smile that Ramona had found so annoying for the past three weeks.

Ramona sulked. Somewhere above those cold, wet clouds the very same star was shining that had guided the Three Wise Men to Bethlehem. On a night like this they never would have made it.

Mr Quimby sang on, 'Oh, I feel like shouting in my heart . . . '

Ramona interrupted her father's song. 'I don't care what anybody says,' she burst out. 'If I can't be a good sheep, I am not going to be a sheep at all.' She yanked off the white terry-cloth headdress with pink-lined ears that she was wearing and stuffed it into the pocket of her coat. She started to pull her father's rolled-down socks from her hands because they didn't really look like hooves, but then she decided they kept her hands warm.

She squirmed on the lumpy terry-cloth tail sewn to the seat of her pyjamas. Ramona could not pretend that faded pyjamas printed with an army of pink rabbits, half of them upside down, made her look like a sheep, and Ramona was usually good at pretending.

Mrs Quimby's voice was tired. 'Ramona, your tail and headdress were all I could manage, and I had to stay up late last night to finish those. I simply don't have time for complicated sewing.'

Ramona knew that. Her family had been telling her so for the past three weeks.

'A sheep should be woolly,' said Ramona. 'A sheep should not be printed with pink bunnies.'

'You can be a sheep that has been shorn,' said Mr Quimby, who was full of jokes now that he was going to work again. 'Or how about a wolf in sheep's clothing?'

'You just want me to be miserable,' said Ramona, not appreciating her father's humour and feeling that everyone in her family should be miserable because she was.

'She's worn out,' said Mrs Quimby, as if Ramona could not hear. 'It's so hard to wait for Christmas at her age.'

Ramona raised her voice. 'I am *not* worn out! You know sheep don't wear pyjamas.'

'That's show biz,' said Mr Quimby.

'Daddy!' Beezus-Mary was shocked. 'It's church!'

'And don't forget, Ramona,' said Mr Quimby, 'as my grandmother would have said, "Those pink bunnies will never be noticed from a trotting horse.'"

Ramona disliked her father's grandmother even more. Besides, nobody rode trotting horses in church.

The sight of light shining through the stained-glass window of the big stone church diverted Ramona for a moment. The window looked beautiful, as if it were made of jewels.

Mr Quimby backed the car into a parking space. 'Ho-ho-ho!' he said, as he turned off the ignition. ''Tis the season to be jolly.'

Jolly was the last thing Ramona was going to be. Leaving the car, she stooped down inside her coat to hide as many rabbits as possible. Black branches clawed at the sky, and the wind was raw.

'Stand up straight,' said Ramona's heartless father.

'I'll get wet,' said Ramona. 'I might catch cold, and then you'd be sorry.'

'Run between the drops,' said Mr Quimby.

'They're too close together,' answered Ramona.

'Oh, you two,' said Mrs Quimby with a tired little laugh, as she backed out of the car and tried to open her umbrella at the same time.

'I will not be in it,' Ramona defied her family once and for all. 'They can give the programme without me.'

Her father's answer was a surprise. 'Suit yourself,' he said. 'You're not going to spoil our evening.'

Mrs Quimby gave the seat of Ramona's pyjamas an affectionate pat. 'Run along, little lamb, wagging your tail behind you.'

Ramona walked stiff-legged so that her tail would not wag.

At the church door the family parted, the girls going downstairs to the Sunday-school room, which was a confusion of chattering children piling coats and raincoats on chairs. Ramona found a corner behind the Christmas tree, where Santa would pass out candy canes after the programme. She sat down on the floor with her coat pulled over her bent knees.

Through the branches Ramona watched carollers putting on their white robes. Girls were tying tinsel around one another's heads while Mrs Russo searched out boys and tied tinsel around their heads, too. 'It's all right for boys to wear tinsel,' Mrs Russo assured them. Some looked as if they were not certain they believed her.

One boy climbed on a chair. 'I'm an angel. Watch me fly,' he announced and jumped off, flapping the wide sleeves of his choir robe. All the carollers turned into flapping angels.

Nobody noticed Ramona. Everyone was having too much fun. Shepherds found their cloaks, which were made from old cotton bedspreads. Beezus's friend, Henry Huggins, arrived and put on the dark robe he was to wear in the part of Joseph.

The other two sheep appeared. Howie's acrylic sheep suit, with the zipper on the front, was as thick and as fluffy as Ramona knew it would be. Ramona longed to pet Howie; he looked so soft. Davy's flannel suit was fastened with safety pins, and there was something wrong about the ears. If his tail had been longer, he could have passed for a kitten, but he did not seem to mind. Both boys wore brown mittens. Davy, who was a thin little sheep, jumped up and down to make his tail wag, which surprised Ramona. At school he was always so shy. Maybe he felt brave inside his sheep suit. Howie, a chunky sheep, made his tail wag, too. My ears are as good as theirs, Ramona told herself. The floor felt cold through the seat of her thin pyjamas.

'Look at the little lambs!' cried an angel. 'Aren't they darling?'

'Ba-a, ba-a!' bleated Davy and Howie.

Ramona longed to be there with them, jumping

and ba-a-ing and wagging her tail, too. Maybe the faded rabbits didn't show as much as she had thought. She sat hunched and miserable. She had told her father she would *not* be a sheep, and she couldn't back down now. She hoped God was too busy to notice her, and then she changed her mind. Please, God, prayed Ramona, in case He wasn't too busy to listen to a miserable little sheep, I don't really mean to be horrid. It just works out that way. She was frightened, she discovered, for when the programme began, she would be left alone in the church basement. The lights might even be turned out, a scary thought, for the big stone church filled Ramona with awe, and she did not want to be left alone in the dark with her awe. Please, God, prayed Ramona, get me out of this mess.

Beezus, in a long blue robe with a white scarf over her head and carrying a baby's blanket and a big flashlight, found her little sister. 'Come out, Ramona,' she coaxed. 'Nobody will notice your costume. You know mother would have made you a whole sheep suit if she had time. Be a good sport. Please.'

Ramona shook her head and blinked to keep tears from falling. 'I told Daddy I wouldn't be in the programme, and I won't.'

'Well, OK, if that's the way you feel,' said

Beezus, forgetting to act like Mary. She left her little sister to her misery.

Ramona sniffed and wiped her eyes on her hoof. Why didn't some grown-up come along and *make* her join the other sheep? No grown-up came. No one seemed to remember there were supposed to be three sheep, not even Howie, who played with her almost every day.

Ramona's eye caught the reflection of her face distorted in a green Christmas ornament. She was shocked to see her nose look huge, her mouth and red-rimmed eyes tiny. I can't really look like that, thought Ramona in despair. I'm really a nice person. It's just that nobody understands.

Ramona mopped her eyes on her hoof again, and as she did she noticed three big girls, so tall they were probably in the eighth grade, putting on robes made from better bedspreads than the shepherd's robes. That's funny, she thought. Nothing she had learned in Sunday school told her anything about girls in long robes in the Nativity scene. Could they be Jesus's aunts?

One of the girls began to dab tan cream from a little jar on her face and to smear it around while another girl held up a pocket mirror. The third girl, holding her own mirror, used an eyebrow pencil to give herself heavy brows.

Make-up, thought Ramona with interest, wishing

she could wear it. The girls took turns darkening their faces and brows. They looked like different people. Ramona got to her knees and peered over the lower branches of the Christmas tree for a better view.

One of the girls noticed her. 'Hi, there,' she said. 'Why are you hiding back there?'

'Because,' was Ramona's all-purpose answer. 'Are you Jesus's aunts?' she asked.

The girls found the question funny. 'No,' answered one. 'We're the Three Wise Persons.'

Ramona was puzzled. 'I thought they were supposed to be wise *men*,' she said.

'The boys backed out at the last minute,' explained the girl with the blackest eyebrows. 'Mrs Russo said women can be wise too, so tonight we are the Three Wise Persons.'

This idea seemed like a good one to Ramona, who wished she were big enough to be a wise person hiding behind make-up so nobody would know who she was.

'Are you supposed to be in the programme?' asked one of the girls.

'I was supposed to be a sheep, but I changed my mind,' said Ramona, changing it back again. She pulled out her sheep headdress and put it on.

'Isn't she adorable?' said one of the wise persons.

Ramona was surprised. She had never been called adorable before. Bright, lively, yes; adorable, no. She smiled and felt more lovable. Maybe pink-lined ears helped.

'Why don't you want to be a sheep?' asked a wise person.

Ramona had an inspiration. 'Because I don't have any make-up.'

'Make-up on a *sheep*!' exclaimed a wise person and giggled.

Ramona persisted. 'Sheep have black noses,' she hinted. 'Maybe I could have a black nose.'

The girls looked at one another. 'Don't tell my mother,' said one, 'but I have some mascara. We could make her nose black.'

'Please!' begged Ramona, getting to her feet and coming out from behind the Christmas tree.

The owner of the mascara fumbled in her shoulder bag, which was hanging on a chair, and brought out a tiny box. 'Let's go in the kitchen where there's a sink,' she said, and when Ramona followed her, she moistened an elf-sized brush, which she rubbed on the mascara in the box. Then she began to brush it onto Ramona's nose. It tickled, but Ramona held still. 'It feels like brushing my teeth only on my nose,' she remarked. The wise person stood back to look at her work and then applied another coat of mascara to

Ramona's nose. 'There,' she said at last. 'Now you look like a real sheep.'

Ramona felt like a real sheep. 'Ba-a-a,' she bleated, a sheep's way of saying thank you. Ramona felt so much better, she could almost pretend she was woolly. She peeled off her coat and found that the faded pink rabbits really didn't show much in the dim light. She pranced off among the angels, who had been handed little flashlights, which they were supposed to hold like candles. Instead they were shining them into their mouths to show one another how weird they looked with light showing through their cheeks. The other two sheep stopped jumping when they saw her.

'You don't look like Ramona,' said Howie.

'B-a-a. I'm not Ramona. I'm a sheep.' The boys did not say one word about Ramona's pyjamas. They wanted black noses too, and when Ramona told them where she got hers, they ran off to find the wise persons. When they returned, they no longer looked like Howie and Davy in sheep suits. They looked like strangers in sheep suits. So I must really look like somebody else, thought Ramona with increasing happiness. Now she could be in the programme, and her parents wouldn't know because they wouldn't recognize her.

'B-a-a!' bleated three prancing, black-nosed sheep. 'B-a-a, b-a-a.'

471

Mrs Russo clapped her hands. 'Quiet, every-body!' she ordered. 'All right, Mary and Joseph, up by the front stairs. Shepherds and sheep next and then wise persons. Angels line up by the back stairs.'

The three sheep pranced over to the shepherds, one of whom said, 'Look what we get to herd,' and nudged Ramona with his crook.

'You cut that out,' said Ramona.

'Quietly, everyone,' said Mrs Russo.

Ramona's heart began to pound as if something exciting were about to happen. Up the stairs she tiptoed and through the arched door. The only light came from candelabra on either side of the chancel and from a streetlight shining through a stained-glass window. Ramona had never seen the church look so beautiful or so mysterious.

Beezus sat down on a low stool in the centre of the chancel and arranged the baby's blanket around the flashlight. Henry stood behind her. The sheep got down on their hands and knees in front of the shepherds, and the Three Wise Persons stood off to one side, holding bath-salts jars that looked as if they really could hold frankincense and myrrh. An electric star suspended above the organ began to shine. Beezus turned on the big flashlight inside the baby's blanket and light shone up on her face, making her look like a picture of

Mary on a Christmas card. From the rear door a wobbly procession of kindergarten angels, holding their small flashlights like candles, led the way, glimmering, two by two. 'Ah . . . ' breathed the congregation.

'Hark, the herald angels sing,' the advancing angels carolled. They looked nothing like the jumping, flapping mob with flashlights shining through their cheeks that Ramona had watched downstairs. They looked good and serious and . . . holy.

A shivery feeling ran down Ramona's backbone, as if magic were taking place. She looked up at Beezus, smiling tenderly down at the flashlight, and it seemed as if Baby Jesus really could be inside the blanket. Why, thought Ramona with a feeling of shock, Beezus looks nice. Kind and—sort of pretty. Ramona had never thought of her sister as anything but—well, a plain old big sister, who got to do everything first. Ramona was suddenly proud of Beezus. Maybe they did fight a lot when Beezus wasn't going around acting like Mary, but Beezus was never really mean.

As the carollers bore more light into the church, Ramona found her parents in the second row. They were smiling gently, proud of Beezus, too. This gave Ramona an aching feeling inside. They would not know her in her make-up. Maybe they would think she was some other sheep, and she didn't want to be some other sheep. She wanted to be their sheep. She wanted them to be proud of her, too.

Ramona saw her father look away from Beezus and look directly at her. Did he recognize her? Yes, he did. Mr Quimby winked. Ramona was shocked. Winking in church! How could her father do such a thing? He winked again and this time held up his thumb and forefinger in a circle. Ramona understood. Her father was telling her he was proud of her, too.

'Joy to the newborn King!' sang the angels, as they mounted the steps on either side of the chancel.

Ramona was filled with joy. Christmas was the most beautiful, magic time of the whole year. Her parents loved her, and she loved them, and Beezus, too. At home there was a Christmas tree and under it, presents, fewer than at past Christmases, but presents all the same. Ramona could not contain her feelings. 'B-a-a,' she bleated joyfully.

She felt the nudge of a shepherd's crook on the seat of her pyjamas and heard her shepherd whisper through clenched teeth, 'You be quiet!' Ramona did not bleat again. She wiggled her seat to make her tail wag.

Beverly Cleary is one of America's most
popular authors and her many successful stories,
including the best-selling *Ramona* series,
have delighted children all over the world
for many years.

Beverley Cleary's books have earned her many
prestigious awards, including the American
Library Association's Laura Ingalls Wilder
Award, presented in recognition of her lasting
contribution to children's literature. She lives in
California and is the mother of grown-up twins.